He's Gone

He's
Gone

A Novel

Deb Caletti

Bantam Books Trade Paperbacks
New York

A Bantam Books Trade Paperback Original

Copyright © 2013 by Deb Caletti
Reading group guide copyright © 2013 by Random House, Inc.

Published in the United States by Bantam Books,
an imprint of The Random House Publishing Group,
a division of Random House, Inc., New York.

BANTAM BOOKS and the rooster colophon are
registered trademarks of Random House, Inc.
RANDOM HOUSE READER'S CIRCLE & Design is a registered trademark of
Random House, Inc.

LIBRARY OF CONGRESS CATALOGING-IN-PUBLICATION DATA

Caletti, Deb.
He's gone : a novel / Deb Caletti.
p.   cm.
ISBN 978-0-345-53435-4 (alk. paper) — ISBN 978-0-345-53436-1 (ebook)
1. Married people—Fiction. 2. Missing persons—Fiction. 3. Secrets—Fiction.
I. Title.
PS3603.A4386H47 2013
813'.6—dc23
2012025421

Printed in the United States of America

www.bantamdell.com

2 4 6 8 9 7 5 3 1

To the six cherished people who most understand what this book in particular means to me: Evie Caletti, Paul Caletti, Sue Rath, Sam Bannon, Nick Bannon, and Ben Camardi. Thank you for being there from the very beginning.

"We don't see things as they are, but as we are."

—ANAÏS NIN

"Transformation . . . Transformation is a marvelous thing. I am thinking especially of the transformation of butterflies. Though wonderful to watch, transformation . . . is not a particularly pleasant process for the subject involved."

—VLADIMIR NABOKOV, 1951 CORNELL LECTURE ON THE METAMORPHOSIS AND DR. JEKYLL AND MR. HYDE

He's Gone

1

I used to imagine it sometimes, what would happen if one day I just didn't come home. Not that I ever considered running off—I could never actually do that, even if I occasionally had that fantasy about driving south and checking in to some hotel. Someplace with bathrobes, for sure. I love those. But, no, the thought was less about escape and more about some cruel intervention of fate. What if, say, the clichéd bus hit me as I crossed the clichéd street? The Mack truck. Whatever it was, something terrible would happen and my family would have to return home to find all the daily pieces of my interrupted life. My husband would see my cup of coffee, half finished, a curve of my lipstick on the brim. My mother would see my flannel pajamas with the Eiffel Towers on them in the laundry basket and the ChapStick on my nightstand. My book would be on the bed, open to the place I'd left off, and my hair would still be entwined in my brush. There would be my really expensive wrinkle minimizer, which honestly didn't minimize much of anything, and my phone charger still plugged into the wall. *This is how it would look*, I would think. *This stuff here*.

Whenever I had to get on a plane, I played that game in my

head, too. I worried about what people might find afterward, at my house. You know, if we went down in a fiery ball, wearing our yellow flotation devices with the helpful little whistles attached. Does anyone else do this? Fixate on impossible and pointless mental puzzles? I don't know. Flying used to be fun, but after 9/11 I did this stupid thing where I would wonder if I should have hidden certain stuff before I left home. Not that there would be much to hide—I'm not guilty of too many things. But I'd worry about those few old love letters, the ones I'd kept from the early days with my first husband, which Ian would have hated to discover. And that half bottle of Vicodin from that root canal, which I'd kept in case I was hit with some emotional crisis I couldn't handle. Oh, and that red lace thong-thing that Ian gave me one Valentine's Day. I don't know what he was thinking. If I never came home, my daughter might see it and think I actually wore it. That particular mental image might scar the poor girl for the rest of her life.

That's pretty much been the extent of my secrets. I guess you could say my conscience works overtime. And while I never actually moved the red lace thong or hid the pill bottle before I traveled, I *did* wipe up spilled stuff in the microwave and remove that big slab of fluff from the dryer vent that wasn't supposed to be in the dryer vent. I made sure my house was clean. Tidying up my domestic crimes so no one would find out that I made messes and couldn't keep my appliances under control, which is probably some home version of the wear-clean-underwear-in-case-of-an-accident idea.

These head games—I guess they're you, in your small way, trying to psych out the here-gone-ness of life, or maybe they're about the awareness that comes after a certain age of inevitable grief hovering nearby. Or maybe they're just about wanting to be good, even in death. Avoiding humiliation even when you're stone-cold gone. I don't know. But what I do know, what I've thought about since that day, is that it was always me I imagined suddenly missing. I never imagined finding anyone else's pill bottles or the slippers that had formed to their feet, now ditched under the bed. I didn't think about discovering someone else's breakfast dishes or the change from their pocket left out on the dresser, their presence sitting right next to their absence.

That morning, well, the objects around me have no more significance than they did the day before. It seems wrong, doesn't it? His reading glasses on the nightstand don't send me some big message. His water glass doesn't tell me the things I should know. I'd been dreaming—I was up high somewhere and I was scared and there was some kind of pounding noise, but when I open my eyes, I realize it's a dream trick and that the sound is real. It's outside my window. Our boat must have gotten loose or something, and it's banging against the dock.

I lie there, catching up to the facts of my life as one does before first getting up, looking at the white of the curtains and trying to guess what the weather's like. Dim white, likely cloudy. In Seattle, cloudy is a good prediction no matter what the season. I don't check to see whether he's there next to me or not. I guess I just assume he's there, because it's still early. We have one of those astronaut-foam-type mattresses, where you can thrash around and the other person won't even notice. I think the advertisement shows a glass of water, which sits still and undisturbed on the bed in spite of some guy jumping next to it. Anyway, the dog can get up there, and you won't even know it until you open your eyes and find him staring right at you.

I roll over. I'm trying to remember as best as I can. I recall *expecting* to see the hill of his shoulders turned away from me, his tidy black hair on the pillow. But I see only the empty bed next to me. Wide, empty, glorious space, and I stretch my legs over to his side and I'm happy about it, that space. I listen, trying to determine if he's home. There's that stupid banging, but the house seems still. Maybe he went for a run, or to work, even though it's Sunday, which wouldn't be unusual. Yeah: I realize there are no footsteps, or the sound of the toaster lever being pushed down, or the hum of television voices. He's likely gone, and I'm relieved. I'm sure I'm not the only wife who feels that—the small relief at his absence. I love him very much, I do; but the house to yourself . . . No need for conversation or company or the press of his presence . . . Ah—coffee in bed, the thrill of aloneness, and a couple of Oreos on a paper towel for breakfast—bliss.

But first there's that banging.

I get up and walk downstairs. God, I feel it then, the banging in my own head, a nasty throb from too much wine at that horrible party the night before. BetterWorks, Ian's software company, had released a new product, something that would change the way we share large video files. I don't really know the details. I should, but I don't. I want to understand it all, but my mind has its own instant off switch that's tripped by lengthy explanations, instruction manuals, and rules to board games read aloud. I have a college education, but, I swear, the minute someone wants to enlighten me about how a fax works or how to play hearts, the mental doors slam shut.

The party was one of those swanky affairs, held in the beautiful lobby of the BetterWorks offices on Queen Anne Hill. The night was all shiny black behind those high, high glass windows, and the city sparkled below us. The Space Needle was right there, in all its George Jetson–Tomorrowland glory. Ian's partner, Nathan Benjamin, was at the party, and I like Nathan. I

liked him even before I met him years ago, because he has those
two first names, which makes him sound friendly. But the room
was full of other people, too, of course—programmers and project managers and investors and investors' wives, eating fancy
little foods off tiny napkins and making witty conversation, and
later in the evening the party spilled over to the wide, damp lawn
of Kerry Park, which lays adjacent to BetterWorks. All night I
pretended not to be shy, even though I'd rather have been home
eating popcorn and watching the Travel Channel. I kept pulling
at my hem, because Ian had bought me this tight black dress and
asked me to wear it and I was mad at myself for agreeing. A
Band-Aid would have covered more and cost a lot less. I had
heels on, and the floor was slippery, and I kept thinking of the
way my sister, Amy, and I used to roller-skate in our garage
when we were kids, inching our way around by clutching the
workbench and then the bicycles and then the lawn mower.

Reasons for too much wine, right there.

"Oh, no, Poll. Pollux, boy. He didn't let you out?" My Pollux,
my sweet black mutt, he's getting old. He has to be taken outside
the minute you wake up, poor guy. I wipe up the puddle. The
thrill of unexpected alone time gives way to irritation. It's him
I'm irritated with. Ian. Overlooking my, *our,* sweet old dog, who
now looks ashamed. The pee requires practically half of a roll of
paper towels, and there's that banging and my pounding head.

I step over my heels, which have been abandoned by the door.
What a night. I can't remember ditching them there, or even
coming home and getting into bed, to tell you the truth. This
isn't normal for me, I should also say. I rarely have more than a
glass of wine, two at the most. I've been truly drunk maybe only
twice in my life, once way back in high school with Tommy Tru-
ello and wine in a box. We drank it before going to dinner at the

Velvet Turtle restaurant on our way to the homecoming dance. I was spinning and sick the rest of the night. It scared me. I don't like to lose control.

Pollux recovers his dignity and trots behind me as I open the door to the back deck. The front end of our small sailboat has come loose, and it's slamming into the dock with each wave of the lake. I'm glad Ian isn't here to see it. He'd be pissed. I kneel down; I make a couple of grabs for the boat before catching it, and then I examine it for scratches. It looks okay. I even run my hand along its surface, in case there's something I can't see but he'll surely notice. I was the one to tie it down when we came back in from our sail Friday evening, so it'll be my fault that the rope hasn't been secured properly. Narrow miss. He'll never know, and I'm glad. Ian doesn't make those kinds of mistakes, and he's not particularly patient when anyone else does.

He'll never know I was out here in my robe, either. He'd have an issue with that, as crazy as it sounds. He's possessive, and it gets irritating. From the way he acts, you'd think the sight of me would draw in the crowds of drooling men out there on their boats. My mom robe, with the bleach stain on the front and the Kleenex in my pocket, is sexy as hell, and all of them will be lining up for sure, just waiting to get a glimpse of me wrapped in terry cloth. Not a big thrill, I promise you. Maybe our neighbor, old Joseph Grayson, might think so, but he's stoned half the time.

It *is* a cloudy morning, but they're the kind of clouds that are rushing off as if they have better things to do. The sun is fighting its way out. I tie the boat down and I'm struck by how beautiful it is on the lake. It hits you sometimes like that, and so I stand there and take it all in. After we'd been married for two years and Abby had graduated and headed to the UW dorms, we moved to Lake Union from The Highlands, that neighborhood on the other side of the bridge that held so much of our tangled history. We (well, Ian) bought our large houseboat at the end of the dock. Whenever I say *houseboat* to people who aren't from the city, they think we drive it around. I have to explain that it's not a boat but a floating home, like in *Sleepless in Seattle,* only Meg Ryan had better hair than I do. Ian has better hair than Tom Hanks, but Pollux has better hair than all of us, and he's so humble about it, too.

The view from our home is similar to the one from Ian's office up on Queen Anne Hill, but at the houseboat it's spread out in front of us rather than seen from above. Lake Union, the Space Needle, various boats chugging past, seaplanes landing—you feel as if the city is *yours* out there, that you belong to it, and it to you. *I never want to live anywhere else,* Ian said once. *I could die here and be happy.* I knew what he meant. It feels so great right at this moment, even after wiping up pee and with a bad headache and with the feeling that things had gone wrong again between Ian and me the night before. I still feel mostly good, because some ducks paddle past, and then so do a pair of kayakers. The woman in the back waves and I wave, too, and I breathe in and notice that the daffodil bulbs in the pots on the deck are coming up, little arrowheads of green.

I decide against going back to bed. I put a pot of coffee on. *Ian must have been in a rush to get out of here this morning,* I think, because he hasn't even made any coffee, and Ian needs his coffee. I also think this: *He could be out at Louisa's right now, bringing us home a pair of foamy lattes and some raspberry muffins, and if he shows up with that fabulous white bag and two cardboard cups, I'll just consider this batch of French Roast my coffee appetizer.* So the pot burbles and I pour Pollux his same old brown breakfast that he's so thrilled about every single day, and I take that perfect first cup of the morning onto the deck, along with a couple of aspirins. I sit on one of the Adirondack chairs we have out there. I smell the arrival of Northwest spring, and the smell of bacon cooking somewhere, and the smell of gasoline drifting over water. All three of those smells I love. Pollux trots out again, with water droplets on his beard. He squints into the early sun and looks out over the lake like the patron saint of sailors he's named for. What a good boy.

I sip that coffee, and the steam rises up in the coolness of morning, and Pollux lays his old self down in a spot of sun. I have one of those moments where you simply feel grateful. My headache is giving up, and the irritation is leaving, too, maybe swept away in the first exhilarating rush of caffeine. A sense of peace takes its place. A rare moment of peace, the kind you take in and vow to hold on to but never can. Those moments are gone at the first traffic jam or botched bank statement, in spite of your best intentions. But it's there now.

I have no idea is what I'm saying. What I keep trying to say.

I have no idea that my husband has vanished.

2

Every now and then you hear someone say it: *I've got no regrets.*
It always seems astonishing to me. It sounds so bold. And freeing. And kind of wonderful, but hard to believe. I mean, if you
have a conscience at all, you'll have regrets, won't you? If you're
honest about your mistakes, small and large? Or even if you only
face the facts about how things in your life didn't turn out the
way you imagined they would. I have regrets from just yesterday, when I yelled at Pollux for laying down right in the doorway. I have regrets from back when I was fourteen and I kissed
Ethan Gunter out by the Totem Bowl on my first date ever, even
though I didn't like him. He was a little strange. He wore a weird
felt hat, and I didn't exactly say yes to the kiss, but I didn't say no.
I was already giving things just because other people wanted
them.

And if you're a parent—well, right there. Can you honestly
say you have no regrets? With all the ways you mess it up, when
it's your best and most important dream to get it right? Parental
regrets, those are at the top, all right. Oh, I wanted to be a perfect
parent, I did. I read all the books. But my dream of perfect was
gone already before my daughter was born, the moment I chose

her father. I didn't know that when I was nineteen. But you can't avoid messing up somehow as a parent, can you? I imagine that even those mothers with their perfect organic baby food and their perfect preschools and their perfect gifted programs still send their kids screaming from their loving arms. Too much perfect will likely result in years at the therapist's office, same as too much imperfect.

But I have other, non-mothering regrets, too. Big ones. The biggest. I have wanted other people's lives and other people's houses, and once, this one time, I wanted another woman's husband. I wanted Ian badly, and what a mess that made. Well he also wanted me badly. Still, you don't toss that kind of guilt away in some flip comment like *I have no regrets*. I've been selfish, but I'm not at heart a selfish person. I've hurt people, and I'm ashamed of that.

And this is what I'm thinking about as I wait for him to come home that morning. I'm thinking about our life together and how it came to be. This isn't some sort of fateful timing; I think about it a lot. Too much. It bothers me. I'm still trying hard to understand where I am and how I got here. My mind picks it up and works on it whenever I have spare, quiet moments, same as some people pick up their knitting.

Peace and gratitude, the peace and gratitude I feel there on that dock with my fingertips rubbing one of Pollux's silky ears— as I said, it's a slippery thing. I guess that a sense of peace is slippery for everyone. Regular life and its noises barge in, little daily earthquakes, and any feeling, especially happiness, isn't allowed to just *be* for long. But for me, it often feels especially hard to hold on to. When it's good, I don't always feel that I've earned my life or that I got it fair and square.

Of course, there are a hundred reasons why Ian's divorce happened, most of which have nothing to do with me. I sometimes forget that. It was a marriage of two real and flawed people who had met very young and who'd barely fit together then, and later not at all. Not for a long while. It would have been someone else if it hadn't been me; I know that. Still, in a way, I'd stolen it. Him. I'm not a good thief. I'd be the one in the bank heist saying, "I'm so sorry. Really. Whatever you can spare. This isn't even a real gun." I'd have to return the next day to give the bags of money back with a note of apology. No matter what the reasons, no matter how well things turn out in the end for everyone, you do wrong and it sits with you, and that's probably how it should be.

If Ian had gone to Louisa's, he'd be back by now, I realize, so I pour myself another cup of coffee. I rearrange the chairs outside so that I can sit in one and put my feet up on another. Someone's dog is swimming out by the adjacent dock. Pollux stands and watches, as if weighing the pros and cons of his own cowardice. He hates the water. As far as athletic endeavors go, he takes after me. More than once, I've rowed a kayak smack into the path of a large boat and then, to Ian's embarrassment and mine, screamed when I finally saw it coming at me. If reading counted as a sport, I'd be a gold medalist. I was an expert at the V-sit in high school P.E. Abby, though—she takes after her father. She's my daughter, and she's *athletic?* It seems a miracle. She's brave. When she was in Little League, she'd stand there at home plate as the baseball whizzed right past her face, and she didn't even flinch. I *always* flinched.

That's where Ian and I fell in love—a Little League game. Our daughters were on the same team. I met Ian when he was there being a *father.* Maybe it wouldn't have happened if we'd met somewhere else. If we bumped into each other on the street or at Safeway, say. I think, for me, something about those gangly twelve-year-old girls with their ponytails sticking out of their caps and the *ping* of the ball against the metal bat and the cheering—the dust, and the cut-grass smell, and the mothers in their sleeveless tops—it felt like safety, like the kind of childhood you wanted to give your kids, so different from the kind I thought I was giving my daughter. Yeah, that's it exactly. I think I wanted Ian for her, for Abby, as much as for me. He was a better idea of home.

Of course, he had his own daughter out there. And Abby had her own father.

Ian and I caught eyes at a baseball game, and then we fell in love, and then more deeply in love, and it was passionate and important. So it sounds unromantic to say this, but I wonder if it could have easily been another man for me, just as it would have eventually been another woman for Ian. I was looking for rescue. Because up there behind the chain-link barrier of the team bench stood my own husband, Mark Hastings, assistant coach of the Pink Dragons. The girls chose their own name, and Mark ranted about this one night in bed, going on about how wrong it was that the Cardinals and the Braves and the Giants were gone now in place of the Sweet Rainbows and the Angel Kittens, and probably he had a point. He'd used the word *integrity*. Sports brought out the heroic in him. Sports were the country he was patriotic about. Still, the parents thought he was too intense. I could hear them talking. You could see it on his face right there, as he gripped the chain link of the dugout in his fingers and shouted, *Follow through! Follow through! Don't be scared of the ball!* Those parents had no idea. His face would get into mine, right up close, and he would scream until I couldn't hear anything anymore. That hollow, faraway sound would come into my head, the one you hear when you hold your breath and dunk your head underwater and stay there for a moment. His mouth would be moving, but I would watch it as if it were something separate from him, a curious undulating creature. People flinch at loud noises, or a baseball, or a raised hand, but after a while a flinch can become a permanent condition.

I went to every practice, and so did Ian's wife, Mary. Mary, who had the name of a Madonna but who was a real person, as we all were. I wonder how that name worked on Ian, though, with his Catholic upbringing and with his own religious mother. Subconsciously, or whatever. I remember seeing Mary there at those practices before I met Ian, talking on her cellphone. I remember an overheard conversation about her husband, who was away in Europe. I remember how she flirted with one of the fathers, Jessica Halloran's dad, a too-handsome short man who built up his muscles to make up for his stature, the way short men often do. He'd made some joke about her big breasts, which she seemed to somehow be known for, the way some people are known for a particular talent, like playing the piano. She enjoyed his appreciation, I could tell. He lifted her up over one shoulder and carried her around, and her dark hair fell down his back. She laughed teasingly, and after I met Ian, this image replayed in my mind. It said something important about their marriage, I thought, something maybe even he didn't know.

He showed up at the second game, home from his trip. I only vaguely noticed the back of his expensive-looking T-shirt and jeans as he stood next to another dad during the pregame parent meeting. It was sunny, and all of us were gathered on the side-lines of the baseball diamond in our suburban neighborhood. There was a pool down the street, and an elementary school, and a tennis court. Here, every life looked the same from the outside. Same house, different floor plan; same cars; same backyard pa-tios with barbecues and Costco faux-ceramic pots; same women with their matching outfits and manicures. My own hands were plain and I knew my own secrets, and so I felt different. My front door was painted in a designer shade just as theirs was, but what happened behind it was mine alone. I thought so, anyway. Probably I wasn't the only woman whose stomach clutched up in worry whenever her electric garage door went up, that rumbling, grim sound that meant a husband was home. But I felt like I was. The suburbs are one of the loneliest places on earth.

On that sunny spring morning of the Pink Dragons' second official game, though, as my tennis shoes got dusty from the newly raked baselines, and as the team mom passed around some new, unnecessary handout, Ian turned and looked at me and held my eyes, and something passed between us. I've always known right away when someone is going to be important in my life. I'd felt this way with Mark, too, and with all the people who've been significant to me. Something shifted. An internal mountain range moved over. One look, and it felt huge. I felt it in my whole body. It seemed like an arrival: of God or fate or the future. Change, announcing itself with silent but circuit-blowing undercurrents.

You could call it love at first sight; we did. It had all the required components of love at first sight—eyes connecting, an electrical charge rarely experienced in a life. Walk around someplace with a lot of people—the mall, an airport—and you realize how great the odds are against such a thing. But rarely, too, do you happen to meet a person whose jagged notches match perfectly with your jagged notches, their key to your lock, damaged roots meeting rightful, barren soil; there are too many metaphors here, but you get the idea. I've come to believe that love at first sight is more likely recognition at first sight—a complicated, instantaneous recognition made by a shrewd and cunning inner Cupid. It doesn't have to be ruinous if what you are viewing from that deep, crafty submarine scope of the unconscious are the best qualities of old Mom and Dad. But if it locks on to the worst ones, as so often it seems to do, the key opens the lock, and you're a perfect match, and love at first sight is also disaster at first sight, only you don't know it yet. You can't know it or hear it over the roar in your chest.

Out on the dock that day, with my coffee cup warming my hands, I relive that particular feeling: I *recognized* him. We barely spoke, yet there it was. This is the part I often play over and over again in my mind—our matched gaze, the sense of importance. Our meeting felt like a reunion. I didn't attribute this to anything tragic or doomed, not then, anyway; I didn't see the ancient, wrecked ruins of childhood all around us. No, it felt magical. A coming together again after a long time apart. There was a sense of relief at his appearance in my life—the way you feel when you've been standing at the roadside for far too long and then the tow truck arrives. *Oh, there you are*, I wanted to say. *Finally.* He felt the same way, he'd tell me later. *Like we'd been living in wrong, separate countries, lost to each other until right then*. Yeah. Just—at last, *you*.

We caught each other's eyes, and then he smiled. He looked slightly taken aback. He made some joke, and I laughed. I laughed the way Mary had laughed with small Mr. Halloran, and my laugh felt tacky to me. This is what happens within the daily confines of the suburbs, flirtations and affairs and bored people making passes at other people's spouses at drunken summer parties as the kids play tag on the cul-de-sac. I didn't like it. I hated it, actually. It was a cliché, for starters (well, that entire neighborhood was), and it was cheap. The kind of cheap of slurred words and vicious gossip and dirty secrets. It wasn't the kind of life I wanted. I liked to go to sleep at night knowing my conscience was clear. I liked simple days of pancakes and the library and helping Abby with some school project involving glue and old magazines. And I liked to think I was a better person than that.

I was aware of his presence throughout that whole game, though. I would watch Mark pace along the baseline, socking his fist into his mitt with a resolute *thwock, thwock*, and I would cheer for Abby when she came up to bat, her eyes serious under her little helmet, and I would watch that new set of shoulders, which were now hunched on the bleachers near me. I had no doubt he was aware of my presence, too. He would glance over his shoulder every now and then. Something had unfurled inside, like a plan, but a plan that had materialized. I guess that's what fate feels like. I might as well have been sitting in a red plush seat in a theater, watching a film, because I knew that what was going to happen had already happened. It was being set into motion, and it was thrilling and terrifying but, more than anything else, it was a *fait accompli*. Yes. Even though I hate it when someone throws a French phrase into their narrative, that's the right phrase. Something had finally begun, which meant other things were over. My life wouldn't forever be what it had been. It was one of the largest moments of my life. Still, if I could undo it all now, I would. I would be braver than I was. I would do things the right way.

You want to be a person who holds your head high, but you are not always that person. This is what happened when our eyes met. Love *and* wrongdoing were that particular truth.

Inside the houseboat, the phone rings. I've been thinking so hard about Ian that I'm sure it's going to be him, calling from his office. I take my coffee cup inside, and Pollux follows me dutifully. He's such a hard little worker.

"You'll never believe what the idiots across the street are doing now."

It's not Ian.

"What?" My mother has regular disputes with her neighbors. Garbage-can conflicts, encroaching tree branches, cats using her flower beds for litter boxes.

"They've been cleaning up their yard, and—what a fool I am—I thought it looked *great*. A nice big patch in the middle of the lawn . . . I'm expecting maybe a hydrangea, some nice heather . . . but, no. Can you hear that?"

I can hear her TV on in her living room, that's all, and the regular old buzz from the open phone line. Since my mother booted her companion, Douglas Hanks, from her home years ago, she's lived alone. Douglas Hanks had a roving eye, and, in a last fit of fury, my mother stomped his cowboy hat flat and tossed his collection of 78s. Right afterward, her hair went white, as if shocked by the cruel vagaries of love.

She's back again. "It's a damn *chain saw*! It's been going all morning!"

"I don't know how you can stand it," I say. "What are they doing, cutting down a tree?"

"I *wish*. You ready for this? They're making a totem pole! A fucking totem pole!" The women in my life—my mother, my sister, my good friend Anna Jane, even my daughter—they swear like construction workers. I'm the nun in the family, as far as that goes.

I picture it—a tower of vacant eyes and downturned mouths, the wings of a raven outstretched on top—and I want to laugh. The neighbors are a retired couple who golf a lot and wear matching sweatshirts. They have an American flag flying out

front, too. It *is* bad, though. The large windows of my mother's
Northwest contemporary home face that yard, and the totem-
pole raven will be permanently staring in. "Oh, no. Chain-saw
art."

"You should see the old guy who's doing it, too. He's even got
suspenders. He looks straight out of *Deliverance*." My mind
clicks along. *Deliverance,* Burt Reynolds, a flashback: my mother's stashed copy of *Cosmo* when Burt Reynolds was the first
male centerfold. I was maybe seven or eight when my sister and
I found it in her cedar chest. It's funny what you remember. I can
still see Burt with his deep-black hair and furry body on that
white rug, an ashtray beside him. He had those rugged, 1970s
sideburns, from the days of gas shortages and Shake 'N Bake and
Moon Boots. Isabel Eleanor Ross, my mother, she liked rugged.
A collector's item, she'd explained, before snatching it back. Ha.

Right then she gives her voice a hillbilly twang. " 'Did you
ever look out over a lake and think of somethin' buried underneath it? Man, that's just about as buried as you can get.' "

"You lost me," I say.

"It's from the movie. I just watched it again last weekend.
Held up pretty well, I thought. Some of those old films look ridiculous now."

"I made Abby watch *Born Free* with me once. God, I loved it
when I was a kid."

"You cried like a baby over that lion."

"*Elsa*. We couldn't get through more than twenty minutes of
it. Abby made fun of me for days. 'I could see why that made you
cry, Mom. I was sobbing myself, it was so bad.' She thought she
was hilarious."

My mother has stopped listening, though. She's peeking out
her front window again, I'm sure. "I'm going to chop that thing
down in the middle of the night."

Well, she might, too. The evidence supporting that possibility piles up like a memory traffic jam: The time she pulled the stakes out of the Beckers' tent after she and Patty Becker got in an argument on one ill-fated family camping trip when we were kids. The time she poured a drink on my father's lap when some woman started dancing provocatively in front of him at a party. The time she screamed *Creep!* at my high school boyfriend when we found out he'd been cheating with Carla Cummings, whose talent, if I recalled correctly, was woodworking. Which brings us full circle.

"Remember Carla Cummings?" I say.

"Who?"

"She won some award in high school for wood shop. Bobby's girlfriend after me."

"Well, it's not her. It's some old geezer. Honestly, I'm supposed to look at this thing the rest of my life?"

I open the fridge, take a couple of spoons of apple crisp from two nights ago. Apple crisp—a reason to love life. I drop Pollux a bit. He keeps licking his lips afterward, which shows what good taste he has.

"Hey, Mom? I've got to go. I think Ian's home."

And it's true. Someone has stepped onto our deck. You can feel when this happens. The houseboat is a large two-story home, one of the largest of the three hundred twenty four on the lake, but there's still a slight dip whenever anyone sets foot on the house's floating platform.

"Where's he been? It's Sunday morning! You two have another fight?"

I should never tell her anything. "He was just getting us coffee."

"Well, that's better than pulling the wings off insects."

"Stop," I say.

"It's brutal. I should call PETA."

"That stuff is his father's. You know that."

"I'm going to fill *my* yard with garden trolls and flamingos. See how those idiot neighbors like *that*."

"Good luck, sweetie. I love you."

"I love you, too."

I wait for Ian. And I wait. Since he doesn't come right in, I listen for the creak-woosh of the outdoor faucet turning on—maybe he's giving the plants a bit of much-needed water. But that doesn't happen, either. I expect to hear him talking with the neighbors or dumping his trash in the recycling, *something*, but there is no other sound.

I open the front door. A padded envelope falls across the doorway. I pick it up. It has his name on it, but that's all. I don't think twice about it. He gets packages all the time. I set it on the kitchen table, where he'll see it when he comes in. The funny thing is, I'm not even curious.

A few hours pass. I eat a bowl of raisin bran for lunch and promptly rinse the bowl, because raisin bran has a death grip if you let it sit. I'm getting a little pissed—at least he could have left a note. I call his cellphone. It rings and rings, clicks over to his voice mail. *This is Ian Keller; I'm not available to take your call . . .* I hang up. I call back and leave a message. I huff around at his bad behavior

"You know, *I* would never do that, Poll. I wouldn't. It's inconsiderate." Pollux agrees, I can tell by his eyes. Dogs are most helpful as an excuse for talking to yourself.

I think about what to have for dinner. I stare at the contents of the freezer for far too long. I consider making some cookies for

Ian, which means I want them for myself. Instead, I gather up a load of laundry and toss it into the wash.

On the way back downstairs, I pass our small office. It's part den, part hobby room. Ian's desk and leather chair and books are squeezed in there, but so are the two cabinets of thin drawers, the narrow table, and the shelves with supplies stacked neatly on them. After that day at Kerry Park a year ago, that supposed picnic, I don't think he touched this stuff again. Everything in the room looks the way it has for many months: the spreading board, the boxes of glass-headed pins, the killing jars, and the small bottles of cyanide. They were his father's things, passed on to Ian while he was still married to Mary, an old pastime of Paul Hartley Keller's that Ian dutifully tried to take on. I avoid that room. I work from home, doing part-time website design and graphics work for a handful of clients, but I prefer to spread out across the kitchen table rather than use that office. I don't like the pictures on the walls, those rows of monarchs and painted ladies trapped behind glass. It *is* brutal. He once showed me how to relax a butterfly's wings so that they could be spread open and pinned down, but I couldn't stand to watch. I had to leave. I told him I thought the whole thing was gruesome.

People have collected butterflies for years. Scientists, he'd argued.

I don't care, I'd said. *It's creepy. It's cruel. You're not a scientist.*

It's a way of appreciating their beauty, Dani. Think of it as paying them homage. You're keeping them perfect forever.

You pay homage by taking their lives? That makes sense.

If you don't get it, you don't get it.

I don't get it. I thought you hated hunting, I'd said. *You think hunters are terrible people.*

It's not the same thing at all. Look, Dani, I used to do it with my dad, okay? It means something to me.

I'd end the argument then, because Ian's father, Paul Hartley Keller, was the shiny, unattainable prize of Ian's childhood. His love and approval were always just out of Ian's reach, which meant that Ian's feelings for him were as unpredictable as a compass with no true north. We had dinner together, Paul and Ian and me, not long before Paul died, a meal in a restaurant with white napkins and fine wine. He'd flirted with the waitress in spite of his fleshy jowls and the droops of skin under his eyes. He must have thought she didn't notice these signs of age, or maybe he didn't notice them himself. To his credit, in spite of the jowls, he looked like a large lion with a gray mane, powerful like that (all right, even virile), but I could hear him breathing heavily. It made me wonder if I remembered any of that CPR we did on that Annie mannequin in high school. How many puffs, how many chest compressions? Paul Hartley Keller's ego—it was sizable. It was his personal butler, opening doors for him, announcing his presence, never leaving his side. It served him well, too—attracting people to him and then pushing them away when he was through. Ian could become a defenseless, angry, needy (take your pick) little boy around his father. That much was clear. *How are things going with your start-up?* Paul Hartley Keller had asked at dinner, long after Ian's company was successful. *It's going great*, Ian had replied, seething, stabbing his meat with the tines of his fork. *Profitable. Too profitable.* Ian was being a bit oversensitive, I thought. Paul Hartley Keller, well, I've got to say, he charmed me right out of my good sense.

The butterflies . . . I'm sure Paul didn't want that crap in his house anymore. Paul also went through his garage once, shortly after Ian left Mary, when Ian barely had two snitched forks from his old house. Paul gave Ian a bunch of stuff for his new place. He was trying to be helpful in his own way, probably. "It's the dream kitchen of the 1970s," Paul had supposedly joked, which was pretty hilarious, I thought, and true, too. There was a harvest-gold fondue pot, an air popcorn popper, an electric carving knife, and a microwave big enough to drive. Most of it was useless to Ian, but he kept all of it anyway. He saved that stuff for years.

Mary had encouraged the butterfly collection, the passed-down hobby. In their home, Ian had an entire voluminous "bonus room" for his supplies, not just the two cabinets we've made space for. He had a wall of bookshelves and oak worktables to spread out the plates of glass and foam boards. He had an antique umbrella stand for his father's old nets with the polished maple handles.

For the most part, I keep my mouth shut about the butterflies, in spite of my feelings about them. That kind of silence is what you end up with when you get together the way we did. At first you're sure that love is larger than any obstacle, but then love comes to feel flimsy measured against what's been lost—family and friends and a history. There's pressure to make it all worth it. So you keep quiet about things you maybe wouldn't ordinarily. To keep peace. To keep you both believing that a lack of conflict means you're happy. Happier than *before*. He'd fallen prey to disappointment in his previous life, and I didn't want history to repeat itself.

This is how it goes: When you go looking for rescue, you end up trapped in your own weakness. You are a butterfly who needs to lay her eggs and sees the perfect leaf, realizing too late that the leaf is not a leaf at all, but the green cotton shirtsleeve of her captor.

The afternoon passes, and Ian has still not called back. It's getting late. I keep checking the clock. Ian is usually considerate about these sorts of things, unless we've had a fight. We haven't had a fight, not exactly. I don't think anyone yelled. Raised voices, maybe, which is different than actual yelling. Truthfully, I'm having a little problem remembering who said what. In the car on the ride home, he was pissed, but I stayed silent. I hadn't wanted the night to slide further into ugliness, especially since we were dressed up. It always seems worse to fight when you're dressed up, doesn't it? The disappointment is larger. Arguments aren't supposed to happen when you have your fancy purse or when it's Christmas or when you've gone to the trouble to curl your hair. As he drove home, his handsome mouth was set in a line, and *wrongness* lay between us. But the night had become a blur of late hours and too much wine, and in the car, the party began to feel far away already, and in my bright kitchen on that sunny Sunday, it feels like weeks ago. I pick up my heels off the floor. They're caked with dried mud, and I rinse off their bottoms.

I try to read, but I'm restless. *Restlessness*: unconscious unease. I don't yet recognize this uneasiness. I'm still just thinking that it's taking him too long to call back. Mostly, I'm irritated. I'm guessing that he's sending me a message about the night before, how displeased he is. Great. Super. Got it, thanks. I stay busy filling in the blank space of his absence with my own stories. He's pissed, which means a fight is inevitable when he gets back. Or else he's at work. Maybe Nathan's there, too, and they're having some long talk. He's been wanting to get the oil changed in his car for weeks, too, and that place nearby us always has a long line. I'm trying to guess what might be in his head—something I've spent a lot of time doing over the years of our relationship, that's for sure.

I'm not uneasy, not yet, but then I decide to go outside and look down the street for his car. It feels a little plaintive and a lot pathetic, but I can't help myself, and when I head out, I remember doing a similar thing once, when I was already divorced but Ian hadn't left Mary yet. He was coming to see me and he was late, really late, and I walked out into my neighborhood street without my shoes on. It was a summer night, and the asphalt was cool on my feet, and I wore a sundress and perfume, and I stood at the entrance to our cul-de-sac and looked for his car, which never came. He just never came, and it ended up becoming the second time we tried to break things off.

Now, though, I step from a house that's ours. Our own home, on our own dock-street, which is full of activity—Josh Harban fussing with his sailboat, Joanie Andresen washing her windows. Mattie and Louise are coming back from a trip to Home Depot, from the look of it. Their arms are strung with plastic bags, and Mattie holds a blueberry bush in a pot. "Plumbing problems," Louise says to me, and raises one arm of bags as proof of her home-repair intentions. "Ha, at our age, isn't that the truth."

"*Your* age," Mattie says. "Don't put us in your category yet, right, Dani? I don't get ads from AARP."

I smile. "I'm staying out of this. Good luck, though."

"I get the fun part," Mattie says. She nods toward her new, robust plant.

"It's as big as a second-grader," I say.

"Blueberries for the whole dock."

They head toward their house and I walk on. Houseboat living is close. Everyone knows one another's business. I could tell you a lot about my neighbors, and we've been here only a year: Mattie and Louise are a happy couple, or else they fight quietly. Jack and Maggie drink too much, which is obvious on recycling day. Kevin and Jennie are exhausted parents with short tempers and a new baby who squalls throughout the night, and the Andresens' daughter has friends who look like trouble. Here, problems aren't hidden behind perfect lawns and SUVs. There *are* no lawns, of course, only unruly gardens spilling from flower boxes and pots. White lights are strung merrily down the dock in every season. It's as quirky and jovial and messy as Joseph Grayson, the aging hippie next door, who races his electric toy boat out on the lake on sunny days. He chases the ducks with it sometimes, which seems mean. They handle it well, though. They ignore him and swim on, looking especially bored, which is basically the same strategy I use whenever I walk past a scary guy at a bus stop.

I reach the parking lot at the other end of the dock. And that's when my restlessness turns to worry, because Ian's car is there. I can't believe it. The black Jaguar is parked right in its spot next to Blue Beast, my old Honda. It's there and locked up, just as it would be if he'd left it for the night. I think: *He's got to be around here somewhere, then.* Yeah, you could walk up to Louisa's for breakfast and you could run into a friend and you could talk as long as Ian might want to talk, and you'd still be back by now. You could go to Pete's Market, but you'd have to examine every item in every squished aisle in that small place to be gone for this long.

The car—something is wrong. Something isn't right here, I know, and I clutch my sweatshirt jacket closer to my body as I walk back down the dock. There is some terrible squeezing beneath my breastbone, near my heart, in that place where we feel all loss, both imminent and actual. I listen again for Ian's voice, maybe laughing with Jack Long or with the other software guy on the dock, Josh Harban, who lives with his quiet wife. Maybe he's helping a neighbor with a fixing-type problem. Something is always breaking down on one houseboat or another. But the stories I'm using to fill in the blank space are becoming more and more far-fetched. Ian's not very social with our neighbors. He's polite, always, even to the point of primness. He takes pride in his good manners. But he's not willingly the stop-by-and-chat sort. And he wouldn't be anyone's choice to help with a repair. Jack Long is the one who fixes things around here. We have a hammer and a screwdriver for hanging pictures, and that's about it. They're a part of the small, orderly tool set that Mary gave Ian one Father's Day, which folds open to reveal an indented place for each object. That set has barely been touched. I did use the measuring tape once, to buy a correctly sized rug.

I stop by Jack and Maggie Long's place. Ian is friendliest with them, of all the neighbors. Jack works near Ian, and they sometimes drive in together. *Everyone* is friendly with Jack and Maggie, though. They've lived on the dock longer than all of us, and so they're Dock Mom and Dad, Mayor and Mrs. Mayor of Fairview Moorings. They were the ones cooking bacon that morning, I can tell now, even hours later. Their house still smells of it when Maggie opens the door.

"Dani!" Maggie's got her pink polo shirt on and a pair of jeans shorts that show her thick, sturdy legs. Their cat, Lulu, slips past me and escapes out the door.

"Hey, Maggie. I was wondering if you've seen Ian."

"Ian?" She scrunches up her face. "No. We've been inside all morning. You okay? You're worried."

"I'm sure it's nothing. I just can't find him."

"Aw." She waves her hand in the air, pushing away my concern. For all she knows, I might be one of those nervous wives who fret when their husbands drift toward the food table at a party. I am not one of those nervous wives.

"His car is still in its spot. He's not answering his phone. . . ."

"He's probably having a little guy time, right?" Maggie says. Jack—now, he would like guy time, football-buddy time, slog-back-a-beer-and-talk-about-wide-receivers time, but not Ian. I don't think Ian even knows what a wide receiver is. I can hear the TV on in Jack and Maggie's living room, a baseball game by the sound of it. "You want to come in?" Maggie steps aside in invitation. On the houseboat docks, this is what you do. You go into one another's houses; you visit. Someone is always heading in or out of someone else's place, carrying a bottle of wine for an impromptu dinner or a plate of fresh-baked cookies. Ian and I, we sort of stick to ourselves. The neighbors probably think we're snobs, but we're mostly just quiet people. Ian had done all that, the neighborhood parties, back with Mary in the suburbs.

No, Ian likes being home. When he's mad, though, he can get punishing. Not answering his phone. Snippy retorts. Hard, icy shoulders turned away from me.

"Thanks, but I think I'll head back."

"One time Jack got pissed at me and walked all the way to his brother's place in Kirkland. Across the floating bridge! I didn't hear from him for two days. I almost called the police. Wait a sec. Hey, honey?" she shouts. "Have you seen Ian around?"

"What?" The baseball noise dims incrementally.

"Have you seen Ian, from next door?"

"Not since yesterday." The volume rises again.

"You guys looked great last night," Maggie says. "Some party?"

"Ian's work."

"You guys moved in, and I said, 'Now, that's a beautiful couple.'"

"That's very kind."

"I could never get my ass into a dress like that!"

"I don't think mine was all the way in, either." I smile.

"My husband stopped looking at me like that twenty years ago."

I laugh. "Oh, I'm sure that's not true."

"He'll turn up," Maggie says.

But he doesn't turn up.

I call Nathan, who says that he hasn't seen Ian since last night. I call Bethy and Kristen, his daughters, who both seem to find it amusing that I can't locate him. *He's probably at the movies. Maybe he took a trip.* I stop at old Joe Grayson's to ask if he's seen Ian around, but no. I consider calling Ian's sister, Olivia, who lives in Kirkland. I try to imagine Ian walking across the floating bridge to his sister's house, same as Jack, but I can't see it, Ian in his nice, expensive shoes, the back of his sports jacket flapping in the gust of passing cars. I think about calling Mary's house, speaking to Mary. I imagine this, too. *I've lost our husband*, I would have to say. She kept him in fine shape all those years, and look what happens now that he's in my hands.

And what if it goes like this? I make that humiliating call. Mary answers. She says, *Oh, he's right here, but he doesn't want to talk to you.* He's relaxing in their family room, in front of that huge, movie-theater-sized television that everyone has in the sub-urbs, sitting in the soft folds of the leather couch that everyone has, too. He's eating fish crackers from an enormous Costco box, snack-ing on cut-up vegetables from an enormous Costco platter, and Mary simply hangs up her phone and resumes her rightful life.

I keep making trips down the dock, watching the street, look-ing at his car as if it has something to tell me. More than any-thing, I want to shout, *Where are you! Where, goddamn it!* I feel like screaming at him at the top of my lungs, though this is obvi-ously a bad idea. First, it's pointless; second, it would scare the poor kid bagging groceries at Pete's. I'm sure he already thinks I'm a lunatic after watching me try to pick out a cereal.

Finally, I write a note. I tape it to the banister so Ian will see it when he walks in. *Call me! I'm worried sick. Left to look for you!* It'll look crazy and slightly hysterical when he finds it, but who cares.

I grab my purse and clip Pollux to his leash. I stick him in the passenger seat of my own car, where he sits like a good boy and watches the streets intently for his own kind as I drive to Better-Works. I look at those tall panes of glass and that metallic sheen and that curving sculpture outside on the lawn and wish, wish, wish, for Ian to turn a corner. *Be there! Please!*

My worry is turning into something more urgent now, bordering on panic as the afternoon turns dark. BetterWorks has high security; software companies in Seattle are all like that—employees wear important identifying badges around their necks and doors open only with the touch of a particular palm. You can't even make the elevator work without swiping a certain pass in front of the red button. I thought it was funny the first time I saw it all. As if hidden behind those doors was the recipe for a nuclear bomb or an imminent cure for cancer. It reminded me of that old Willy Wonka movie, when the chocolate-factory spy sneaks in to obtain Gobstopper secrets. But now the security is maddening. I find the evening guard, and I have to wait outside while he checks Ian's office. He seems amused that I can't find my own husband. Obviously, I've been rather absentminded to lose something that important.

"He'll show." He grins, as if Ian is likely in a hotel room somewhere, doing it with some younger woman who doesn't have to touch up her roots. When Ian does show—I'm going to be *furious*. And I'm going to tell him what an ass his security guard is. That guy better watch it, if he values his job.

I want to keep looking, to keep *doing something,* but I have no idea where to go or what to do. I drive around aimlessly for a

while. I drive around the streets near his work. And then I have
an idea. His gym. He has this gym membership. I don't think he
even goes there anymore, but maybe he does. He could've walked
there. He could've walked there after spending the day somewhere else. Maybe he's swimming laps in the pool, blowing off
steam.

The place has only a few cars in the lot. Pollux waits in the
Blue Beast. I know what a stupid idea this is the minute the bell
chimes my arrival. He's not here. In those bright lights and that
pumping music, I feel my own desperation.

"Welcome to Fifth Street Gym! My name is Elizabeth! May I
assist you with a membership today?" Elizabeth's hair is up in a
perky blond ponytail, but her eyes are tired under the fluorescent
lighting, and her self-tanner is the unfortunate shade of a split
apricot. I ask about Ian. Apparently, confidentiality isn't an issue
here. Don't expect privacy if you're a member of the Fifth Street
Gym. She flips through a file of cards with one small, muscled
arm. I have to spell his name twice.

"He hasn't been in since December. The membership's ex-
pired. Would you care to renew? We've got family plans." I
shake my head. I thank her. The bell cheerily ding-dongs my
exit. All at once, I am scared. In the car, Pollux's eyes catch the
light of the streetlamp and glow in that sci-fi way dog eyes do.
His sweet, chocolaty gaze turns into two beams of spooky green
lasers.

"Nothing," I tell him.

I drive back home. I slam the keys down on the counter, storm
to our bedroom. I take inventory. Wallet—gone. Phone—gone.
Keys—gone. Laptop—still in its case tucked beside the dresser.
Would he leave without that? Of course, he has more than one—
he has access to a whole *building* full of computers. I fling open
the closet. I search through the hangers of shirts, looking for

something, who knows what. Shoes. Is his luggage missing? I go
to the hall closet and find both of our suitcases still sitting side by
side, a patient, well-behaved pair.

That padded envelope. I'd completely forgotten about it. It
occurs to me that it might hold some sort of an answer. I'm sure
of it now. It's addressed to him, not to me, but inside is the reason
for Ian's absence. It has to be. I go to the kitchen. The lights of the
city sparkle on the other side of the water. My coffee cup from
the morning is still there in the sink. The house is very quiet, and
all I can hear is the laughter of some people on a boat far off on
the lake. Pollux sits by his bowl patiently. What time is it? Past
time for his dinner.

"I'm sorry, boy," I say. I feed him. I eye that envelope. I sit
down on the kitchen chair, exhausted. Years and years exhausted.
Exhausted in the way you are when your whole life suddenly
catches up to you, from that humiliating oral report on the In-
dustrial Revolution back in the sixth grade all the way to the
long, terrible divorce, with every flu and disappointment in between. I am sure that envelope holds the end of the story somehow. I am almost relieved.

It is possible that he's finally left me.

I listen to Pollux happily crunching his dinner. He takes a big,
sloppy drink of water and then sits by my chair. He looks up at
me, waiting. His kind, warm eyes tell me to get on with it. I am
glad for his company. I rip open the padded envelope.

No letter. Nothing but a small object, stuck in the bottom corner. I turn the envelope upside down and shake it. The bit of
gold falls onto the floor, and Pollux gets up and gives it a sniff.

A cuff link. *Ian's* cuff link? Ian doesn't even *wear* cuff links.
Could he wear cuff links without me knowing it? He has that
big belt buckle with the bull on it, and I'd never in a million years
pictured him wearing that, right? That was a present from his

brother-in-law, though. I think it was his brother-in-law. It seems crucial to remember. The sheer amount of things I don't know opens up before me: his first memory, where he gets his car fixed, his mother's maiden name.

This was what he had lost last night, I realize now. It had to be. The sight of it makes me sick.

I go back to our bedroom. If he'd worn those cuff links last night, the other one would likely be in the tray of our dresser drawer, where he keeps his various treasures—an old class ring, a tie clip of his father's, one of his daughters' baby teeth. He would have set it there after getting undressed for bed. I fling open the drawer. The same old things lay in that tray. There is no cuff link. I reach my hand down into the socks and underwear, feeling beneath them. I don't know what I'm expecting to find—a telltale receipt, a letter, a secret. My fingertips hit the edge of something, paper, and I lift it out. It's a photograph. Just a photo of him with his daughters when they were small. He is stretched out on the floor with his shirt off. Bethy is sitting on his chest as if he's the furniture, and Kristen, just a baby, is tucked in the crook of his arm. He looks so happy.

My heart lurches. I would have put that photo in a frame, set it right up on our bedside table so he could look at it every day. I would have done that gladly. But he had hidden it for his own reasons. He had hidden it, the way you hide precious things that you don't want stolen from you. Then again, for a very long time, he had hidden me, too.

I remember. His mother's maiden name is Charles, all right? Okay? Fine.

I check my phone for messages again. I dial Ian over and over. It's late, but I call people from our address book—Ian's sister,

Olivia; his old friend Simon Ash. I phone Ian's college friend
Leon Green, who has a place in the mountains where he and Ian
went to ski once or twice. I try to sound casual. *By the way*. Olivia's concern ratchets up rapidly. Simon Ash assures me that Ian
probably needed a little time to himself, no big deal, and then
starts telling me about his new job. I call the retirement home
where Mrs. Keller, Ian's mother, lives. I don't want to scare her,
so I talk to the night nurse, who tells me that Mrs. Keller's only
visitor in months has been Georgia Smith, her sister. She comes
every day to play cards. She tells me that Mrs. Keller has recently
been having trouble "voiding." I hate the word *voiding,* but this
is no time for petty annoyances. I promise to let Ian know.

I call the motel Ian stayed in when he first left Mary. I call the
furnished apartments he also stayed in when he left her for the
last time.

I call my mother.

"It's a bear," she says, as soon as she picks up the phone. "It's
not a totem pole. It's a bear holding a fish, like he's just caught it.
Dear God, I think he's going to have a chain-sawed fishing hat.
The old coot just quit for the night."

"Ian's been gone all day."

"Lucky you." She's never hidden her feelings about him. Not
since the first day they met. The minute Ian took her soft, much-
lived hand in his cool, manicured one, I saw her dislike. I guess I
saw his feelings of superiority, too. She works at the bank and
loves Target and feels slightly ill at ease in fancy restaurants, and
he doesn't. Ian would never admit that he thinks he's better than
my parents. He sees himself as the ultimate nice guy. But there's
polite-nice and proper-nice and follow-the-rules nice and don't-
say-it-out-loud-but-show-your-feelings-anyway nice. Of course,
after Mark's anger, which spilled its contents like a moving truck
that had flipped over on the freeway, I welcomed polite, proper,

follow-the-rules containment. Ian isn't one of us, but his rigid sense of responsibility has always felt like safety to me.

"I'm really worried." My voice cracks. Tears have snuck up on me, which tears tend to do. I'm not a crier. The possibility of weeping sits in my throat, waiting for its chance. "He's not answering his phone. His car is still here."

She is silent. She is silent for what seems like a long while. "That's strange," she says finally.

My fear—it too often needs a person to second it, as if it's merely a suggestion on the table until someone else agrees it's a good idea. Fear doesn't always seem real to me. Mark would be standing over my body, his face changing into something dark, and I couldn't quite believe it was happening. It seemed too overly dramatic to be true. I've never been very good at listening to my inner voice. It's been one of my biggest faults, and it's gotten me into my worst troubles. My inner voice speaks too softly, or maybe it's connected to some wire that was wrongly bent years ago, same as my old stereo speakers, which never worked at the same time. But now, at my mother's words, fear takes its rightful place. It shoves forward, becomes a rioting crowd of panic, toppling all my fragile reasoning and flimsy stories of the day. "Something's wrong. Something's really wrong."

"Do you want me to come over?"

"No. I don't know. I don't know what to do. Should I call the police?"

"He's only been gone a day, Dani. You had a fight, didn't you?"

"Not fight exactly."

"Oh, hell—"

"Don't say he'll turn up. It's not like he's a lost cuff link . . ." I'm feeling a little crazy.

"Wait until morning. If he's not there, then call."

"Something's wrong," I say.

"Maybe you should call now."

"What if I call 911 and he's in a hotel somewhere? He'll be so mad."

"Wait until morning, then."

She's no help.

"Are you sure you don't want me to come over?"

"I'm sure."

We hang up. I open the front door and look out again, like an abandoned child. I walk down the dock for the hundredth time that day. I am barefoot. The night is cool. Pollux runs ahead and pees on the nice flower box at the end of the dock. The wind has picked up, and the lake water is slanting toward the shore. The rings of sailboat lines clank and clatter, and the dock groans with its own weariness.

I shove through the dock gates that lead to the street and look at the long line of parked cars. Someone's cat rushes out from underneath one, and then he slinks past, looking for late-night trouble. Ian's car shines under the streetlight, black and gleaming as a grand piano. I set my hand on its hood. I peer cautiously into the backseat, as if I might see a crouched figure there. It's empty, except for a file folder and the UW Husky sweatshirt he wears on the weekends. The metal of the hood is cold.

I hurry back to the house, get the spare key to his car. I unlock the Jaguar's back door. I open that folder. What am I expecting, some note? Horrible last words? But the folder is empty.

I lean against his car, under that streetlight. *Please*, I say, to whoever might be listening.

The clanging sailboats and the wind in the trees and the groaning dock and that wide, wide night sky say only one thing back. *He's gone*, they say. *He's gone*, the darkness and the empty street say, too.

3

I should mention that when I was eleven, my father had an affair that broke up my parents' marriage. I was almost the same age as Abby was when Ian came into our lives. My sister and I were left to pick up the fragmented pieces of my mother's heart, which was no small task. Remember that old *Brady Bunch* episode when Greg and Marcia break Mrs. Brady's favorite vase and try to glue it together again? Marcia fills it with water, but the water spurts out in a hundred places, a fountain of tiny holes. That was my sister and me, minus the canned laughter, trying to put something back together that could never be put back together. The job was too big for us, anyway. There was water everywhere.

I don't think I will ever forget the sound of my mother sobbing on the bed that was now hers alone—the thought makes my stomach ache even now. It didn't feel safe in that house. It was scary. I remember the helplessness and, yeah, if I'm honest, the desire to flee. I wanted someone to rescue us then, too (specifically, my father), but no one ever did. Needless to say, I ended up with strong feelings about adultery. Well, everyone has strong feelings about adultery. But that sobbing and that helplessness—

it amped up my beliefs into something close to fervor. The concept was black and white to me. I would never do that. Never.

And, of course, Ian's father was an outrageous flirt and a ladies' man. Paul hadn't exactly been discreet, either, when he cheated on his devoutly Catholic wife. For Ian, well, think of it: mother protection vying with father identification . . . Oh, psychologists could go to town on this one. They'd make a bundle on us. The point is, Ian and I—we'd both come from a legacy of divorce and treachery, from a homeland where the emotional terrain was steep enough that you craved someone to throw you a line. We were each the least likely and most likely to end up where we did; a solid argument could be built either way. How much does history make your life choices inevitable? That's what I want to know. Maybe we don't truly have the option of free will. Maybe we're only following some old family recipe that has been handed down for years, written in spidery, ancient handwriting and splotched with past ingredients.

He called me one afternoon, after that baseball game. He used some excuse—inviting Mark and me to one of their famed barbecues. I learned later that we were the first people he'd ever invited on his own, because Mary determined who their friends were. I'm not being unkind here; that's just the way it was. Mark was thrilled. We'd made it into the suburban in-crowd, and he was as giddy as Jackie Zavier, my best friend in junior high, after we'd been asked to Scott Maynard's Halloween party.

Ian called me from his office. Abby was at school and Mark was at work, and I think Ian and I both knew that the phone call disguised as an invitation was somehow illicit. It was one of those conversations where there's a whole other conversation going on, unsung notes on an unseen staff strung between you, felt if not actually heard. I hung up, and my heart was beating hard. We'd already begun something. I didn't like myself for it, but the truth was, when Mark came home that night, I felt a sense of secret power that I hadn't felt in a long while, ever since he'd raised a hand and struck me for the first time. That power felt good. I didn't want to hurt Mark, I really didn't—even his rage could feel childlike, a tantrum, something you could pity. For a long time I told myself that he hurt me because he was hurt, but I was tired of being the dog he came home and kicked. That dog was digging a tunnel under the chain-link fence and smiling privately.

We went over to Ian and Mary's house. Abby came, too. They lived in the part of our neighborhood where the houses got bigger, where the garages went from two- to three-car. Abby joined the rest of the kids playing kickball in the cul-de-sac. Inside, their home was a showcase of electronics and furnishings and food and expensive beers. Their boat was parked in the garage; a motorcycle, too. Mary was sitting up on the kitchen counter, swinging her legs. She wore a low-cut blouse that showed off her cleavage. She took a pinch of Mark's shirt, pulled him slightly toward her, and told him how great he looked.

"Ian never wears dress shirts," she said. "I love a man in a dress shirt."

I left Mark in the kitchen with Mary and Charlene and so and so and so and so. Mark was loving it there. You should have seen how happy he was. Ian gestured for me to follow him outside. A couple of neighbor men stood on the patio with their beers. Another woman played with her small toddler on the lawn, blowing bubbles with a plastic wand dripping soap. Usually, she'd have been the one I talked to—the quiet person. The one off to the side, fleeing all the show and all the false lilts in conversation, pretending her child needed her when she needed her child. I'd been guilty of that trick, acting as if the baby needed to be changed or fed or put down for a nap just so I'd have a few minutes away from the in-laws or other strangers. Ian lifted the lid of the barbecue, and a big gust of smoke billowed out. There were platters of meat—beef and chicken and even pork chops. I had never seen so much food in all my life.

"So, what do you think?" Ian said.

"It's a lovely home," I said. I wasn't sure how I actually felt about it. The grass was laid out in a large, orderly rectangle, and the walls inside the house were white, and it felt like something important was missing—color, heartbeat. It was that same feeling you get when you talk to someone and they're saying all the right words but there's an echoey lack of the right emotion.

"Not about that. About *this*."

"This." I wasn't sure what he meant. I'd never played this game before. It seemed too soon to admit the energy between us. And, oh, the energy. I felt it right there. I almost saw it, as real as the hot orange of those coals.

"This party."

I could hear the doorbell ring inside the house, the rise of new voices, laughter. "It's a great party."

He stabbed a thick piece of meat, turned it, as the grease sizzled and kicked up a new torrent of smoke. "You're saying the right words, but . . ."

I smiled. I wasn't used to being seen like that, seen *through*. "I don't do these things too often."

"Thank God," he said. "I knew I liked you for some reason."

The new couple opened the sliding glass door to join us outside. "Shut the door!" Mary called. "The smoke!"

It was true; my eyes were watering. I was in over my head, trading one place I didn't belong for another place I didn't belong, but I didn't know that yet. Then the wind shifted, and it carried the ashy clouds over the neighbors' fence.

"Where there's smoke, there's fire," Ian said.

I think I was furious at my parents for their failed marriage, but I hadn't been married yet myself. Fury is easy until you're in someone else's shoes. I didn't understand how complicated a marriage was. I didn't understand my parents as adult people, how their own histories could sit upon them and press and press. Personal histories, generations of marital dynamics creating marital dynamics. That, and all those pages and pages of fine print and hidden clauses and expectations between two people, ways you are bound to a person when you might desperately need to be free. For me, as a married woman, it was fine print and a small child and a frightening man and economic fears (how, how, how, would I take care of Abby?), all of which had me backed up against a high wall. I was afraid to leave. Inside my body, I felt the race against time as if I were in my own thriller movie, where the ceiling was inching down, ready to annihilate me. When I thought about my life, my heart thumped hard, as if I were being chased. I had become so small that I could almost see my own self, one inch high, standing in the palm of my own hand, waving my tiny arms, screaming for my own miniature help. I was getting smaller and smaller and the walls were coming in and something had to be done.

Ian was getting smaller, too, he told me. In his own way, a different way from mine, but, still, he was. Barbecuing and fixing drinks at all those neighborhood parties he didn't care about, turning steaks and handing over a cool glass of tinkling ice and vodka, making empty conversation. He was disappearing in that life, he said. He tried to tell Mary this in every way he could, for *years*, but after a few weeks of promised change, she'd be back to the drinking and the socializing and the spending. His daughters would have new outfits and glittery new eye shadow and new pink phones, but they would be failing in school. He went to work to make more money for the new sofa and the slipcovers and the display of holiday lights, becoming more and more lonely with each receipt and each shopping bag holding the fruits of his labors. That's what he felt he was worth—the new towels and the car stereo and the manicures and the My Little Ponies. He was stuff, not a man. A provider, whoever that is.

It was clear that I needed to get out of my marriage. It was dangerous and defeating, and no one would question that. But for Ian, the decision was murkier, because he was stuck in the impossible labyrinth of that doomed quest—to find the magic place where marriage is happiness. Logically, he knew this was unfair to Mary. I knew it was unfair to her, too. Two different people and the thing they created between them, a botched and imperfect thing, carrying the weight of spilled gravy and relatives and swimming lessons and car repairs—it wasn't fair to look at *her* and say, *This is the life I have. This is all.* It wasn't fair to her to be disappointed beyond reason. Not fair, but that's the way it was. This was what they'd built. They were so familiar to each other that they'd become strangers. *She doesn't know who I am*, he'd say. *I've tried everything I know to get her to* hear *and to* see, *but* she's *happy. She loves her life.* He would also say, *If we met now, I wouldn't even be attracted to her. I wouldn't* respect *her.*

My marriage had the raised hand and the cowering on the kitchen floor as Mark's shoe struck my rib cage, but Ian had water-torture love—the small, everyday drips of disillusionment and loneliness. Both things can wreck the soul, I think. Violence, yes. That surely destroys love. But bathroom hand towels with embossed satin shells that you weren't supposed to use—maybe those could, too.

The screen door screeched open and closed again at that party, and more people tumbled out, carrying wine coolers and bags of chips. Introductions were made. There was talk about a hair salon and about the unfair treatment twelve-year-old Jason got from Mrs. Bryan when *Gared* had actually been the one to provoke him. There was some discussion about Gared's mother. Gared's *single* mother—no wonder he was out of control. And the men discussed a lube job on Rob's BMW. The freaking doctor telling Neal at his exam that he had high cholesterol. He was supposed to have a goddamn special diet! *I could die tomorrow,* Neal said. *I'm not eating broccoli three times a day.* And then Jason himself came running through the party, snatching the neatly coiled garden hose and reaching for the valve, as Jason's father yelled at him to stop and Jason's mother said Mary must have given him M&M's before dinner.

Those marriages fell like burning trees, one after the other, after Ian and I got together. First, though, there was all the gossip and the nasty barbs as we fled that place, as if we'd set fire to it all, everything, each of their houses. But then, later, their houses *did* catch fire, and their marriages burned up. And how could they not, in that dry, barren place? A marriage can be choked by dust and desperation, destroyed by a last, thoughtless lit match. How could people not lose each other there? It was so lonely in that place. I've said it before, but it was.

You ever taste that Red Rock Ale?

I'm not gonna weed and feed my yard this year. All the work, and it still looks like crap after two weeks of hot weather.

You gotta water every day. Buy a sprinkler system, you cheap bastard.

I actually called Lindsay's mother and told her she'd better tell Lindsay that we won't tolerate bullying toward Jasmine.

Ian caught my eyes and held them. Inside the kitchen, Mary fixed the collar on Mark's shirt.

It was possible that I could rescue Ian and that he could rescue me.

That was the start. And as I stand outside with my mother, watching that police car retreat down the street, I think: *Maybe this is the end.* The feelings I'm having—they aren't exactly unfamiliar. I remember a similar dread from our courtship, from the times I wouldn't hear from him for days. I'd feel scared and sick but angry, too. Yes, angry. I'll admit that.

But now we're married. We have our own bed with soft sheets and sweet memories. On Sundays, we lie there together, our toes entwined. A picture flashes:

Do your "Secret Asian Man." He pretends not to know the lyrics of lots of songs. He thinks this is hilarious. The covers are a tangled mess. We are both revved on coffee.

No laughing. He waggles his finger. Of course, laughing is the point.

Come on! I'm not laughing with you, I'm laughing at you!

In that case. He hops on his knees. He gets the air guitar going, and he's wearing that hot stage number, his blue boxers. *Beware of pretty faces that you find. A pretty face can hide an evil mind!* he sings, shimmying around until the big payoff. *Sec-ret Asian man!* he hollers, wiggling his ass, giving it all he's got. I sock him with a pillow for the audience participation part of the program.

Things are different now, I try to tell myself, but my whole body is shaking, unconvinced. Some weird alien tremor has begun, and I can't stop it. The car turns the corner and is gone. What's just happened doesn't seem real, but it is real. A police car means it's real. My mother puts her arm around me. "I just want to know that he's okay," I say. "Just that. Just that one thing."

My chest feels caved in, as if it has fallen in on itself, and I can barely breathe, it hurts so bad. His absence is immense, dark and immense, because once the logical likelihoods are gone, it means that anything else is possible. Anything and everything. He could be anywhere, with anyone. He could be in some foreign country; he could be hurt somewhere; he could be dead; someone could have killed him; he could be driving in some convertible down some road with a new identity in his pocket.

He wouldn't take off without telling his kids, I had told the officer who arrived that morning. Detective Vince Jackson had a beefy head and inky-black hair (dyed, likely) and chubby cigar fingers. But is this true? Ian's children had rejected him after we got together. For a long while, they refused to see him if he was with me, and Kristen had instructed him not to come to her graduation. His idea of himself as a good father had been destroyed. You can run, can't you, if there isn't anything much to leave behind?

"Come on," my mother says. She pulls me to her. She has her old flannel shirt on and her jeans. She'd been working in the yard. So she says. Spying on the neighbors' chain-saw artist, more likely. She smells like fresh dirt and Jean Naté.

We walk back up the dock. Maggie pokes her head out the door. "Dani?"

"He's still gone," I say.

"Oh, no." She holds her hand to her heart. She and my mother lock eyes. They exchange unspoken information that I don't want to witness. "If I can help at all . . ."

The day drags on. I can't do anything. I can't work, of course, or get the mail or make necessary phone calls, whatever those might be. I can't eat or sit still. Pollux is nervous. He doesn't like high emotions. He gets upset at tears and arguments. He looks worried; his forehead is crinkled and his eyes are concerned. I stand and stare out the large glass windows of the houseboat. The sun is going down. Again. Pollux is as close as he can get. I feel him leaning against my legs.

"Do you have anything to help you sleep?" my mother asks.

"No."

"Maybe I can—"

"I need to hear the phone. I hate that kind of stuff, anyway." I hate the way it makes me feel—the thickness in my limbs, the heavy fuzz in my head. The way it confuses my thoughts and blurs my memory.

"You need to sleep. I'm planning to stay."

"No."

"I'm staying."

"Really. I want to be alone."

My mother shakes her head. She washes her hands at the sink, for lack of anything more useful to do. She dries them on the kitchen towel that hangs from the rail of the stove. The kitchen towel has a row of cherries on it. My husband is missing. I don't know how to reconcile these two facts.

"That hairbrush. His toothbrush. In those Ziploc bags," I say.

"They have to do that. You heard him. Did you hear all the agencies that'll be notified? MUPU, NCMA? Some clearing-house . . ."

"Clearinghouse? How is that supposed to do anything?" All I can think of is Ed McMahon and the giant check. Or a large room with hundreds of files with thousands of names. "This is crazy!"

"They have to determine if Ian's even missing, Dani. He might not be. All they're doing is covering the basics right now. That's what the detective said. They'll open an investigation when they have reason to think he hasn't disappeared of his own free will."

"I couldn't even answer the questions. I don't even know how much he weighs."

"You were close enough, Dani. Come on."

"*Identifying marks.* God."

"I know, sweetie."

"He's gone." It strikes me, a blow to the chest. A dark smack of fear, the biggest and most terrible feeling of all: *gone.*

"Ian's not high risk. That's what the man said. He's not high risk for disappearing."

"I don't even understand what that means."

"Alzheimer's, mentally unwell. In danger. That's why he asked about health issues Ian might have, right? That's why the *Unless you think a crime has been committed . . .*"

This seems comforting. There's a procedure for these things. If they aren't alarmed, I can be less alarmed. It's like that trick I do when there's turbulence on the airplane. If the flight attendants are still serving drinks and collecting garbage, there's nothing to worry about. If they're chatting to one another and laughing, the bumps and lurches that terrify me are things they've seen a hundred times before.

I remember all those nights, too, when I worried about Abby when she was late coming home and still an inexperienced driver. She'd known I would worry, though, and she'd always found a way to eventually contact me. Ian knows I'd worry, too. This leads to an equation in my mind, a calculation with a sickening result. There are only two possibilities: Either he can't contact me or he doesn't want to.

"That detective looked around here like I had him hidden somewhere." I twist my wedding ring.

"That's his job," my mother says.

Mind if I look around? Detective Vince Jackson had asked. *Of course not,* I had said, and then he walked around the houseboat with his eyes scanning. He looked in our bedroom. He asked me if anything was missing. *Ian* was the obvious answer, but, no, nothing. Nothing else. Ian and the jeans and black shirt he'd worn to the party. The soft leather shoes. His phone, his wallet, his keys.

You came home, he got undressed for bed?

I couldn't remember exactly. Can't. I've tried and tried. I was so tired. I was groggy, and I headed for bed, and I assume we did what we always do. He might have stayed up to read or sit and watch the lights on the lake. He might have climbed into bed after I was already asleep. I could have been asleep before he even came out of the bathroom.

Detective Vince Jackson raised his eyebrows. He wrote things down. He asked me when my last clear memory of my husband was. In the car, driving home, I said. I was being too honest. But that was the truth. I didn't have a clear picture of Ian walking inside the house, taking off his clothes, coming to bed. I had images of myself dropping my heels at the door, climbing thankfully between the sheets, dismissing him and the whole uncomfortable night. It was the kind of thing that happened regularly, the way you don't even remember the drive to the store. The way your head is full of your own thoughts after a bad night. *That stupid dress; that woman at the party; Nathan, he's a kind man; an altercation; Ian's grim face behind the wheel; forget it all until tomorrow.* The cool sheets, the bliss of sleep.

What's this?

Vince Jackson had popped his head into Ian's study. His eyes went immediately to the board, where the last butterfly had been pinned. It was still there, collecting dust. It wasn't the way to pay homage to something beautiful, as Ian always claimed. It had been pinned and forgotten.

His hobby, I said. I wanted to say, *It was the way he stayed connected to his father,* but it seemed like too much information. Ian would be embarrassed by that, by his own need for the love of the great Paul Hartley Keller. Definitely he wouldn't want such a thing to be revealed to this man, this Vince Jackson, a tough, impenetrable male, who didn't look as if he'd ever questioned his place in the world. Ian's father need—it was the kind of hole you saw and wanted to heal for someone you loved. After trying that routine twice and failing, with Mark, with Ian, I knew something else, too: It's human nature to want to help and soothe and save with your love, but it's also arrogant.

It's a strange hobby, my mother remarked to the detective. I couldn't believe she said that. I was getting the creeping feeling that Detective Vince Jackson suspected me of something here; I could feel the mistrust in the way he moved his thick shoulders through the doorways of my home, looking at carpets and window frames and the comforter I'd picked out at Bed Bath & Beyond. My mother must have felt it, too. *If something is off here, that something was Ian,* she seemed to say.

His suspicion made me feel guilty. Admittedly, guilt can be my default setting. After a social gathering, I'm often left with a vague sense of wrongdoing that I try to pinpoint the source of. Had I laughed insensitively or slighted someone unintentionally? And I always feel accused in Nordstrom. The saleswomen look at my jeans and inexpensive haircut and I'm sure they're thinking I'm about to slip a pair of earrings into my purse. I feel guilty when I eat white bread and when I don't recycle. The therapist I saw during my divorce, Dr. Shana Berg—I loved her—once told me that I was in desperate need of rebellion. The idea of it sounded wonderful, like riding in a convertible on an open road, with a scarf flowing behind you.

Detective Vince Jackson stood outside on the front deck. The lake was busy with its usual merry parade of tour boats and water taxis. The sun was out, and the water sparkled wrongly. I heard a happy shout, someone making a joke, laughter. Two guys on paddleboards rowed past, as Detective Vince Jackson stepped onto our sailboat and looked around for my vanished husband. He made his way down below, to the cabin. I heard him open and close the bench lids. He climbed the ladder back up. *The New View?*

Even the boat's name was some sort of accusation. *It means . . .* I struggled. *The way we were going to do things differently.*

Differently?

We'd been married before. And both of us had divorced parents. I was talking too much. It made me look like I was nervous. I *was* nervous. That man's big hands and blue uniform and the way he wrote things down made me nervous. His hips were packed with heavy equipment—a radio, a gun. The radio kept spitting out loud bits of crackly conversations and codes. I wondered how he knew when to listen and when to ignore it. He was standing in front of my lounge chair, where I sunned myself and drank lemonade and read. *We wanted to have commitment in our lives,* I said.

I followed Detective Vince Jackson's eyes out over the lake. I read the question there before he asked it. The lake—it didn't seem possible. *If he'd fallen . . . You hear everything around here,* I said. *A splash, a call for help . . .*

Can he swim?

He was on the swim team in high school. And there's a ladder right there. I pointed to the edge of the dock. That's why every dock has one; if you fall in, there's a quick way to get out.

How much did he have to drink that night?

A glass or two? I don't know. I wasn't with him the whole time. He drove home. . . . He seemed fine.

How much did you have to drink?

The same. Two, maybe?

He ever run off before? Take a few days? A little breather, a camping trip to commune with nature?

Not exactly.

He looked up from his notebook. I could feel my mother's shocked eyes on me. Well, you don't tell your mother everything.

He didn't come home one night, if that even counts. We were just married. Had an argument. He came right back.

Coulda done the same thing?

We never had an argument like that again.

He continued to watch my face but asked nothing more. *I'd contact everyone you know. Ask around. He's probably cooling his jets over something you didn't even know you did. I'd like a list of everyone in his life we should talk to if we need.*

Okay, good. No problem.

Now my mother was being too helpful. She'd rushed inside and was already rummaging around in my kitchen drawers for a notepad and pen. She was shoving around all the unused coupons and take-out menus, not even looking in the right place. *Here,* I had said, retrieving the pad by the phone. Detective Vince Jackson stayed outside and talked to someone on his radio.

I wrote down names. Nathan. Paula, Ian's secretary. His family. My mother was piping in every two seconds with more ideas.

I wished she would stop. My brain was going a million miles an hour, and yet it also felt stalled and broken.

Bethy and Kristen Keller, I wrote. And, in parentheses, *daughters.*

Don't forget Mary, my mother said, as Detective Vince Jackson slid open the door and came inside.

Mary? he asked.

His ex-wife, I said.

Detective Vince Jackson sat down in the kitchen chair across from me. He sighed. *Mrs. Keller*, he said. *What do you think happened to your husband?*

Images appeared; the options presented themselves. It was crazy, but the one that screamed the loudest (and that maybe— how awful to say—I feared the most right then) had nothing to do with murder or an accident. I could see him straddling the seat of his old riding lawn mower, an expensive one, of course. There he'd be, turning the key, and the engine would start, and so would the engines of all the other riding lawn mowers on that street. He would lay his regrets to rest as the machine made its clean stripes into the grass and as the neighbor men made their clean stripes into their own lawns. Up and back he would go, and Neal would go, and Rob, and Mark, as the *New View* bobbed in now ridiculous, falsely optimistic waters. Because you can never entirely flee disappointment, can you? We have it, too; the bare foot meeting dog barf, the spilled coffee grounds, the discouraging daily stuff that could feel like a life metaphor. Of course, those men don't even live in that neighborhood anymore. Mark lives in a condo on the Eastside, and Neal took off to Israel or somewhere, and Rob and his wife divorced and I have no idea where they ended up. Still, when Detective Jackson asked me that question, I saw them all out there on their Sunday morning lawns, one riding north and then south again, the other riding south and then north, as their wives sipped orange juice and vodka.

I don't know, I had finally answered. *I just don't. I just hope he's okay.*

We all do, ma'am.

I love him, I said.

Love is complicated.

I handed over the pictures the detective asked for, the ones I had nearest—a recent PR photo for the new BetterWorks website, which I'd kept on the nightstand by our bed. Ian looks so handsome in it, in that dark shirt set against the white backdrop, with his strong cheekbones and his black hair and those bright blue eyes against the tan he had then. Oh, the chemistry between us. I handed over our wedding photo, too, the two of us on the courthouse steps, me smiling up at him. Ian has one hand raised, like he's waving to potential voters. I gave the detective another photo, as well. The one I'd found in Ian's dresser drawer. The one of him with Bethy and Kristen, the one hidden under the rolled-up socks.

Good lookin' family, Detective Vince Jackson had said, but his voice was clipped and businesslike.

Now, though, the detective is gone, and my mother is watering my windowsill cactus. Sure, it needs it—it looks like a cucumber left too long in the produce drawer—but still. "Please, Ma," I say. "Go? I've got to call Abby. She's worried sick. She's called me six times. I'll try to sleep, I promise."

"Dani—"

"There's nothing we can do but wait. That's the thing. *Nothing.*"

My mother sighs. Then she collects her purse, her jacket. "My keys . . ." She looks around. She's forgotten where she set them. There they are, by the kitchen phone. "What's this?" She holds it up.

The cuff link. I'd forgotten all about it. "Someone dropped it off yesterday. Ian must have lost it at the party."

"Not really his type."

She's right. It's a small circle of gold with a jade center. Ian isn't much for jewelry, even when I wear it. He'd bought enough of it for Mary. She'd go to the store and pick out what she wanted before every occasion. One thing you learn in a marriage, though—there are always things you don't know about your partner. Always.

"Well, you should tell the police about it. You never know what's important."

My mother kisses my cheek. We say goodbye at the door. I call Abby back. I call Ian's daughters. I call my sister. I call my father. I do my best to get through these calls, because I don't feel like talking to anyone. I feel only like keeping vigil. All I want to do is wait for Ian to come back. And so when the phone calls are over, that's what I do. I sit on that deck outside and I watch the red night-lights of the boats and I stay still and hope, until the evening gets cool and the water gets dark and darker still.

I think about that list of names. Who I've left off. Mark. Should I have written him down? The woman at the party, too, the one talking to Ian on the grass of Kerry Park. The one in the red dress, who had her hand on Ian's sleeve. I'd forgotten her. But, then again, I don't even know her name.

4

"What's this?"

Abby unzips her backpack. She hands over a package wrapped in cellophane. "Banana bread." Another package. "Cookies. Oh, and cinnamon rolls. The frozen kind. I didn't make them."

"Oh, honey."

"Baking helplessness."

I look at her shiny dark hair (the exact color of Mark's) and her lovely brown eyes and all those baked goods, and I realize for the millionth time what a good person she is. No matter how many mistakes I've made as a mother, this daughter of mine has managed to be a fine, fine person.

"Don't you have class?"

"Like I can go to class? You look like shit. I'll make us some coffee."

I watch my Abby, who now lives on her own with two friends in a tiny apartment near the university. During her first year in her own place, I'd get these great calls asking how to make that stroganoff I cooked, or that chicken teriyaki, or if you could bake a pie in a cake pan, or what to do if you needed butter for a recipe but didn't have butter. Years ago, we'd spend hours making gingerbread men with frosting pants and sprinkle hair. But now here she is, making her way around my kitchen like the grown woman she's become. I have a wrong thought then. I could face anything except losing her. I could even lose Ian but never my child. I remember the shift that occurred after Abby was born—there'd been the great big before, where dying grandparents and natural disasters on the news were sad but mostly distant concerns. But then I became a mother, and when that happens, you cross a line that makes all loss a crushing, personal matter.

The coffee pot burbles. Pollux's nose is up, sniffing madly at the baked bounty on the counter, which I have no desire to eat. I'm waiting. Waiting to sleep, waiting to eat, even. Abby pours two cups. "I hope it's not too strong."

"Never," I say.

"I talked to Grandma." Abby sets her fingers around her cup. "She said the police guy came yesterday."

"I called the station again already this morning. I left a few messages. I don't know what to *do*."

"Are we supposed to be making flyers? *Lost Software Exec? Reward?* We should call the media or something. We can organize a search. We can't just sit here. I'm worried sick about him." This is Abby. She's the kind of person who gets in and makes things happen, which she's done from the time she was four, supervising the preschool girls in a game of restaurant while wearing her little red stretch pants and *101 Dalmatians* sweatshirt.

"TV? Oh, honey, I don't know. If we got other people involved . . . What if we had him on all channels, and he *left*? You know, *willingly*."

"You really think that he would do that? He wouldn't do that, Mom. After all that crap with his kids, when things are finally settling down for you guys? Wait. What do Bethy and Kristen say about this? Do they have any idea where he is?"

"Kristen said she'll make some calls. Bethy . . ." I shake my head. "'Maybe he finally got smart.'"

"She's such a bitch."

"I don't think they were too worried until last night, when I told them I called the police."

Abby's forehead wrinkles in concern. "Mom, I don't know how to ask this . . . but was he depressed or anything? I mean, sometimes he can get kind of down. Grandma thought he might be, you know, upset enough to—"

"She reads *Psychology Today* and thinks she can diagnose people. Ian, his religion . . . Suicide's not an option. I don't think it's an option. He loves his work, he loves—"

"You."

Abby and I look at each other. In my head, I play the scene again. We are in the car. Ian's face is grim in the light of the passing streetlamps. We'd had words, but it is more than that. It goes deeper. I could make a hundred guesses—I wasn't friendly enough, my laugh was too loud, I stumbled after drinking that wine, I glared at the woman with her hand on his sleeve. Ian likes things to go right. He likes the towels folded a certain way; he likes the car vacuumed a certain way; he likes an email to be written a certain way. He doesn't like errors of balance or manners or grammar. He never makes mistakes, I swear. Never a misstep. It can get exhausting, trying to measure up. You start to feel as if you're on a perpetual job interview.

After that party, I was tired. This, I do remember. I got into bed. I didn't think about Ian, because I was sick of thinking about Ian. There were the cool sheets, sleep.

"You guys are happy, right?" Abby asks. "It seems like it."

"Of course!" But this sounds wrong. It's too cheerful under the circumstances. It's obviously what you say to a daughter so she won't worry. I'm not sure what it even means, *happy*. We had done so much to find our happiness. We had worked so hard and struggled so much to get *to* it. *Happy* could be like anything else you worked too hard to get—an expensive vacation, say, that you saved for, and gave up other things for, and dreamed of, in some location that you flew long and difficult distances to reach. After hours of jet lag and waiting in dirty airports, you could find yourself on the shiny, disappointing shore, exhausted and sick from foreign water, wondering how you possibly got so far from home.

I go through it again. The party, the drive home, the grim face. The cool sheets. The bliss of rest.

There were more weekend parties at their house, the baseball team's end-of-season bash, the neighborhood gang 4th of July, someone's birthday. Mary must have just finished tossing paper napkins and washing glasses before she began planning for the next get-together. It was distraction, I guess, the way some people keep the TV on all the time so they don't have to hear their own thoughts. When we were with them, it was obvious how the lines between the couples were drawn—Mark and Mary, with all they had in common; Ian and me, with all we did. Mark and Mary were physical people, who wanted to drink and laugh and spend. Ian and I loved books and music and quiet places. He'd take me into their living room and show me his old albums. He had his father's Tony Bennett, and he had the Cars and Leo Sayer (which we thought was pretty hilarious, Leo with his big afro). He had Patty Griffin and Emmylou Harris and the Clash. He'd play me songs he loved that I loved, too, while Mary and Mark drank more beers and margaritas and Bloody Marys and joked with the crowd in the other room.

My friends are asking where you came from, Ian said to me as

John Prine played. *Toby and Renee, especially*. Toby and Renee were longtime buddies of the Kellers. They'd all lived in the same neighborhood in the Silicon Valley before moving to the Northwest. *Renee thinks you're too flirtatious. I think she's jealous because you're beautiful.* I heard the compliment—*beautiful*. I'd never thought of myself that way, with my straight brown hair and all my "too"s—too skinny, too tall, too big of a nose—but I was so happy he saw me that way. I felt beautiful when I was with him. But I also heard the criticism there. And the next time I saw Renee, I watched myself. I kept my energy turned down a notch. It's one of those things you think about later that makes you cringe. God, why'd I do that? But I wanted her to like me, if he wanted her to like me. I wanted that life. I wanted a life with him. A life where the hose was rolled up, and things were in their place, and the remote control had its own little holder. Where I was beautiful, sure, but, much more important than that, where order implied safety and calm.

And, the funny thing was, Mark wanted that life, too. He was there at that house and at those parties because he wanted that motorcycle and a boat like Ian's in the garage. He wanted the perfectly landscaped yard. But he couldn't ever get there himself, by himself. He worked in sales, on commission, and he fought with bosses and quit jobs and bought expensive leather jackets he couldn't afford, and money was another way I felt unsafe. Mary, too, ran up credit cards, never had a job, and didn't really know where their wealth came from. Ian worked crazy hours, building his company. Two A.M., three A.M.—more hiding, maybe, but that Visa bill had gone through the roof again, and someone had to pay it. Ian knew where every penny was. He had IRAs and CDs and ETFs. He had every financial product with an acronym that existed. He was shoring up against the next financial disaster or shopping trip, stuffing money into iron-vault mattresses.

I balanced our checkbook to the penny, as well, and when Mark felt too depressed to work, to sell, when he stayed home and slept late and roiled about the unfairness of people's treatment of him, I would freeze large quantities of cheap food in case the worst came, the way old people who grew up during the Depression hoard canned vegetables.

Ian offered us tickets to a concert, and we all went together. Two other couples, too. Some country singer, I can't remember. I don't like country music, and neither does Ian. The twangy pop kind, anyway. Mark and Mary did. They loved it. It was a way that Ian and I could be near each other, even if we didn't admit it yet. Seats away, still near, amid ten thousand screaming people.

Wait. Clint Black. That's who it was. Black hat, black outfit.

We all went out for drinks later. Mary was working on her third margarita, telling some story that was making everyone laugh. *And then I drove down the ramp, and I didn't see the sign— bam! Nearly took the top half off the car!*

Lisa, married to Gene, screeched with laughter.

Take it to Auto One, Gene said to Ian. *They do a great job. Lisa bashed the Subaru, and it doesn't have a scratch on it now.*

I didn't bash it! The idiot ran a stoplight!

Pretty hilarious, when you didn't have to work your ass off to buy the thing, Ian said. He wasn't joking. His face looked suddenly tight.

Fine, I'll get a job and pay for it myself!

You're careless. That's the problem. He was being cruel, but she didn't seem bothered. She kept laughing and drinking her margarita. I felt a pang of guilt. His cruelty was there, I was sure, because of me. Because their marriage was ending.

I'll do pennants, she laughed. She waved an imaginary flag. She was a little tipsy.

Penance? Ian corrected.

Hey, I love a good penance, Gene joked. *I like my penance every night, baby.*

Ian met my eyes over the table and held them. I would never be careless with something he bought. It was easy to see how things would be very different with us. I respected him and how hard he worked.

And I understood his deep need to be responsible, financially and otherwise. I was the same way. I'd started doing my own graphic-design work part-time after Abby was in school, brochures mostly, travel brochures and new products displayed in three panels. I was teaching myself how to create websites. I had a handful of clients—two tour companies, a husband-and-wife team who sold personal-care products, and a mom who delivered homemade baby food to the "choosiest parents." (I believe we used those exact words.) I spent the school hours in front of my computer, looking at images of cobalt waters and white sand and sensual bottles of eco-friendly shampoo. For days I rearranged photos of vegetables. I would try to put the pieces together in a way that was whole and desirable and enticing. I aimed to please. Well, I sure did.

Sometime after that concert, Ian began calling me in the afternoon. I would be there at my desk and the phone would ring and my heart would quicken. He would call for some made-up reason—an invitation, a news article about a music performer we liked. The cobalt waters and white-sand beach would sit in front of me for too long, and my tuna sandwich (tuna, mayo, potato chips laid inside, white bread, perfection) would find itself uncommonly ignored.

The voice on the other end, the talk, real talk, talk between two people—not talk that was effortful, a counseling session, anger avoidance, careful stepping around land mines, all the things talk was with Mark—it was a new world. I didn't know that's what talk was like. I had met Mark when I was nineteen, and I guess after all those years he had exhausted me. I never knew I was signing up for some battle, but I finally knew that he had won. It wasn't just the anger that had done me in, the moments when he would thrash and rage and a fist would go through a door right next to my face—it was the daily tending of an emotional person. The violent outbursts (his hands on me, his feet kicking) would come once or twice a year, more sometimes, but the mood reading, the way I was a perpetual ranger at a perpetual weather station watching for ominous signs, that was a constant, and that's what defeated me. Our marriage wasn't all rage, of course. Of course we had our good times. Of course there were things I loved about him. I patched that door he'd punched the hole through, though. I hid the damage. I used spackling paste and a flat-edged tool I found in the garage. I painted over it, but you could still see the rough edges where his fist had gone in. I wore long sleeves sometimes, too.

With Ian, when we talked—I got something back, and this seemed like a revelation. I learned things about his work. I learned about his life. I learned about what he wanted and didn't have, and what he had and didn't want. He was calm. He was kind. His life seemed so . . . controlled. But I also spoke. I didn't know there was a door you could open to a whole land of yourself. Or maybe I suspected it but finally saw it was true. There were all these ideas I had, dreams, all this *energy*.

Do you know what Mark told me once? I just remembered this. He told me that he didn't want to hear about my day when he came home. He needed *me* to listen to *him*. What I can't believe now is that I must have gotten in bed with him that night, after he said that.

Still, what Ian and I did was the coward's way out. I know this. I know it now, and I knew it then, although I justified it. Adultery often happens, I am sure, because you are on the sinking ship, and you need to leap but can't leap. You are too spineless, maybe, to leap. The water is too dark and choppy and the sea is too large. Saving your own life, even, isn't enough reason to jump—no, you need the hands at your back, pushing, the hands of something as unavoidable and inevitable and imperative as love. It's got to be something that big, you know, to get you to jump. That life raft down there is too small, and the unknowns are so immense, and you know where the kitchen is on the ship; you know where your own bed is, and the sinking is so slow, anyway, that you've gotten used to it. You really don't want to hurt a person, either; that's the irony. Even if he's someone who has screamed in your face and struck you. Especially not if her only real crime is running up the credit cards and drinking a lot and occasionally ignoring the kids. The compelling forces of capital letter LOVE and another person in that life raft so that you're not alone—they make the leap possible.

Of course, having company in that boat does not alter the fact that you're lost at sea.

I told my first lie, my first real lie, to Mark. Ian and I planned to meet one night at his office. It would be our first time alone. God, I was so nervous. I told Mark I was going out to dinner with two old high school friends. I didn't feel good about the lie. First of all, he could find out, and, Jesus, what *that* might mean . . . But it was more than a fear of repercussions. He had made himself popcorn that night. He and Abby were going to watch a movie while I was gone. No matter how much harm had been done over the years, that popcorn made me feel terrible. The way he settled the bowl on the coffee table, a beer nearby. That little pile of napkins. Napkins could break your heart; who knew.

When I got in the car, though, when I started to drive and was finally away from that house and that neighborhood—I felt free. God, it was thrilling. It was *mine*. It was night and I love driving at night, and I remembered how much I loved it. Something was happening during that drive. I was old and getting younger. I didn't realize I'd felt so old until then. The city lights, the radio, the driving *away*—I felt like I was the self I'd lost long ago. The someone I'd been before meeting Mark, before my life turned down that hard road. I remembered who I used to be and maybe still was. I felt light like that, as if I was sixteen and Journey was playing on the radio and the future was wide open and I had all the time in the world.

I'd forgotten all about that feeling. It came back to me as I drove. I turned the radio on and I felt filled with joy. Lifted and filled, and I loved the city and the streetlamps and the car lights in the rearview mirror and every single soul still working in those high, lit, skyscraper offices. I wished each of them the very best.

I thought it was about Ian, but it wasn't. I know that now. It was about returning. Setting the clock back to that place where you'd turned but should never have turned. It was about undoing the damage and filling the holes and repairing the broken pieces. In a way it was like watching a film in reverse. Mark's hands flew away from my body back to his own sides, and I walked backward out of the church where we were married, becoming the girl I once had been.

It was early summer. The night air smelled like heat and grass

and darkness. Ian stood waiting outside the BetterWorks building, his arms folded. I walked up to him, and he greeted me as if
we were having a business appointment. Someone might have
been working late behind *those* tall glass windows, watching.

He had his head down, and I followed him. We waited at the
elevators, where he swiped his pass. I took in all the perfect lines
and the clean wood and the neatly exposed beams. It was an impressive place. We walked into a hall of closed doors, with windows looking into offices piled with papers and computers. He
unlocked his own door. His office did not have windows that
looked out on the hallway like the others did. Instead, there were
huge panes of glass inside, and the extraordinary city in front of
us, the buildings rising up, the Space Needle, the lights reflecting
on the water of the lake.

"Wow," I said.

He didn't say anything; he only let the door swing shut behind
us. He grabbed my arms and spun me toward him, and we kissed
and it shook me so hard—how much I wanted it, him. I didn't
know I could want like that. I had imagined him kissing me, but
here he was now, up close. Here was his breath, his tongue, his
hands gripping my shoulders and then my hair.

He pulled away. The lights of the room were off, but I could
see his mouth, shiny from the kiss. He stared at me, looked into
my eyes, far, far in. I believed he saw things there that no one else
had. Maybe I didn't even know those things were there.

"Jesus," he said.

"I know."

"There are all these new places," he said.

"There are."

He sat down in his desk chair, one of those high-tech sorts
with metal and black mesh. He did something that I now know

was not Ian-like at all. He spun a full circle, a chair lap of disbelief and even happiness. He exhaled, the way a man does when he can't believe his good luck.

He reached out his arm, and I took his hand. He pulled me into his lap, and that stupid chair tilted and we flung backward and hit the desk, and it was not the way it would have happened in the movies. Our chins knocked together. We laughed.

"Good move, Keller," he said. "Smooth operator."

"I should tell you I can't dance," I said. "Or dribble a basketball. I'm entirely uncoordinated."

"Obviously, I really like uncoordinated," he said.

Oh, I felt sixteen. I felt the giddiness of falling in love, and my real life and past history—a popcorn bowl, a child, my stormy husband and difficult in-laws—were all momentarily gone. We were there in that first thrill you get around anything potent. I suppose it's the same place in which alcoholics find themselves when they fall headfirst for that warm buzz, or what a gambler feels when the bells ring and the horses are let out of the gate and they are running, flying. It's all yours, yours, yours. What it all means, what it really *means*, is too far away to be real; you're just willingly going down. It's such a heady time, before all the consequences. Certainly you're not even aware of the lonely, destructive nights ahead when your knees feel so deliciously weak. *Take me*, you want to say. Not to him, but to *life*. You are at the very center, at the beating heart of *possibility*.

He pushed me up off his lap. I had driven over the bridge to meet him, lied in order to give that night to him, dressed carefully, waited, and anticipated. And we were there all of an hour. He set me back on my feet. He looked me deeply in the eyes again and he said, "I can't do this, Dani.

"I can't do this," he repeated, and then he kissed me again, or

I kissed him, and we thrashed and tore and parted. A kiss only, but, dear God.

I got back in my car, and he stood there at the doorway to his building again, arms behind his back, watching me drive off. I was in so far over my head that I was already drowning. I just didn't know it yet.

I only thought, *I've been saved.*

When Abby goes home, I get my car keys. Maybe it's stupid (it feels like it is), but I leave another note for Ian. I can't stand being in the houseboat anymore. I check my phone for messages, and then I check it several more times to make sure I haven't turned the ringer off accidentally. I want to make sure I hear him if he calls.

"Be a good guard dog, okay?" I say to Pollux. He isn't really a guard dog. He hides in the other room whenever he sees the vacuum cleaner.

The day is moving forward around me. I see a bread truck delivering dinner rolls to Pete's Market. An Argosy tour boat (Ian calls it the *Agony*) is taking a new group of tourists around the lake. For the millionth time, I hear the voice over the microphone telling everyone within hearing distance that *Lake Union is an actual airport runway, with an average of ten seaplane landings a day.* . . . I had gotten my period that morning. My husband is missing, and my body is moving through the month, regardless. He could be dead while I'm hunting in the bathroom cupboard for the box of tampons. I remember to get the mail. My car tabs are due. I will have to get an emissions test.

It occurs to me then that Ian might be truly gone, gone forever, for whatever reason. It hits me: I might be completely on my own now. Alone with emissions tests and taxes and electrical repairs and bills. My God, the world seems huge when you think of yourself against it, all the things you have to stand there and handle. Child-rearing and illness and carburetors. Family fights and auto accidents and health insurance. My relationship with *alone* has always been a love–hate one. I've always loved *daily alone*, when it's you and a book or you and the dog or you and just you, when you're blissfully released from the burden of someone else's mood. When no one needs you, when no one expects anything of you, when there are no demands of you . . . It's such a relief. But *life alone?* Somewhere along the line, I guess I've gotten the idea that the world is a dangerous place and that, in it, I'm a small child in a dark and threatening forest. These are not things you go around admitting. Especially when you think of yourself as a strong person, which I do. I hate to say this, but even as an adult woman, I've felt the need for protection. Not only in empty parking garages, either. It's possible I've felt this way since I was a child. Here's the irony (or destiny—take your pick): The places where I've sought protection have been rickety and dangerous, and I don't know entirely why. Alone in the forest, I had first chosen a feral, hungry dog to shield me, and then I'd selected a companion with two broken legs and an empty canteen. Faced with my own freedom, I've gotten trapped behind glass, same as Ian's butterflies.

The hugeness of *alone*, the panic of it, gathers up my insides and squeezes. After all I'd done to avoid it, maybe it had come to find me anyway. Oh, the cruelty of it. But this is how it goes, isn't it, with the Big Life Lessons? You can run but you can't hide?

He's hurt, he's been killed, he's run off. He's hurt, he's been killed, he's run off. *What do you think happened to your husband, Mrs. Keller?*

"Come on, Blue," I say to the Beast, and turn the key. I drive the route Ian takes to work. Maybe he decided to walk there on Sunday morning. He could have twisted his ankle; he could be unconscious, lying deep in the ravine near Kerry Park, the one adjacent to BetterWorks. There was that narrow bit of grass, the place the party had spilled onto on Saturday night, the place we had sometimes picnicked. There had been good and bad times there, times when we'd brought a blanket and white bags from Kidd Valley stuffed with burgers and onion rings, when we'd eat and kiss and people-watch. But there was that day, too, when he brought the butterfly net. We got out of the car, and I was carrying the bottle of wine and the paper cups I'd brought, and then he opened the trunk. I cringed when I saw the net there. I had the briefest, unkind image of him prancing across the grass with it in the air, like some child on a Victorian postcard. I never would have said anything, *ever*, but he could sense criticism before the thought even finished forming in my head. Ian's an accomplished, sexy, smart man, but his ego is fragile as a bird's wing. Paul Hartley Keller saw to that. *What?* Ian had said that day, the word a challenge. I swear, I hadn't even blinked, hadn't changed my facial expression one bit, but Ian had picked up on the tiniest shift in my approval. *Nothing, Ian*, I said, but it was already too late, and the afternoon was ruined.

The edge of the park drops right off down a steep hill. It's what makes the view of the city so fine there: the height. The park's an added benefit to the staff at BetterWorks. They can go there to eat lunch or take a walk.

Now, though, there's only an empty van in the parking lot, a beat-up green machine with a Seattle-worthy bumper sticker reading CAPTAIN COMPOST. The park itself is also nearly empty, except for a mother with two small girls wearing the city's regulation attire for hip children of hip parents—part expensive hemp EcoWear, part dress-up box. In Seattle, there's always some kid in a feather boa or a tutu and cowboy boots, which demonstrates how supportive the parent is of the child's self-expression. It gets irritating. You wouldn't believe how many little girls have tutus and cowboy boots. This particular woman is delivering a loud, singsongy lecture about friendship, so I'll know what a good mother she is. It would probably surprise her that I don't care whether she recycles or eats organic or teaches her children about diversity. It would probably disappoint her that I don't even notice her for more than a moment and that I don't have the energy to admire her. I'm looking for my husband, who might be lying dead in the tangle of blackberry bushes on that bank.

I walk the path, which winds along the bluff. It would seem crazy, calling out his name. I do it anyway. I step down from the muddy ledge and try to see if anything is there except brambles and ferns and huckleberry plants.

"Ian?" I call. It probably looks like I've lost my dog. The slope is slick and angled. The ground in this city never fully dries out until July. Thorns stick onto my sleeve, and I have to pull myself free. This is futile, I know, a frantic act. Still, I *will* Ian to be there, unconscious after hitting his head. I might see his shirt. A bit of his jacket.

Of course, his cellphone is missing, too. This little fact is hard to ignore. He has it with him, undoubtedly. He could likely call if he needed help. No story I can come up with makes the details fit. None. This is crazy, and now my arms are scratched from blackberry thorns—

"Mrs. Keller?"

Shit! I startle. I am so shocked at the sudden sound of my own name that my foot slides, and I end up on one knee as if I am pleading with Detective Vince Jackson.

He calls down to me. "Do you need a hand?"

I am struggling upright. "I'm fine."

"What are you doing here?" He is wearing those stupid, intimidating sunglasses that seem to be a required fashion accessory for men in blue. He looks huge standing up there.

"I thought . . . I should go looking. Maybe he'd walked here, fallen . . ."

"I think you should go home, Mrs. Keller," he says.

I get myself back up the hill. I have a round splotch of mud on my knee. "I'm sorry," I say. I don't know what I'm apologizing for. My throat closes up, and I can feel the tears start. I'm scared. For Ian, for my future. Even Detective Vince Jackson scares me.

"Try to stay calm. We're doing our job," he says. It's a very policeman thing to say. I notice that he is wearing a wedding ring. He'll go home after work and his wife will be there, wherever his home is. I picture a colonial-style house, a kitchen with a wallpaper border. He'll have something solid for dinner, like roast. Roast, a memory: I knew I would eventually leave Mark after making it one night. This was before I'd even met Ian. I had cooked a small prime rib, overcooked it, and Mark had gotten angry. Furious. I was sure that there was something else bothering him. No one could get that angry about a roast. I'd been sure like that a hundred times before. But he *was* mad about the roast. He was, and when I finally realized that, I knew that something important had shifted in my thinking. It was an overcooked-roast epiphany. You had violence, and then you had the ludicrousness of it.

"It's hard to stay calm," I say. "This is just so awful."

"Go home. Let us know if you hear anything."

I get in my car. My hands are shaking. All of me is shaking so badly. The worst thing is, I can feel that detective watching me.

* * *

I don't go home after all. I'm right there next to BetterWorks, and so I drive into their lot and park in Ian's spot. Abby's right, we should be doing something, only I don't know what. I can't wait for the phone to ring anymore, that's for sure.

I want to go in. I want to talk to everyone there to see if they know anything. I want to search through Ian's office, look at his papers, read the files on his computer. I want to find some telltale message or receipt. I wonder if Detective Vince Jackson is still around, eyeing my every move.

I've seen Ian come out of that building so many times. We always met there in those early days, holing up in his office after hours, breathing each other in and leaping apart when the cleaning woman came to dump the garbage. Ah. But we've spent so much time there in our ordinary life, too, during our not-quite-three years of marriage, after our scandalous days were over. When we lived at my old house, I'd drive over the bridge and meet Ian here after work so we could walk to Costa's for dinner, and after we moved to the houseboat last year, I came even more often. He would meet me in the lobby, or I'd wait by my car until he appeared with his laptop bag slung over his shoulder, his collar undone, and a huge smile on his face. We'd kiss. I'd smell that cologne of his. I love that smell. That smell is him to me.

Fingertips tap on my car window. Oh, God, no! Shit, shit, shit! I picture Detective Vince Jackson's big, guarded face again, staring in at me. It's not a crime, is it, to long for Ian? To be there, where he's most likely to show up? He didn't just *disappear*. He's *somewhere*.

But it isn't Detective Vince Jackson who's tapping at my car window. It's Nathan Benjamin.

"Dani?" His voice is muffled through the glass. His two first names make him seem friendly, as I've said, but so does his great hair—longish loose curls—and his warm eyes. He has nice-person hands, too. They aren't lean and manicured; they're guy hands, with uneven nails. Even though Nathan is very good looking, he is somehow regular and approachable. He still wears a wristwatch, the kind with the sun and moon rotating in small dials.

I roll down my window. I put my hand to my heart. "You scared me."

"I'm so sorry. That's the last thing you need right now."

"This is horrific," I say.

"The police were here a minute ago. A detective. He was asking questions."

"I saw him. Did you hear what you just said? 'The police were here.' This isn't real."

"Do you want to come in?" he asks. "Come sit in my office? I can get you something to eat? Drink? Some company? Do you just want to be nearby?"

"I think I'll get going." The idea of playing detective is rapidly losing its appeal. I'm not sure I can face those people in there.

"All right." He sets his hand on the ledge of the window. He pats it.

"We'll talk," I say.

"We'll talk," he agrees.

I leave him standing there in the empty spot next to Ian's parking place. Two nights ago, right there on that lawn, it was spring, and there was music, and there were waiters passing drinks.

Later, it's like a wake at my house. On a normal weekday, Ian would be arriving home any minute. I'd have cleared my work crap from the kitchen table and set it for two as dinner cooked.

A pasta dish, stir-fry. I'd light a candle for us, and I'd put on makeup. But instead of Ian and me eating dinner and watching some show we liked, people are arriving at my door as if he's already dead. Abby has been calling everyone, and my father is here, my mother, too, and my oldest friend in the world, Anna Jane. Bethy and Kristen are in the kitchen, sobbing onto the shoulders of their friends, and Ian's sister, Olivia, asks questions of me as if she's a prosecuting attorney. Of course, she sounds that way every Thanksgiving. It's how she is. My father is on the phone, talking to I don't know who. Hospitals, morgues, police departments of other counties. He's working from a list he found on the Internet. I hear my mother say, *Why are you doing that right now? Sometimes you just need to be here*, but he ignores her. *We don't need you to be the hero,* she says, and then looks at Anna Jane and rolls her eyes.

I'm grateful for what he's doing, though. It's motion, and I can witness some sort of progress. He, Nathan, and Ian's friend Simon Ash have also gone door-to-door on our dock, talking to people, asking if they've seen Ian or heard anything. They drove up and down our streets and the streets near Ian's work. They returned looking exhausted, but Simon promised to do the same thing in Ian's old neighborhood the next day. Olivia suggests calling airlines. Simon tells her that they won't give out information unless there's a subpoena. They argue this point. Simon is a contract lawyer and Olivia is an elementary school teacher, so he seems to win. She purses her lips and turns away.

Abby has taken one of our wedding photos and cropped me out, making flyers with Ian's face on them. Underneath, it says: *Have you seen this man?* She gives a handful to everyone to post. Paula, Ian's secretary, takes a copy and promises to print more at the office. She'll hand them out to everyone there, and she'll assign various employees to various jobs, such as questioning various store owners in various locations. Someone has made a color-coded map. Bethy's boyfriend, Adam, is walking around and talking on his phone, plugging one ear with his forefinger to hear better. My sister calls and insists on taking the next flight out, reluctantly changing her mind after I beg her not to. I am worried that all these well-meaning people are working so hard when Ian might be gone because he wants to be gone. I tell my sister that I don't need her yet but might need her later. *Later*— what that might entail, I have no idea.

In spite of this onslaught of help, I am desperately hoping they'll all leave soon. I can't *wait* properly with all of these people and emotions and relationships in the room. Most of all, I want to sit and rock and listen for him to come home.

Finally, everyone does leave, everyone except Abby, who has packed a bag and moved into our back bedroom. No one has ever slept there before. The bed is Abby's from our old house. Boxes from our move are still stacked in there, the tape lifted once and then patted back down. It's all the stuff you look at and don't know what to do with now that it doesn't fit into your new life.

Abby cleans up the mess from the impromptu vigil. She picks up the cans of soda the girls left on the deck rails, empties the overflowing garbage, and gathers the Subway wrappers from the sandwiches that Anna Jane brought because *we still had to eat*. Then Abby hunts through the canvas duffel she's brought. She takes out a paper bag with a bottle of Jack Daniel's in it.

"I got this on the way over. It seemed necessary. I don't even know what this stuff is." She removes the cap, sniffs. "Holy crap. That just burned a fire through my nasal passages." She pours us each a large glass.

"Honey, that's way too much." Abby isn't a drinker. She tries to pour some of it back through the narrow neck of the bottle, but most of it spills on the counter. It'll probably take the varnish right off the wood trim. Ian won't be pleased.

We each have a few swallows, which is followed by an array of gasping and sputtering and coughing. "It *is* nice and relaxing," Abby says after a while. We sit in silence, until the alcohol catches up to us.

"I've got to go to bed," Abby says.

"Okay, sugar."

"Is it okay to ditch you?"

"Of course."

"Double hugs," she says, and leans down to give me two.

"Double hugs," I say.

I try to sleep, I do. I even undress and lie down. The house is quiet and dark now. I listen to the crickets outside and to some far-off airplane. It's too hot in here. Someone has turned the heat up way past where we keep it. I can't stay in the same sheets Ian and I have recently been in together. Maybe some people would find that comforting, but I don't. It's a bed of mixed emotions. Beds often are, even in the best of circumstances. I get up. In the living room, Pollux lifts his chin from his pillow and watches me, decides it's not worth the effort to follow. He tucks his chin back down again. He's been up way past his bedtime, too, with all those people around. I open the sliding door to the deck and sit down in one of the Adirondack chairs. I pull my robe around me. My phone is in my pocket in case Ian calls.

If you have taken off somewhere, I am going to be so fucking mad at you, I tell Ian, wherever he is. The moon is large and white (he's under it, too, somewhere) and the water out there shimmers with light. I can smell the deep murkiness of the lake. The dock groans and creaks and sways a little—soft, lulling rhythms. The *New View* sloshes and bumps against the dock.

The party, the drive home, the grim face.

I try and try to remember.

The cool sheets. The bliss of rest.

I take my phone from my pocket. Her name and number are still on my list of contacts. I dial.

You have reached the office of Dr. Shana Berg. If this is an emergency, please dial 911 . . .

I listen to her voice, wait to leave a message, but there's a beep on my phone. It's the double ring of another call coming in. It's midnight. It's him, of course it is. Who else? He's heard about the commotion here tonight, and he's feeling bad that he's worried all those people. I feel sick with fear and relief. I feel joy, and fear and sickness, but, thank God, whatever it is, now I'll know. I punch the button on the phone and wait to hear Ian's voice.

"Dani?"

"Yes?"

"It's Nathan."

"Nathan?"

"I'm sorry to call so late. I really am. So many people were there tonight . . . I wanted to talk to you, but . . ."

"What, Nathan? What? Do you know something? You know something."

He is quiet. For a moment I think we've lost the connection. "Nathan?"

"I think maybe we should meet."

When I was a child in the suburbs of Seattle during the 1970s, we lived next door to Mr. and Mrs. Harris, who were quiet and kept to themselves, even on Halloween, when they turned their porch light off. They were the only ones who did that, the one dark house on that street. One summer, I was sure that Mr. Harris had done in Mrs. Harris and their small dog, Trixie. I hadn't seen Mrs. Harris's large, floral-clad rear end bent over in the garden for a number of days, and I hadn't seen Trixie flinging her small body against our shared fence whenever we let our cat out. But Mr. Harris kept coming home from work every night at six P.M., same as ever. It seemed possible that Mr. Harris had buried Mrs. Harris right under one of those flat, cement squares of their back patio, because he was a funeral director and because school was out and I was bored. For a long while, it was my understanding that this was where they put all the bodies from O'Dooley's Funeral Home: beneath their patio, under the Harrises' barbecue and Mrs. Harris's tomato plants, the very place where Mrs. Harris sunned herself on a tippy, webbed chaise longue, slathering on the Sea & Ski and drinking Tab out of the can.

I spied on Mr. Harris for a few days and took notes in a spiral pad I'd decorated with a cool STP sticker. He washed his car. He hauled out his garbage cans. He turned on their sprinkler and forgot to turn it off until late at night, when the lawn was soaked. I watched too much *Dragnet* with my father, too much *Adam-12*. I read *Two-Minute Mysteries* and *Encyclopedia Brown* and *Nancy Drew,* and funeral directors seemed likely capable of anything.

Mrs. Harris and Trixie returned, though, after apparently spending several weeks at the local Travelodge. I heard my mother tell my friend Becky's mom that Mr. Harris had gotten involved with someone he worked with at O'Dooley's. This was extraordinarily creepy. Thrillingly so. I couldn't imagine how Mrs. Harris could let Mr. Harris touch her after a day at work, let alone fathom an O'Dooley's *couple*. I was ten, and the funeral home was in a large, chalky mansion in town, and I pictured Mr.

Harris and some woman with pancake makeup doing it in a red velvet casket.

Mrs. Harris was alive and well, but her marriage was dead, and even though I didn't realize it then, the mystery was likely deeper than I ever could have imagined. Human nature deep. I've said it before, but in marriage there are things you don't know about your partner. Always. The real thoughts in his head as he drifts off to sleep with his shoulders turned away from you—you can't even guess. But you want to believe you *do* know. That a person *is* knowable. You need this belief. It's a necessary denial. How can you go about everyday life otherwise? How could you ever water the tomato plants and unfold your chaise longue and enjoy a summer afternoon if you knew there were things buried under the cement patio of your very own yard?

"When can I see you?" I say to Nathan Benjamin.

5

"Mom? Mom!"

I rise through the shadow layers of sleep, untangling nightmare images from waking ones. When I open my eyes, I'm almost surprised to find myself in my own bed. Abby is there in her pajamas with the dancing dogs on them, the ones my mother made her for Christmas. Her face has the sweet plainness of no makeup, framed by shoved-up, bedraggled hair. But she also has that look she gets, a mix of worry and concentration. I first saw it when we made the papier-mâché horse for her third-grade report on *Misty of Chincoteague*.

"Are you okay? Jesus, you scared me."

"A bad dream . . ."

"You were crying out."

"I don't know. It's already gone. I don't even remember."

The abrupt yank into wakefulness is confusing, until my real life efficiently barges in and takes over duty again. I hate that disorienting moment in the morning, I've always hated it—that brief empty in-between before you remember your life's plotline. The blankness is the perfect setup for a nasty surprise, and I'm not fond of surprises. It can go either way, of course. Sometimes what returns to you upon waking is good news. *That's right, I've fallen in love!* Or, *Oh, yeah! Today my new boots are coming in the mail!* But, other times, what reappears is the knowledge that your child is sick or that the kitchen flooded the day before. The bad stuff forgotten in sleep comes rushing back, and it's new all over again. Every single time, it's a split second of fresh pain or joy or thrill or doom.

My husband is gone.

"God," I say. "Ian." I can hardly believe it. I just . . . It's impossible.

"That stuff we drank probably didn't help. My head feels full of fluff." She rubs her eyes. "I can make you some breakfast. Pancakes?"

"We've got forty pounds of baked stuff. Banana bread . . ." That fact also comes rushing back.

"Cinnamon rolls, oatmeal–raisin cookies . . ." She counts on her fingers. "I need coffee."

Pollux trots in at the sound of voices. He puts his paws up on the side of the bed, looks at me hard.

"Okay, I know," I tell him.

I put on my robe. I grab my phone, which I'd placed next to my pillow the night before. Nathan Benjamin, that's right. My stomach flips in dread. I'll be meeting him that afternoon.

I don't know why I do it, but after I get up, after I let Pollux out, I go to Ian's closet. I run my hand across the row of colored dress shirts. I choose one and put my face to it, sniffing deeply. I don't do it because I'm longing for the lost, missed scent of him. No. I know it's crazy. But I'm wondering if I just might find the lingering smell of perfume.

* * *

After that first time I lied to Mark, Ian and I began to meet regularly. Oh, those were intoxicating days. I was elevated by love. I felt connected to all people and things, struck by our common humanity and the beauty of it. I'd see the moms and dads at Target buying stuff to play Easter Bunny, and it would feel so damn sweet. I'd go to the garden department of some store and I'd take it all in, the abundance of flowers, the fat bags of bark, us folks with our endlessly optimistic desire to grow things. I noticed the big and small all around me—the lovely curve of orange peels, the bittersweet tenderness of twilight. I wanted to be a better person, certainly better than the one I was being then.

Sometimes I would go to Ian. I'd drive to Seattle during the day, thirty minutes each way, for a half hour of being together in his car somewhere, away from the eyes of anyone he might know. Or he would come to me. We'd meet on his way home from work, at one of the wooded trailheads that surrounded our neighborhood, or at a park in the next town over, a dank, dark, and eerie place seldom used because it was dank, dark, and eerie. I usually got there before he did, checking my makeup in the visor mirror while I waited, sucking on mints, playing music especially chosen to evoke the feelings I most wanted to have then. I'd watch and watch for his car (a silver Audi, in those days), and then there it would come, oh, God, and he would park, and I could see through the windows that his jawline was somber and almost resigned until he leaned over the passenger seat to unlock the door and let me in.

It's been days. It's been too, too long, he would say, and that's exactly how it felt no matter how much time had passed. Eons. Slow, loud ticking clocks of days until our meetings, where the time would go so fast, you might become sure that some cruel, punishing time warp truly did exist. How could the very same minutes go so slow and then so fast? Scientific mystery. His car was one of the few corners of his world I was allowed into, and I claimed it—*my* seat beside him. It sounds pathetic and insignificant, meeting in his car, but it was also oddly wonderful. The car was contained and protected from intrusion and from the complications and hazards of real life. A space small enough to be perfect. These were moments of time in a private, enclosed domain that belonged to only him and me. He would put a CD in, one of our favorites, and then he would lean in and we would kiss and kiss some more until my lips got numb. It was the sort of passion that could never fade, you were sure, that could never be lost among laundry and bills and the needs of children.

Just kissing, though. Always just that at first. See, it wasn't an affair that was all about sex. (*Affair*—what a trivial word. It sounds like a party with frilly dresses.) No, it was the much more dangerous kind of relationship, the marriage-breaking kind about meeting your soul mate.

What if this is nothing more than lust? he asked once. He asked a version of that question many more times still. And I would answer. I would give all the reasons, making an argument. I fought for it. The sinking ship was going under, under, under, and I was in the lifeboat and I was struggling to get him in there with me. I was grasping his hand and pulling more than my weight to haul him over the round rubber side of that small, perilous craft. He had swum there himself, though. He had pursued me. I shouldn't forget that. I couldn't have lifted him in without his desire to get in. Still. I had argued on our behalf.

You're the one I should have always been with, he would say, after my logic had softened his and brought him back to me. *I see a lifetime in your eyes*, he said once, too, a line I would have made fun of if I had heard it on TV but that choked me up in real life. He meant it. There were small acts of electrifying teenage romance, too: He would twirl my hair around his finger; he would look long and deep into my eyes. I can feel his round, hard shoulders and the buttons of his shirt under my fingers as I write this. I can feel my own heartbeat. More music, more kissing, his hand at the back of my neck, pulling me to him with want. The damn parking brake.

And then a utility truck would arrive. Or something. Some guy on his lunch break, taking a sandwich out of a brown bag and looking our way with a lurid grin. The dream would shatter, and the trees of that park would suddenly loom, and the clock would be noticed with alarm. Ian would take a pinch of his shirt and sniff. *You didn't wear perfume, did you? Not even hand lotion?* I would shove away the thought—*How did I get* here?

He would kiss me goodbye. I would leave his car. He would roll down his window. He would mouth *You.*

I would sit inside my own car for a long while, old Blue Beast, holding on to that thing that was mine and mine alone for as long as I could. This is a confession—*another* confession. Every irritant and questionable comment from him got suppressed in support of those victorious moments of *freedom*. I guess you don't turn away a rescuer in hopes of a better one. You're thankful. I'm guessing that when a prisoner is let out, even the penitentiary parking lot looks beautiful.

Because, soon enough, I would be pulling into my own driveway, going inside, taking some hamburger from the freezer. I would be the audience as Abby practiced her oral report on primates, both of us turning our heads toward the door as Mark walked in, both of us pausing to read his face for signs of what the evening would bring. I would feel relief if his eyes were smiling and relaxed and if he came in joking, tossing his keys on the counter. Maybe that would mean a bike ride later, a roughhouse game with him and Abby. But if his eyes were hard, if he thought the world had done him wrong while he'd been out, it meant stepping carefully. Either way, after Abby was in bed, I'd go up to our room and disappear into a book. Blessed books—they're a place to be alone, and no one else can come in. I put up my book barrier because I didn't want him to touch me. You came to hate sex with someone who betrayed you with violence. You'd do anything to avoid it. His mouth felt all wrong by then anyway.

As I sat in that car, though, during the suspended time that came between meeting Ian and heading home, I was filled with the elation of a changed future. I was a butterfly, with the weight of two rose petals, yet with the power to fly thousands of miles.

While I'm on the way to meet Nathan Benjamin, I phone Detective Jackson. I leave a message for him. I want to call and call and call, but I hold back. This will make me seem unstable, I think. But maybe I'm supposed to call more often than I do. I don't know what the protocol is here.

I look around for Nathan at the Essential Baking Company, one of those chic, organic Seattle cafés, which I have to admit I usually love. Artisan bread, beautiful pastries behind glass—I'm always in favor of butter and sugar. Today, though, even five jillion glorious fat calories seem criminal. I am aware of some jazzy music playing in the background, and of greasy fingerprints on the glass case, and of the bright smiles of the girls in aprons. The latte machine grinds loudly and, all at once, being in public feels wrong.

Nathan rises from his chair and comes toward me. He takes my arm and puts one hand on my back, the way you help an old woman cross a street. His jacket is wet. There are little drops on the shoulders. It's been raining, and I haven't even noticed.

"I didn't know—I ordered. I didn't think you'd want to—" He's waving his hands in lieu of words. On the table are two chubby white cups with latte hearts formed in foam on the top, along with dishes of croissants and carrot cake. When someone dies, people bring casseroles. When someone vanishes, baked goods multiply. Who knew?

Nathan sits down, knocking over his propped-up umbrella. He shrugs off his jacket, but I keep mine on. I want its good tangerine-ness around me. That coat had seemed like such a wonderful secret splurge when I bought it (a tangerine coat!), and we are still allies many wearings later. There are reassuring things in its pockets, too. There's a ticket stub to an "opposites attract" wedding movie Abby and I saw together and an open pack of cinnamon gum. I'll take all the comfort I can get as I wait for Nathan to tell me what I know is coming.

"Not the quietest." Nathan's eyes are apologetic. His watch has stopped at 10:15.

"Maybe I don't want to hear what you have to tell me."

"What are you thinking?" He reads my face. "Oh, hell. Dani, no. Not that—" Poor Nathan. All of this has rendered him incapable of finishing sentences.

"You have something to say." I imagine Ian away from this rain, on a beach towel in some sunny place.

"Not what you're thinking!"

"No? That's not why we're here?"

"God, no." He shakes his head, but I see it, I am sure. The flash of a lie, the brief sidestep of eye contact that means deception.

"I'd rather just know. I can't take this not knowing."

"That's not it at all. Something else . . . Something else entirely. Ian and I . . . I didn't want you to hear this from someone else and think . . . I don't know what you might think. Or what anyone might think."

I put my hands around that warm cup. I wait.

"What I need to say . . . Well, Ian and I had a meeting the morning of the party. A conference of sorts. Did you know? Because, that night, you were acting like you always did toward me. I thought, *Maybe he didn't tell her*."

"He didn't tell me."

He pauses. I see how hard this is for him. "Dani, I offered to buy him out."

"What?"

"I wanted to dissolve our partnership. I offered to buy him out."

"You did? Why?" I'm shocked, as shocked as Nathan had guessed I would be. Ian had told me nothing about this. When he came home to pick me up for the party, it was all about that stupid dress, the right heels. God, I can only guess how Ian would have reacted to an offer like that. It would have seemed like a betrayal to him. His radar for disloyalty was overactive to the point of paranoia anyway.

"Ian . . . How do I say this? He's difficult. His exacting need for perfection . . . Goddamn, it's a great thing. I'm not saying that's not a great trait to have, especially in this business. But I gotta say, it's making me crazy. It gets me down. Every little . . . *mistake*. I sound like a pussy here."

"No, I know."

"I'm sure you *do* know. He and I were colleagues before, right? But I didn't have that much interaction with him day-to-day, year-to-year like this. A few weeks ago, I sent him this email about a shipping-date issue that could affect our entire year's profit, and he responded by correcting my grammar. *Which*, not *that*, you know? He's done that kind of shit before, but I was pissed. The proverbial last straw. I was *furious*. Goddamn, I've never been so angry. I ran a red light and almost got myself killed. I made a decision right then. I love the guy, I do, but I don't want to go on working with him. Life's too short."

He shakes his head apologetically. I want to tell him that I understand completely, but this seems wrong with Ian missing. A blond woman with a large purse and two shopping bags knocks into our table, causing my foamy heart to spill over onto the table. Nathan jumps up, grabs some napkins, and begins soaking up the liquid, which is spreading quickly toward the table's edge. I can hear the woman loudly placing a complicated coffee order. No one needs a cup of coffee like that, unless you're out to prove you can get exactly what you want. Nathan ditches the soaking napkins into a trash can.

"Don't you hate assholes?" Nathan says.

"I do."

"Maybe you get to a certain age and it hits you. You're so damn sick of being nice and polite."

"I know."

"A lot of good it does."

He's right. He's so right. Where *does* it get you? You tell yourself you're trying to be a good person, but there's more to it, isn't there? *Nice* is akin to not walking under ladders or stepping on cracks. It's a superstitious hedging of bets. A part of you thinks your good behavior will ward off evil. Well, apparently that's not true. "You get fed up, I guess."

"That you do." The drippy coffee napkins have splotched Nathan's shirt.

"So you and Ian had a meeting."

"I had gotten some people together, investors, to see what my options were. I invited a couple of them. I called us together, away from work, on a weekend. Neutral time, neutral territory. We met over at Starbucks, by work. Nine A.M., after he had his coffee; you know how he needs it. Witnesses, in case he put his hands around my throat. I told him I could offer him enough to make it worth his while."

"What'd he say?"

"I think he felt ganged up on, with those other guys there. He asked, 'Why?' He seemed honestly baffled. I said, 'God help me, Ian, if we keep working together, I'm gonna kill you.'"

I've been staring into my cup, swirling what was left of that heart, but I look up at Nathan then. He blushes.

"What did he do?" I ask finally.

"He didn't do anything. He just stared at me. He was shocked. And then his face got hard. Distant. He looked at me as if he'd already dismissed me. It felt permanent. I don't know . . . He got up and walked out. I didn't see him the rest of the day. Not until the party."

When you love a person, you come to know so many things about them. You know what they'll order in a restaurant, and you know that they'll cut the scratchy tags off their shirt collars and that they get cranky when they need to eat or when the bed sheets have become baggy. You know by the lilt and rhythms of their voice if they're talking on the phone to their mother, or their daughter, or their lawyer. But, maybe most of all, you know their relationship to criticism.

And Ian's relationship to criticism—well, the people most sensitive to criticism are usually the best at handing it out, aren't they? Ian always made sure that *no one* would think badly of him—not God, not the lady wearing prissy shoes on the train, not some omniscient "they," not the ever-present ghost of Paul Hartley Keller. There would be no misplaced commas or wrongly used salad forks, and when you were on his arm, you could not stumble or stammer, either. And no one, by God, *no one* would find him irritating enough to dismiss.

"Wow," I say. "I don't know how to see this."

"I don't, either, actually." Nathan rubs the back of his neck.

"What does this mean?"

"I just thought I should tell you. It sounds so bad. God, it sounds *guilty*. Maybe I watch too much TV. I *do* watch too much TV. But it sounds like—I hate to say this, but I want to before anyone else does. It sounds like some kind of *motive*."

The rain drips down the windows. It's really coming down. I like rain, but right now it seems so cold and terrible. Ian might be out there in that weather somewhere, hurt. Dead, even. There are enough reasons not to think he's dead, though, to believe that he's run off, and Nathan's news provides another one. It sits like a horrible stone in my stomach. I can't help it—I feel bad for Ian, wherever he is.

Nathan and I look at each other, saying nothing. The word— *motive*—it hangs there between us. Neither of us moves. We are both paralyzed. But the blond woman takes her extra-skim-no-no-no-whatever to her table and settles in comfortably, and the latte machines continue to grind and steam all of those desperate attempts at control.

Ian's gone-ness—it's a deep black chronic pain, and it never lets up. But then I drive back home and the stupid Fremont Bridge goes up. For a brief second I'm only irritated. Irritated the way a normal person is when the stupid bridge goes up, when we are all sitting there waiting and waiting as that impossibly huge rectangle of iron rises inch by frustrating inch. Waiting as the lone sailboat meanders across as we twiddle our thumbs with our shut-off engines. I realize what I've done. I've had a two-second reprieve from the sick, heavy feeling in my gut and heart. I've forgotten. I feel terrible about this. My worry is another kind of superstition, a form of prayer that will keep him safe, and I've let down my guard.

I drive down Fairview, the street that hugs the lakeside. Right away, I notice Ian everywhere. For a second I think I'm in a horrible dream. I wonder if I'm going crazy. Then I realize that Abby has been busy posting flyers. Ian's face looks out from the telephone poles along the street. He's staring at me everywhere I look. It's disturbing. I park the car, and he's right there. It gives me the creeps. Once, there was a flyer for Louise's missing parrot in the exact same spot. The parrot was finally found in a tree, and when Mattie climbed a ladder to get it, she fell and broke her leg.

I try not to look at Ian's parked car, either. That car seems especially cruel. Normally when I see it there, it means he's home. But now it's cold and elusive, keeping its own secrets.

I hurry inside, away from all those Ian faces. Pollux, bless him—he's thrilled to see me. He jumps up on my legs, his tail going a million miles an hour. Before all this, I often wondered how old Poll viewed the passing of time while I was gone. Did he ever worry I wouldn't come back? How long was an hour to him, or a day? When we went on vacation and had to leave him in a kennel, it always upset me. He looked sad, and that place was sad, too, with its flecked-linoleum floor and barking dogs and the odd gray-haired owner, who preferred animals to people. On the counter, there was a Lucite holder of pamphlets about dog training, and they'd been there long enough to become defeated, the print faded and the edges curled. The place smelled like sawdust and Lysol and dog. Pollux might think we'd left him there for good, and I couldn't bear that idea. Before we'd go, I'd explain that we'd be away for a week or two, and I would tell him how much I loved him. I could only hope that somewhere in his sweet little brain he would know I'd never leave him. But what would it mean to him, to be left there? As the days went on and he kept waiting, a day might mean a week, and a week might mean forever.

"I'm back, boy. I'm back." I put my face to his fur. My voice wobbles with tears, but he refuses to join the drama. He escapes my grasp, sits by the door like a gentleman. He's moved on to the practical matters of his bladder.

There's a note on the counter from Abby. *Putting up flyers with Zach and Janna. Back in a few.*

I stand there in my coat with my purse over my shoulder. I am in my own home, and I am wholly and utterly lost.

Pollux's rump is inappropriately merry as he jogs down the dock. It's quiet out here right now. The gray drizzly sky makes everything look gray. The lake is gray, and the ducks paddling by are gray, and the windows of the houseboats reflect gray. Rain drips from plant leaves and gutter spouts. Most everyone is at work except for Jennie and her baby, and old Joseph Grayson, who's smoking another joint, by the smell of things. I walk Pollux to the end of the dock, and he goes through the daily (and ridiculous, if you ask me) ruse of deciding where to pee. He walks in circles and sniffs and walks in more circles, as if thoroughly considering his options, and then, of course, lifts his leg on the same old flower box he lifts his leg on every single time.

I'd tucked Ian's car key into my jeans, and now I unlock that cold, callous Jaguar. I open the door for Pollux, and he hops in and sits down. You can see how pleased he is—he's never been allowed in this car before, which shows a lack of faith on Ian's part. Pollux is always a respectful passenger.

I am about to get in on the driver's side when I notice a long scratch on his door. I've never seen it before. Where did *that* come from and, more important, *when*? With all the looking I've been doing at that car, you'd think I'd have noticed it. Maybe it's been too dark, or maybe I haven't been clearheaded enough to observe carefully. I don't know. I have no idea. It's a nasty scratch. Deep. Could have been anything—a key, a branch, a hurried, misjudged left turn. You don't really want to park on the street here, but there's not much choice. Some kid buying beer at Pete's could have gotten wrathful after his fifth drink. Ian will be furious.

I get in on Ian's side. I sit in his seat. Detective Vince Jackson already looked inside here, so I assume I'm not disturbing anything important, evidence of some kind, if there is evidence. The idea of *evidence* seems overly dramatic. That empty file folder and the sweatshirt are still in the back. Maybe I watch too much TV, same as Nathan.

I put my hands on the wheel, because that's where Ian places his own hands nearly every day. I plead with him. *Where are you? Please, just let me know. Please!* The not knowing and the waiting . . . Not knowing and not knowing and not knowing, and waiting and waiting and waiting. It is killing me. Ian stares at me from that telephone pole. Ian, on our wedding day, wearing that grin. The way he's looking at me makes me shiver.

His car smells like leather and his musky-clean cologne. The seat is closer to the wheel than usual, something Detective Vince Jackson must have done, because it's way too close for Ian. Perfect for me if I were driving, but Ian's nose would be right up to the windshield like that. I reach down and scoot the seat back so that I'm exactly where he'd be. Where I last remembered seeing him. I stretch my foot to the pedal. I close my eyes and try to bring him close. I try to feel him. I try to get him to speak to me, some mad metaphysical exercise that goes nowhere. When I was twelve, I'd saved my allowance and bought a Ouija board, hoping for supernatural communication. In my heart of hearts, though, I knew that when the teardrop pointer moved, it was only Jackie Zavier, pushing it with her mood-ring fingers.

I change tactics. I fish through his glove box, finding nothing but the car manual and extra fast-food napkins. There's a package of wet wipes. An ice-scraper. A brittle rubber band. I look in his ashtray and find a few quarters and too many pennies, the wrinkled foil from a roll of mints, and a white pill, which upon closer inspection proves to be a Tylenol. I have a flash of what I am sure is a brainstorm, the obvious overlooked answer, and I check under the plastic mats, finding only dirt crumbles and gravel, the lacy skeleton of a lone dried leaf. I get out and open the trunk. There's the spare tire and a set of jumper cables and the red plaid blanket he keeps there in case of emergency.

I give up my investigation. I get back in the car, just so I can be with him. I imagine his profile; his black hair combed neatly, his Adam's apple. His manicured hands are on the wheel, and one reaches for the radio dial to turn up a song we especially like.

Car dance for me, he'd say. He says this often, and I'll do some goofy upper-body-only move, shaking imaginary maracas. We have a version for various places. Bed dance, couch dance. Various jazzy commercials might come on, which inspire us.

Oh, you are fine, he would say, smiling, sneaking side-glances as he drove.

I'm a pro, I'd say. *I'm thinking of going full time.*

If anyone should full-time car dance, it's you, baby.

That night, driving home after the party? We weren't joking then. His jawline was tight. Light from streetlamps illuminated his face in flashes. I rode beside him, wearing that stupid tight dress, my shoes off, thank God. We both smelled like party aftermath—alcohol and other people's cigarettes.

I look over at my passenger now. Pollux sits in his seat politely, gazing out the window, as if we are driving down a pleasant country road while he enjoys the view.

I need to call Dr. Shana Berg's office again. I don't want to. But I need to. I had told Abby that I didn't remember what that dream was about. I do, though. And, I have to say, it bothers me. It bothers me a great deal.

6

Memory is such a sadistic, temperamental little beast. You can forget where you just put your car keys but remember that you gave your sixth-grade teacher a bottle of Love's Baby Soft Musk for Christmas. You can sit in some dentist's office, filling out a form, unable to recall your husband's cellphone number (a number you call at least once a day), but, great, there's the address of your old house from childhood: *115 Sterling Court*. My sister is especially adept at summoning lyrics to forgettable songs—"Muskrat Love," for example. She can do all of "Sail On, Sailor." *I sailed an ocean! Unsettled ocean! Through restful waters and deep commotion!* That's all I know, but she does the other verses. She shows off about it. Words from my junior high fight song have come unbidden while trying to fall asleep at night, and I know "Afternoon Delight," but she's the queen. I wonder if some brains have an area reserved for songs from the seventies.

"Afternoon Delight," my God! *Oh, mighty Rose Hill Royals, give us a score!* Both of those inconsequential songs conscientiously remain there, awaiting my need of them. Why, then, *why* does this magical, powerful entity that's our very own brain hold out on the most critical things? How does the most vital stuff slip through its Vulcan starship efficiency? Or is it actually there, maliciously hiding somewhere in all those gnarled, twisty crevices? Sneaking out for a bit of that sadistic, tip-of-the-tongue taunting? It's your own brain. It should be on your side. So often it's your very own self that betrays you, that's the thing.

"Did he change his clothes when he came home after the party?" Detective Vince Jackson asks.

"I don't remember," I say. "I assume so. I went straight to bed."

Definitely I watch too much TV. When Detective Vince Jackson called that morning to ask me to come to the police station, I imagined us in some frighteningly blank room, empty of everything except a desk and two chairs and a microphone. There would be a hidden camera up by the ceiling and one of those two-way mirrors with a bunch of people watching on the other side.

Do you need a lawyer? my mother had asked. I'd phoned her in a panic to tell her that Detective Jackson wanted to speak with me.

Of course I don't need a lawyer.

She watches too much TV, too.

We sit at Detective Vince Jackson's desk. There are other desks around, with other officers and detectives. Phones are ringing. His desk is a mess. There are stacks of file folders and papers, and there's a coffee cup with an American eagle on it and a cardboard burger container from Jack in the Box. He asks my permission to record our conversation. His memory is terrible, he says. He's taking notes, too. He taps the end of his pen while he waits for me to answer. That part *is* like TV. He leans back in his chair, and it makes a terrible sound, like a squawking bird.

"You're sure he *came* home with you?"

"Yes. Of *course*." I don't like his sarcasm, not at all.

"But you can't remember if he changed his clothes, took off his shoes, his tie . . ."

"No tie. They're very casual. Software guys—no ties, even for parties. No suits. A sports jacket, rarely."

"His wallet is gone. His phone is gone. Keys. Briefcase?"

"He doesn't use one."

"So, wallet, phone, gone. Everything he was wearing the night before is gone. Far as you know, he could have left again in the night?"

I don't like that idea, him leaving that night. It's possible, though, isn't it? He could have just walked away, or someone could have met him right outside, picked him up. It seems a more urgent act, a desperate getaway.

"I guess. But it wouldn't have been unusual for him to put on the same clothes the next day. On the weekends, he just throws on whatever's draped over the chair."

"But you say you didn't hear him that morning. You didn't hear him on the phone, hear the door open, anything?"

I shake my head. "Nothing. I'm so sorry."

"The toilet flush?"

"No."

"Are you always such a sound sleeper?" *Tap, tap, tap.*

I don't respond. I feel helpless. I feel a million miles of desperation inside. It stretches out like the most lonesome, dusty road, with no gas station for miles.

"I'd like you to go through his closet thoroughly and give me an inventory of what might be missing. Anything. A gym sock, whatever."

"Okay."

"Obviously we're still trying to determine if he left of his own accord."

"What have you found? Have you found out anything?"

"His phone's off. Hasn't been used since that night. Neither have any of his personal bank cards."

I already know this. I've called the phone company, and the bank, too. I've called every day. Still, when he says it, the news hits. Something about it is permanent, ominous. It feels like suicide. But it could also mean a solid plan, a plan developed over months, when a second marriage proved as disappointing as the first, when that particular failure would have been too disgraceful or just too much trouble to face.

"I'm sorry, Mrs. Keller."

I don't know what it means, this apology. Is he delivering some news, death news? Is he telling me something his experience told him was true right now, this minute, without any closet inventory or further investigation? Detective Vince Jackson reaches into a large desk drawer and shoves a box of Kleenex toward me. It's true. I've been crying. This is what the apology is for.

"God," I say. I blow my nose. A female officer hands Vince Jackson a folder. Behind me, the water cooler glugs as someone pours a miniature cup. I have the feeling that I'm overstaying my welcome. I collect my purse. I stand up.

"Inventory." He hands me a sheet. It's a list, to operate as a helpful reminder. Who knew there were such things?

"I'll get it to you right away."

But he's not interested in what a good student I am. He doesn't care if I've always been someone who follows the rules or has never been in a police station before this moment. He turns his attention to the folder he's been given.

I leave the ringing phones and the business of missing persons and robbed 7-Elevens and bar fights and prostitution behind me. I went to traffic court once.

I should have told him then, I know. I will say I'm sorry for that, right here. I am sorry. I didn't tell him because I was embarrassed. I wasn't trying to hide anything. It felt shameful is all. No, I'm not always such a heavy sleeper. The evening—a lot of it had dropped down behind some heavy curtain of haze and forgetting for a very particular reason. I had taken one of those Vicodins that night, before the party. The ones I'd been given after a root canal and never needed. It was a chickenshit move on my part, pure cowardice. I hate those parties. I thought the pill might give me a shot of false confidence or at least take the edge off the social discomfort. Ian wanted me to wear that ridiculous dress, and then there would be all that work chatter I wasn't a part of and the people who knew him from his previous life, who knew Mary, who knew enough to be able to judge and compare. And there'd be all those women he worked with, too—the smart, sexy women he often told me about when he came home. I'm not one of them. I'm old enough to feel embarrassed in that dress. I've never felt beautiful, no matter what anyone has said. I was in the middle of a good book, too, one that I would have done anything to get back to.

I was supposed to show Ian's coworkers and benefactors and colleagues what a prize he'd won, that's how it seemed, and I just didn't feel up to it. I'd be an honorable mention, at best, and I am fine with that, personally. I don't want to be more. I'm someone who's unsteady in heels, who wipes off my lipstick the second I get the chance. That's who I am. He would have told me to stop looking so uncertain, and I was too tired right then, too life-tired, to tell him to shove it.

So I took one of those Vicodins. I had taken one once before, prior to Ian's office Christmas party. I'd liked the soft, easy confidence it gave me. I had felt magnanimous, the most socially generous I'd been since Yvette Bolo's slumber party in the sixth grade, when I knew full well that my appearance had raised the event from *desperate* to *nearly normal*. My own group of regular friends set me on the top rung of popularity among Yvette Bolo's weird ones, and that night I was middle-school nobility among Alicia Gess, who wet her pants in the second grade and never lived it down, and Katherine Graves, who had some kind of illness that made her thin and pale and gave her seizures, and Felicity McNulty, who would commit suicide in her senior year.

Of course, at Ian's Christmas party, I hadn't also had those two (two plus) glasses of wine. It was stupid, I know. I would never have admitted this to Ian. It was a secret I would have kept to my grave.

That evening, my mother and Abby sit on my bed, with Pollux curled up next to them on the floor. My mother is wearing jeans and an Eagles sweatshirt—not the band but the baseball team my nephew, Justin, plays third base for. Abby is back in her pajamas (sensible girl—she prefers pajamas to real clothes whenever possible), and her legs are folded under her. Pollux is wearing what he wears every day: shiny black fur, a classic. Abby holds the inventory sheet from Detective Jackson on her lap, and a coffee-table book of Ian's acts as a hard writing surface. I can see by the spine that the book is *One Hundred Butterflies*, by Harold Feinstein. Mary and their daughters had given that book to Ian, and there's an inscription on the first page in Mary's hand: *Happy Birthday, Daddy! Love, Your Girls.* Inside, there are lush photos of the Peruvian Nymph and the Painted Jezebel, the Jungle Queen and the Wanderer, with their thin brittle bodies and jeweled tissue wings. Ian wouldn't like Abby writing on top of that book. *You should have taken it, if you cared so much about it,* I silently tell him.

"Someone could take stuff from my own closet and I wouldn't even know it," my mother says.

"That green satin vintage dress?" Abby says.

"Ugly bridesmaid disaster, 1960s. Don't you love it how some words get swankied up to make them sound better? Vintage? Come on! Try *old*."

"Substance abuser, addict. There's another one," Abby says.

"*Substance* sounds so benign. Like a helpful cleaning product." I have the irrational thought that my guilt about those pills is leaking into the room. I've never had a secret that I wasn't sure everybody somehow knew. When I lost my virginity at sixteen, I was certain my mother could see it on my face, though she'd just kept on browning beef for dinner, if I recall correctly. And now Abby only stretches out her legs and pets Pollux with her foot. "I love that dress, actually," she says.

"You do?" my mother says.

"I used it to play movie star."

"You should have told me before. It's yours. Next time I see you, remind me. I was going to give it away to the 'Truck In Your Neighborhood' people. Hey, you want your grandpa's old concertina, too?"

"You shouldn't have said anything," I tell Abby. Once my mother starts giving stuff away, you can't stop her. She'll give you the shirt off her back, as they say, which really happened once when my sister admired a cardigan she was wearing. She'll do anything for the people she loves.

"What's a concertina?" Abby asks.

My mother mimes pushing bellows in and out. Hums something disastrous.

"No, that's okay. Maybe you should give it back to *him*?"

My mother snorts. She gives her head a shake of disgust. You're either for her or against her. If you're for her, the generous heavens open up. If you're not, you get what's coming to you. You have to watch your step with my mother, and my father failed to do that, or failed at the end, anyway. Well, he rejected her, and that's hard to forgive. That little woman in the Eagles sweatshirt is fierce love and ferocious loyalty, all standing guard in front of a vulnerable heart.

I kneel down in front of Ian's closet. I take out a stack of jeans from the bottom wire basket.

"Check the pockets," my mother says. It's more an accusation than a helpful suggestion. I shoot her a look. As I've said, she's never liked Ian. Still, I reach my hand into each one.

"Any missing pairs?" Abby is ready with her pen.

"I can't tell. I don't think so." I try to picture him in his favorites. I have a sudden flash of his ass in jeans, a pair that's thin and fading at the knees. Yes, they're here in my lap, neatly folded. I don't know how many pairs of Levi's he has. He's never even worn the black ones. They still have the tag on them.

"Shoes?" Abby prompts.

I look down at the row of them, toes pointed out as if they're rather wearily waiting at the starting line. He has stiff leather dress shoes, and black boots, and tennis shoes that are old and hunched and still green from cutting his former lawn. He has a pair of those ultra-white-bright men's running shoes that can look silly paired with calf-high socks. He has more shoes than I do.

"He has more shoes than you do," my mother says.

"That's not a *crime*," I say.

"Mother, concentrate," Abby says.

"Running shoes . . ." I am trying to remember.

"The phone," Abby says.

"Get it?"

Abby hops up. She abandons *One Hundred Butterflies* and the inventory of my missing husband's clothes. She steps over the dog, who decides to follow her out in case something exciting is going to happen that might involve him.

"Every time I answer that phone and it's not Ian, it kills me," I tell my mother. I pick up one of the grass-stained shoes. I picture him back in his old neighborhood, wearing them. Of course, if he had stayed there, none of this would have happened. You can drive yourself crazy playing that game.

"It looks like a goddamn Nordstrom Rack in there," my mother says.

I guess I married Mark for rescue, too, but a different kind of rescue. Once again, our dark, buried selves, working from their subterranean lairs. Mark was tough. I knew he'd never take shit from anyone. He saved me from my own lack of bravery by being the dangerous one. His dangerousness perhaps spoke of fearlessness, and fearlessness spoke of power, and being chosen by someone with that power made me feel powerful, too, and oddly, wrongly, absurdly, safe. As I said, we're not supposed to admit to things like that: our awareness of our own weakness, our sublimation to the most helpless parts of ourselves. Men can, I suppose. Or can't, for their own reasons. But it's even worse for women. Feminism was supposed to chase away all of those embarrassing vulnerabilities. At least, you were supposed to be aware that acting helpless was something shameful. So was the tendency to hide your own fear behind the toughness of bad boys, if you had that. I had that. I'm being honest here.

The bad-boy lure . . . What is it? Is it a caveman thing? A cavewoman thing? A reaction to some archaic evolutionary urge that's warning you that it's dark and that people with clubs lurk in that dark, ready to do you harm? Protection can seem like a good idea. Hell, protection feels *great*. I remember one time when Mark and I were riding a bus after we'd gone Christmas shopping downtown. We had just met. I was nineteen, almost twenty. He was twenty-two. We look so young in those pictures. That day, we were carrying shopping bags. The bus was crowded, and we were standing. The driver shifted gears to go up one of Seattle's steep hills, and I lost my footing and lurched against this guy. He looked me up and down and said something to his friend in Spanish, which made the friend laugh lewdly. Mark stepped forward then. I swear to God, he puffed out his chest. It was gorilla-like, it really was. Gorillas, you know—they're mob leaders. Even in the zoo, when they look at you it makes you nervous. *Watch it*, Mark said to the guy. He *snarled* it. He snapped like an animal, even though his voice was low. It wasn't a voice I'd ever heard him use before, not then, anyway. And the guy—he held up his hand in a mean-no harm way. *Hey*, he said. *Hey*. He backed up. They got off at the next stop, and who knows if it was even theirs.

I loved that. I've got to say, I did. I sort of love it even now.

Not every woman feels this kind of thrill, I'm sure. Some are probably even offended by that kind of chivalry and machismo. Maybe only some of us are drawn to valor, we who already feel defenseless in the world for whatever reason. When I met Mark, I was emerging from a childhood of divorce and uncertainty, where there'd been crying and upset, where the mighty oak that was my mother had been felled. Long after their marriage was over, the moods under that roof felt dangerous. I wanted out of there. I was a butterfly, thin and transparent, and if you looked, you could see my heart beating.

Mark looked, and he saw. He saw my heart beating, and he saw my jeweled tissue wings. A butterfly wears its skeleton outside its body. Men can love this idea as much as women do, maybe more. They can love to rescue. They can need it as much as we do, propping up their own strength with it, same as we do ours. Being a man, being a woman, being a human being—it all hangs on such fragile architecture.

I'm especially embarrassed to admit that I loved how Mark smoked cigarettes. It was heedless and incredibly sexy. He wore those jeans and that white tank undershirt. What a cliché, but, *God*. He had curly black hair and Elvis eyes and he spoke in velvet undertones. He'd smoke while leaning against his car on a hot summer day, and then he'd put out the orange-lit tip with the toe of his boot and it all made me feel safe, ironically or not, subconsciously or not, fated or not, *safe*, and so I married him. I could blame my age, but even at twenty-two you know when you are hiding things from yourself. Still, Mark and I married right after college, and I licked the envelope closed. There. The rest of my life. So I thought.

It went like this: I wanted him to be larger than me, and so he was. And when he was, I didn't like it. And when I didn't like it, I broke the contract. When I broke the contract, the one that said I'd be smaller than him, he lashed out. I'd signed, though—the large print had said, *Me, weak. You, strong*. But I wanted a caveman only every now and then. You realize this. I wanted to be able to be small but large, too. I wanted to be both. These were the themes of our relationship: Dominance, control. Abuser, victim. It's what you get when you give up your power, when you don't realize that your strength is your self-respect. No one has the right to abuse you, sure, but no one should hand over that right, either.

I should have known better is all I'm saying. With Ian. I'd let myself be rescued before, and look what happened there.

* * *

"White shirts," I say. "Blue, black."

"They all look the same to me," my mother says.

No. Not at all. I can picture Ian in each one. This is when I see him most clearly, looking at his shirts. I can see thirty Ian's all in a row, draped from every hanger. The blue button-down is a favorite of his. In it, he leans forward over me in bed, blue shoulders, smelling like shaving cream, kissing me good morning before he takes off for work. That orange one—sitting beside me on the airplane during our trip to Sante Fe. That white shirt—he married me wearing it.

Abby returns to her place on the bed as she reports on the call. "Evan Lutz? Another friend of Ian's."

"Employee." I picture Evan with his red hair and beard, his office decorated with his collection of Happy Meal toys.

"He's got a lot of friends," my mother says.

"Mom?" Abby has an odd look on her face. Oh, no. She holds that book again with both hands.

"Tell me."

"Evan said his girlfriend was sure she saw Ian at Bagel Oasis yesterday."

I put my hand to my heart. I'm not sure I can breathe.

"Yesterday?" my mother says.

"That's what he said."

"Did you tell him to call that detective?"

"I did."

I am holding the sleeve of an olive 100 percent cotton number. Terrible to iron. I am holding it by one cuff. It might look like we are holding hands. Olive shirt: romantic dinner date at Mario's. The candle kept blowing out, and the waiter returned repeatedly to relight it.

We are all silent. It is great and horrible news. I feel sick. My mother tries to lift some stain off her jeans with her fingernail. Abby just looks down at that book.

"We don't know," my mother says finally.

Abby opens the book at random. She gazes down at an image, which proves too remarkable not to share. "Wow," she says. She holds it up, shows us. It is breathtaking, all right. Lush, velvety blue wings rimmed with soft corduroy brown. *"Ulysses,"* she reads.

"Well, isn't that perfect," I say. "Ulysses. Maybe Ian'll be back in twenty years, too." Shock—it's quickly being replaced by anger.

"I don't know about you guys, but when I see something beautiful like that, all I want to do is trap it and suffocate it." My mother rolls her eyes. She huffs with disgust again.

A hand over a mouth. Arms pinned back. A struggle to breathe.

It's not here. His favorite T-shirt. I can see him in that shirt perhaps most of all, sitting across from me on that picnic blanket on one sunny summer afternoon. It's funny what becomes a favorite shirt. My own is a big white cotton thing, beloved because it's big and white and cotton. But his—it's got a guitar on it, with wings. It was a promotional item from a product release from the company he used to work for. He's had that thing forever.

I grab the stack of T-shirts, toss one aside and then another. I look through the laundry hamper pile, already dumped out.

"There's a T-shirt. It's not here. A pair of running shoes, too."

"Okay," Abby says. But she doesn't write anything down. She just closes *One Hundred Butterflies* and sits there with a worried face.

"Pollux," I say.

"What?" Abby looks confused, as if maybe Pollux is being unjustly accused of making off with Ian's stuff.

"He's been too quiet for too long."

It's that mother sense you develop. That never-ending surveillance for potential disaster that is always, always working after you have a child. It ticks steadily behind the scenes, no matter if you're cooking dinner or if you're on the phone or if you're checking your missing husband's closet for clothes he might have packed when he left you.

There's a crash in the kitchen. It's the sound of a knife dropping on the floor, at least. Something else thudding, too.

I dash in there, and Abby and my mother follow. Pollux has pulled down a corner of Saran wrap with his teeth, and he has banana-bread crumbs on his beard.

He runs over to the back door when he sees us. He lies down, as if to convince us he's been there all along.

"Goddamn it," Abby says. "Look at this, you bad boy!" He's gotten a few cookies, too. "Come here!"

Of course, he doesn't. He gets up and starts to woof and trot around, back and forth and back and forth in front of that glass door, wild-eyed with wrongdoing. He is not innocent and we know it, and there is nothing for him to do now but bark and bark at that dark night.

7

I try to call Evan Lutz at his Happy Meal office the next morning, but he doesn't answer. I am tired of waiting around and doing nothing. Minutes are now posing as hours, and hours as days. The crew calls in: Paula, Ian's secretary; Simon Ash; Bethy; my father. No one has any news. I call our bank again to see if there's been activity on our account. I open Ian's laptop for the hundredth time and look at that damn password screen in frustration until I slam it closed once more. I call Detective Jackson but only get his voice mail. I picture him on the other line right then, speaking to Ian, delivering a stern message about his bad behavior. This feels great, even if it's only happening in my own head. Ian is susceptible to humiliation, and Detective Jackson is really hammering into him. There, you bastard. Bagel Oasis? You go into hiding, you at least ought to do it right. You go to the Caribbean or something, you asshole. Not some cheap sandwich shop a few blocks from your very own office building.

It occurs to me: I'll lose the help of the police now, won't I? It's unclear what exactly Detective Jackson has been doing as he waits to open a proper investigation, but I've been mostly grateful he's around, regardless. His presence has felt like action when there's been no other forward motion, no leads, no calls about our posters, nothing. So what do I do now? I should freeze my bank accounts, that's what.

"Going to BetterWorks," I tell Abby. She's eating cereal, and I can see her five-year-old self there at the table. She's still the same determined little person with those intent brown eyes. Years ago, I'd be getting up to make her lunch. Sandwich, fruit, treat, and a love note written on a Post-it. I'm struck with a heart stab of longing for that time.

"Want me to come?"

"No."

"You okay to drive? You look like hell."

"I'm fine." Oh, how we love and overuse *fine,* our all-purpose little evasion. *Fine* means *not fine. Fine* means *Pity me. Fine* means *Don't ask.*

"Last night, you were—"

"I know. Bad dream."

"Same one?"

"I have no idea."

"Maybe we should try that Jim Beam again tonight. I won't pour so much."

"Wasn't it Johnnie Walker?"

"I get all those alcohol men confused."

"Wait. Jack Daniel's."

"Isn't he a country singer?" She chuckles at herself.

Pollux sees the jacket and the keys. He waits for the magic words but gets the other ones instead. "You stay with Abby," I say to him.

"God, don't look so disappointed, Poll. You're making me feel bad." Abby plucks a bit of cereal from her bowl and gives it to him.

"Poor you, left behind," I say.

* * *

I am failing at this, I think, because I'm supposed to be sure of something here. Sure that he's left me. Sure that he'd never leave. Sure that he's fine, or not fine. Alive, or not alive. I'm supposed to have some kind of knowing, deep in my bones. But I have no knowing. I am sure of nothing. Deep in my bones, there is only hollowness. I am so hollow that I can feel the wind outside whipping through me as a truck speeds by, driving too fast on our street. I can feel my body shudder—that's how empty it is. The wind has upended a bit of trash on the street. It's a piece of paper, which scurries end-to-end, corner-to-corner, for a few brave feet. It's making a run for it, and I run, too, to catch it. Suddenly that paper seems potentially important. Everything does. Everything might be. It has critical information, I know it. I pick it up. It's only someone's old dry-cleaning receipt. *Aloha Fine Dry Cleaning. Silk blouse (2). $14.99 plus tax = $15.65.*

Ian and I—we made love for the first time in a forest. It was in that spooky park, which didn't seem so spooky once you got out and walked down some of the trails. It was beautiful in there, really. It was the beginning of summer, and light filtered through the trees, making lace-doily patterns against the boughs. We weren't the type for some motel. I guess it felt more honest that way. Nature was more authentic than renting some cheap room for a few hours. We didn't want it to be like that. You had to separate yourselves out of the cheapness of it all somehow—give some dignity to what was otherwise tawdry.

He carried the blankets. I carried a bag with a few snacks and drinks. Premeditation. We assumed we'd walk down the trails, same as we had a few times before, and that some perfect spot would call out to us, some flat, leafy glade that would both welcome and hide new lovers. But off the path there were only ferns and bushes with stout, sturdy leaves and thorny trails of blackberries that stuck to your skin, making pinpricks of blood. I tried to joke, because Ian was thrashing this stick back and forth as if it were a machete and we were in the Amazon. He was so serious right then. He didn't laugh or make some crack back at me. I felt guilty about this, like I wanted what was about to happen more than he did. Every branch that snapped under my feet sounded as loud as a cracking spine.

Eventually there was a spot of soft ferns, well away from the trail and any eyes that might see us. Ian laid down the blanket with his usual precision. He reached his hand out to me and I went to him. Finally he smiled, though his eyes still looked solemn. I knew that this was a momentous occasion, less because it was a transition for us than because it meant the breaking of his vows. His, not mine. The crisis always seemed to be about his marriage, his loss. I felt a curl of resentment that I ignored. And the truth was, I *didn't* feel the guilt of that vow-breaking in the same way he did. My vows had felt broken since the first time Mark raised his hand to me. They had been broken again when he threw me to the ground and kicked my ribs. Why do they always say a marriage is *crumbling*? It sounds so gentle, like toast. Mine didn't crumble. Big chunks fell off and crashed into the sea, causing tidal waves to rise. I wanted Ian. I wanted him to make love to me. I wanted that *union*.

And, in spite of his solemnity, Ian wanted it, too. He pulled me to him. We always had passion, and it lit up there on the forest floor. He undid his pants and put my hand around him, and if at any time I felt a sense of my own infidelity, it was then. Not because my hand belonged to only one man, but because I had held only one man for so many years. Ian felt different. It was like momentarily wearing someone else's slippers. Your feet know the feeling of your own, and any other pair is wrong.

Passion—well, honestly, I was fighting to hold on to it. I felt too aware of twigs in my back and the possible sound of footsteps and the awkwardness of bra clasps. I was acting. Maybe it was like most first times, when things squeak and fumble, when you're thinking too much. The first time can be a mission to be accomplished or a line to cross. We fixed that later.

But that day it was the effort of the outdoors and some slight embarrassment at my choice of underwear, that kind of thing. I am never exactly smooth when I want to be. It was one of those memories that become more embarrassing with time, after you know better. The next Christmas, Ian gave me six tiny thongs, and I realized my mistake. Tall mother undies, even satin, were still mother undies. I cringe at that even now.

Regardless, the mission was accomplished. The line was crossed. We lay together only briefly afterward before hurriedly dressing. If you've ever thought that an affair might be romantic, believe me, there are a thousand reasons why it's not. Especially when the motivation is as serious and life-changing as love. This isn't some sort of cautionary message of morality, don't get me wrong. Do what you want. But there were no long hours of looking into each other's eyes is all I'm saying. Someone always wore a watch. And even then I could feel it, the way my options were dwindling as my old ship was beginning to sink, the prow tipping upward in the black waves.

I love you, Dani. God, I love you so much. We were meant to be together.

I love you, too, Ian.

Shit! Look how late it is!

Oh, no! Can you hand me my—

I'll probably break out with poison ivy. That'd be a trick to explain.

Mark came home that night, and I set dinner on our plates and plates on our place mats and poured milk in our glasses, something I had done hundreds of times. Hundreds. But now all of that, a *lifetime* of that, was a fate I had suddenly, narrowly missed. At the table, Mark talked about work, the leads that were given to Gary when they should have gone to him, something, I don't know, because playing over his face were images of forest leaves and light patterns among branches, skin on skin, bodies that now didn't seem to fumble awkwardly but moved effortlessly in the replaying. I watched Mark cut his pork chops, but over the top of his hands, like those plastic sheets in some medical book showing ever deeper layers of the human body, were Ian's hands, set on the curves of my hips. As I picked up the dishes that night, I was aware of the long red scratch from a blackberry thorn that was hidden under my sleeve.

Later that evening, I watched Mark brush his teeth at our sink. His shirt was off, and he was wearing a pair of baggy boxers. His white stomach hit the counter edge. *He's gained weight*, I thought uncharitably. There were small round rolls spilling over the silly elastic of his shorts. Then again, I had thin white lines on my hips from being pregnant with Abby, and my breasts had started to sag.

You didn't notice I got my hair cut, he said.

Ah, you got your hair cut. I was in bed already. Abby had gone to bed, too, an hour before. I had a book on my knees. I read the same lines over and over. Lines about some forest floor, a couple tangled passionately, a couple now separated and filled with longing.

Too short? I think it's too short. Makes my face look fat.

My heart had become closed and stingy, unable to offer any reassurance. I shrugged.

Thanks, he said.

What? It looks fine. You worry more about your hair than I do.

He brushed, spit into the sink. Wiped his mouth on a towel. Shoved the towel back onto the rack.

Can you? I gestured in the direction of the towel. *It's all clumpy.*

You giving the home tour tomorrow? Who's going to see? He wasn't angry, he was joking. Trying to kid me out of some confusing mood I was in.

I will. It's inconsiderate. I work hard to keep things nice.

He got in bed beside me. *You do. You keep things really nice.*

I was engrossed in my book. Much too engrossed in the riveting plot to notice his eyes on me, questioning, or his fingertips stroking my arm up and down, up and down. My skin was shriveling from his touch; it felt disgusting to me. I wanted to scream at him to stop. He was staring, and it felt like he could see too much. He hadn't seen me for years, but now there I was with my butterfly skeleton outside my body.

Are you okay? he asked.

I'm fine.

He was still waiting.

I went for the all-purpose fatigue-and-illness excuse, our other favorite evasion. What would we do without it—all the honesty it's helped us avoid, all the intimacy? *I'm tired, is all. I think that dinner didn't sit well with me.*

You need a Pepto-Bismol? Brief flash—forest floor interrupted by the realization of daily issues like stomach upset. Somehow you don't picture a lover fetching Pepto-Bismol. I felt a little panicky at the flimsiness of the dreamy light flickering among evergreens. Soul mates would still occasionally eat at some bad taco truck or get the flu. My husband had seen me give birth, and he was still here.

I'm okay.

I turned the page, even though I hadn't read it. Mark reached around on the floor by the bed, found the remote, and flicked the TV on.

Mark . . . I'm reading.

He gave me that long look again, and then he turned the volume low, low enough that he'd have to lip-read to watch the show. I set my book down now that he'd ruined it with moving mouths and silent dialogue. Really, I couldn't even hear it. Still, I turned my shoulders away from him in a huff.

I could feel it in my chest, the spinning piston of irritation. Mark felt it, too. He began to stroke my arm again.

Something else had happened that day, I could tell. I could feel it in Mark's needy fingers. It was remarkable. It was temporary. But it was good while it lasted: The tables had turned.

It changed things, making love with Ian. It was like losing a second virginity. Marriage sends you back to some sanctioned state of purity in regard to sex, and now Ian and I had broken that, and we'd broken it together. It was not done lightly and the ramifications were not inconsequential. God, do you hear that? It sounds like I'm discussing contract negotiations, not pleasure. I guess it *was* a contract negotiation of sorts, contract *re*negotiation. We thought about our relationship differently after that. We thought about our marriages differently after that, too. It solidified things between us. Not entirely. But we went from the liquidy state of Jell-O to the point where you could drop the fruit in it. We would have had a mess if we'd taken it out of the mold right then, but you get the idea. Not the best metaphor. Whatever.

I wanted Mark to know after that. The marriage was finished in my mind, and staying now felt intolerable. His eyes were the wrong eyes and his body was the wrong body and my life was the wrong life. Even if Ian and I didn't ride off into the sunset together, I knew that the marriage was irretrievably broken if I could have those kinds of feelings for someone else. Before then, every time I faced the thought of leaving, every time I sobbed after some frightening altercation or held my pillow in the night or watched his jawline for signs of mood, it felt too large. *Over* was just too big. *Alone* was even bigger.

They call an abusive relationship a cycle of violence, when really it's a cycle of hope. It's a cycle of misguided optimism. One day that optimism is gone, if you're lucky.

Here are a few things (the few that I care to disclose): Mark came home one afternoon and told me he'd quit his job, just like that. With a baby and a mortgage and me not working yet. He'd gotten into a fight with his boss. No matter where he worked, he was always getting into a fight with a boss. And there'd been sexual-harassment charges at another workplace. Another thing: On Christmas Eve, his sister told me that he'd once dislocated his own arm while beating her up when they were teenagers. Another: He spent more than we had. And this: One night, after shoving me hard onto the bed and screaming in my face and battering me, he left. He left for hours. Where? A porn theater, he admitted later. I washed the clothes that he wore that night. They smelled of cigarettes and of old men in overcoats slunk down in worn velvet theater seats. The woman who washed those clothes—it's like talking about someone I once knew.

You can get too small to save yourself. You married a tiger because a tiger is large and fierce, but he's fierce to *all* humans, even you. Especially you, because with you he can hide behind the word *husband* and the doors of your own home and no one will ever know. You start to understand that if living with the tiger is bad, leaving the tiger is going to be worse.

The point is, I forced myself to see the good in Mark because of my own cowardice. The ways he was a great father to Abby. The bike rides. The baseball practices. The times we were a regular family, joking, taking vacations. Running out to the waves on some beach, holding hands. Thanksgiving, when he said that what he was most thankful for was me. He made me laugh sometimes. Your hatred lies low, disappears in your fear of what it might mean to leave. I reminded myself instead of the endearing way he'd crack up at his own jokes, or the joy he showed coming back from some trip to buy lumber, or his earnest, good intentions with some self-help book. It's like the thing you do when you don't have money (well, I did it, anyway, after I was divorced)—you turn the radio up because the car's making some noise you know is going to cost more than you can pay.

I was "in denial," which sounds like I was "in" some foreign country, which I guess I basically was. I stayed in denial until I saw the slightest shadowy figure of a rescuer who might have held a ticket out of there. Ian wasn't even a real rescuer. He made no promises. He hadn't yet decided what his own life and marriage needed to be. He was merely the *illusion* of a rescuer. That was enough. Even if it was a trick of the eye, it suddenly appeared that I wasn't facing the tiger alone. You stand there and look and look and look at the tiger. You stare and stare at his teeth. And then, seemingly all at once, standing there a second longer is worse than the possibility of being eaten alive. There was no knight, not really. No sword. But I was ready anyway. Finally I could say, *Enough.*

Finally I could say, *Go ahead and eat me, fucker.*

I remember reading something once, in one of Ian's books. It reminded me of us. The Aztec goddess of love, Xochiquetzal, held a butterfly between her teeth as she made love to young soldiers on battlefields. It was a promise of rebirth, should they die while fighting for freedom.

On the way to BetterWorks, I pray. As I drive past all of the photoflash images of typical Seattle—the six coffee places, the thin, speeding bikers, the cafés featuring sustainable food—I silently ask for my family's safety and well-being. This is what I settle on after some initial perplexity about what to pray *for*. You know: If he left home, do I pray he returns? If he's swimming in the sea somewhere, do I pray for a shark attack? Or do I pray for mistaken identity, for Evan Lutz's girlfriend's bad eyesight, for it to have been some bank employee with Ian's profile she saw there in Bagel Oasis? I don't have a great deal of confidence that God is really listening to me, anyway. There's probably some strike-out system Up There, and I'm sure I've gotten more than my share.

I pull into the BetterWorks lot. My stomach is roiling, a boat riding ocean swells. Ian might come out of those glass doors right now. He might spot my car and bolt. He won't exactly want to see me, will he, after ditching me in such a cruel way? I didn't even know he had reached that point. Being disappointed is one thing.

I am struck with a blow of frigid air from the air-conditioning when I walk in. He keeps it too cold in there. Kitty and Jasmine are at the reception desk. They're chatting and laughing together, but when they see me they stop. It's not one of those social situations for which there are rules. Kitty collects herself enough to speak.

"Mrs. Keller!"

"Is Ian in?"

She looks baffled. Kitty and Jasmine glance at each other. My voice is bitter, even to me. Those embarrassing moments that seem worse later—this will become one of them.

"He's not been in since . . ." Kitty waves a hand in a small circle, treading emotional water.

"Last Friday. Saturday. The party," Jasmine says.

"Saturday. The party," Kitty repeats.

I guess I'm relieved. I've been worried he's in his office, wearing his missing clothes, eating another lunch from Bagel Oasis. But Nathan would have told me if he'd seen Ian, wouldn't he? Nathan has a good heart.

"Is Nathan in?"

"Not yet, Mrs. Keller."

"I'm actually here to see Evan Lutz."

"I'll buzz him," Kitty says, which leaves Jasmine to deal with me. Her eye contact is awkward. I realize I haven't showered. I probably look a little crazy. I pat down my hair. I have a sudden fear that I'm wearing only socks, but, no, thank goodness, my shoes are there.

I remember: Jasmine is a part-time employee. She's a student. Something-something, I don't know. "How's graduate school? How are your classes going?" Jasmine tilts her head, troubled, but I persist. My husband may have left me in some cruel, unimaginable way, but I can still manage. *I* can be kind. And I'm just fine. See? *Fine.* He might have left me because my clothes aren't sexy enough, or because I am annoyingly forgetful about tying boats down, or because I waste food, or because his daughters hate me, but I'm perfectly okay without him. "Business marketing?" I say to Jasmine.

"Right. You know, busy . . ."

Kitty saves us. "He's on his way," she says. I don't have the three different passes with secret fingerprints that allow the elevator to work. You'd think Ian's building was the goddamn CIA. Now here is Evan. Red beard, crumpled shirt. He looks about twenty, though I know he's a good deal past that. Apparently, years of playing medieval video games can contribute to a youthful appearance. There are two kinds of computer guys, I've found—you have the ones who dress in food-splotched clothes, who eat out of pizza boxes, and who can't make socially appropriate eye contact, and then you have the ones like Ian. Casually but expensively dressed. The feel of money and the lifestyle of perfection that programming code requires. The former have cars that run on soybeans and cow manure. The latter have foreign sports cars with leather seats and some satellite fantasy woman who'll help them out of their traffic woes.

I am getting used to the look I get from Evan as he takes my hand. I imagine it's the same one you give to the dogs at the pound, the ones you won't be bringing home. It's a mix of apology–guilt–pity that draws down the mouth and the corners of the eyes. I hate pity, which is probably one of the reasons I've never told people about what went on between Mark and me. I don't believe in self-pity, either. I believe I'm responsible for my own messes, even this one. Reasons are not the same thing as excuses.

"Dani . . ." Evan has chubby fingers and the sort of squishy palms that make shaking hands unpleasant. I hate shaking fat hands. It's one of life's unpleasantries, along the lines of sitting in a seat still warm from someone else's butt or smelling a stranger's fart in a bookstore. But now he's walking and I'm following. Evan is my day's fate, like it or not. We're in the elevator, then out of the elevator. He's apologizing again and again. "I'm sorry. I'm so sorry . . ."

More useless pity, I think. We arrive at the doorway to his office before I realize it's not pity at all. He's really apologizing.

I look at all those Happy Meal toys on his desk and shelves—
the little cartoon cars and Ronald McDonalds and Disney characters, some I even remember from the bottom of Abby's toy box.
That *Lion King* one, right there. A rubber Simba and his lion
girlfriend—her name escapes me. And that power-woman with
the red-laser eyes. She has a trigger on her back that makes them
spit fire.

"Hailey feels *terrible*. She only met them once, you know? So
she got confused."

"What?"

"I really am so sorry. I was telling her everything, right? And
I said that Ian hadn't been seen in days, and she said, 'But I just
saw him. He was at Bagel Oasis today, getting lunch.' I didn't
even question. I just assumed it was him. We even called the
police department, like your daughter said to. And then Hailey
and I were talking this morning again. And she said something
like, 'He probably has women around him all the time, good-
looking like that. That hair . . .' And I thought, *I don't think
Ian . . .*"

I was hearing: *women*. I was hearing: *all the time*. Ian is good-
looking, all right, but not exactly known for his hair. It's cut
rather seriously. Trim. Handsome, but . . .

Evan is shaking his head. "Ian's *hair*? And then I just went,
Oh, shit!"

My stomach makes an odd flip. Ian hasn't been seen, that's all
I'm getting.

"Nathan. She saw *Nathan*, not Ian. She didn't know. She only
met them that once." He's repeating himself. "We are both so
sorry. She feels *terrible*. She didn't even go in to work today, she
was so upset."

I might throw up. The Happy Meal room also carries the sickening scent of cold French fries. The smell of old grease is coming off Evan's clothes, too.

There's a hand on my arm, and just in time, because the floor appears to be moving. "Dani?"

It's Nathan, Nathan with the fabulous, noticeable hair. Nathan who isn't Ian, and who looks nothing like him.

"Let's go to my office or something. Let's go sit down."

There is more following, and then Nathan shuts his door behind us. There are no toys here, thank God. The windows show another wide, gorgeous vista of the city. There's a couch, and pillows in warm fall colors. There's a bookcase filled with books. Not only science books and tech magazines, I can see, but novels and biographies, too. There's *On the Road* and *To Kill a Mockingbird* and *The Phantom Tollbooth*. I love that. His desk is a bit messy, which is somehow comforting.

I sit on his couch. He's gone and then he's back, carrying a cold bottle of sparkling water, which he hands to me. He sits on his desk chair, facing me. He is hunched forward and his hands are folded together. If someone were spying on us, it might look as if I was hearing his deepest secrets.

"It wasn't him," I say.

Nathan gives a single shake of his head.

"We still don't know anything."

He shakes his head again.

I look out at the city. So many stories are there, in each of those windows and tiny cars. Every single person has his or her own story line going on at that very moment, one that involves the urgency of *right now*, but with motivations and themes that go back generations. Out there are lost fortunes and broken hearts and great ideas and daughters who've never truly left home.

Nathan's office is strangely cozy and confessional. It calms me, though maybe it's all of those books, all of those life stories. Books can have that effect in a room. It reminds me of Dr. Shana Berg's office. She also has a bookshelf and a couch with pillows in fall colors.

"I was the best I could be," I say. It sounds bad, even to me. I rather hate myself for letting it slip out.

"What do you mean?" Nathan's voice is soft. His cellphone rings, but he only glances at it and then shuts it off.

I don't answer at first. How to explain? In my marriage with Mark it had been clear, the state things were in. We had even gone to marital counseling a year or so before I met Ian. Dr. Frederick Mercury—yes, that was the psychologist's name, poor man, he could never be called "Freddie." He listened without saying much all that time. I got to wondering, you know, what we were paying for. But after a few months, near the end of our time with him, he only looked at us both. He said, "I have to question if you can fix something so broken." Just that. The comment still hurts, even now. But it was clear is what I'm saying.

"Some of his clothes are gone."

"You really think he left you?" He leans back in his chair. He runs a hand through that memorable hair.

"What else?"

"He could be injured somewhere. Dani, I don't want to be blunt, but he could be—"

"He's not dead. He's left me."

"In that case, he's left you, his kids, me, our business . . ."

"He'll come back to those things. He won't come back to me. I believe that."

"But *why?*"

"He lost so much because of me. The kids, all that money. Their friends. You have to be so much *more* to make it all worth it. . . ." Nathan is one of the few people in our lives who would know to what I'm alluding. When you have our history, you don't exactly advertise it. It's always awkward, that moment when you're asked, "So how'd you meet?" You skirt the truth. *Through friends,* you might say. You don't say those friends were your kids, who played on the same baseball team when you both were married to other people. But Nathan's known Ian for a long time. He's been through the gory details with him.

"He loves you. He's crazy about you. His eyes follow you. I mean, you're gorgeous and you're kind and you're funny. . . . You see the world in your own way—"

"No, don't do that. I don't need you to say that."

"It's true."

"I don't want you to say that. It doesn't matter. There are always these *things*. I can't seem to get it right for him."

"That's how he *is*."

"I didn't see it, not really, until we got married."

"Maybe he was trying to be better than who he'd been."

"Maybe."

"For as long as he could."

"The way he flirts, though—even at that party."

"It doesn't mean anything, you know that. It's Ian being his charming self." Nathan rubs the arms of his chair. He's at a loss. "You deserve better, Dani. So do I, actually."

"Where is he, for God's sake? Nathan, *where*?"

"You know what I think? What I honestly think? I think he's feeling unappreciated. That night, he was pissed. At me. At you, too. I mean, I noticed. I saw." Nathan meets my eyes. He waits for some acknowledgment from me, but I don't know exactly what he's referring to. *What* did he notice? *What* did he see? "He's like the kid on the playground who picks on people and then sulks when they don't like him for it. We'll appreciate him now, won't we?"

Nathan's hostility surprises me. But, really, why should it? This is what happens when nice people are pushed too far. We give too many chances, and so when we've finally had enough, we are well and truly done. When a nice person shuts a door on you, it's shut for good. "I want to go into his office," I say.

Nathan smacks his forehead. "I'm an idiot. Of course you do. You want to *look*."

"There's got to be *something* . . ."

Nathan gathers up his keys in one swoop, grabs his coffee cup. We head down the hall to Ian's corner office. Nathan unlocks the door. Ian's office is so different from Nathan's. You can tell that Nathan handles the creative end of their partnership while Ian manages the technical side. Ian's choice of furniture is contemporary and high-tech. His own couch is made of black leather panels stretched onto linear brushed metal. His coffee table is a thin iron structure topped with fragile glass.

For all of Ian's precision, his office is a disaster. It always has been. I remember being surprised by this on my first visit; it seemed so unlike him. His desk is dominated by his huge computer screen, and the screen is flanked by magazines meant to be read and mail meant to be sorted. There are boxes and piles of paper and masses of file folders on a round table in one corner of the room. Computer components are stacked in another corner, their cords neatly wound and tied with rubber bands. A bookshelf is haphazardly decorated, as if the task had been abandoned halfway through. There's a tech-magazine award that Ian had won (a glass pyramid on a black stand—he won it two years in a row, and we have another one in our office at home) and a chunky clay pot painted garish colors, made by Bethy in elementary school. There's a photo of us that I gave him. In it, we're leaning against the *New View,* and the sun is setting.

I take it all in. It's not the office of a person who never makes mistakes, and something about this makes my heart soften. He's a complicated man, but I love him. I am choked up, about to cry.

"I don't know where to begin," I say.

"All this mess . . ."

I am overwhelmed in front of those piles of file folders and stacks of paper. There's too much. Each item represents a thought that had once crossed through his mind. I could be there for days, just searching for a single receipt or a small jotted note that might tell me what his plan had been. And there had to have been a plan. Ian's not exactly spontaneous. Look how long it took him to finally leave Mary—two and a half years of both mental and actual back and forth. He researches the layout of the parking lot before going to the Opera House. He keeps a log of his gas mileage.

But if I am there to learn something, anything, it suddenly offers itself. I only have to run my eyes over that room, past his desk, to what's lying on the floor. There is his blue gym bag, with the Mariners logo on it. He isn't a baseball fan, so where it came from, I don't know; he's had it for years. And while he hasn't been to the Fifth Street Gym in a long time, he sometimes goes for a run after work. He comes home sweaty and tired and starving.

The gym bag—I know what it means before I even look inside.

I lean down to pick it up. The slippery nylon is so familiar, as are the woven handles. I'd forgotten about this bag and what is likely inside it. *Stupid, stupid, stupid.*

"Look." My voice is unsteady.

"His gym bag?" Nathan doesn't get it.

I set it on Ian's desk and unzip it with shaking hands. Yes, there it is. That T-shirt. Ian's favorite one, with the winged guitar. And there are the running shoes. There are also a pair of sweatpants and shorts I hadn't realized were missing. A zip-up sweatshirt, too. An empty water bottle.

I hold the T-shirt up for Nathan to see. I feel a flip of nausea that turns to terror.

"Dani . . ." Nathan might not know what this means, but he can read my face. He puts his arms around me. The T-shirt is between us, in my hands.

I can feel my heart beating against Nathan's chest. There are no certainties now. Every possible thing is possible all over again, same as the day Ian disappeared. We don't know anything. He could be anywhere, with anyone. He could be in some foreign country; he could be hurt somewhere; he could be dead, maybe even murdered; he could be driving in some convertible down some road with a new identity in his pocket.

Or worse. The terror in my chest is saying that: *Or worse*. My sheets were muddy that morning. The heels I'd worn to the party had been muddy, too, but so had the bottoms of my feet. My missing memory of that night—it's the plumpest blackberry out of reach, hanging past the thickest thorns. *What* had Nathan seen? My heart is thumping hard against Nathan's chest—it is fear, a shadowy kind of fear. Because there are all the ways I've disappointed Ian. But there are all the ways he's disappointed me, too.

8

I drive back home. In reverse now, I pass the Java Jive and the Black Cat and the Sureshot, the Allegro and the Tully's and the Pete's and the Starbucks, Starbucks, Starbucks. Next to me, a man in a Fat Boys Plumbing truck sips from the tiny lip of a white lid, and two girls with multicolored hair cross the street to get in line at Cool Beans. Tattoos snake up their arms and wind around their necks. In this city, colored hair and multiple tattoos are as commonplace as middle-aged women in turtlenecks. A golf sweater would be an act of rebellion here.

Something is rattling in my car, in old Blue Beast, and I roll my window down at the stoplight to see if I can hear where the sound is coming from. I get the car-trouble-panic feeling, where every noise elicits internal calculations of credit-card balances. Once, I worried all the way across the bridge from Seattle to Bellevue, an hour-long ride, because of a rattling Tic Tac box. You spend time as a single mother, and money disasters haunt you. The sound of breath mints can mean you're about to go under.

All I need now is for something to go wrong with the damn car.

"Come on, Blue," I plead. Old Blue has been with me a good long time, and I've likely taken it for granted.

I try my favorite radio denial trick. I haven't used that one in a while. But I can still hear the noise, even over the music, and I also quickly realize that the thumping sunny beat isn't an option, nor is a nasal-y announcer talking about a jewelry sale and the way you can prove your love for her with a diamond engagement ring. I shut it off. Those things don't belong in the world I'm now in.

The noise seems to only get worse when I accelerate. I make it home. Nothing falls out of the car on the way, so maybe we're okay for a while. I park on the gravel strip in front of the dock, a few cars away from Ian's. That car has an attitude now, rigid and withholding. I need some privacy for the call I'm about to make, so I stay put. I fish my phone out of my purse.

I can tell right away that the message has changed. Right after *You have reached the office of Dr. Shana Berg,* she's supposed to say, *If this is an emergency, please dial 911 . . .* But now it's different. *You have reached the office of Dr. Shana Berg. I will be out of the office . . .*

A long weekend? Gone until Tuesday. She offers the number of her colleague, Dr. Hank Helprin, but I don't want Hank Helprin, even if his name has *help* in it, which ordinarily I might have seen as a good sign. Shana Berg knew me at my worst, and right now I need someone who knows me.

I am angry with myself for being too much of a coward to speak with her earlier. But I am also relieved. I'll admit that. I'm not the best at facing facts, but, then again, who is? It seems like every one of us spends a good part of our time here on earth doing what we can to avoid the truth.

* * *

I flip fast through the day's mail, insanely hoping for a letter from Ian. There are coupons for a new Thai restaurant, the electric bill, a QFC flyer, nothing. I look for the millionth time at our bank and credit-card balances. No activity. There have been no calls about the flyers. I write a few apologetic emails to my handful of design clients; I haven't worked, obviously, in days, and now those urgent matters will have to wait—the blue border versus the green, the change of fonts from Baskerville to Book Antiqua. I return another call from Ian's sister, Olivia, and one from my father, who's been phoning daily. I talk to Detective Jackson, who only tells me once more that they're doing what they can. They've checked airline flight lists and patient admitting sheets; they've kept his alert status active across our state and other states. *Our next step is for you folks to do an interview on the local news,* he says.

I tell him that I'll discuss it with Bethy and Kristen, but I don't do this. When news of our affair broke out among Ian's friends in that suburban neighborhood, it was, for Ian, one of the most painful parts of the whole mess. People talking about him. People *judging* him. That prick Neal Jacobs had called him an asshole under his breath at curriculum night—Neal, who had slept around on business trips; he'd told Ian that himself. But Neal hadn't fallen in love. He hadn't *left*. Mary's friends Charlene and Candy wouldn't speak to Ian, either, and he was the only parent not invited to the Stroms' home when they were taking photos before Bethy's prom. This wounded him. I didn't get the whole pre-prom gathering at the house of whoever-had-the-best-backyard, anyway. They served food at those things. Prom—all the dances—had become a precursor to some future out-of-control wedding, with the makeup artists and hair salons and limos. I didn't think it was such a hot idea to encourage kids to believe they led movie-star lives, even for a night. That job they'd get after college—a limo ride would cost them a month's groceries, and it was unfair to imply otherwise. Still, Ian had been so hurt.

Ian would be destroyed if I put his personal business on the news. I know it's crazy, but I still care what he would want. Even if he's sipping a margarita somewhere (the drink keeps changing in my mind—margarita, piña colada, tequila sunrise—all tropical, usually involving an umbrella), I care. And, one more thing, if I'm being honest? The shame has always belonged to us both.

I call my sister. One of her kids is practicing the recorder in the background. I hear the notes. *C. C. C. A. A. A.*

"Stephanie," she says. "It's driving me nuts."

"You should have heard Abby her first year playing violin. Just put on your headphones."

"But then I won't hear if one of them is burning down the house."

I laugh. She can always make me laugh, even now. "Thanks for your message, Ames," I tell her. "You forgot to hang up, though. I heard you walking around, gravel crunching, and then I think you dropped me into your purse. It sounded like a construction site in there."

"Thank God that's all you heard. Have you changed your mind yet about me coming out? It doesn't feel right for me not to be there. I want to! If you keep saying no, I'm going to come anyway."

"I might need you later."

"Stop saying that. You've got to have faith that he's alive and that there's a reasonable explanation for all this. I'm coming out there."

"You're here for me just fine from there, sweetie. Really."

"I feel like I'm not doing anything."

"You are." She is. Just hearing her voice helps.

We're interrupted. It's Justin, and he's whining. "In a minute!" she says to him. She kind of snaps actually. Even good mothers snap every now and then.

"It's okay, Ames. I'll let you go. I promise I'll call if anything changes."

"He's got a new magic kit. He wants to show me the disappearing coin. Remember the disappearing coin?"

I do. "Yeah."

"Remember magic shops? With the joke toys? The plastic barf? The fake gum? You loved those. You always bought them with your birthday money."

"The snake in the peanut can was my favorite."

"Believe me, I know."

"*You* always bought bad perfume from Mom's Avon catalog."

"I loved bad perfume! Jovan Musk Oil? Charlie?" She pauses. "It's going to be okay, Dani-Dee."

When she says it, I believe it. I have a moment of inexplicable, soaring hope. Maybe it's the feeling that comes when you're around your own people, even briefly. Or maybe it's just the stupid memory of old magic tricks, that coin resting in its green plastic case. It hadn't really disappeared. Of course it hadn't. It was right there all along.

I try to rest. Abby is over at her place, catching up with her life and getting more clothes. I need a break from Ian's gone-ness. I can hear Mattie and Louise joking around with Maggie Long on the dock. I lie down and put the pillow over my head. It seems wrong for them to be laughing when their neighbor is missing. When you're grieving, you think everyone should be grieving, too. People at the beach, or some couple celebrating an anniversary, or a soccer team getting cherry Slurpees at 7-Eleven—they should all be ashamed of themselves.

Pollux is curled up in his little donut shape beside me. He's snoring like an old man. He started snoring in his advancing age, and I know he can't help it, but, God. There's some other noise, too—a high-pitched buzzing, with the annoying rise and fall normally associated with the whine of mosquitoes and chain saws. It is old Joe Grayson with that damn remote-control boat. You'd think the novelty would have worn off by now. This is your brain. This is your brain on drugs. Here's how old hippies end up. Playing too enthusiastically with the Christmas-morning toys of ten-year-old boys.

I give up and get up. Pollux dutifully rouses but regretfully so. "You can stay there," I tell him. "I never said you had to follow me everywhere."

One look into those melted-chocolate eyes and I regret my tone. I rub his silky head. "I'm sorry, Poll. Want a treat?"

We both have a piece of one of Abby's oatmeal cookies. I chew and swallow cheerlessly. The food sticks in my throat. Even swallowing requires some sort of deliberate attention I don't have. The problem is, there are words jogging endless loops in my head, like some fitness freak running off the calories of a carrot stick. *He flirts; it doesn't mean anything. He flirts; it doesn't mean anything.*

I've always managed to think of Ian's flirting as an embarrassing trait that only I noticed, akin to spotting your spouse's dandruff. If I brushed it off, no one else would see it, either. But *It doesn't mean anything* says that Nathan (and other people, no doubt) is aware of it, too. *It's how he is.* Am I a cliché? You can't trust a cheater? I understand the few facts I have. Apparently, none of Ian's clothes are missing, but you can get clothes. No money has been taken from our accounts, no credit cards used, but Ian might have stashed money for months. He could have fallen dead, but where, when? He'd been with me. Our history— it still seems like the obvious answer.

He's innocent, though, until proven guilty, right? Well, then, I deserve proof. At least I'm entitled to that.

I unzip his laptop bag. I reach down into the pockets, feeling for something, anything. I open the top and turn on the machine as if I have a right to it. Of course, I've tried this before. Once again, though, there's that white empty rectangle, blinking unwearyingly, waiting for the secret word that will let me in.

I know you, I say to it.

He'd be stretched out on a webbed deck chair with her next to him, staring out at that stunning cliff-edge promontory that overlooks the Bahia de Cabo San Lucas. He would be smoothing tanning lotion over the cliff edges of her shoulder blades, sharing words about the cliff edges of their relationship. They'd both be drowsy from sex and sun and piña coladas. The drink is piña coladas this time, because that's what we drank then. He'd be tan already after six days away from home (he's always tanned quickly). He wouldn't have shaved in that time and so he'd have stubble, and he'd look so sexy it would be hard for her to resist reaching over and grabbing the bulge under his red swimsuit, or the moons of his ass, if he was lying facedown. He'd have those sunglasses on. Are they missing? (Is the swimsuit?) Those glasses are his favorites—expensive—and he looks great in them.

Their room would be cool, a retreat from the hot sun, and that resort is beautiful, with the winding trails along the water lit at night, the palm trees lit, too, with white lights circling their trunks. The food—real guacamole and shredded pork in handmade tortillas—is fresh and satisfying. He'd pay. He'd scan the bill for error, as she looked at her folded hands set against the bright pattern of her sundress. Something about this careful accounting would make her feel as if she shouldn't have ordered dessert.

They would walk the festive street after dinner. The town—it's not her kind of place. No, it *would* be. He'd be looking for an improvement of some kind. She wouldn't mind the bar scene there, the constant party. She'd be more like Mary in that way. She would only laugh when she saw the women dancing and kissing each other. She wouldn't need to analyze it. She wouldn't lean over and say that it seemed done for show.

Her hair would be swooped up, and he would take her hand and pull her to him and kiss her bare neck. They would head back to the hotel in their rental car, but he wouldn't run over the rabbit that had been sprinting—not fast enough—across the midnight-dark road. He would not weep with guilt over it. The night would not turn bad as they walked the beach in front of the hotel. He would not look out onto the sea and say, *If I were a good man, I'd be here with my wife right now.*

They would not go back to their room with a distance between them, cactus prickles along her guilty spine, the room too hot and then too cold. He would not turn to her in the night to make love, and she would not try to be tender where he was sunburned on his shoulders.

They would only swim in the sea, and he would lift her, weightless, so that she could wrap her legs around him. They would kiss with saltwater lips and brush sand from their legs. They would admire each other's lean bodies, and the sun and swimming and sex would make them ravenous. Night again, they would marvel at the glowing phosphorescence on the beach and at the way nature made the best magic. *Gracias*, they would say to everyone. Inside, the only feeling they would have would be *gracias*.

* * *

"BethyKristen," my mother says. She's breathing down my neck.

"Tried that," I say. "Like a hundred times. We started with that two hours ago." I sound like an eye-rolling adolescent on TV, but I'm exhausted. I've run the gamut of emotions today, and my ill temper is all that's left.

"*Your* name?" Abby says. She's leaning over my other shoulder.

"Come on, folks. We've tried that a million times, too." I type it in again anyway. Nothing.

"One, two, three, four," my mother says.

"He would never choose something that obvious."

"Twenty-six, fourteen, five, twelve." Abby elbows my mother. I can hear the barely stifled laugh that's about to erupt from her. My mother snorts out her nose. She can't hold back, begins chuckling.

"You guys," I say.

Abby swats Mom. "Stop that, Grandma."

"You're the one." She gives Abby a little shove back. For God's sake, they're two kids in the back of the car. "Try six, seventeen, two, five hundred."

Abby snorts out her nose now. This has been going on for too long, hours, and now they're sliding into fatigued hilarity, where an exhale from a cushion could become fart-like high comedy.

"Just try some random word," Abby suggests. I rub my temples.

"Like *boner*," my mother says.

They both crack up. "Grandma!"

"We're done here," I say. This isn't exactly funny. This is beyond inappropriate.

"You can't give *up*," Abby says. "Maybe it's a combination of words."

"Like *priest boner*." Mom's shoulders are going up and down in suppressed hysterics.

"Clown boner," Abby says. They both bust up. My mother's eyes are watering, she's laughing so hard.

"God," she says.

"Try that one," Abby says. More hysterical laughing.

"Fine. We're done. Jesus, people."

"Monarch," my mother says, out of nowhere.

I type. *Tip, tip, tip.* And, oh, dear God, the enchanted doors part. They do. It's a miracle. The password screen disappears. I can't believe it, I really can't. Small icons of possibilities show themselves.

"I got it!" my mother yells. "I got it!" She starts jumping up and down, and Abby is jumping with her, and they are hugging and squealing as if my mother just won the Chrysler LeBaron on *The Price Is Right.*

Well, of course you shift loyalties when you're being unfaithful. Of course you do. I've always felt that a heart is meant to be given to only one person at a time. And, too, when it moves on, it moves on for good. Hearts are pretty decisive, unlike heads. The loyalty shift—it showed itself in trivialities. When I got a new client or worried over my mammogram results, it was Ian, not Mark, I wanted to tell. When Ian was stressed about making a product deadline, he talked it over with me, not Mary. If I saw some funny or sad thing—a toddler making a crafty escape from his stroller, an odd couple with especially tall hair, a rickety old lady crossing a busy street—I shared it with Ian. Ian got it into his head that he wanted this newer, faster motorcycle, something Mary would never approve of, and I encouraged it. I was *go-for-it*. I was *let's-do-it*. I wouldn't have wanted Mark to have a motorcycle, to tell you the truth. As the other woman, though, you're the one who's supposed to open the windows to a bigger world. That's your promise. A bigger world with more sex, or something like that.

We closed in around our secret and grew something that was just ours, selfishly and totally ours, and there aren't many things like that in a life, things that are just yours. Of course, the moment you let it out into the world it's not yours anymore, and, of course, you want it out in the world. I wanted to go to restaurants, to movies. We both did. After more than a year of sneaking around, fourteen months from the day we met, I was tired of lying. I was tired of negotiating the parking brake. We were all over each other once, my shirt nearly off, when there was a tap at the car window. It was a policeman, patrolling the park. We had to hand over our licenses as I clutched my top to my chest. We both felt like guilty teenagers, only worse—there were different last names and addresses on those licenses, and there were those wedding rings, and we were too old to be caught in a car. The guy probably went back to the station and told everyone and had a good laugh. Ian hated to be laughed at. I didn't mind. His ego had been battered enough that the touch of a fingertip caused a bruise, and mine had been battered enough that it didn't even know when it was being pummeled.

During that time, I have to admit, there was something thrilling about turning my back on Mark every night in bed. He was right beside me, but I left him and went to this place in my head—it felt like an actual *place*—where I could relive that day's conversation with Ian, the loving words, or a touch, or a long gaze, or talk of the future. I could feel Mark shifting around in bed, but I shut him out. It was powerfully punishing. He sensed my retreat and went either stony or desperate. He used to twine a lock of my hair around and around his finger to help him sleep, like a child with the corner of a blanket, but when he did that then, I'd pull away. My hair was my own. I didn't want to be used for comfort anymore. People who kick dogs—they pet them, too.

I let Mark find out. I suppose it's what an employer with any heart does before a round of layoffs—he drops hints of cutbacks and profit losses before delivering the pink slip. There were those shoulders turned away from him, first of all, and long stares out windows. Finally, an email left where he could see it.

I left an angry man by having an affair. As Dr. Shana Berg said, it wasn't a very good plan, but it was a plan.

You snip a thread, and . . . Wait. I'm remembering my first communion, when I was eight. My father grew up Catholic, and, therefore, so did we. At least, we check-marked the regular boxes—baptism, first communion. I was dressed like a little bride. White dress, white veil, white shoes and stockings. It's one of those things (like Christmas trees, neckties, camping) that make the human race particularly hard to fathom. My father had the car running and my mother was yelling that we were late, when I noticed a fuzzy nub on my thick tights. I made a quick cut with my kiddie scissors, and as soon as I got into my father's baby-blue Chevrolet Impala, the unraveling had begun. One small clip and so much damage can be done. The tights were in shreds by the time we reached the church. My mother noticed as we walked up the path; she let out a shriek that turned the head of Father Dominique, in his white robes with the gold trim. My stockings kept unraveling and unraveling until they were ribbons of disgrace, drooping across my leg as I received the white wafer on my tongue in front of that crowd. My mother was furious. We ate cookies and drank punch at a party afterward, as the run slithered down into my shoe. No one thought to just take the shameful things off.

A single snip is what I'm saying.

Of course, things got broken after Mark found out about Ian and me. The first thing was the tile countertop in our kitchen, as he slammed his fist into it again and again. Things get broken, and no matter how well they were put back together, you knew where the crack in that tile was.

A quick look at Ian's documents and his email tells me there are no immediate answers on his laptop. There are no suicide notes on his desktop or flight itineraries in his mailbox. There is no email from another woman left where I can see it. Delving further will take hours, and I'm too depleted for that.

"I can't," I say. "Tomorrow."

"We need fooood," Abby whines. She used to get like this whenever we went school-clothes shopping. I'd buy her an Orange Julius to bribe another half hour out of her.

"I can run out and get us teriyaki," my mother says.

I groan. Nothing sounds good.

"You've got to eat," Abby says. "The ass of your jeans is getting baggy. Eggs?" I rub my eyes. Decisions about food can sometimes feel mammoth and complex. Should we have Italian or Mexican? Should we land the troops on the beach or attack the enemy by air? I feel this way on an ordinary day.

"I'll handle it," Abby says.

My mother is already rooting around in my fridge, which is irritating me. A fridge is as private as your purse, or else I *am* hungry, hungry enough to be rattled by anything. We all hear it: My stomach growls like a creaking door.

"I hope an alien doesn't burst out of your chest," Abby says.

My mother finds what she wants. "Help is on the way," she

says, holding up a bottle of red wine. Ian makes fun of the fact that I like my red wine cold.

It's a wine crime, I replied once. *Arrest me.*

Don't let Nathan see that, Ian had said. Nathan is a wine connoisseur. He has one of those mini-cellars in his town house. The wine choice is always up to him when we have dinner together, but he's not a snob about it.

He wouldn't care. He never even swirls his glass.

I'd *care.*

Next time, I'm really gonna go crazy and drink red with fish. Twenty-five years to life.

Hilarious.

I hope you're a tree stump in your next life. Joking was one way to deal with his criticisms. There were other ways. Distraction, anger. You try everything.

Thanks.

Tree stumps don't worry about what people think of them. It'd be very freeing.

Pour me a glass, smart-ass, he'd said.

"Pour me a glass," I say to my mother.

She holds three wineglass stems in her hand expertly, tucks the bottle under her arm like a well-trained sommelier. It's rather impressive, actually. "Let's get some air."

Mom tries to open the sliding door with her foot. "Let me get that," I say. It's beautiful out on the lake. Spring air is mingling sweetly with hopeful, dusk light. The evening smells so good, I could drink it from a great big cup. The edges of the waves are silvery-white and bittersweet. The *New View* sloshes merrily against the side of the dock. Abby clatters pans in the kitchen. Pollux rediscovers his youth and bounds with great speed out the open door.

Mom settles in a deck chair, pops the cork. It sounds wrongly celebratory. She pours me a glass. I gratefully sit in the lounge chair beside her and sip my wine. It's a cheap bottle bought from Pete's—I'm not a connoisseur. I buy bottles because they're on sale and I like the label.

"Monarch." My mother leans back and smiles. She is still pleased with herself.

My mind works the knot, endlessly so, but I'm not getting anywhere. "He wouldn't have committed suicide," I say. I've said this a hundred times by now. I stare out at the lake, at a large sailboat, the *Lucky Lady,* which swoops past. The captain waves at us, and his windbreaker flaps cheerfully. He has no idea we're discussing a person taking his own life.

"I wondered that at first. But Ian thinks too highly of himself to do that." My mother's cheeks are already red after only two sips of wine.

"You know it's not a high opinion. You know it's hiding—"

"Oh, God, please. Don't say it. 'Self-hatred.' 'Low self-esteem.' I think we used the same excuse for Mark."

I stare at her, shocked. Hurt. She flutters her hand, implying that she means no harm. It stings, though. Well, the truth does. "You keep confusing the one who's saving you with the one who's drowning you."

"I don't think now's the time for relationship advice," I say.

"Now's exactly the time."

My chest is burning; I can feel red cinders under my skin, the buried fire of anger. I don't want to fight with her. Best to stay on her good side, anyway—when she's mad, watch out. "I was *saying,* I don't think he would have committed suicide. It's against his deepest beliefs. His religion . . ."

Back in the day, Ian's mother went to a school taught by Jesuits. Her room at the care facility still has a gory, sad-eyed Jesus on a cross above the doorway. The lessons of Ian's childhood are there in bottomless, sunken grooves, even if he doesn't go to church. The concept of sin is real to him. He's shocked me more than once, talking about Adam's rib or "the flood." I always want to laugh, but he's serious. I had some naïve belief that we were all sort of past that stuff. He went to graduate school, you know? I mean, he's a logical person. He's studied math and science. But, to Ian, logic and religion are sold separately.

"Christians are so mean," my mother says.

"Remember when I shredded my tights at my first communion?"

"You had first communion?"

"You sewed the dress."

"Don't remember."

"I was a little bride."

"I should never have let your father talk me into that."

Pollux is sniffing around the edges of the dock, intent on some canine investigation. He's perilously close to the edge. My mother has her eye on him, too, the way she probably watched us as toddlers near the neighbors' swimming pool. "He won't fall in . . ."

"No. He hates the water."

"He looks like he's going to fall in."

"He's a very capable dog."

"He barks when the doorbell rings on TV," she says.

"Don't say that so loud. You're a champion dog," I say to him. "A prizewinner."

Now Abby opens the door with *her* foot. "Gourmet meal for three."

I jump up. "Let me help . . ."

"Damn, that looks good," my mother says.

"Hey, I'm a grilled-cheese maestro, what can I say."

"Dill pickles, too." I feel the momentary delight of a perfect meal—grilled cheese, potato chips, sliced dill pickles. In the grimness of these days, I wouldn't have thought it possible, but there it is. Brief moments of goodness are shockingly persistent. You're in the dark, darker, darkest, and yet there's a dog sitting beside you, on his best behavior for a dropped crust, and there's an industrious line of ducks paddling past, and there's a grilled-cheese maestro. Life insists.

"You okay?" Abby says to me. "Pickles make you teary?"

"I'm so grateful for you guys." It overwhelms me then, the gratitude.

"It's just grilled cheese. It's not . . ." Abby searches around for the right word, and then delivers it with a nasally French accent. "Boeuf bourguig-*non*."

"Crêpe de Paree," my mother says with her own French accent, though she sounds like an angry German soldier. She rolls the *r* heartily, so that *crêpe* becomes *crap*.

"Pour me a glass," Abby says.

It feels good out there, a rest, and so we sit on the deck long after the sun goes down. Abby fetches us sweaters from the hall closet. The lake turns the deep gray of a ship's hull.

As we're sitting there, I remember something. I've never told anyone this. I'd sort of let myself forget it, actually. But when Ian and I were moving to the houseboat, we had a fight. We were going through a storage unit he rented when he first moved out of Mary's place and into that furnished apartment. Two years into our new marriage, we were finally moving to a place that was our own, and it was time to deal with all that old stuff. The storage facility was creepy—one of those warehouses with pulled-down metal doors along cold cement hallways, where it smelled like rancid paint and dead people's belongings. It was a

mausoleum for objects, or maybe some kind of object purgatory—
the place between the hell of the dumps and the good old life
back in Grandma's living room.

We stood in that small, dim cubicle and sorted through boxes.
This, get rid of it. That, keep. There was so much that I had
never been a part of. There were a lot of old wedding gifts that
Mary had foisted off on him in some effort to burden his conscience. Champagne flutes. Silver trays. The boxes of butterflies
and the collecting equipment had been stored in there then, too,
and so had all that crap from Paul Hartley Keller's garage, the
fondue pot and the carving knife and such. The wooden cabinet
that Ian's grandfather made was there then; it was heading to
our new dining room.

I didn't know how to help sort—there were books with in-
scriptions from old girlfriends and an ugly painting of an Indian
woman kneeling beside a creek, which had been in his and
Mary's bedroom. There were boxes of photos and children's
crafts made for Daddy and old college textbooks. I could see
Ian's mood deteriorating. He had started out ready to tackle the
task and was quickly slipping into defeat. Who wants to look at
the past laid out like that? Who wants to touch every yearbook
and that first box of personalized business cards and all those
discarded items of marital joint property, from the chip-and-dip
dish to the silver wedding goblets? Seen together, it doesn't add
up to much. Especially when a good lot of it was now called a
mistake.

If you don't know what to do with it, just leave it! he'd snapped.

Be nice! I'd said. *I'm trying to* help *you here.*

*Do you think this is easy? Show some sensitivity. Look at all this
stuff! I'm throwing half my life away.*

Right then I was sick to death of his criticisms and outbursts
of self-pity, I really was. After all of the fighting with ex-spouses

and the mediations and the attorney bills and custody evalua-
tions and apartments and waiting and divorce and remarriage,
after all of that, we were finally moving into a new place that was
free of the past. And right then, too, I suddenly felt as if I could
leave him. I could. Even after all of that. Or *especially* after all of
that.

I looked around that cold place. He came with an awful lot of
stuff.

Don't do it on my account, please.

He was holding a lamp in the shape of a cowboy boot, something he'd had in his childhood bedroom. *I can't believe you just
said that.*

I wanted to say more. No, I wanted to take that eerie, cold
freight elevator out of that place where I didn't belong. I wanted
to get away from the weight of him. But I didn't do any of that.
Instead, I picked up what looked like the bust of someone. Some
fired-clay bust—a crude attempt to replicate what must have
been Paul Hartley Keller.

Oh, my God! I laughed. *What's this?* I could barely lift the
damn thing. Mary was happy to get rid of *that*, I was sure. *Is this
your father?*

No. Ian's jaw tightened. I'd offended him. Great.

It looks just like him. At least, it had Paul Hartley Keller's high
forehead and recessed chin, done in amateurish clay pinches.

It's me.

I looked at it. I laughed. I couldn't help it. It slipped right out.
*You? Oh, my God, this is disturbing. Where'd you get it? This would
give me bad dreams.*

*It was a gift. Mary commissioned it for me as a surprise. When I
first bought the company. She had some idea of it going in the lobby.*

I'm glad you didn't put it there! It'd scare people.

You know, Dani . . .

People would scream when they walked past it. I was cracking
myself up. Really, the thing was hideous. It looked exactly like
Ian's father.

You know, I can see how you'd make Mark so mad.

I stopped laughing then. I looked at him in that dim cell and
he looked ugly to me, as ugly as that pinched-clay bust. I set it
down. I didn't say anything more. I shoved my anger far down,
where even I wouldn't be able to see it.

But how many things stay buried, really? Not memories, not
anger, not pieces of shipwrecks, floating to the surface and landing on a beach somewhere years later.

That bust ended up in the trunk of my car, along with boxes
of his old straight-A report cards and more stuff Mary didn't
want from their closet, including a hand vac that had been a
birthday gift to her that she was still pissed about. We left the job
half done; we'd gotten a late start, and our attitudes had wors-
ened, and so that stuff rode around in my trunk for a good week
afterward. That night, we went to Kerry Park with a blanket
and a bottle of wine. We actually had a nice time. It was only the
third night in our new houseboat.

It was time to forgive and forget, but I didn't forget. When
Ian went to work the next day, I opened my trunk. I hauled out
that bust, and it took some doing, too. Jesus, that thing weighed
a ton. I lugged it down the dock, and I had to set it down once or
twice when it got too heavy.

I can see how you'd make Mark so mad. It was a vicious, vicious
thing to say. He had no idea the kind of terror you felt when
someone's fist was in your face.

It was much harder to accomplish than I thought it would be.
I really had to work at it, and I was sweating. I set that goddamn
thing on the edge of the dock. And then I shoved.

It took longer for it to sink than you'd imagine. I watched as that Paul/Ian face slowly, slowly, dropped down into the murky water.

God, it was satisfying. I felt joyful. My heart did a little victory dance. But then I immediately started to worry. Ian never asked me about it. I don't think he even realized it was gone. Still, I envisioned chunks of it floating up for him to see. I worried about it for days. My anger itself was a crime, I was sure.

"Things are biting me." Abby swats at her ankles. "Let's go in." Her cheeks are red from wine, too. It's a genetic trait. Three swallows of wine by any of the women in our family, and we're all as rosy and flushed as fat men moving pianos.

I'm glad we're heading in. Now that I remember that statue under the water, right beneath us, I feel uneasy being out there.

We bring the dishes in. There's the pleasant clatter of china and silverware in an evening hour, a sound that usually means all is well. Abby is sponging off the counter, and my mother's hunting for where she put her car keys. She looks in her purse and coat pockets and in the dish by the phone, where we always put ours. She picks up the cuff link, which I'd set there. She holds it aloft, as if she's found a pearl in the oyster, or maybe the crucial evidence at a homicide scene.

"Dani! Did you ever tell the detective about this?"

I shake my head. "I forgot all about it."

She narrows her eyes at me. She's given that same look to teenagers lingering too long in our street, and to ill-behaved children in stores, and to men ogling my sixteen-year-old self when I was wearing my tube top and shorts.

"There's been a lot on my mind," I remind her.

"Where'd you get it?" Abby takes it from my mother. She holds it in her palm and shakes it as if she's playing Yahtzee.

"Someone dropped it by here. They must have thought it was Ian's."

"Doubt that. It's kinda Vegas. He's got better taste."

"That's what I said," my mother pipes in. "Not Mr. Classy's type."

Abby returns the cuff link to the bowl. "God, Grandma. Ian's *missing*. Be nice. He could be hurt somewhere. He could be . . . I mean, no clothes are gone that we know of. His cards haven't been used. . . . I don't even want to say it." Her voice catches. I put my arm around her shoulders. I pull her close. I agree with her about my mother's words. There should be reverence for what is lost, no matter how it has become so.

"Well, I never understood that, why people talk nicer about someone when they're gone. Why? Their bad luck makes them a better person? You're an asshole alive, you're still an asshole dead. Personally, I think it's just covering your bases. In case God's still nearby listening in, we'd better be nice or he might throw some of the same bad juju our way." She's looking in her jacket pocket again for her keys, then finds them in her purse, the first place she looked.

"I don't know why we do it," Abby says. "I just know it feels bad when you talk like that. I care about him. I care about him a lot."

I look at my little, now-grown Abby. She's so strong. I'd have never talked to my mother like that. Abby always says what she needs to say, without fear of consequences. She'd never be someone who would lose her voice while looking for rescue.

Maybe we all try to give our parents what they most ask for, what they most value but don't have, whatever that is— perfection, compliance, success, strength. The liquidy caterpillar evolves into adulthood in that chrysalis. It becomes something new. For better or worse, it emerges.

9

My sheets are a tangled mess from the bad dreams, and half of them are on the floor. They look like they've had a rough night. When I sort out my bed, I can still see the faint marks of mud on them. I took off my shoes after the party; I know I did. I remember that. My feet were killing me. There's an explanation. Still, that dream replays again and again. . . . His hand on my mouth. His grip on my wrists. Dreams tell you important things, don't they? They tell the truth? I am desperate for my sleeping mind to say *something* to me, to convey some information about his whereabouts. After all, there are people who have dreams like that. My college roommate, Fiona, had a dream about hurricanes the night before one hit in her own hometown, and she dreamed of boys falling out of windows before a brokenhearted student jumped from the balcony of a fraternity house. I want to have a dream that shows me where Ian is—in some woman's car, driven off a cliff; living in an orange stone house in San José del Cabo; in a Motel 6 the next town over; anything. I'll take whatever I get as long as it's an image handed over to me in deep slumber by some sympathetic higher power. But the psychic airwaves have remained mute.

I keep having that same nightmare, and it's beginning to haunt me. It's shaking my sense of myself. When I wake up after that dream, I worry that I have experienced my own metamorphosis, that I have become something horrible. The repetition is making this feel true. It's probably only fear speaking. *It isn't information, Dani, you idiot*, I tell myself, *just your worst ugly doubts let loose, your subconscious unraveling its darkness. Knock it off.* But it's not that easy. A dream can be meaningless, but a dream can feel so real.

Here it is: The contents of my heart are what leave me uneasy.

Of course, our dreams were real, too, Ian's and mine. The dreams for our future. They were meaningless perhaps, or at least misguided, but they were real to us. After Mark found out about our affair, though, Mary found out, as well, and then everything went crazy. Visions of *happily ever after* have a hard time weathering *crazy*. Mary threw Ian's clothes out onto the lawn (bit of a cliché, that), and she once turned into a madwoman, driving her big black Explorer toward Abby and me as we walked down the sidewalk, veering away at the last moment. It was another wonderful memory to paste into Abby's baby book. Mothering regret number four hundred seventy-five. Your dreams always take some direct hits.

The tribe, the Greek chorus, whatever, chimed in, too. Anyone who'd been to your wedding, or *any* wedding, or who was in a marriage and deeply needed to feel the strength of the institution just then (most likely because they were feeling its *vulnerability* just then): they needed to be heard. They needed to shake your shoulders and look you in the eyes and tell you how wrong you were to do what you did and how foolish you were to do what you were planning. They do these things because they think they know what's best, when they can never know the universe that lies between you and your spouse in that bed, the speeding comets and stars burning up, the black holes. They shake your shoulders because your marriage is marriage in general and it's capable of tumbling in a gust or even a breeze. One failed marriage seems threatening to all of them. The butterfly effect. One butterfly flaps its wings and it can supposedly cause a hurricane weeks or months or years later.

Two mothers from school, women I didn't even know, called me up to ask me to rethink my relationship with Ian. That's a polite way to put it. And then, Ian's old friends Toby and Renee phoned Ian and asked him to go for a ride. They drove him back to their house, where several other friends sat in a circle in their living room, waiting for him. They attempted to bring their wayward one back to them, as if he'd turned to a life of heroin or had joined a religious cult. Which was the cult, really? That neighborhood with all its mirror-image houses and identical people—well, an argument could be made, is all I'm saying.

Ian and I sat in that damn car again. This time, we were parked on the leafy campus of the university. It was near his work but not near his work. I loved it there. On other days, we'd met on that lawn with a blanket, under the old Denny Hall clock, the ancient elms standing sentry on either side of a stone walkway. You could feel relaxed among students. Lots of young couples were out there on blankets. This day was different, though. We had met there to bring in the field reports and discuss strategy. It was clear that we were being defeated. Ian could take Mary's anger but not her tears. The sad look in his children's eyes crushed him, as did the judgment of his friends. Neal and his wife, Rory, all those people they used to have over to their house—their disapproval was Paul Hartley Keller a thousand times over. And Mark. A broken countertop, a shattered wind-shield (he'd put his fist through it—how that was even possible, I don't know), the smashed glass of a painting that had hung in our home . . . His most useful weapon was his strength, while Mary's was her weakness. Oh, we wanted out so badly, didn't we? Ian and I struggled so hard to get free. Still, I caught Abby getting cereal out of the cupboard one morning, actually tiptoe-ing, trying not to make noise. That was the feeling in our home. Glass was everywhere, cracked in its spiderweb fashion, barely holding together. The slightest move or sound might cause the final, drastic break.

Home—it felt unfair to use that word. It's a word cross-stitched in delicate thread, a word for wedding cakes and the flushed cheeks of sick toddlers, a precious, priceless word. But it had become a bad word then, a place to avoid.

All the damage we'd caused—we'd harmed other people, and even each other. And all the damage that had *already* been done before that, between us and our "loved ones," all the damage over the damaged generations, people trying their best to love one another and maybe feel a little safety in the process . . . Ah, human beings. We cause problems to solve problems.

The situation brought out the best and worst in all of us, though the truth of who we really were was still in there some-where. When you're holding on, *fighting*, for your security, all kinds of sudden transformations and tactics are possible. Mark became the perfect husband for a short while but then changed strategies, taking sadistic competition to new heights. Mary ex-ploded first but then changed strategies, becoming the perfect wife. She cut down on her spending and eliminated the parties; she cut down on her drinking, which had gotten excessive. She read books and tried to discuss them with him after he acknowl-edged his need for depth in his life. She bought him that motorcycle he wanted. She grew her hair long like mine and turned to him for sex every night, or so he confessed later.

I think we need to separate for a while, he said to me. It was fall, appropriately. The leaves were falling; we had fallen in love; things had fallen apart. The leaves were vivid orange, red, yellow, but, of course, those leaves were dying.

All right, I said. I didn't feel *all right*. I felt used and abandoned, as we all did in one way or another. I felt like wailing my protest. But I also felt relieved.

I need to do everything I can to save my marriage before I end it.

I heard the illogic. If you know you're going to end it, you're not doing what you can to save it. But I understood this, too, the primary conflict: What does it mean to be a good person? Do you owe someone else your life? When you want to be a good person and you're not being one (in their eyes or your own), you've *got* to twist the logic to be able to live with yourself. Your heart knows when it's over. Something *dies*. You know it, whether you're ready to face what it means yet or not. So what do you do? The least you can do is check-mark the right boxes. Therapy, whatever. Marriage counseling, "trying." How else do you sleep at night?

I know.

He sobbed into his hands. We held each other and grief filled my chest. *I love you so much,* he said. *I love you so much,* I said. It felt like the future was over, or at least our vision of it—the joy and the possibilities. This way, that way, this way, that way. The torment of indecision. This way, our future was over. That way, Mark's and Mary's were. It was devastating. It was "the right thing." You weren't supposed to choose yourself.

It was temporary. To go back to something that was already broken even before you stomped on the shattered pieces—the destruction is too great. Mark's revenge could go on for a lifetime. Mary's best behavior couldn't. A choice like ours . . . Well, somewhere inside you know that you're pulling the plug on your dying marriage the minute you enter a relationship like that. You're closing your eyes and turning away and cringing, but you're still pulling the plug.

It's over, I told Mark. *Between Ian and me.*

He said nothing. I could read his face; it held righteous conviction. He was taking the higher road. His intention was to move on but to never forgive. I realized I'd given him a permanent excuse to do what he never had an excuse to do before. If I stayed, that is. Now I could never stay. As Dr. Shana Berg said, it wasn't the best plan, but it was a plan. The sorry old soldier that I was put the butterfly between my own lips and promised myself rebirth.

Mark made me scrambled eggs because I was depressed and devastated. Let me repeat that: *Mark* made *me* scrambled eggs. He assumed my tears were contrition, and my lack of appetite was remorse. My weakness had transformed him from killer to nurse, though he was still the kind of nurse who might put deadly medicine in your IV while you slept.

He took my hands. His touch made me cringe. When it's over, even your skin knows it. He looked into my eyes.

I want us to know everything about each other. No holding back. I want to know *you.*

I said nothing. I was a thousand miles away by then. We were in our bedroom, but I was at some gas station in the desert, with a warm breeze at my back and a credit card in my own name in my wallet.

I want you to know *me.* He squeezed my hands. He paused. Then: *I had a near miss, too. A woman at work. Maria. Diego.*

The name was familiar. I remember passing a desk where a dark-haired woman sat. There was a picture of two small boys in a frame. *We talked. A lot, you know? I met her after work. We had drinks. Nothing happened.*

Outside, someone started up his lawn mower. I heard the revving, the chomping of grass and fallen dead leaves. In my head, a semi truck whipped past on that desert highway, and my hair caught in my mouth. The keys to a fast car were in my hand.

Finally my marriage was over.

"Mom, what are you *doing*?"

"This . . ." I shove those sheets in. I pour some bleach into the rising water.

"Laundry? *Now?*" She is shouting over the sound of the washing machine. She holds the phone with her hand over the mouthpiece.

"I just want them clean." I think of Lady Macbeth. How can I not? I think of Medea. There are ancient themes here, as I replace the cap on the Tide.

"It's for you." She nods her head toward the phone.

"I didn't hear it ring."

"Over this noise? What a surprise. It's Bethy."

I shake my head. "I don't want to—"

"Mom!"

"No!"

"Fine."

She turns her back to me and leaves. She's pissed. I am a contemporary parent; we can't stand the displeasure of our children. I clang the lid of the washer down. It starts to rumble vigorously. Ever since I moved it here from my old house, it hasn't worked correctly. Maybe it's the floor or something, the occasional tilt of the houseboat, I don't know. What I do know is that it tries too hard. It shimmies its little appliance heart out. One time I came back to find it in the center of a room, as if it had attempted escape but had given up.

Right then the thought crosses my mind: *I'll have to ask Ian about it when he comes back*. And then comes the sick rush of truth. The truth I've been avoiding all morning. It has been one week. One week without even a phone call. One week must mean he's never coming back. One week could mean he's dead. *Don't think it!*

I pour a cup of coffee. Abby made it strong. My grandma would have said, *Strong enough to curl the hair on your chest*. It was one of those things that you were pretty sure was a joke at age seven but were a little uneasy about anyway.

"I told her you were in the shower." Abby gets a bowl for cereal. She slams the cupboard door. She looks at me disapprovingly. She gets that look from my mother. I am part of the unfortunate generation that first had to please our parents and now has to please our children. We never got our time in the sun. No wonder we rebel.

"I at least need my coffee before I take her on."

"They want to see you. Can you blame them? Their father is missing! You've got to talk to them, Mom."

Still. All the best parts of you can end up in your children, can't they? His power, your generosity, but in the appropriate amounts. It can give you some faith that maybe there *is* a bigger plan in action, one that might succeed, even if we poor misguided souls continually do our best to fuck it up.

I want to get back to that laptop. I want to sift through all of Ian's electronic stratums, all of the things he keeps hidden deep down beneath a password. It is the thing to do: Lift up and look underneath. It's important to *see*. This is all about unfaithfulness, I'm sure. How can it not be? It runs through our bloodlines, and it runs through the history of us. Maybe more than that—I can see his hand on the back of that woman's dress that night and her hand on his sleeve. I need to find out who she is.

But first I have to meet Bethy and Kristen. I do the right thing, of course. I return the call after my bolstering cup of coffee, and I arrange a meeting. I will go to them, because going to them is how it generally works. Our house "never felt welcoming," Bethy once told Ian. I suppose it wouldn't if you walked in shooting your shotgun eyes at everything there, at every piece of furniture or artwork that wasn't from the old homestead. If you walked in as a reporter, ready to write down the details to bring home to Mother, then those details could be made ugly and certainly "unwelcoming." Every verbal misstep of mine, every look that did or didn't pass between Ian and me, a rug they thought was ugly, a runny sauce—they were all good stories to snicker over later, or even right then, just loud enough for me to hear. Perhaps if we had hung their family portrait over the fireplace, perhaps if I had made their mother's recipe for stroganoff but failed it miserably, then maybe I could have somehow once and for all shown that I acknowledged their mother's superiority. We could all move on then. I had trumped their mother with Ian, and that was the problem.

This sounds bad, because I got what I deserved from them; I know that. They were a family, and I had helped to ruin that. It was understandable for them to make their point again and again. Still, it had gotten tiring, and that's what I am now, tired. If people in general cannot see the dark universe that sits between a couple, well then children, most of all, are unable or unwilling to see it. I guess it's true no matter what the situation: A parent's experience is an unknowable one. How, after all, can a child fathom what it means to be a parent, let alone a parent of a certain generation, with a certain personal history, with a certain spouse, with even a certain child?

I get ready for my meeting with them. I take a shower, and then I become stuck in front of my closet. As the clock ticks, my indecision about what to wear shifts from a nagging concern to an all-out panic. On certain occasions, the choice of black pants versus a black skirt can feel full of meaning and possible consequences. I stare at my clothes, paralyzed, and then, worse, begin heaping desperate piles of options on my bed. And shoes—God. Why is it that heels, boots, covered toes or bare ones, all carry different messages? It becomes about nuance, appropriateness, sensitivity. Fashion is a communication problem to solve, and I have enough trouble speaking with words, let alone footwear.

Then again, every encounter I've had with Bethy and Kristen has prompted this same fashion crisis, along with those other self-destructive acts you commit right before a dreaded social outing. Cutting your bangs, for example. Spilling coffee on a just ironed blouse. Some people just bring out every small part of you, all the little self-hatreds, and so the evil inner trolls take the scissors out of the drawer and chop the hell out of your hair. I swear to God, the more anxiety I feel about an imminent event, the shorter I cut my bangs. I've gone to many intimidating places looking like a nine-year-old on picture day.

When I look into my closet now, all of my clothes suddenly seem old and defeated. It's the museum of my life—there are stretch pants in there and even (way back) a blue silk jacket with humongous shoulder pads. I need to find something that is not exhausted from history and pale from too many washings. I need energy and confidence; good luck, old clothes. Good luck to you. Jeans and a T-shirt, my standby pals? No. Bare arms are too vulnerable and unprotected. Tennis shoes? Too childlike. Boots are more authoritative. Ian's daughters will want things from me I can't give, like *answers*.

A time like this could bring Ian's daughters and me closer in our mutual loss and fear, but of course this won't happen. The usual suspicion in their voices has amped up now, and every time we've talked, their words have been cuts and slashes. It's another form of the hatred that's always been there, but still the animosity gathers in the center of my chest. It isn't fair to feel this way about them, but years of sniping remarks and spiteful glances have worn me down. We need Ian between us. He's both the cause and the solution to our rift.

That noise in my car is getting worse. I try to ignore it as I drive on the floating bridge over Lake Washington. You don't go get your car fixed when your husband is missing. The waters of the lake are choppy on one side of the bridge and still as glass on the other, yin and yang. I pass the pricey lakefront communities and make my way toward the foothills of the mountains, which are now home to repeating, ever-multiplying suburban neighborhoods with names like The Highlands, High Point, Manor Grove—images of upper mobility and lofty outlooks. Did I mention that our old neighborhood was called "Tuscany"? What degree of self-delusion did it take not to laugh at that sign (with its cascading waterfall) every time we passed it? There's a QFC and a Bartell Drugs right down the street. There's a *Supercuts*.

Mary still lives in the house that she and Ian had owned in "Tuscany," and Bethy has stayed close by. She now resides in a nearby apartment complex. It's mildly shabby and has another grand name, Forest Ridge. I park under one of the carports and walk up the dim green stairs. It's a place for people in transition—

kids in their twenties and newly single fathers, one of whom, I'm guessing, is right then bringing out his recycling. He looks out of place in his elegant clothes and expensive shoes; I hear the wine bottles clatter into the bin. Bethy went to college for a year, but then she quit. She works at the same video-game company where her boyfriend, Adam, has a job. Ian helps pay for this place, this apartment where Bethy now lives with Adam and their cat, Missy, but it isn't my business. I see Bethy's and Kristen's cars down below, parked next to each other. He paid for those, too.

Music is playing behind the door, which is marked with a brass 5. The sound is turned down at my knock. The clothes I've chosen (boots and a newish skirt and shirt) are doing nothing to help me. They are only clothes, after all, and I'm on my own. Bethy lets me in, and the smell of just-fried food makes a run for it out the door. The music had been from a video game, I see. Controllers have been set down in an abrupt muddle of cords on the coffee table, and the television screen shows two now-frozen futuristic warriors, one woman and one man, dressed in red and black and holding enormous complicated weapons at their sides. *Remember how thrilled we were at Pong?* I want to say to someone, but there is no someone here. *Remember Kerplunk and Lite-Brite and Which Witch?* There are losses upon losses, aren't there?

"Bethy." I reach out to hug her. She endures my embrace as if she's being tortured but will never give up state secrets.

Adam doesn't move from his spot on the couch. There's a bag of Doritos open on the table and an empty plate with crumbs on it. Kristen sits on a bar stool at the counter, which divides the kitchen and the living room. She stirs something in a cup with the tip of her finger. "Hey, Dani," she says.

I go to her, hug her shoulders. There's hot chocolate in that cup, whipped cream on top, melting quickly into a white pool. She sucks the tip of her finger, wipes it on her sweatpants. We've had a few moments of connection over the years, a good conversation, a shared love for a book. It would give me hope until the next time I would see her, when she'd avoid eye contact and talk only to her father. Still, a friendship seemed possible, unlike with Bethy, who was older and closer to her mother. Maybe after years and years, Ian's daughters and I could know one another as people and not players in a triangle. Maybe after years and years they wouldn't move the camera so I'd be cut out of every picture they took of Ian and me.

"Hey, missus," Adam says.

"Adam." I never know what to say to him. He played football in high school, and he's got one of those amused-but-snide jock grins. That's how he is. Frat boy without the frat. His dark hair is cut cleanly, and Ian likes that. He thinks the haircut says good things about the kid. But the grin makes Adam seem arrogant, even as he shakes your hand and says all the right things. I can't find conversational ground. I sound parental every time we speak. I don't think he's ever asked a question of me since I've known him. Same for Bethy, come to think of it.

"You can sit down." Bethy gestures to an old lounge chair, the kind where the footstool pops out, probably something from Adam's parents' basement. "Kristen!" Bethy jerks her head toward the couch, indicating that Kristen should be sitting in the living room with us. Something about this (the huffy frustration, the older-sister toss of the hair) makes me realize how young Bethy still is and how hard she's trying to manage an unmanageable situation.

Kristen slips off her stool. In her pink socks and too-long sweatpants, she, too, looks like the near-child she is. She pulls her sleeves down over her hands. She sits on the couch with Bethy and Adam. The couch springs lost their virility long ago; Kristen sinks down into the cushions. Adam is trying to grow a goatee,

but it's a scrappy, weed-filled parking lot. And Bethy—her fingernail polish is chipped. There's a stain on her shirt that her
mother probably could get out. I see it clearly: Ian's daughters are
harmless. I had given them so much power, but they're just kids.
Kids who are as scared about their father's absence as I am.

I feel a sudden softness toward them and a deep regret for all
that's passed between us. "I haven't heard anything," I say. "His
phone is still off. Nothing on our credit card. The detective says
they're doing everything they can, there's not much to go on.
Have you guys—"

"No. Not a word. I think he'd call us if he was going to call
anyone." Bethy picks at her polish.

"Maybe he *can't* . . ." Kristen's voice wobbles.

Grief creeps up my throat, tightens it. I need to be the grown-
up here. I need to keep it together. "Oh, honey." I reach forward
to hold her hand, which is still tucked up into that sleeve. It's a
good idea, but the execution is awkward, and so I only end up
patting her covered wrist. "I know, sweetie. But we don't need to
go there yet. He could be anywhere. Let's not go down that road
yet."

"He's been gone a week," Kristen says. "A week seems like
he's *dead*—"

"Don't," I say. *"Please."*

Adam leans forward now, too. He puts his fists on the
knees of his jeans. "Mrs. Keller made us a list of all the places
he might be. We've spent the last few days driving around and
driving around." I'm confused for a moment—*Mrs. Keller.*
That's me, but not me. Mary hadn't changed her last name. Now
we share it.

"Give anything you can think of to the police," I say. *"Any*
ideas."

"Well, that's what we want to talk to *you* about," Adam says.

"That's why we called you here." I sit back. Adam's voice has become authoritative. He's suddenly become the one in charge.

"It doesn't make sense," Bethy says.

I can suddenly see that they have a plan. They've discussed how this will go. The softness I felt toward them—it's hurrying the hell out of there. In its place comes the uneasiness you feel alone on a dark street or in an elevator with the wrong kind of stranger.

"It doesn't make *any* sense," I agree.

"His car is still there. Where'd the dude go without his car?" Adam's dark eyes bore into mine. I can imagine him on the football field, staring at his opponent through the eyepiece of his helmet. The funny thing is, he reminds me of Mark.

"You said you went to bed. You got up and he was gone," Bethy says. "It doesn't make sense. You would have heard something." She's repeating herself. My uneasiness is growing. I am on that dark street, and now there are footsteps behind me. I am on that elevator, and now the stranger is standing too close. The smell of whatever they cooked is making me feel sick.

"We had this late night, wine—"

"How do we know he *got* home?" Adam puts his index finger in his ear to scratch an itch, twists it like a screwdriver. This manages to make him look both idiotic and threatening. Adam is like one of those chimps you see at the zoo (chimps: frat boys of the primate world), throwing their shit one moment, and then eyeing you in a way that makes you think they're capable of pulling a knife.

"Because I *said* he got home."

"Do you realize there's a scratch on his car?" Adam says.

"Yes. I saw it."

"It wasn't there when we saw him last," Bethy says.

"He keeps that thing *immaculate,*" Adam says.

"What are you suggesting? It could have come from any-where. You know what it's like on that street."

"You would've heard him if he left. He wouldn't disappear without you knowing." Bethy's voice is rising. I am shocked to find myself in an interrogation, and the shock has opened a door onto a blank, empty room in my mind. I have no idea what to say.

"That's exactly what happened." My voice is desperate. Even I can hear it.

"People don't just disappear," Adam says. "You were with him. It looks like that car was driven down some forest road—"

"I don't like what you're implying. I know we've had a rocky history—"

"That's besides the point," Bethy says.

"That *is* the point," I say.

"You're not exactly giving us a straight answer."

"I don't *have* an answer, Adam. If I had an answer, I'd know where your father is."

"I know where *my* father is," Adam says.

You can want to slap someone, you really can.

"We have some questions. His car is still there, and it's scratched." Bethy ticks the points off on her fingers. "His phone isn't working. None of his clothes are gone. You were the last one with him. I, for one, don't get how you didn't hear him leave."

"This is ridiculous. This is crazy. If you have concerns—"

"Oh, we have concerns, all right," Adam says. He leans back now, too. His legs are open, and one arm is draped across the back of the couch. *Dare me,* his body says.

"If you have concerns, you should take them to the—"

"Oh, believe me," Bethy says. "We definitely—"

"You guys!" Kristen shouts. "Stop!" Her face is red. She's cry-ing. My heart is beating so hard I think I can hear it. "Stop!"

I get up. A twist of hatred has broken loose, and I feel capable of the worst, wrong words. Forever words. "I think we're done here."

Adam stands. He folds his arms. It's another junior high school bully move, a jock move, a Mark move, a move to remind you that he's the big guy. I look at the warriors on the television. I suddenly remember that Adam has been in trouble with the law, something about a break-in. A "scrape." Before he'd met Bethy, supposedly.

Bethy's eyes are hard, and now those children don't look so harmless, not at all. I notice that her shirt has silver cat hairs on it, and I can smell the animal's litter box.

"Wait," Adam says. "Bethy . . ."

They look at each other. Bethy hesitates.

"There's one more thing," Bethy says. She glances at Adam again.

"Come on, for Christ's sake," Adam says. "We're already into the next month."

"Dad writes a rent check," Bethy says.

Kristen pulls at those sleeves. "Car payment."

"He sends them the first Saturday of every month."

The first Saturday was the day of the party. The day of his meeting with Nathan. The day he usually sends money to the children who have sided against him.

Sometimes you look at someone and you see your whole history together, right there. The life between you flashes before your eyes, all right. I looked at Bethy then, and Kristen, too. I understand their hurt and anger; I have for years. But I've given every outreach and showed every kindness to make up for my wrongs. I have done everything I can to understand and understand and understand. Still, I will never understand their cruelty, especially to their own father.

"We need a check," Bethy says.

It's dangerous in there. Bethy's cat comes in and jumps onto the couch and walks across Kristen's lap. That cat has green eyes. It starts to scratch at the woven fabric of the couch, its claws catching in the threads. Kristen swats at it to stop. The cartoon warriors hold their weapons. The space between us needs only a lit match for things to blow up, I can tell that. I know I'm sealing my fate with what I do next, but I don't care anymore. You reach a point where you've had enough.

"Go ask your mother," I say, and I slam the door behind me.

"Really? That's your response?" Abby is talking on her phone. She turns her back to me when I come in and then disappears down the hall. "If you're not going to be supportive, this conversation's over."

Pollux is hopping around in reunion joy, his toenails making too much noise for me to listen in. I pick him up so we can be better spies. "Shh," I whisper to him.

I can make out a few words. *Police say. That won't help. Grandma's been.* A questioning lift to her voice includes the word *Vicki.* Abby is talking to Mark. Vicki is the woman he's been seeing for more than a year now.

One of the disappointing truths about divorce is that when you have children together, you are never free of the one you've tried so hard to leave. Never. You have to tolerate their presence at graduations and weddings; you hear about a birthday gift they're about to get; you catch their murmurs on the other end of a call. You feel them there but not there. Their partner is mentioned in regard to some restaurant they all went to (she ordered the veal), and you hear that your old father-in-law's in the hospital for some liver problem (he always did drink a lot) when you phone your child just as they're heading over to see him. In small snippets and snapshots, you witness the ex's aging and feel the past receding and the ways he's different now yet still exactly the same. You see him in a photograph from a vacation your child took with him and his partner; his hair is thinning and his waistline has grown, but it's still him. You see the gifts he gives your child and the relationship she has with him, and then you hear about some nasty comment he made—it's still him, all right. Every now and then this distant proximity allows sentimentality to sneak in, but, thankfully, it's quickly squashed. People keep being who they are, and you can tell that even from snippets and snapshots.

"Sorry," Abby says when she appears again. "Dad."

You hear about him, so of course he hears about you, too. He's there in the wings of this crisis, reveling in my misfortune, I imagine.

"He can be such an ass."

"Don't even tell me."

I can only guess what he would have to say. Mark has never been one to "wish the best" for me, his former wife, "the mother of his child." Some divorced people use these terms, though to my trained ear it sounds like more of the self-serving campaigning that divorced parents are so fond of. See how well behaved I am with that asshole? See how generous I am to that bitch? Maybe Mark's just more honest. People talk about *co-parenting* and *open communication* and *not talking bad about the other parent,* but look closer and listen for the edge in their voice. I've come to believe that co-parenting is one of those mythical creatures like Sasquatch, which some people swear they've seen but that likely doesn't exist. Most often, co-parenting actually means that one person is especially adept at keeping their mouth shut. But in our situation, well, Mark doesn't even bother with good intentions or illusions. He's kept his vitriol at hand. He hasn't eased his victorious grip on it over the years, not one bit. He's forgotten all about the battering. For him, it has somehow faded off into some inconsequential bit of married life, toothpaste-cap squabbles. Instead, he throws around my wrongdoings like cartoon bad guys crashing carts of melons so that the police won't catch them.

My anger lately . . . It was wrapped and bound in silk threads all those years. But now what lies beneath is apparently growing too big for its soft-spun manacles.

People don't just disappear, Adam had said. And Detective Jackson had asked about anyone who might wish to do Ian harm. It seems overly dramatic, TV movie-ish. But I think about this question as I set old Poll boy back on the floor. I really think about it.

Mark would wish him harm.

Mary.

His children, even.

Nathan, though it seems unlikely.

I don't want to say it or even think it. But, looking at it objectively, I suppose you could add me to that list. I suppose you could.

Of course, Ian is his own worst enemy.

Monarch, I type, and the magic doors open again.

10

I can hear the rain on the roof; I can hear it on some plastic tarp old Joe Grayson uses to cover his firewood. I can hear it on the lid of our barbecue. This is how it is in Seattle, even in the spring. Moody, always. The raindrops jump on the surface of the lake, a raindrop ballet on a water stage, and the houseboat tilts in the wind. The rings and ropes of the *New View* clang against its mast. Outside, it is a palette of grays again. Here, you get to thinking that summer will never come. Living in Seattle is like living with a depressed person, one who might all at once cheer, one who might suddenly rage.

The file is named *Dani*. I open it with a sick heart. This will be the letter; I know it. A goodbye, regrets, the name of a city where one could begin a new life, or maybe a plan involving pills and a mountain road.

I read until I realize the words are familiar. I've read this letter before. Years ago.

Dani —

I know we agreed not to write or speak, but did you hear that Raising Cain has a new album out? Okay, that's the worst excuse

*ever for writing. But I miss you so much. There have been so many
things I've wanted to tell you, from this great new brand of coffee
I tried to the news that Nathan and I are moving products to three
new countries. I can't believe you don't know these things, and I
can only wonder what I don't know about you. I've driven past
your house late at night and have seen Mark's car gone. Is he putting it in the garage now, or . . .??? Are you okay? My imagination
is going wild.*

*I am struggling. This is the hardest thing I've ever done. The
counseling is awful—understandably it's all about her rage and my
betrayal, but the reasons behind the "affair" have been lost. My
head, my screaming conscience, wants to feel for Mary what I
should feel. But everything I say and do is a lie, except for what
I do with my children. We even took a family trip to Disneyland,
happiest place on earth, and Mary held my hand and I rode with
the children on the rides and I felt like a ghost. Everyone tells me
that the only way I can have my family and friends is if I have
Mary, too. I feel blackmailed. I'm dying in this place.*

There are other letters, too. So many others. He's kept them
all, and they are organized carefully, lovingly even. His letters to
me are there, and so are mine to him. My heart squeezes; I feel
my chest collapse in grief. It's all there. Our history.

Ian –

*First things first! The name of that coffee! How could you have
held back on information like that for even a day?*

It's another kind of rain I'm hearing now. Rain on the roof of
that house I'd shared with Mark. The gutters are clogged with
leaves, and water is whooshing out the drain spouts. I am in the
spare room where we keep the computer. Abby's aquarium is in

there, too, and it burbles and bubbles, more water, but the water is murky and the thing needs cleaning. I see Ian's email in my in-box. I haven't heard from him in over six months. My heart fills with a love and an optimism that feels perilous.

There is so much to say, and so much not to say. I hadn't been to Disneyland with Mark and Abby. No. Mark had moved out the day after Thanksgiving, six weeks after Ian and I stopped seeing each other. The just-washed gravy boat was still on the counter from the dinner I had made the day before. After he left, everything in the house made me unbearably sad. That gravy boat. The toaster, the kitchen table, the coffeepot. My grief extended to every single item—a butter knife in the sink. Most especially, the artwork Abby did the year before, which hung above her bed. Looking at it, my body cracked open, and my insides, my heart, spilled out onto the floor. Those suns, you know, drawn in Magic Marker above blue houses with green lawns.

In December, I met with an attorney. It wasn't what I had ever envisioned for my life, but it was my life, which is as good a definition of *surreal* as any. Those were my shoes down there, walking on the plush carpet of the attorney's office. I wrote a check that nearly depleted what I had left in my checking account, because two brochures and one set of business cards and three websites cannot keep a family afloat. I tore off that check with shaking hands and I handed it over, and it was *all* surreal— the check, the person who was my lawyer now, me. That woman writing the check seemed in no way capable of managing what was happening. She might not make it back to her car in the parking lot, first of all.

During that time, I talked to Mark every night on the phone. My mother disapproved of this. She didn't understand that I needed to keep the tiger happy with bits of meat; a whip and a chair would not be enough. It wasn't only his anger I had to control, I knew. I also had to balance his despair with demonstrations of my own sadness; I had to build his broken self-esteem and sense of victory with a show of my own failings. I could lead us all where we needed to go without disaster, I thought, managing his moods as I had for so many years before. This felt manipulative and imperative. We saw him every few days, too. He would come to the door and we would have a few minutes of awkward conversation while Abby got her shoes. I would watch their backs retreat down the walkway, and I'd be filled with guilt and mourning at what he no longer had. He'd taken stuff from me, but I took things from him, too. I saw it every time they walked away together.

Mark came over for Christmas that year, our first one as a separated couple. I guess that's what you do when you're figuring out how to be apart. He came for a few hours. It was just the three of us, and Abby was hyper and silly, becoming the court jester so that everyone smiled and no one got their head chopped off. There was a hunt for batteries for Abby's new pink camera. Empty boxes and wrappers were strewn all over the floor. Mark acted like the father that he was and showed Abby how to use her camera. Then he put the new DVD into the machine so that she could settle down and watch it, and he took my hand and led me to the bathroom and raised my skirt and lifted me onto the sink and made love to me insistently, quickly. I let him, because it was easier that way, but when it was over, it didn't feel easier. I felt sick. I wanted him gone. I wanted him away. He kissed Abby goodbye and then left shortly afterward, and I locked the door behind him. I locked all the doors, I shut the blinds, shut my mind. Every image that came to mind was a wrong one.

The rain was falling, and the aquarium was burbling, and I was typing. No, I was carefully choosing words.

First things first! The name of that coffee! How could you have held back on information like that for even a day? I will definitely have to check out that new album, after I visit the divorce attorney, alas.

I am glad to hear from you. A thousand things to say, but mostly . . . I miss you, too.

Oh, the pain and terror of those months, which Ian would never know about. It was all unspoken in those lines. The fear, fear, and more fear, of Mark's anger and economics and the *future*—they all hid behind the lightness of my words. The weight of that fear would send him running, so I never shared it. I loved that man. I wanted him back. But I was hiding so much, *I* was. I was hiding my own need, most of all.

In that aquarium behind me, there was a tiny Disney figurine that Abby had gotten from who knows where, I don't remember. Maybe it had been on a birthday cake. It was Ariel, the red-haired mermaid, sitting on a rock. We had fastened her next to the stone castle and plastic plants. She had given up her voice to live among men. I had done the same.

Of course, Ian and I started back up again after those emails. *My heart is in your teeth,* he would say to me. *My heart is in* yours, I would say back. It was a lyric from one of the songs he'd first played for me. I don't even know which song anymore. It was a pact between us. It meant: Be gentle.

I look and look everywhere on that laptop. I read letters and documents and find the websites he visited. He's obviously in the market for another pair of Italian shoes. He has three pictures of a city in Spain: Andalusia. There is the website of a Mediterranean restaurant in Seattle. He has recently opened several medical pages about thyroid conditions. I look and look, but there is nothing there. Nothing but us.

That night, sitting in the dark, I dial those familiar numbers again. The houseboat tips and rocks in the wind, and something—a leaf, a branch—ticks against the glass of my window, startling me. I listen to Ian's voice, which calmly suggests once more that I leave a message. I beg that voice to tell me something, but it only speaks those usual, guarded words. We are both there in that same night; he is somewhere out there. I only hope he is alive. I can hear the *New View* bump and squeak against the floats. The chains that anchor the houseboat to the dock creak and groan. It can be unnerving to live in a floating house. I sometimes fear that I will go to sleep one night and, without my knowing it, the house will come unhinged. The restraints will slip; the house will have a mind of its own. Who knows what might happen then.

I end the call. You could want so much from a phone, and still it sits there in your palm, being its cool little technological self.

I sit in bed with my legs crossed, as the house is rocked by waves. That statue I had dropped into the water, the one I still think of as Paul Hartley Keller—it's down there somewhere, staring up from the murky depths, tangled in seaweed, perhaps, likely covered now in slippery brown algae. The image disturbs me. I feel agitated. I get up, look out into the night, and then I pick up my phone again. I step around the creaky parts of the floor. I don't want Abby to hear me. She's been so great—the least she deserves is a good rest.

"Hello?"

His voice is sleepy. I've woken him. "Nathan?"

"Dani? Have you heard something?"

"The police are parked on my street. I saw them here tonight."

"You sound scared."

"They're watching my house."

"They're probably watching underage kids buy beer at Pete's."

"I don't know. It looks like him. Detective Jackson." I'm silent. The silence and the darkness and the whispering feel confessional. I look at the lights across the lake, the pointed tip of the Space Needle, the yellow-white-lit windows of the cityscape.

"Those guys all look alike."

"He's been gone a week."

"I know."

"It feels different now that it's been a week."

"To me, too."

"Maybe he went to Spain," I say.

"Spain?"

"I saw these pictures on his laptop. A city in Spain. Andalusia."

"Oh, Dani . . ." He sighs.

"What?"

"I don't know if you remember. You probably don't. I went there a couple of years ago. I'm sure I sent him some photos."

I can't imagine Ian there, anyway. Not really.

"His Spanish is terrible," I say.

"He'd be all freaked out about drinking the water."

"You're right." I remember his long fingers plucking bits of lettuce from his plate when we went to San José Del Cabo. He can be prissy about disease—germs, a coughing person in close quarters. He thinks he has every ailment in those articles: *Ten Signs of a Heart Attack. The Twelve Most Undiagnosed Killer Diseases.* Of course, I'm not any different. I get a bad headache and I'm sure I have a brain tumor. My back pain means some sort of cancer. This is probably what happens to people who think too much about pleasing others. You stay on high alert; you do what you can to avoid being left, because rejection could come from any direction. Even your own body might decide to call it quits.

"Spain, no," Nathan says. "He'd be more like . . . Cape Cod."

"Cape Cod?"

"No, no. I'm not suggesting anything. I just mean, not there. Not Spain. He'd think . . . dirt and grime and bad traffic."

I don't respond. I listen for stirring, Abby waking . . . I want her to be able to sleep, yes, but, truthfully, I feel bad about this phone call. Ian himself would disapprove. Calling a man late at night? It's not exactly appropriate, even if we're discussing *him*. But the house is still. No one's caught me doing anything wrong.

"I went to see Bethy and Kristen today, and when I was leaving, I thought I saw him. This man had his back turned to me, he was unlocking a car door, and I could have sworn for a minute it was Ian. His same body frame . . ."

"I saw his haircut in Starbucks. I saw his coat in the bank," Nathan says. "I even called out his name, and this guy turns around and he's, like, ten years older with a goatee."

"Ian tried to wear a goatee for a while."

"I remember that."

"I think goatees look evil."

"Some facial hair is definitely malicious. Those little mustaches."

"The Hitler ones."

"Right. And even those bushy mustaches on big guys in camouflage jackets."

"The walrus ones."

"Yeah."

There is more silence. I hear him breathing. It reminds me of the hours Ian and I used to spend on the phone together, being in the same place when we couldn't be in the same place. When he lived in his apartment, we once watched *West Side Story* together over our phones after the kids went to bed.

"There was a woman at the party," I say to Nathan.

"I can't hear you. You're whispering."

"There was a woman at the party."

"Okay . . ."

"Red dress."

"I'm not good at this. I never remember what people are wearing. I don't even remember what *I* was wearing that night."

"She was talking to Ian."

"Dani, there were, like, two hundred people there."

"Out on the lawn, at the park. After all the speeches, when the party was winding down? Some people were still dancing, but mostly everyone had started to drift outside— Why are you avoiding me on this? You know exactly who I mean."

"I'm thinking. *You* were wearing black."

I smile a little in that darkness. Nathan is sweet. "Blond? Long hair. Big . . . How else to say . . . Big boobs. Really big."

"Oh, right. Desiree Harris."

"Men—you definitely remember the *boobs*."

He chuckles, guilty. "Um, she was kinda advertising."

"Kinda?"

"She's in marketing."

"How fitting."

"She's new. Hasn't really proven herself, not in my opinion."

"He had his hand . . . you know, on the back of her dress." I hold my hand up in the dark, replicating the move.

"I could see why you were pissed, okay? But it was just Ian being Ian."

"You did know who I was talking about."

"It wasn't anything."

"I don't believe that."

"You're totally barking up the wrong tree. I'm telling you. And *Desiree?* No."

"Why not?"

"She's not his type."

I don't want to argue with him, but he's wrong. The exposed breasts, that showiness that spoke of parties and drinking and liking a good time—it was Mary all over again. Even if these were precisely the things Ian claimed he'd grown weary of, you could miss your old life. Even if you wanted that divorce, there were parts of a person and parts of your past that inspired an illogical yearning. "She caught him by his cuff. You know, grabbed his wrist."

I could see why you were pissed . . .

All at once, I remember it. I see it. I shut my eyes, and it's there. Black sky, starry night, the music drifting toward the lawn, the back strap of my heels digging into my skin. I should have worn them around the house beforehand to break them in. I was looking for Ian—I wanted to go home. I had spent the last twenty minutes stuck in conversation with a middle-aged couple who were raving about their trip to Fiji. They had told me about the locals and the food and the place they stayed, and I had heard the expression *Like Hawaii used to be* so many times that I lost count. The wine (three glasses, three and a half) and those Vicodins (two, yes, I had taken two, not one, I admit it) were swarming uneasily in my head, and I had responded to the couple with a thickness in my mouth that I didn't trust.

My calves ached from standing. My energy for small talk had been used up, and the dessert table had only lemon tarts left. Where was Ian?

Wait. I could hear his laugh. People chatted in small groups on the lawn, and some car engines were starting up as folks headed home. There he was. And, oh, look. Perfect. There she was, too, in that red dress, and he was moving her toward the building, his hand guiding her. She made some joke and caught his sleeve, and I couldn't read his face.

I felt a rise of anger. Bitterness clawed through the comfy blur I'd arranged for myself. It really pissed me off, it did. I had put up with all his ridiculous comments and monitoring, the ways he was sure some man might see up my skirt or take my friendliness as flirtation, and now this. He guarded me like the prize jewel in his personal museum, and yet I'd never given him reason to doubt my fidelity, never. He was the one. He was. His insecurity—it meant you tolerated his criticism and his ego. Well, I was done tolerating.

I could see why you were pissed. The grass, my muddy feet. His grim face.

"I think I should talk to her," I say to Nathan. I'm thinking about that cuff link.

"Dani, you know, this is crazy. I understand that you want to pursue every avenue, but he loves you. I'm sure there's an explanation, yeah, but not that one. I mean, I think it's time we face the possibility . . . He might . . . Something might have happened—"

"Don't say it, Nathan." Dead. He's dead. *Don't think it, don't think it, don't think it.*

"Okay, I understand. I get that. And he could've only checked out for a while. That could be. He's punishing us. Believe me, I can see it."

"If so, he's a bastard."

"That's fair. More than fair."

"You know what I thought today? What if we never know? What if things just go on and on like this, and we never find out where he is or what happened to him?"

"We will."

"But what if we don't? Can you imagine living with questions like this? Forever questions? Wondering for the rest of your life?"

"You gotta hang on here. Ian is logical, isn't he? Methodical. There will *be* a reason."

Yes, but Ian held to that reason and the "right ways" of doing things, he *clutched* that restraint and that logic and that perfection, because, just on the other side of all that, sitting so, so close, was irrationality and anarchy and every hideous thing let free. On the shadow side of perfection is fear of uncontrollable rage, but I don't tell this to Nathan. I know this because I've seen it. Once. I saw it in that very same park, during a picnic gone wrong.

Your history, dear God, it follows you. It's under your skin and in your cells and it flows through your blood, and so you can't escape it. You grew up hiding from the storms under your own roof, and so you look for lightning to live with, even to marry. Your second-grade self is told by your arrogant father that you're no good, and so to you no one else is, either. Of course, the two of you, he and you, you rescue each other. You dodge the big shadows and cling to each other, two lost souls, as night falls on that lifeboat.

How could Ian *not* collect butterflies, same as his father?

"There are lots of possibilities, Nathan. Reasons behind the reason, even."

"And then there are just plain accidents," Nathan says.

But I don't believe that Ian has had an accident, and I doubt Nathan does, either. Something's happened, something bad, and I am becoming surer of it. I am so angry, for one thing. I want to rip those shirts off their hangers and tear them with my teeth. All this anger means something.

* * *

Dr. Shana Berg had said it all those years ago. *You must be furious.* Her office was in a house on Capitol Hill in the city. It was an old Seattle foursquare, with crown moldings and high ceilings. The waiting room had stiff chairs and outdated magazines, but I liked the musty smell in there. It was a good kind of musty. It made me feel as if people had lived there for years, weathering the good and bad of life. Dr. Berg appeared in the waiting room and called my name, adding a question mark to the end of it. It was a good place for a question mark, all right. I rose, and she shook my hand in a way that was both kind and efficient. Things were going to get handled, the handshake promised. Well, I had a lot of hope. She had gray hair cut bluntly and a warm face with wrinkles, which I decided were signs of wisdom. I needed wisdom. Poor thing, she probably went home and burned her meat loaf like everyone else, but I required more from her than that.

Mark and I had been separated for a solid year by then. I had filed for divorce shortly after he moved out. *Filed*—it sounds so orderly. As if you place a finished marriage in its own efficient folder and shut the drawer. The truth was, Mark had gone nuts, and there's nothing orderly about nuts. He was fighting for custody of Abby. He vowed to keep fighting for as long as it took. He had fired his attorney and had become his own, and you know the saying about people who do that. He'd made it clear: He would not lose. This had become the ultimate sporting event, and he was wearing his cleats, and he would break every rule as long as it meant winning. He was running up enormous debt on our credit cards. He was making ominous nonverbal threats. He sat outside the house with his car running. He climbed in an open window to make himself a sandwich with my groceries. The sliced turkey was missing, and so was the journal I kept by my bed.

After Ian's email, we had begun to meet in secret again. The hands and mouths and desire—it was a place to disappear into and aim toward. When I looked into his eyes, I forgot my loss. I forgot my terror, even. There was a future here, not just this turbulent and painful past–present.

Several months later, Ian left Mary and moved into Motel 6. I visited him there that first night. It was like a hospital room, without the calming assurances of sterility. The walls were white, the floor was hard linoleum, but there was a hair in the bathtub, and the soap had been used. It was a thin surfboard sliver on the sink. I remember that. The room was too hot and the thermostat was complicated. There was no television, and the bed was hard; there was no comfort anywhere, aside from one white towel hanging from the bar in the bathroom. Of course, the mission was doomed. The place was prison cell more than hospital, come to think of it, which I guess was what he felt he deserved. The wrongness of leaving his children and the lure of the leather couches he'd bought with his own money sent him back within two days. He wanted to be a good father and a good man. He wanted to live a life more true to himself. He didn't think he could have both of those things without paying dearly. He was right. I understood his terrible conflict. I couldn't have left Mark if it meant leaving Abby. Even in my situation, I could never have done that.

I told Dr. Shana Berg my whole story as she listened, her hands folded carefully in her lap. I looked to see if there was a wedding ring on the telltale finger, but there wasn't. Her hands were bare and they seemed strong. They were the kind of hands that would be able to grow things and chop an onion and start a fire in a fireplace. That's right—there was a fireplace in her office, too. I almost forgot. A brick one that maybe didn't work any longer, but it added a warmth to the room, anyway, even unlit. A hearth.

I spilled it all—my fear and worry, Ian's indecision. I spoke of
Abby. I spoke of exhaustion and defeat and financial panic. I
spoke of sleeplessness and longing and of the helplessness I felt
being stuck in one place for so long. But Dr. Shana Berg kept
talking about anger.

I'd be furious, she said.

I don't know if I'm furious so much as terrified, I said.

*You've got a bully that you're trying to pacify and a guy who can't
make up his mind that you're trying to pacify. I'd be* pissed.

*Anger doesn't feel very fair. That'd hardly be nice. I got everyone
here. It's my own fault.*

Nice can be a place to hide.

Well, she was probably right. *It's all I've known. Since the first
grade, when Mrs. Franklin sat me next to Michael Mulls, the bully,
to "be a good influence."*

How tiring, Dr. Shana Berg said.

*Isn't that what we learn? Don't talk back, be seen and not heard,
don't ask for that candy bar in the store?*

*You probably wanted to pull out Michael Mulls's chair right be-
fore he sat down.*

I laughed. I loved the idea of it, even after all those years. *Can
you imagine?* I said. What a thrilling thought. *I never could have
done it.*

Why not?

It would have been wrong. I was always trying to be good.

Good. She let the word sit there in the room.

Such a simple word. I shook my head. *It's supposed to be so clear,
too. Good, bad, right, wrong.*

Good has been complicated for you.

*Well, look. I was always so nice, and now I've got this scarlet A on
my chest.*

Nice is often just powerlessness with a smile.

I quit seeing Dr. Shana Berg after Ian moved out for the last time, a few months after his first attempt. I got too busy. I was taking on as much work as I could, and I was trying to build a life with Ian. I started canceling appointments. It seemed like a waste of time. It wasn't cheap, either. I didn't like the direction she and I were going, anyway.

Oh, boy, that must have made you so mad, she said, after Ian went out to dinner with Mary. Even after he left home, he was still doing stuff like that. *You probably want to tell him where he can shove it.*

She was the only one I was getting mad at. Dr. Shana Berg, she just kept kicking the opossum who was playing dead. But that opossum was playing dead because it was a survival mechanism, built into the DNA from the time opossums first walked our fiery earth and useful every damn day since.

After Nathan and I hang up, I sit there in the bedroom. Night is the worst. Ian is *gone;* I can't see him or talk to him or reach him or ask him a simple question, and the truth of that becomes agonizing after dark. And then there's the bed, our bed. A bed has stories. It has a complex past. It lacks the innocence of other furniture. In it, there are memories of lovemaking and angry shoulders and secret thoughts in your own head and silly conversations before sleep. Ian and I once spent hours talking about candy we liked from childhood. Cola-flavored Bottle Caps, tiny Chiclets, peanut butter Mountain Bars, Zotz. He remembered how raw your tongue got from sucking on those extra-large Sweet Tarts. I remembered the planetary rings of the half-eaten jawbreaker. We've argued in our bed and made up there. We planned a vacation and wrote grocery lists there. A bed is a couple's own small continent.

And then there's the darkness itself. In darkness, every line sunk down deep can be reeled in. Every vulnerability, every black thought—they surface. There are the noises, too, the ones you never hear in the day, some squeak that might be a footstep, a disturbing hum from an otherwise silent appliance; there is the ticking clock and your own loud heartbeat. Your sweater over that chair is an ominous, bulky form. Your coat on a hook is a stranger in your bedroom. Ghosts never show themselves in the daylight. Nightmares don't come during an afternoon nap.

Sleep might mean that dream. His hands would be on my wrists, pinned above my head like a butterfly's wings on a foam board. *The best way to kill one*, he told me once, *is to press its thorax between your thumb and forefinger. It takes a lot of practice to apply the right pressure. Not too much or too little; enough to stun it without damaging its body.*

I curl up on our continent, pull the covers up. I could wrap myself in white sheets and be transformed in sleep. But, no, the wind is still pitching our house, enough that the door swings and then clicks closed. A banging starts. That damn boat has come loose again. I remember that sound from the morning he went missing. It's the sound between before and after. I'd been happy then. Or, at least, I'd been innocent.

I get up. *Damn it!*

Pollux rouses and his eyes blink, confused at these unexpected nocturnal events. I open the back door. The wind knocks over the card my friend Anna Jane sent, which Abby had propped on the kitchen counter. It's cold out there. I'm wearing only a T-shirt and a pair of underwear, and goose bumps crawl over my skin. I kneel on the dock. It occurs to me—kneeling and praying. Maybe that's what I should be doing every single night. Getting down on my knees.

I look around. I try to figure out what's going on. A cleat is a little loose, that's the problem. I can see that now. It's jiggly, and the rope frees itself as the cleat rotates. I tighten it with my fingernail. That'll work for now. I'll have to screw it down properly in the morning.

I reach out for the rope, and I secure it to the cleat as best as I can. The *New View* is tight against the dock now. It's so dark out there, and the lake is choppy in the whistling wind. All the lights of the houseboats on the dock are off. I feel uneasy. It's unsettling, it really is, the way this home of ours is surrounded by water.

11

Mary was the one who had the balls enough to finally make Ian choose between us. That's why he moved out for the last time. You know, good for her. I was oddly proud of her. I wish I had been the one to be strong like that.

Ian brought me to a small lakefront park near our neighborhood to tell me. There we were, in a park in public during the daytime, where anyone might see us. It seemed so open. It felt strange to not hide.

We don't have to hide anymore, he said, reading my mind. He held my hands. He looked deeply into my eyes. *I've decided.*

I wasn't sure what my response was supposed to be. Excited? Respectfully somber? Mary must have been devastated, and I'm not a person who rejoices in my own victory. In any competition, I always feel bad for the loser. Watching sporting events on television, even a cooking-show contest—I am sad for the defeated team, or the one in second place, pushed behind the winner at the end of the season as the confetti falls from the ceiling. Those poor women with their failed cupcakes, even. They did their best. I once won a spelling bee in sixth grade, and I shared my candy with Allison Leffler, who got the silver ribbon.

Ian, too—this was thrilling and long-awaited news, but he looked exhausted. His eyes were tired, dead. We were both exhausted. We'd had one passionate and adulterous year and another one and a half years of mutual, hellish marital collapse. It did not seem like we were at the start of something great, more like we were in the middle of an impossible, arduous race that might never end. There were no rainbows on the horizon for us to skip toward.

We walked back to the car. I was still glancing over my shoulder, expecting to see Neal or Rob or Jason's mother, all of whom might stone Ian and me if they saw us together. There was a baseball practice going on nearby, the little team in their red striped shirts and important socks, and you could hear the metal ping of ball against bat, the cheers of support—*Go! Go! Go!*—for the red-striped runner. That baseball game where we'd met seemed like a lifetime ago.

Ian's decision to leave changed everything with Mary, of course. Gone was the hand-holding and talk of change and sex every night and even the hairstyle that looked like mine. He was going to pay. People play nice until they know it's really over. It makes you realize how much of a relationship can be a strategy to get your needs met.

Mary was thunderous once more as the marriage crashed down, cataclysmic, as Mark continued to propel my attorney's bills into stratospheric figures. The person you want to leave is the one you'll have to divorce. Now, there's a piece of advice; remember that. It was Shakespearean. It was ordinary. Dr. Shana Berg shrugged her shoulders. *In long-standing marriages, ninety percent of the divorces involve infidelity. No one likes to leave alone. But no one likes being left even more. So it goes.*

So it goes? I had said. The world was crashing and burning.

Remember when you were pregnant and it felt like no one had ever been pregnant before?

I nodded.

These things happen.

This was not the way we should have done it. That's one thing I know.

She bobbed her tea bag in her cup. *It wasn't the best plan, but it was a plan.*

"We'd like to go over your story one more time," Detective Jackson says on the other end of the phone.

"I don't understand."

My mother and Abby and my dear friend Anna Jane watch me anxiously. *What?* my mother mouths at me. Anna Jane begins picking up breakfast plates. When nervous, she always gets busy. When her own mother was ill, she was the one who interviewed doctors and picked up prescriptions. This morning, she'd arrived at the houseboat with coffee cake. My sister had sent a box of homemade chocolate crinkles, with their cracked desert landscape of powdered sugar. Oh, the women in my life, we feed our misery.

"We'd like you to come in."

"I'll do anything you need, but I don't understand. . . ."

"Some people have some concerns."

"I'm sure you mean Bethy and Kristen. We have a history, Detective. They don't exactly love me. They see me as the reason their father left their mother."

My own mother lets out an angry huff, and Abby covers her face with her hands.

"They have some concerns about the state of your relationship with Mr. Keller."

"They've always had concerns about the state of our relationship."

"We can discuss that when you come in."

"Fine." I hear the edge in my voice and regret it.

"Oh, and we'd like you to bring in your personal computers. His and yours. This is voluntary, of course. It may give us some helpful information." He sounds cheerful, as if we're exchanging recipes. "We're not charging you with anything."

"Oh, my God, I hope not."

I hang up. I put a hand over my mouth, in shock. I think I might be sick.

Anna Jane moves away from the dishwasher, sets her arm around my shoulders.

"They want me to come in. They want the *computers*."

My mother slams her hand down on the table, causing the remaining dishes to jump. "Goddamn it. I am so goddamn mad. What are these fucking idiots doing? What a fucking waste of time. It's those girls, isn't it? And their *mother*. You want to look anywhere, it should be *there*."

Anna Jane's voice is soft. "I think you need an attorney."

"Oh, God," Abby groans.

"I don't need an attorney."

Pollux feels the anxiety in the room. He begins to whine and trot around.

"Bruce had a drunk-driving offense." Bruce was Anna Jane's brother.

"You never told me."

"He was so embarrassed. Anyway, they used this guy . . ."

"Your father's divorce attorney, he was a real tough bastard," my mother says. "Frank Lazario. I'll never forget *his* name. Scary to even look at. Probably Mafioso. He had one of those alcoholic noses. . . ."

"Grandma, the guy's probably dead by now."

We're all silent. No one has anything else to offer. This is the extent of our experience with lawyers. "I'm not getting an attorney. They can look at the computers all they want. I have nothing to hide. They're not charging me with anything."

I sound so brave and sure. I think of Detective Jackson outside at night, watching my street.

"They're just doing their job," Abby says.

"That's right. Let them have what they need. Maybe they'll find something on his laptop that we didn't find. This is good. This is okay."

"That mother. That's who they should be talking to," my mother says. "If I were her, I'd want to kill him."

Anna Jane catches my eye. We have a silent, mutual recognition of my mother's insensitivity. "Hey," she says, as if she's suddenly had a brilliant idea. "If you need a lawyer, you could always call Mark."

I laugh; I can't help it. My mother chuckles, too. Even Abby tries to suppress a grin but smiles anyway. The year that Mark acted as his own attorney has become family lore. He'd been nicknamed Perry Mason and Atticus Finch and, most often, Clarence, as in Darrow. The humor grew as the bills mounted and the situation became ever darker.

"Sorry, Abby," Anna Jane says.

But even Abby knows that this is what we do when things get their blackest. "Hey, no worries. I'll call him and see if he's got an appointment."

"I only want the best," I say. "Gotta keep me out of the slammer." The idea seems so ridiculous, it's only right to joke. "Can you see it? Me in the exercise yard?"

"With your book. Sitting in a sunny corner," Abby says.

"At least you'd never have to worry about what to wear again." Anna Jane knows me well.

"There's always a silver lining," I say.

"Maybe you'll meet some nice dyke in there," my mother says. My mother always goes too far.

I pick up Pollux to stop his pacing and whining. I put my face against him. "It's okay, boy. Everything is all right."

He squirms dangerously, does a half flip out of my arms. It's a wild circus move. He's as unconvinced as the rest of us.

I try to keep the panic down. The idea of me being charged with something, arrested . . . It's too far-fetched, and that's a good place in which to rest. This would never happen. But other things that would never happen already have. I woke up one morning to find that my husband had vanished. That should have been impossible, too.

Anna Jane comes to the police station with me. It's a Sunday, the day of the week when people go to church or stay in bed late and read the newspaper. It's the day of French toast. But I am going to the police station. Let me say that again. I am going to the *police station*. Because my husband is missing. Because they want to ask me questions about his disappearance. God, even as I write these words, I still can't believe it.

Anna Jane drives, which is a good thing, because I haven't yet dealt with that rattle in my car. All I need now is to get stuck somewhere. On the freeway, even; I can just see it.

I hold our laptops, Ian's and mine. The cords are wrapped neatly, the way Ian likes. It looks as if they are heading into the shop for repairs. One time, I was about to bring my laptop in to be fixed and had left it on the table as I went to get a jacket. By the time I returned, Ian had formed that cord into a tidy figure eight, secured with a twist tie from the kitchen drawer. He hates displays of carelessness.

"Can I help?" Anna Jane asks. I shake my head. I am walking

into a *police station*. They want to look at our *computers*. It'd be like having her carry bloody sheets or something.

"For the millionth time, I think this is a mistake. You're not listening—Dani, look at me."

I look. Her forehead is creased with concern but maybe anger, too.

"You should *not* do this. Why are you brushing us off about it? A person has a lot of private stuff on a laptop, Dani."

"Mrs. Yakimora is going to be pissed about the breach in client confidentiality. Now everyone's going to know she does tax returns at a discount."

"I don't mean your *work*, Dani. Come on. You know what I'm saying. Emails, websites you've been to? All that."

"Amazon? Macy's? There were those criminal pillowcases I got on Overstock. I've got nothing to hide."

"God, you're stubborn. I tried. Okay. It's your decision. You know, we're here. Whatever you need."

"It's the right thing to do."

"This will all be over soon." Anna Jane sighs as if she's not so sure.

It's been eight days. It feels like my new life.

I am with Detective Jackson for what feels like hours. After he is finished with me, I have to find Anna Jane. This time, Detective Jackson and I were not sitting at his desk by the water cooler. We were in a white, nearly empty room, and now I am lost. Finally I locate Anna Jane, who is sitting in a waiting area. She's thumbing through a magazine, same as the time she came with me to the doctor's office after I had that suspicious mammogram.

"*Good Housekeeping?*" I say. Oh, perfect.

"Halloween pumpkin ideas from two years ago. A cake that

looks like a graveyard." She shows me the picture, sets the magazine down. She collects her purse from the chair next to her.
"What happened?"

We push the doors open. God, it feels good to be out of there.
"Well, they didn't keep me." I put my arms around myself so
that Anna Jane won't see me shaking.

"They better not have kept you. You were in there a long
time." Anna Jane looks worried. Maybe she realizes this, because
she puts her sunglasses on, hiding her eyes. We walk toward her
car. I head for a silver four-door sedan.

"Over here," she says.

The wrong silver four-door sedan. Cars basically look the
same to me even when I haven't just been sitting in a police station being questioned. I am nearsighted but rarely wear my
glasses, which probably contributes to the problem. Ian gives me
a bad time about it. I'll head purposefully to a black car I think is
his and wait to be let in, and then I'll see some baby seat in the
back or realize he's across the way, unlocking a different car door
entirely. *Black Jaguar?* he'll say, lifting his eyebrows. He's offended, I think, that I could confuse his Jaguar with anything
else.

"Get in. Let's get out of here," Anna Jane says.

It's a relief to be in her car with her, with the doors shut, surrounded by the comforting smell of leather seats and Anna Jane's
lingering perfume. She's so familiar to me, with her broad cheekbones and soft brown hair. She's family. There aren't too many
people who see the whole crazy picture of your life, from junior
high (when we'd met) until now. We shared a locker. I wore a
now cringe-worthy pink satin dress in her wedding, a size bigger
than normal, as I was pregnant with Abby. I was with her during
her mother's illness and listened to her cry when she found out
she was unexpectedly pregnant for the third time. She cried

harder after she miscarried. She stood up for me during all my life markers—wedding, pregnancy, divorce—and I did the same for her. Now this.

"I want to go somewhere far away." Wait, did I leave my purse in that place? No, thank goodness, there it is.

"You better stay right here." She's joking but not. She backs out of the parking space while simultaneously reaching toward the backseat. She tosses me a water bottle. That's how efficient she is.

I look over my shoulder, too, making sure it's safe for her to go. I drive along with other people, which makes Abby crazy. When she catches me doing it, we have the same *You're control-ling/ I'm trying to be helpful* argument that all anxious people find themselves having regularly.

"So?" Anna Jane sneaks a look at me.

"It was fine."

"What does that mean, Dani?"

"I managed. It was all right. He did get a little . . ."

"What? He got a little what?"

"Aggressive, I guess. A little aggressive. Repeating himself. Details. What I remembered."

"Jesus. This is crazy."

"Did he do this that night? Did he do that? What I heard and didn't hear. Making me say it again and again."

"God, Dani. Like this isn't bad enough without them ques-tioning *you*."

"Well, Bethy called him, right? They told him all these things—"

"Of course they did."

"Same old bullshit stuff."

"I can understand being worried, but, come on." Anna Jane turns on her signal and pulls neatly out into traffic.

"They told him we weren't getting along."

"You've never gotten along."

"Not them and me. Ian and me."

"Oh? And how would they know that? Spy cam in the fruit bowl? Jesus, people."

"Ian had lunch with Bethy a few weeks ago. According to Bethy, when she asked him how he was, he answered with one of those *I'm okay*s that don't sound okay. She asked how *I* was, how *we* were. He said we were fine but shrugged it off like something was bothering him."

"She thinks she's on fucking *48 Hours Mystery* or whatever it's called."

"I know."

"And big deal, anyway! Who doesn't shrug stuff off? I told my brother I was fine last week after Peter and I had gotten into some argument. I don't even remember what we fought about now."

"That's what I said, too."

"And isn't that one of Ian's specialties? The *I'm okay* that's not okay? That passive-aggressive thing, that care-about-me-I'm-suffering-silently thing? How many times have you told me—"

"It makes me want to scream."

"I'd want to strangle him," she says. "Goddamn it, did you see that? That guy pulled right out in front of me."

I saw. My foot is jammed down hard on my own personal passenger brake. "Ian and I are happy. We're mostly happy. What does happy mean? We're not happy all the time."

"Who is?" Anna Jane snitches another sideways glance at me, weighing my words. "What does Bethy know about that? She's, like, sixteen." Nineteen, and she knows it, but Anna Jane is right. Nineteen cannot know *this*.

"He asked if there were any problems between us. 'Anything bigger than who gets the remote?' I said no. I said I love Ian deeply. I said that we had been through a lot to be together, and I wanted it to stay that way."

"Of course you do."

"Bethy, though—"

"That girl is a troublemaker. And I know you guys don't like to say bad stuff about Mary, but what's up with the dressing your daughters like they're sexy little hot stuff when they're in middle school, huh? What're you trying to do? Yeah, honey. Great idea. Show your ass like a baboon. That's what we want to teach our girls to be?"

Oh, how I love Anna Jane. I know how upset and concerned she is. Her hands are gripping that wheel. But the words she offers are purposefully everyday ones, and the kindness of that makes me want to cry. You'd never guess where we've just been and what I've just been asked. You'd think we were sitting at Starbucks, having a latte, gossiping over a shared slice of pumpkin bread on a fine spring day.

We go to Safeway. Anna Jane needs lunch, or so she says, which probably means she thinks *I* need lunch. A grocery store is a wrong, outlandish place when your life has tumbled into anguish. The music and the clanging shopping carts and the cakes with *Happy Birthday* written in neon-blue icing, the donut case, the row of international foods—none of it makes sense to your assaulted brain. What *doesn't* seem surreal now, let alone something as ordinary as a grocery store? Anna Jane sends me to get some fruit while she collects sandwich fixings, and I try to open one of those plastic produce bags. It won't open, though, on either end, and when I lick my fingertips and try again and it still won't, I almost sit right down by that display of red and black plums and weep.

I can't find Anna Jane. We didn't make a plan of where to meet, so we're in that grocery-store hell of missed connections, where the store becomes a complicated maze with a moving cheese, more frustrating after the brief glimpse of a familiar shirt color, now disappearing. Flour, sugar, baking mixes; no, not there. Cereals, so many—virtuous choices and self-indulgent ones, the whole aisle screaming *good* and *bad,* with righteous bran and decadent pastel marshmallows. Even cereals judged. Whatever happened to those Kellogg's variety packs with the six small boxes you could slice the back of and use as waxed-paper-lined bowls? Did they make those anymore? Or the fabulous and garish cereals of my youth—Quisp and Franken Berry and Kaboom, with its smiling fruit faces that turned the milk a disturbing purple-brown? So much of your life just *goes.*

So much of your life is loss—contemplating loss, avoiding loss, dealing with loss. Objects go, cereal goes, time, places, people. The whole place is starting to spin. Frozen dinners, frozen vegetables, hard squares of spinach and corn. I decide to stay put. Isn't that what you're supposed to do when lost? I feel suddenly awful. *Did he take off his jacket, Mrs. Keller? Where did he put his keys? What did he say before going to bed? There's an awful lot you don't remember, Mrs. Keller.* My stomach lurches with alarm. My God, my God, my God. I am near the refrigerated beers. Someone might see the way I look and my location and jump to the wrong conclusions, but I can't move. I'm nauseous. The beers with their hip names and labels (What happened to Schlitz? What happened to Hamm's and Olympia?) swim in front of me, and I feel clammy. I start to sweat. A man comes down the aisle, rolling his cart. There is nothing in it but a steak and a *People* magazine.

"Are you okay?" He has a big beard and kind eyes. I am gripping the edge of the refrigerator case.

"I feel a little . . ." I wave my arm in a circle.

"Here." He grabs a beer, sets the cool bottle against my cheek; he smells like past-tense cigarette smoke. I'm grateful for his ingenuity. The man glances around for someone to give me away to. He seems slightly panicked. He feels, I imagine, the way I did that time in the second grade when I had to walk Sandra Waldo to the office when she was about to throw up.

I hold the bottle against my cheek. That morning, as I wrapped up our laptop cords, I had racked my brain to make sure there was nothing on my computer that would look bad. I didn't want to keep things from the police, I wasn't hiding anything, but I didn't want them to misconstrue something innocent. But what was there for them to see? Pamphlets in process, website designs? Our old letters, Ian's and mine—so what?

But I had forgotten something. Somewhere between the flour and the sugar of the baking aisle, I realized this. I'd forgotten a letter. A day where I'd had enough. It was private, my own private thoughts. I hadn't even sent it.

"Maybe you should sit down," the man says, and then all at once there is Anna Jane.

"Dani, honey, there you are! I just called your phone. Are you okay?"

"Dizzy or something," the man says.

"Oh, no."

"Take care, huh?" The man rolls his cart away, relieved, I'm sure. It was a narrow miss, and now he's off to his peaceful evening of red meat and celebrities.

We pay for the groceries. We leave that beer bottle behind, the one I'd held to my face. It seems wrong. Someone might pick it up and take it home, bringing traces of my horror with them.

"I'm fine," I assure Anna Jane.

But I'm not fine. I'm sick with dread. Is this how it feels when your life is over? I had told Detective Jackson that Ian and I were happy. That I hadn't been thinking about leaving.

Now I've been caught in a lie.

My divorce from Mark dragged on. After a months-long investigation, a guardian *ad litem* had given her recommendation to the court regarding custody of Abby. Mark was outraged—the two weekends a month he'd been given were unacceptable. The evaluator had been biased, Mark claimed. She was a woman, for starters. She was on my side for that reason alone. He actually said that. He threatened to fight until he got what he wanted, and what he wanted was equal time and no child support. We'd go to trial, he said. My legal bill was rising—thousands and thousands and thousands. It was unlikely I'd ever dig myself from the wreckage.

But, unexpectedly, he changed his mind. It happened out of nowhere one day. He was finished. Probably he'd met someone. My attorney moved fast then. A person who changes his mind suddenly can just as suddenly change it back. Once more I stood by that aquarium next to our old fax machine, and I madly sent signed pages. My hands were shaking, because it was that part of the movie where the music's ominous and she's about to escape, but you know he's still in the house with that knife. Everything was *hurry, hurry, hurry*.

And then, all at once (an all-at-once that lasted more than a year and a half), the divorce was final. *Final*—another tidy word, a declaration a fed-up parent makes after sending each quarreling kid to bed with a decisive shut of the door. *That's it! That's final! No more!*

Wouldn't it be great if that really were true—*final*? But the kids never stop quarreling, even behind their own doors. *Final* is wishful thinking.

It was strange to have those papers signed. Like any big project or crisis that takes every waking and non-waking moment of your life, it was odd to have it concluded. A move, a college degree, a wedding—something long-strived-for is completed, whatever the outcome, and there is a huge space where it all once was. All that open time now, and a continuing nagging sense that there's something you need to be doing.

Still, it was shocking, freeing, fabulous. I was new. Yeah. Exhausted and weather-beaten, but new. I loved my bare, ring-less hand. I loved that so much, because it felt like my very own hand then. Just Abby and me eating dinner—whatever we wanted for dinner, whenever we wanted it—it was as close to joy as I've ever felt. Impromptu takeout brought a soaring sense of independence and liberation. My clothes breathed and expanded in all that new closet space. I could fix the damn vacuum-cleaner belt myself. Mark had always handled that job before, leading me to believe it involved some mechanical proficiency beyond my abilities. Well, look there. It was inanely simple. The vacuum-cleaner belt was a glorious fuck-you. So was barbecuing. So was starting the gas mower. Even when my finances were keeping me up at night in fear, the vacuum-cleaner belt felt like victory.

There was triumph, but there was also crushing sadness. There were all the things that were gone now, and all the things that had been left behind or abandoned. Not only family vacations and silver anniversaries, but objects. The crappy garden tools he didn't want because their wooden handles had become worn after being left outside in the rain—they were in the garage. The oil stain from his car was still stubbornly there, too. The wedding album (yes, Abby, hats were in then; stop laugh-

ing) was moved to the back of the closet. That extra-large cellphone, our glorious, exciting first (which he'd bought even
though we couldn't afford it), had been dumped in the garbage
with the coffee grounds and old lettuce. It had been my job to
pack up the last of the clothes he'd left behind when he moved
out. I stuffed them into large green plastic bags, the kind you use
for grass clippings and garden trash. I handed them over to him
in a parking lot, eyes averted, as if it were a sordid, illegal exchange.

There was no question that it was a necessary divorce, but that
didn't make it less painful. You don't think it will hurt, leaving a
marriage like that, do you? But it's the same misguided thinking
that makes people ask, after your mother dies, how old she was.
If she was ninety, the bereavement isn't supposed to be as crushing. But of course it is. Of course. There's no equation for loss.

The thing is, there was all that hope once. That's at the beating center of what's gone. Hope for the life the two of you might
have had together, sure, but for me, even more, the hope that I
would have given my child something whole; at least, something
so much *better* than this. That's what tore me up the most. The
childhood I was giving her. Now that she lived in two places,
Abby always kept her bag packed. Clothes spilled from it, but
still. Every other weekend she had to remember the shoes that
went with the outfit, the books that went with the homework,
the gear that went with the sport. It was such an effortful endeavor to move between houses that she left the stuff in that bag,
like a tired salesman waiting to leave on his next, wearying trip.

Somewhere in there it sinks in, the ways that it's over but
never over. Divorce is a chronic illness. After the diagnosis, you
live with it your whole life long.

* * *

Ian had moved into a furnished apartment after he and Mary finally separated. I hated that place. It was newly built, and it
smelled temporary. I tried to see its finer points when I visited,
but its narrow living room seemed confined and claustrophobic,
even with its large windows. There was a loft with a bed. His
children stared out at me from photos on his nightstand after we
made love.

And Bethy and Kristen refused to see him. Fifteen and thir-
teen now, they were not easily forced. There was a court order,
but they would visit only at their own home with Mary there,
insisting on old family nights where the four of them had dinner
and watched movies and made popcorn. Mary shrugged her
shoulders about it. There was nothing *she* could do.

I felt squeezed in that narrow apartment. I waited in the hall
once while Ian talked to Mary about a crisis Bethy was having at
school. There was always a crisis, an illness that was sure to turn
life-threatening, an emotional outburst that undoubtedly meant
a psychological calamity. I looked out at the lights of the city and
wished myself anyplace else. The game was getting tiring, but it
was a game I'd put in motion. I hadn't stopped it, for my own
selfish reasons, and now look. He was talking to his wife on the
phone—a woman who'd just sent him a topless photo to lure
him back; oh, the lengths she would go to that I never would.
She wanted or needed him more, I guess, and now his children
wouldn't get in his car without her, wouldn't see him in his new
narrow apartment, wouldn't hug him or meet his eyes kindly
without their mother present. That bed next to the staring
photos—I wanted out of it, but it was the one I had made.

How do you make a life that is really yours? How do you
identify it when you see it? First, you don't take one that doesn't
belong to you. You're dead in the water from day one if you do
that. In addition, though, I imagine you have to look inside your-

self and listen without fear. You can't see clearly otherwise. I've learned that, at least. I loved those ring-less, independent hands. I hated the small ways in which Ian was beginning to criticize me, ever since he left Mary for good. But I shut my eyes and saw no red flags, and I focused instead on his beautiful profile and the times we'd drive in the car with the windows down, singing loudly along with the songs we both loved. I told myself these things: He knows the names of trees. He thinks my third-grade picture—loud, plaid dress, huge teeth—is adorable. He freely confesses to crying at movies where the lovers are separated by death or war. He made me a bracelet out of Red Vines. He will never abruptly quit a job because he fought with his boss. He is generous with Abby, and they have fun together. He will never strike me. Back then one of his finest and most reassuring qualities was that he wasn't Mark. Another was that he wasn't *no one*.

You're everything to me, he'd say.

I heard it in his voice, the clutching. And so I treaded water, rescuing the rescuer. *I'm here*, I'd say. *I'm not going anywhere*.

Some people have a blind, undying optimism. I, for one. I do. Did. It's dangerous. It's naïve. Maybe optimism is partly a desire to not face facts, because facing facts might require action. Facing facts might mean admitting how powerless you are. Maybe facing facts, too, would mean acknowledging failure and then another failure, and so you keep "trying." You keep seeing the positives because you're a coward.

I don't know.

I once visited my sister in Santa Barbara, just after my nephew, Justin, was born. As I've said before, it's strange the things you remember. We ordered a pizza. I even remember what kind. All-meat, part of a "Family Feast," one of those stomach-churning combos that come with the same pizza dough in various forms—breadsticks, cinnamon rolls; dear God, you vow afterward to do broccoli penance.

Who wants to cook, though, right? Because, here we are: The baby is a week old, and my niece is a toddler, and everything is wet. Along with wet diapers and laundry, my sister's shirts are wet, Nick's shirts are wet, and I've got those damp splotches on my shoulders. There are spilled cups and tipped bottles and leaking bodies. Amy's and Nick's eyes—they're intermittently vacant and love-filled. I'd forgotten how exhausting all that was, but, oh, oh, oh, that wrinkled back of a baby's neck, those milky folds. Those tiny T-shirts that snap at the sides.

Anyway, Buck, Amy and Nick's dog, hears the pizza delivery guy drive up. Actually, I swear, Buck hears him start up his car at the pizza place, because he begins to pace as soon as we get the paper plates out and set them and the roll of paper towels on the coffee table. Buck's a sweet boy, but God help the UPS guy who passes through their gate. The mailman is his archenemy. He sees himself in the starring role—his family against the kidnappers, the fate of the world on his furry shoulders. It's all up to him and he won't let anyone down. Probably livens up his day a great deal.

The enemy is a pizza guy getting out of his car; he's about twenty-one, with a thin build and shaggy hair, forced to wear that humiliating red vest and collect the dollar-off coupons. He goes home smelling like charred crust and red sauce, poor kid. But Buck starts to growl at the slam of the car door, and Amy can't lunge, because she's holding the baby, and Nick is unaware, because he's hunting around for his wallet.

The doorbell rings. It's the enemy's first mistake. Buck is a weapon unleashed; he brings all he's got. He flings his meaty

German shepherd body against the door. It's a side of him I've never seen. His teeth look huge in that snarl, capable of doing real harm. He's standing on two legs and is taller than you'd imagine; he's looking eye-to-eye with that pizza guy through the door's three triangles of glass. He's barking and leaping furiously, and if that pizza boy had any thought of pushing the red button to release the nuclear bomb on a major city in the United States of America, well, he'd be thinking twice now.

Buck—wow. It's impressive, but it's scaring the shit out of me. I get up and knock over Stephanie, my two-year-old niece, who's walking around with some hard plastic toy piano; they clatter to the ground with dramatic C notes. I'm trying to reach Buck's collar, then Nick appears, and he grabs Buck and manhandles him down from the door with some effort. Buck is still trying to leap and Nick is yelling at him, and Nick shoves his wallet at me. Buck is drooling with protective fury.

Whew. I open the door. The delivery boy's face is kind. He's just trying to make beer-and-rent money.

"Sorry," I say. I think we're sharing a moment of nerves and mutual shock. I imagine that he can't wait to get the hell out of there. Behind us, Buck is frothing at the mouth as if he's become possessed by the devil.

And this is when the pizza delivery guy says: "Oh, look at your dog. He's excited to see me!"

Poor, poor soul. Poor, innocent sucker. It stuck with me, the way that boy tore off the credit-card receipt and handed over the goods, smiling. Buck was rumbling a low warning in the back of his throat. But the boy only said a cheery thank-you. He strode down the path; he might as well have been whistling.

What could have accounted for this, his ignorance of the obvious, his lack of insight? Was he, too, nearsighted? Was there any part of him that *did* see what he should have been seeing, I wonder? Did he not read that look in Buck's eyes that said that Buck would gladly sink his teeth into his thin, very white throat? There had to be a part of him that saw those fangs and the damage they could do. I believe that. We know the truth. Whether we want to admit it to ourselves or not, we know.

12

I once counted up how many days of Abby's life I didn't spend with her because of shared custody. Don't do this. It hurts too much, first of all. Second of all, as I've tried to say before, you can't count loss. Mark took Abby skiing for the first time, and I never saw it. They went camping, and she caught a fish that I never witnessed her catching. She sprained her ankle when they were on a hike, and I didn't know they'd been to the emergency room until after they'd returned home. If a child falls in a forest and you aren't there to see it, do you feel like shit for years after? She goes away for a weekend and comes back with a new haircut. She rides a horse for the first time, away from you. Put a number to that.

Sometime after I first met Ian, I had taken Abby to our suburban neighborhood pool. I had just parked in the busy lot. I was collecting my bag and our towels and was searching for my book, which had slid under the seat, when I looked up and saw Ian there, with Bethy and Kristen. It was unplanned, but it felt like especially good luck, the kind of good luck that makes you secretly believe in fate.

"Look who's here! Guys! It's Abby and her mom!" Ian had

said. His smile was bright against his summer tan. His sunglasses were on his head. I could tell even from there that he smelled like suntan lotion. I was so happy to see that man.

We hugged hello. Just the day before, we'd spent a few illicit hours wrapped in each other's arms on a blanket on the university campus. We were secretly in love and I was buoyant with it.

We walked as a group from the parking lot to the pool entrance, Abby and Bethy talking shyly, Kristen dragging a snorkel against the sidewalk. We parted ways as soon as we got in, because Ian was meeting Neal and his kids. But for those few moments, during that walk, as Ian and I each held a stack of towels and toted a bag, I imagined us as a family. A restructured family but still whole. The three girls and us, heading to the pool for a day of fun. This was what it could be like.

I was such an idiot.

Of course, you have your losses, and your children have theirs. In that iconic stepfamily, the Brady Bunch, there were no ex-wives or ex-husbands, and Jan didn't resent Peter for the attention he got from her own mother, Carol. Marcia, Jan, and Cindy didn't return home after a visit with their father, sporting new clothes and cellphones, eliciting feelings of jealousy in Greg, Peter, and Bobby. Mike Brady didn't hate the girls' father; Carol didn't think Mike spoiled his boys. Greg didn't bring up his mother and the good old days every two seconds, inspiring murderous annoyance in Carol. Cindy didn't start wetting the bed, causing Carol to believe that her daughter was damaged for life and that it was all her fault, and Bobby's mother didn't phone every week (usually right during the middle of the Brady family dinner) to argue with Mike about school-picture money or Bobby's missing shin guards.

Here is a stepfamily recipe: Take your pain and his loss and the children's anger. Add his ex's intrusions and your ex's incon-sistencies. Fold into a house with at least one shared bathroom and mutual holidays. Blend.

Anna Jane kisses me goodbye after a quick lunch at the house-boat. I wonder if she is as relieved to get away as that man in the store had been.

"I feel bad leaving you all alone," she says.

"I'm fine."

"I can wait for Abby to get back."

"No, no. You'd better get going. Traffic over the bridge . . ."

"I'll call you tomorrow." She gives my arm a final squeeze.

I watch her drive away. I know she'll turn and wave, and so I wait until she does. I don't want to wait, but I force myself to. And then, the very second her car turns the corner, I head back. That letter, that lie—I need to do what I can to find out what happened to Ian, and fast.

The party, the drive home, the grim face. The key, the dog, the heels. The cool sheets. The bliss of rest! Goddamn it! Remember!

The cuff link.

I could see why you'd be pissed . . . An argument.

I do remember. And I know I need to talk to Desiree Harris. Now.

"Dani?"

It's my neighbor, Maggie Long. She wears a pair of culottes— who knew anyone still had those? She's run out to meet me in those swingy, skirt-like pants; she even leaves her front door open, she's in such a hurry to catch me. She's probably been watching for me out her front window. Her brown hair is pulled back in a butterfly clip. *Butterfly clip*—the words make me think of a thorax pinched tight between thumb and forefinger. All those beer bottles in the Longs' recycling bin—the alcohol is beginning to show on Maggie's face. Alcohol really ages a person.

"We've been talking about you," Maggie says. What had Ian been thinking, going away like this? There was no way everyone would not know his business now. *Our* business. You want everyone to think you're perfect, and you do this? You blow it all up in one big move? Was this just a last giant fuck-you to everyone? To me and Nathan and his kids and his father and everyone who'd ever loved him and let him down? The police have visited every neighbor on the dock, of course. We've called every person in Ian's life. Unless he has a very good, innocent reason for being gone (and what might that be? A kidnapping? Amnesia?), we'll have to leave this place if he ever comes home. Domestic drama in a sprawling suburban neighborhood was bad enough for him; on this small dock, it would be intolerably humiliating. Every time he stepped out the door, there would be Jack or Maggie Long or Mattie or even old blissed-out Joe Grayson, with their awareness of his failures. Every day he walked into his office . . . He couldn't live with that. I know that about him. Even if he comes back, our old life is over.

"I appreciate it," I say to Maggie. "This has been hell."

"I can't even imagine." Maggie shakes her head, but it's an obligatory move. It's the comma between two sentences, the pesky have-to before she gets to what she can't wait to say. "Listen, Jack and I—we were going over that night. Replaying it. You guys went out to that party . . ."

"We did."

"Later on, in the early morning, did you hear that boat?"

"No." My chest clutches up, bracing for some blow.

"I can't believe you didn't hear it. It was sitting out there for a few hours! I'd forgotten all about it. This motor—one of those obnoxious ski boats. You know how the sound carries."

"What did it do?"

"Nothing. I just remember waking up and hearing it, and Jack rolling over and saying, 'Fuck!' and thinking it was some stupid kids sitting out there drinking on Daddy's toy. I put a pillow over my head and went back to sleep."

I don't know what to think about this news. I try to make some connection in my head, but there are noisy boats all the time, at all hours. It's one of the negatives of living on the lake. I stand there with Maggie Long like an idiot, as she looks at me, waiting. I don't know what she's trying to tell me.

"Is it possible?" she asks. I shake my own head now. I have no idea what she's getting at. She sighs. She squinches her nose, as if it's distasteful to have to say. "Could he have left that way? By boat?"

I feel the air leave me, as if she's socked me in the gut. I've played so many scenarios in my head, but never that one.

"Jack said, 'His car is there, you know?' I didn't want to mention it to you, but Jack said, 'You gotta tell her. Maybe she hasn't thought of it.' The car doesn't mean anything, you know, necessarily."

"It never occurred to me."

"People get picked up on the docks every day."

For dinner, for a boat ride to a Husky game. Not to disappear into a new life. I rapidly flip through the images: Ian standing at the dock with his wallet and cellphone, waiting to hop a ride. A boat cruising up, sloshing and rocking our home as I slept like the dead.

"I looked at my clock, too." Maggie Long's eyes are bright. This is more excitement than she gets on an ordinary day, doing the books for that accounting firm, or cooking Jack a medium-rare T-bone. God, she looks as excited as Pollux does when I shake the treat box. "I made sure to check the time. One-thirty. I always look at the clock when I hear an unusual sound in the night. You never know when it might be important."

It's obvious that she's imagining herself the star witness at some trial. Thank you, Miss Marple! Thank you, you fucking nosy neighbor! This is as helpful as those psychics who claim they saw the missing person next to a red fence in a yellow field. I wonder if Maggie and Jack had their big revelation after their first six-pack of the night or their second. Maybe the news team could come, and Maggie could be interviewed. She'd be the perfect one to say, "They were just normal people. They kept to themselves. We always thought they were a little *too* quiet. . . ." All of her friends could come over to watch KING 5 at six. They could scream and point at the screen when she came on. They'd reassure her that she hadn't looked fat on TV at *all*.

I'm losing my mind. This is getting to me. It's changing me in ugly ways. I am transforming. There is all this anger, which is burning away my soft silk threads. I *like* Maggie. She's only trying to be helpful; I know that. My rational self does. The self that began disappearing eight days ago, when Ian did. The self that is utterly gone now that Detective Jackson has my laptop with that letter on it.

Maggie grips my arm. Her eyes shine. I remember this, from my adultery and divorce in the suburbs—how thrilling your tragedy can be to other people.

Desiree Harris is not listed anywhere. I am searching the white pages on my phone with no luck. If I had my damn computer, this would be easier. I try to call Nathan, knowing he'll have ac-

cess to her cell number, but there's no answer. What now? *Think,
think, think.*

Kitty, the receptionist. She could get that information. But it's
Sunday, and she won't be at work. Kitty what? What's her last
name? Wait. Something funny. Bizarro? Maybe Bissaro? *Please,
please, please.* I try my phone again, but those damn online white
pages are useless. I hunt for her name in the phone book that,
thankfully, we still have under the kitchen counter. It's been
years since I've used a phone book, and, wow, the print has
grown smaller. How do people even read these things? I hunt
around for my reading glasses. Katherine Bissaro, there it is,
thank you.

She answers. "'Lo?"

"Kitty?"

"Yes?"

"This is Dani Keller. I'm sorry to call you at home, but I need
your help. I'm trying to reach Desiree Harris, but I don't know
her number. You don't happen to have that, do you?"

"Not *here.*"

"God, Kitty, I'm sorry to ask this of you, but can I meet you
over at BetterWorks and get it from you? It's an emergency."

She hesitates. "Yeah, uh, hold on a sec." I hear her speaking to
someone on the other end, and then she's back. "Mrs. Keller? I
live, like, two miles away. I usually bike. My boyfriend, Jesse,
said he'd give me a ride over. I'll call you back."

"Kitty, that would be amazing. Thank you so much. I really
need to get in touch with her."

"No problem. If I can help at all about, you know, Mr.
Keller . . ."

"Thank you."

I'm an idiot, though. Because when I hang up, I realize I
haven't given her a way to reach me. Wait, if she has Desiree

Harris's number, she'll certainly have mine! And what about caller ID? I don't need to worry. But I do worry. As the minutes pass, I'm getting more anxious. I need to get a hold of this Desiree immediately. I need some answers before Detective Jackson comes up with answers of his own. How long does it take to go two blocks? I wait five minutes exactly, and then I phone BetterWorks.

There is ringing, and then the answering system picks up. Of course, it's Sunday. I try one of the back lines, but there is only more ringing, endless trilling. I wait four more minutes exactly and try again. And again.

Finally, "BetterWorks."

"It's me. Dani Keller."

"I just got here." She's out of breath. "Let me find it for you."

"Fantastic," I say. "Thanks so much again."

She puts me on hold. The piped-in music comes on automatically—some jazz piano number. I feel a weight on my chest, as if something's pressing there. It's hard to catch my breath. I felt this way once before, when I fell off the monkey bars in elementary school and landed flat on my back. I remember the recess teacher's big face looking into mine, the orange balls of her necklace dangling over me. I thought I was dying. No air, no ability to even gasp . . . Wait—twice. I've felt this way twice. I'd gone to court for a temporary order of separation from Mark, and I met my attorney in her office beforehand. This same thing had happened. She pulled a paper bag from her desk and made me breathe into it. I thought it was darkly humorous that she kept a stash of them handy. When my bill grew, I understood even better why they might be necessary.

Kitty is back. "Mrs. Keller? I know I took a long time, but I was talking to Doug, and I was thinking that it's against policy to give out those numbers."

"What?"

"It's against policy. I was thinking maybe I should call Desiree and give her your number."

"Kitty." I try to breathe. "Do you understand that this is an emergency?"

"Just stay right there. I'll call her now."

She puts me on hold again. The jazz song ends, and another begins. It's the screaming-horns kind of jazz, and I want to claw at my own skin at the sound of it and at this waiting, waiting, furious, crazy waiting. Ian doesn't even like jazz. Why he has jazz on his answering system is beyond me. I once played a mellow guitar-type jazz album at a dinner we held for some colleagues of his, and he said, *I thought you had better taste than this.*

I stamp down a feeling of fury, the way you make sure a fire is completely out at a campground. It doesn't do much good. Cinders are flying everywhere now. I make a deal with myself. If she's not back in ten seconds, I'm going to get in my car and *drive* over there. I'll talk my way past that guard. I'll get on the damn computer and find the number myself. It'd be quicker than *this*.

"Mrs. Keller?"

"Yes, I'm here."

"Desiree isn't answering."

I keep the cry of anger down with great effort. I imagine Desiree Harris at Nordstrom. She's in the dressing room. Her cellphone is ringing, but she has a new red dress half over her head. Or else maybe she and Kitty *did* talk. They talked and Desiree is avoiding me. That's what's going on. Of course it is.

I try not to sound as furious as I am, I really do. "May I have her cell number please? As you can imagine, this is rather important."

Kitty sounds nervous. "We can't give those out, Mrs. Keller. It's against the rules."

"My *husband* made those rules. You might want to remember that."

Oh, the dripping venom, the bitch tongue. My old self is gone, and good riddance to her, the pathetic, self-defeating Goody Two-shoes. Ian gives me a hard time about the way I pour on the nice to every salesperson, barista, waiter, telemarketer, or person I bump into in an elevator. A guy came to repair our furnace once, and I asked him if he needed something to drink. I asked how long he'd been in furnace repair. I told him that it must be gratifying to do his job, to provide something people needed so badly, warmth on a November day. Ian was disgusted. *You act like you're personally responsible for everyone's self-esteem.* He was right.

Kitty's voice is strained, stretched tight as glass. "I'm so sorry, I can't . . ."

I open my mouth, where a string of vicious words are waiting—I can feel them pressing in my throat. Instead of speaking, I slam that phone down so hard that the plastic case smacks against the wall, which causes Pollux to leap to his feet in alarm. His eyes are chocolate pools of distress.

I dial Nathan. I reach Tim's Shoe Emporium instead, whatever and wherever the hell that is. *Goddamn it!* I try again.

"Dani? You okay?" Nathan says this instead of *hello*. "I'm sorry, shit. I see you've been calling me. I'm in my car. I couldn't hear over the radio."

"I've got to reach Desiree Harris and can't get her number. I tried Kitty, but she won't give it out. Kitty called Desiree herself, but she says she's not there. I don't believe it. I think she's avoiding me."

"I'm not . . . I'm at . . . Just a sec." I hear him place an order for a number three with a root beer, and an intercom voice gives him a total.

"You're at *Taco Time?*" I'm shocked, actually. It seems so

wrong. A detective is about to catch me in a lie about my missing husband, and his business partner is ordering a beef soft-taco meal.

"Dani, you sound awful."

"You've got to get her to meet me. Or at least talk to me on the *phone*."

"I don't think this is a good idea—"

"Nathan." I attempt to infuse my voice with reason. I unclench my fist, where my nails have left little red crescents in my skin. "She might know something. I've got to reach her."

"I'm worried, Dani."

"No one's more worried than I am."

"That's not what I mean. I mean, this might not look good. It feels . . . aggressive. I don't want anyone to get the wrong idea."

"It's not aggressive, Nathan. It's *desperate*. If she doesn't want to talk to me, there's a *reason*."

"She's probably afraid."

"Exactly."

"No, I mean, you calling like this . . ."

"Afraid of *me*?" Ludicrous. I can't even imagine it.

"Yes."

I don't say anything.

"You should hear your voice."

I shut my eyes. It's a two-second form of prayer without words. "Nathan, please help me," I beg.

"Let me call her," he says.

I hear a voice on the intercom again. *Hot sauce or ketchup with that?* And then there is the rustle of a paper bag. I summon every atom of calm I might have in my sorry cells.

"Thank you, Nathan," I say.

* * *

Picture this, my first meeting with Paul Hartley Keller:

Ian and I are drinking a glass of wine in that narrow furnished apartment. It's just the two of us so far. Ian keeps looking at his watch. Paul Hartley Keller is late.

Our knees are touching. Ian rubs my leg. I reach for my glass on the coffee table.

"Darling," he says. "If you hold the glass up there, you warm the wine. Hold it by the stem. Or with your fingertips."

"Ian, relax. Why are you so nervous?"

"I'm not nervous."

I feel a prickle of irritation. "I won't embarrass you."

He leaps up at the knock. I stand, too, and pull my black skirt down. *We're going to the Twilight,* Ian had said earlier in the week. *You know that black skirt you have? That tight white satin shirt? That'd be perfect.*

Ian answers the door. I can see where Ian gets his looks, first off, and his taste for expensive things. Paul Hartley Keller, even with his fleshy jowls, is a handsome man. He's got a full head of gray hair, brushed back from his face, and icicle-blue eyes under bushy brows. He's a big man. His suit is dark, beautiful, and he has a cashmere overcoat. His voice is large, too.

"Hell of a lot closer to civilization than your last place," he says as he comes through the door. He is huffing badly; I hear a little wheeze that makes me nervous. But he fills that room. I feel his energy the minute he steps inside. This is much better than I was imagining. All at once, the night seems to hold possibilities. I'm actually excited for it. Who knows what might happen. You can tell this about Paul Hartley Keller right off: He makes things *happen.*

"Dad." Not a hug, but a handshake. "This is Dani."

"Mr. Keller," I say.

He looks me directly in the eyes, holds my gaze. "Paul. Please." He takes my hands. "Oh, your hands are so warm," he says.

Ian stands around. He's waiting for something, I can tell. What? Some acknowledgment of his new living arrangements? The apartment is stylish; there's a view. The building is new and it still smells new. The furniture it came with is leather. The appliances are stainless, though Ian never uses anything in the kitchen except the microwave. But, really, what is there for Paul Hartley Keller to admire?

"Shall we?" Paul Hartley Keller says. "I left the car unlocked."

"Not exactly a dangerous neighborhood," Ian says, and meets my eyes. I smile, but I think he's being overly sensitive. Paul Hartley Keller takes my arm, a firm grip, and stands close to me in the elevator. I slow my pace to his on the way to the car, aware of his effortful breathing, but the truth is, it's better for me, too, with the shoes I'm wearing.

"Aren't you a breath of fresh air," he says. "A beautiful one like you, I bet you're a very powerful woman."

I laugh. "Well . . ." I say. We arrive at his Mercedes. It's new. Gorgeous. Brushed silver.

He knows what I'm thinking. "Silver fox like me, eh?" I almost blush. I feel nervous, but it's the good kind of nervous, the kind that's hiding a secret center of giddiness. He opens the front door for me. There's a moment of awkwardness, as I don't want to sit in the front, but I do so anyway. This leaves Ian to sit in the back. I glance behind me, give him a brief look of apology. He looks like he's about seven years old back there.

Paul Hartley Keller asks me what I do, and I tell him about my graphics firm. I use the word *firm,* though you could hardly call it that. I admit this. He chuckles. "Creative professions have the highest job satisfaction in the world," he says. Maybe he's making this up, but, oh, well. Who cares? He pays the parking attendant with a folded bill and doesn't wait for change. It's a small, thrilling world in that car; it smells lush, lush leather and breath mints, and it *feels* lush. Music is playing, and the ride is like velvet. Ian keeps poking his head between us from the backseat, interjecting comments.

"I can't hear anything back here," he whines.

"You want me to turn this down, just say so." Paul Hartley Keller's hand hovers near the car's stereo system.

"That's fine," Ian says.

"It's the José Granada Trio," he says to me. It's some sort of flamenco. He turns it up a notch. "Like it?" I do like it. I like it a lot. It's unusual and sexy and fun. He snaps the fingers of one hand as he keeps a casual but commanding hold of the wheel with the other. He smiles as if to say we share the joke. He's the kind of man who'd be a great dancer, though. He'd guide you with a strong, definite hold. He'd know what to do.

The city looks especially beautiful through those tinted windows. Paul Hartley Keller pulls up to valet parking at the restaurant. The college kid opens the door for me. He's dressed in black valet pants, a vest, and a crisp white shirt. It's crazy, but I feel somehow glamorous getting out of that car. My legs feel longer; I'm more elegant.

Paul Hartley Keller has his hand on the small of my back as we go inside. We walk in together. Ian is behind us somewhere, separated at the revolving door. All these stories I'd heard about his father, and now look. He's utterly charming. He's not at all what I'd been expecting.

Paul Hartley Keller seems to know the hostess. We're seated at a perfect table by the window. And this place—wow. There is a view here, too. A wider, more expansive view than the one in

Ian's apartment or office; it's of the city and the sound and the mountains beyond. It goes on forever.

Ian is already looking at his menu. "What's the rush?" Paul Hartley Keller says. "You have a train to catch?" Ian sets the menu down. The restaurant is glittery with candlelight. I glide my napkin to my lap, where it feels as delicate as an orchid.

Paul Hartley Keller orders wine. The sommelier arrives with a white towel over one arm. Paul Hartley Keller sniffs and swirls and nods his approval. The wine is poured—red. I make sure to hold my glass with only my fingertips.

"Better than this," Ian says. He holds his glass out to me, cupped in two hands. It's cruel. I redden. I don't know why he wants to skewer me.

"Private joke?" Paul Hartley Keller says.

"The way Dani was holding her glass earlier."

"She could keep it on the table and lick from it like a cat, and she would look lovely doing it." He clinks my glass. I clink his.

"Are you having the trout?" Ian says to me. He's forgotten that I don't like white fish.

"The grilled bluefin is excellent," Paul says.

"I'll have the petite filet," I say to the waitress when she returns.

"Ah, the girl likes her meat," he says. It sounds seductive, electrifying. I may be a powerful woman after all, who knew? Paul Hartley Keller tells us in great detail about a trip he's thinking about taking, a cruise, but not the kind where a hundred people are huddled together on deck chairs. He likes his space. He likes the best service. The Greek Islands, the Aegean Sea, Santorini, Ios. The way he describes them, they sound like luxurious chocolates in a blue silk box.

"I should tell Dani my Microsoft story," he says.

"I could tell her. I know it by heart," Ian says. He's becoming snippier and increasingly rude as the night goes on. The wine is amazing. A gentle heat blows through and disappears after each sip.

Paul Hartley Keller tells me how he warned Bill Gates about the idea Bill had to develop a computer for a regular person to use. " 'Doomed to fail,' I said to him. 'The average person doesn't want to mess with that technological bullshit.' He was sitting right there in my own living room. Just a kid. And Paul on my other side. The *other* Paul."

"Oh, no," I groan appreciatively. "Now, there's a big *if only* . . ."

"How are things going with your start-up?" he asks Ian.

"Six years, it's still a start-up?"

"Whoa," Paul says. He holds up his hands as if to ward off a blow. "The best companies can take years to get off the ground."

"It's going great. Profitable. Too profitable. Fifty percent of my stock may go to my ex-wife." He looks up at his father. I can see it for what it is. It's a line of connection thrown out his father's way. Paul Hartley Keller lost a fortune to Ian's mother when *they* divorced.

Paul shrugs.

"It's been tough, you know?" Ian's eyes are soft in the candlelight. They are almost pleading.

"You've been sitting in the middle of this for over a year," Paul says. He spins the wine in his glass, sips again.

"I know. It's hell."

"What're you doing this halfway for? Get in and finish the job. Move on." Well, obviously, I couldn't agree more. He touches the cuff of my blouse with the tip of his finger. He looks in my eyes. "I'm a man who always finishes the job."

I feel a warm rush, and I am ashamed of myself. It's attraction, but it's also turning to disgust. I'm not sure who attracts me and who disgusts me. I look at Ian, and I swear he has shrunk; it's the wine or maybe the terrible, terrible yanking ropes of lineage and years of humiliation, but I swear Ian looks about a foot tall. He's a tiny man sitting in that chair.

The waitress arrives. She has our plates balanced on her arms. Poached salmon and grilled bluefin and my filet with fine Roquefort potatoes. "Diane," Paul says. The waitress has no name tag, so he obviously knows her from another visit. "When is your birthday? Let me guess. . . ." He waits; he looks her over. A man at another table is signaling his need for her with an upraised hand. It makes me nervous—the other diner wants his check and Diane is still hanging around, as if she has all the time in the world. "October," Paul Hartley Keller declares.

"November." She giggles. She has auburn hair. She has a long, thin neck like a ballet dancer.

"I knew it. Scorpio! Dynamic, passionate . . . aggressive." He lifts one eyebrow at the last.

She laughs again. "Ah, yes. Watch out, mister." She shakes my steak knife at him before setting it down next to my plate. I have an ugly feeling. Jealousy, repugnance. My own shine is dimming. "Anything else?" She pours him more wine without asking.

"That's quite enough," he flirts. He watches her ass as she leaves.

Definitely enough. My mood is turning sour. His charm is shriveling in my eyes now, too. That disgust I feel—it's making its rounds. First it was Ian who disgusted me, then Paul. But I'm disgusted with myself the most.

We decline dessert, but he relishes his. He licks the spoon with a fat pink tongue.

On the way out, Paul sees someone he knows. He takes her hand, kisses her cheek. Her eyes shimmer. "Oh, your hands are so warm," he says.

Paul asks the valet to call us a cab. He has people he's going to meet. His fingers look like stout sausages as he hands over his credit card to pay. Ian and I don't speak. The cab takes forever to get there. We stand at the curb, waiting and waiting, as the glittering people come and go.

Eight months later, Ian got a call with the news. Paul Hartley Keller had had a massive heart attack. He was dead. It happened at "a friend's" apartment. I tried not to imagine the scene but did anyway: Paul Hartley Keller eating oysters in bed, post-sex. A "powerful woman" with her powerful thighs wrapped around his waist. It was a complete fabrication, but this is what I imagined when I thought of him dying. There were other factors, too, though, I guess, other than lust and desire. I remembered that wheezing when we walked uphill toward his car. And he had that diet of rich food and flattery that was obviously bad for the heart.

Not three days before this call, Ian's divorce had been finalized. Paul Hartley Keller would never know it had happened.

Ian didn't cry at the news that his father was gone; he only seemed stunned. Days afterward, stunned. He didn't sleep. Abby was at Mark's that first night, so I was with Ian. He sat on that temporary couch in that furnished apartment, and he stared out the window at the city lights. He was not an angry little boy then; he was a sad and lost man.

"It'll never be different now," he said.

It would never have been different, anyway, but I didn't say that. We can need so much from people. That need is so thick sometimes, we can barely see through it.

Ian dressed in his most beautiful suit for the funeral. He

shaved carefully. I held his hand during the short service at the funeral home.

They were there at the graveside service, scattered across that dewy green lawn. The butterflies. The one silently weeping behind her sunglasses. The one in those high, high heels, which were sinking into the grass. The one in a red dress, obviously defying conventional black in some way she felt Paul Hartley Keller would approve of.

I don't believe he's gone, Ian had said. Not: *I* can't *believe he's gone.* Not: *It doesn't seem real that he is gone.* But: *I don't believe he's gone.* He was probably right about that.

We got married three months later. Three months to the day of Paul Hartley Keller's death. To Ian, it was more important than ever to prove that he was a man who could finish the job.

13

Really, why would Desiree Harris pick this particular place? *This* is where you go to meet a woman whose husband has disappeared? A husband you may have been involved with? The bar of the Sorrento Hotel—it's a meeting place for lovers. You sneak there for drinks in the rich, lavish, candlelit room downstairs; you sink into a plush couch or a wingback chair and sip drinks and feed each other smoked salmon with your fingertips. The Sorrento Hotel bar is a hidden, seductive den, where the waiters make themselves respectfully scarce. Sometimes there is a well-dressed man sitting at the piano. He plays dreamy, pensive pieces, but he, too, is politely preoccupied, immersed in the keys or else looking up at some faraway image in his own mind, his eyes closed. Ian and I had met there, in our early days. We even sat on the very couch where I am sitting right now. Feeling safely unseen, I'd draped my leg over his, and we'd breathed each other's breath, and love was enough reason for anything. It was *the* reason. It was planetary orbits and cells dividing and sunsets in God colors.

Now, though, I just watch the door. I keep my eyes on it, waiting for her arrival (still imagining her in that dress) or for Nathan's. He'd insisted that he come, too. He didn't feel that I should meet Desiree Harris alone. What did he think I would do? Wrap my hands around her throat in the Sorrento Hotel parking lot? Stab her with an appetizer fork? All I want are answers, and I want them *now*. Why is she so nervous to meet with me, anyway? That's what I want to know. Most people would do anything to help a woman whose husband was missing. Most people would not pick a dimly lit, let's-finish-this-upstairs hotel bar to meet in, either. But maybe that's what you did when you were the type of person who flashed your breasts around like you were offering a roll from the breadbasket.

Had she and Ian met here, too? *There*'s a question.

This is taking entirely too long. Who would be late to a meeting like this? Jesus. I reach inside the zippered pocket of my purse and feel around. Yes, it's still there, that cuff link. I order a glass of wine. And then I call the waiter back and switch to something stronger. I remember the brown fire that Abby had brought over that night after Ian disappeared. Maybe it'll scorch my throat so that every word I want to say will be charred away to harmless ash. I don't trust myself. Inside, I'm blazing. The answer to all this, the reason for all this pain and fear and unknowing—I'm sure it's going to walk in that door at any moment.

A man in a light spring suit arrives. He has newsman hair and a shiny, wholesome, Christian face. A woman follows behind him, looking over her shoulder. She wears a tiny knit dress and has a straw purse. Meeting secretly, probably. I never noticed things like this before. Even in high school, I was the sort of person who didn't realize that pot was being sold in the upper parking lot. I lived in a different, more innocent world than anyone else. I kind of liked it there. The first time I saw a bong, I thought it was a fancy decanter for vinegar and oil.

My whiskey arrives. I swirl the ice expertly, the way Paul Hartley Keller might, the way Ian might. I take a swallow and try not to shiver and sputter. How do people drink this stuff? And now I need to go to the bathroom. It's an amusing trick my body plays with me, ha-ha, one of its personal favorites. Whenever I can't easily leave a place—the doors of the theater have just shut, for example, or I am jammed in the airplane window seat next to two sleeping businessmen, or I am waiting to meet the skittish possible lover of my husband—I am sure to have to go. Badly. I begin to worry. It becomes an impossible problem: The place is filling up, and if I get up now my spot will surely be taken. Will I miss her if I make a quick trip? She might leave if she doesn't see me. Of course, I could leave my coat on the seat. I could ask the waiter to keep watch. I am busy with these highly complex mental calculations that are all part of this particular syndrome when I feel a tap on my shoulder.

"Mrs. Keller?"

It is Desiree Harris, and I don't even recognize her. She wears a somber blue skirt with a short-sleeved white blouse. It is buttoned. She has flat black shoes, the kind you wear if you're planning to walk a long distance. Those shoes surprise me. They're practical. They might even have insoles she put in herself. Nobody finds Dr. Scholl sexy, likely not even Mrs. Scholl. *Seductive* and *practical* are never friends. They never even say hello to each other. They each make fun behind the other's back.

"Desiree." I stand up. And then, dear God, what is wrong with me? I offer my hand! I smile politely! Why did I smile politely? I am instantly furious at myself. It's the furnace repairman again but worse. Way worse! I can hear Ian's voice in my head.

You asked the guy how long he'd been in furnace repair. No one's in furnace repair. It's not like being in real estate, or in financial planning. He's a furnace repairman! You've elevated the entire profession with one preposition!

"I didn't recognize you. I was waiting over there—" She gestures toward one of the neighboring couches, already filled by the Christian newsman and another guy. I was wrong about him and the woman in the dress. The men's knees are touching, and their eyes are furtive. "We only met that once, and your hair was up. . . . Nathan said he was coming?" She looks at her watch.

"You can sit down," I say. I've recovered the proper tone. Authoritative, pissed. We aren't having a tea party here.

She chooses the wingback chair to my left, sets her purse beside her. The leather of that bag collapses as if exhausted. "Hope this is okay." She spins a finger in the air in reference to the room. "I live nearby. My car battery was dead, so I had to walk."

"It's fine."

"I'm so sorry about what's happened—"

"What *has* happened?"

She tilts her head as if she hasn't heard correctly. "Ian? Disappearing?"

"I assume you know something about that." I swirl my ice cubes meanly.

"Me? I don't know *anything* about that."

Her voice is so earnest that I can't help myself. I look at her face, really look. It's tired, too, I can see. It's the kind of face that belongs to someone who has been unlucky in love; maybe she has a child at home. I realize I don't know a thing about Desiree Harris. It worries me. I've been a fool, perhaps. Dear God, maybe there is no answer to be found here. What if there is no answer to be found here? My anger begins to dissolve; panic is waiting to replace it. Because what then? What if I'm wrong about Desiree Harris? And then it happens. She looks down at her hands. She's lying. I see the lie hurry past and dart from view.

I reach into my purse. I have the split-second fear that my fingers won't touch that circle of gold, that I won't find anything there. But it is there. Thankfully it is. It's real. I need it to be real, because if not *this* story, then . . . Please, let it be this story. Let him be back at her place right now. I hold the cuff link in my palm. It looks as guilty as a packet of cocaine or an empty condom wrapper. "Did you give him these?"

Desiree Harris puts a hand to her chest. Her left hand. She wears a ring on her middle finger, as many single women do. Is this to accentuate the fact that the ring finger is bare? Maybe that's the point, I don't know. "Oh, my God, no. No, I didn't give him that."

"You've obviously seen it before."

"Someone's gotten the wrong idea."

"You mean *me*?"

"I mean whoever saw me. Someone saw me, right? I was afraid of this. I was just trying to do a favor . . ."

"You brought this to our house." I know that. Somehow, I do.

"I did bring that to your house. I found it on the grass, after you two left. The party? I decided to drop it off. And then when I heard he had gone missing, I felt weird about what I'd done. The timing. Not leaving a note . . ."

"And why would you feel weird?"

"Because I could have just given it to him on Monday."

The waiter hovers nearby, asking without asking if she needs anything, but Desiree shakes her head. *What* is taking Nathan so long? Someone else should be hearing this. It's not adding up, in my opinion.

Now the man is at the piano. He's settling in, adjusting his sheet music. Desiree Harris leans toward me. She reaches out her hand. I think she's going to touch my arm, but her hand simply hangs there in the space between us. I'm glad she doesn't touch me. Her eyes are pleading. "I was curious. You know? That's the only thing I did wrong, I swear. To wonder. To *look*. I wanted to see where he lived. Where *you* lived." She waits for my understanding, but I give her nothing back. She tries again. "You just seem so . . ."

The man begins to play. The glassy notes fill in around the conversational murmurs and the soft clatter of utensils. I have no patience for this. "What?"

"Lucky."

The word shocks me. No, what shocks me is the way I suddenly get this. I understand this, too well. I see it for what it is, for what it does and doesn't mean, and it feels like a blow. What Desiree is saying, well, I'm not the only one who has ever wanted someone else's life. Desiree—her roots need touching up, and her lips are self-consciously lined with pencil, and even in the sparkly candlelight I can see that tired purse. It looks like a purse that works hard, trudging along from errand to errand, sitting in grocery carts and hanging off her shoulder as she waits in line at Marshalls. It's a bit beat up. A pen has leaked ink in the bottom corner, leaving a dark splotch.

"You didn't give him this? As a gift?" I look down at that stupid cuff link. My voice sounds far away.

"No, of *course* not. Why would you think I did?"

I stare down into my glass. I know why I thought she gave it to him. Something happened that night that I *did* remember but didn't want to. He'd wanted to go back and look for that cuff link. Badly. It had meant a great deal to him. It was *important*. When we were finally, finally in the car after that dreaded party, he told me he needed to go back. *Needed*. I had assumed that need was related to love. What is more imperative than love? What drives us more toward *need*?

Ian, really? Please! I've got to get out of here. I want to go home!

I'll only be a minute. I'm sorry if this night has been such a torture. *I'm tired, is all.* I slipped my shoes off, set them on the floor mat. *What do you have to do?*

I lost something.

What? Your wallet?

No.

What?

Never mind!

Your phone?

Just let me look, would you?

He was seething. He got out of the car, slammed the door. He headed for that Kerry Park grass. It was one of those interactions that could make you furious—the held-back information, the something hinted at but not revealed, the refusal to hand over what had been dangled in front of you. Yes, fury rose up in me. I opened my door. I strode over to him. The woman in the red dress, and now this.

Ian!

Stop it.

What are you doing? What have you lost that's such a big secret?

Never mind, I said! Jesus. How much did you drink tonight?

Less than you, I'm sure.

Look at you. You can barely walk.

He was right. I was stumbling on that lawn. *I can't see, that's why! It's too dark out here. You won't find anything, anyway!*

Not if I don't look, I won't.

What is so important? Jesus, Ian!

Not everything about me is your business.

Ian! Damn you!

No shoes, wet grass, mud. I grabbed his arm. I felt it between us then, the possibility of rage. I had felt it one other time. I knew what could happen.

He knew, too. He shook off my arm. He stepped back. *What is wrong with you?*

The fury crackled there between us. We faced off. He weighed his options. Finally: *This is ridiculous*, he said. *Fuck it!*

He did not look for whatever it was he'd lost, after all. He returned to the car instead. But he was pissed about it. Pissed at me. He drove home with that face, that stone-chiseled jaw. We drove in silence. You marry the person you love, and you marry their shadow self, too.

With Desiree now, I try again. It sounds crazy, but I am actually *hoping. Please, please, please, let it be so.* "The two of you— you had some sort of relationship?"

"No, not at all."

"You don't know where he is?"

"No, of course not."

"Flirtation?" I saw it with my own eyes that night.

"Friendliness. He was friendly. He joked. I joked back. He always mentioned his wife. You. Always. I saw you at the party. I don't know . . ."

I am silent.

"I mean nothing to him," she says.

I feel unwell. My head is beginning to swim. Desiree is still trying to explain. She has no idea that I likely understand this better than she does herself.

"Have you ever walked down a street at night and looked into some window?" Desiree says. "Maybe you see a person in there, in a beautiful room? It's so intriguing, and you don't even know why exactly. You just want to know more. Maybe you wish you were inside. Maybe you wish that room were yours. That's all. That's all it was."

I shouldn't have drunk that stuff. It is swirling bitterly in my stomach, and something else is happening: My chest is caving in again. I can barely get my breath. I try to suck in air, but there is no air.

"Are you okay?" Desiree gets up, heads toward me, and that's when that damn purse takes the opportunity to rebel from its life of drudgery, or perhaps it's merely an attempt at handbag suicide. It leaps from its spot, clatters down toward the tiny glass table, causing my drink to slide across its surface and fall to the other side. Everything is falling, crashing down from high ledges. The ice cubes lay there on the carpet; the liquid drips off the side of the table and soaks a dark spot into the rug. The waiter appears immediately—I'd been wrong before if I thought they were off somewhere minding their own business. He has napkins. It's like that day at the Essential Baking Company with Nathan and the spilled coffee but worse, much worse. The waiter and Desiree are blotting things, but the napkins aren't up to the job, and now there is Nathan himself, finally, taking my elbow, asking if everything is all right. The napkins are sopping wet with brown liquid, dripping everywhere, and Desiree's purse contents are spread out for all to see—a bottle of hand sanitizer, a tampon, a pink tube of mascara with the label worn off.

"I'm so sorry I'm late," Nathan says. He looks at me and at Desiree and the mess around us as if he doesn't know what to think.

"We're done here," I say. I grab my own purse and I leave them there. I get the hell out of that place. *He flirts; it doesn't mean anything. He always talks about his wife. Always.* Desiree Harris is just a woman.

She's just a woman, and she does not have the answers I need.

Please, I say to whoever might be listening. *Please, no.*

My stomach churns. I am sick with fear. Because I can feel my fingernails in his skin. Even right then I can feel them digging in.

* * *

As they say, the ink was barely dry on Ian's divorce papers when we got married. It had been nearly four years since we met at that baseball game. He didn't want an actual wedding, not without his daughters there, and so we went to the courthouse in the city. I wore a cream-colored dress, and he brought me a bouquet of white roses as a surprise. Ian's old friend, Simon Ash, and his wife, Theresa, stood up for us. It was the first time I'd met them. My family wasn't there—Abby wasn't—and it bothered me. But I kept my mouth shut. These were more red flags that I ignored. Maybe they should make those flags in another color.

I didn't know then what I know now, that emotional rescue is, at the heart of it, a lack of respect. If you're the one being rescued, it's a lack of self-respect. If you're the one rescuing—lack of respect for the other person. You're demonstrating your belief in your own weakness or in theirs. It's insulting.

Not that I was with him only because he was rescuing me. I loved him. Oh, I did. My heart ached with it. I didn't see him clearly, not at all, but I loved him. His eyes got teary, too, when he said his vows. *Forever*, he said. You could believe a day like that could bring a whole new start. He'd been short-tempered and critical since his divorce, but who wouldn't be? His daughters wouldn't speak to him. His father had died. I was the equivalent of having all your eggs in one basket. I *was* the basket. No wonder he started imagining that men were interested in me when they weren't. No wonder he accused me of flirting. *Toby and Renee noticed this about you from the beginning*, he'd say. I've never been a flirt. In high school, I blushed when boys talked to me. Ian was just experiencing temporary insanity. In no time, he'd go back to being the man I fell in love with. His behavior made some sense, if you thought about it. The security of marriage would cure him. Oh, the arrogance in the idea that your love can cure. Good luck with that.

The whole mess—we were clichés, all of us. First, Mark and me. We played out the typical woman-leaves-husband story. In this sordid tale, she tries to leave and he attempts to destroy her for it. During the divorce, he keeps being the asshole he was in the marriage and devises lengthy, expensive legal maneuvers, while she keeps being the victim she was in the marriage and falls apart. There is a separation agreement, a parenting plan, one restraining order, one divorce decree, and a partridge in a pear tree. He gets an apartment and schemes revenge, and she stays in the family home and leans too much on the children for emotional support, ensuring their need for later therapy. He dates bimbos, joins a gym, gets a fresh new look (hair, tattoo), and throws himself into new, weird, short-lived interests (astrology, singles bars, religion). She reads self-help books and tries to be more assertive and marries the first post-husband man she sleeps with. He buys the children expensive gifts he can't afford but doesn't show up for birthdays or school events as promised; she struggles with money, gets a puppy, and sews Halloween costumes involving hundreds of sequins, which still does nothing to alleviate her guilt. He disappoints; she hovers. The children (or child, in our case) trudge back and forth and eat two Thanksgiving dinners in one day and vow never to marry unless it is for forever.

And Ian and Mary performed the man-leaves-wife drama. Here, he cheats and hides it, and she finds out but pretends not to know until he finally confesses, after which she tries to meet him at the door in a trench coat with nothing on underneath. He half-heartedly "tries to make his marriage work" while she goes to Nordstrom, maxes out their credit cards, and then sees an attorney secretly after a session of "couples counseling." In this version, *he* gets an apartment and marries the first woman he sleeps with, and *she* reads self-help books and joins a gym, gets a fresh look (hair, tattoo), and finds new, weird, short-lived interests (yoga, online dating, religion). Their children rally around her and don't speak to him, even *on* Thanksgiving, and vow not to marry unless it's for forever.

After Ian and I wed, we morphed into yet another tired and overused contemporary family story. We were the "blended family." There are usually two versions of this, too, I've found. In version one, the kids don't accept the new partner, and in version two, they do. In our first scenario, the children blame the new wife for every change they see in their father, from a too-fashionable style of sunglasses to a never-before-seen assertiveness. The new wife gets chilly hugs and the-way-Mom-does-it-better stories, as the daughters (usually daughters) act like mini-wives, scheming to rid the house of the intruder who is monopolizing Daddy's time, money, and affection. They give sentimental gifts involving old photographs, ruffle his hair in ways that seem disconcertingly seductive, and deliver information back to Mom that requires her to phone Daddy immediately after their weekend with her "concern." Daddy (he's always "Daddy") alternatingly plunges into grief or walks around unaware, little bluebirds of Daddy love tweeting around his oblivious head. If during one visit they don't step on the backs of the new wife's metaphorical shoes or don't pull the metaphorical chair out from under her, he's sure that all the bad feelings are now in the past. He magically forgets everything that came before; it's a clean slate in his mind. He's performed some misplaced act of contrition on their behalf, sure of their goodness. Next time, they will step on the backs of her shoes and pull the chair out from under her. This is the stuff of fairy tales.

In scenario two, the children are fond of the stepparent but must hide those feelings from the real parent as if they are potentially world-endingly nuclear. Which, of course, they are.

Yet, in spite of the clichés, there are the snapshot moments where the pain of it belongs to no one but you. The banality shatters, and what is suddenly, horribly there is all yours. Like watching war on television, or some earthquake, any tragedy—it's just another war or earthquake or tragedy, until you see that dead arm with a watch on it or a child's shoe sitting among the rubble.

Example: That second Christmas Eve after our separation, Abby was celebrating with Mark and his family at his parents' home, and Ian was still with Mary and their children at his. I should have at least made other plans, but I stupidly hadn't foreseen the danger. I wasn't alone but ALONE, me and that cheap, scrawny tree I'd bought at Safeway because it was all I could afford and all I could wrestle onto the top of old Blue Beast. The weeping and aching that came that night were so old and so far in that nothing felt worth that kind of agony. Even with fists in walls and heels in ribs, leaving Mark felt like a mistake.

Example: Bethy and Kristen finally agreed to see Ian after we'd been married for several months. They met him for one hour, over lunch, at a Greek café near his work. Mary had dropped them off, and she waited in her car to pick them up. He'd hoped it was a first step, a new beginning. Maybe they would look at him and remember that he was their dad and not some villain. But they'd come to deliver news. Kristen's middle school graduation was coming up, and they thought it best that he didn't come. It would make their mother too uncomfortable. That night, he sat up alone in the dark again. I brought him a blanket and a pillow. It was obvious he would be sleeping on the couch. His voice was miserable but angry, too. He glared at me from across the room. *I am missing so much of their lives*, he'd said.

Example: Abby likes Ian. We'd take her and her friends to

dinner, and we watched movies and went on hikes. He practiced with her for her driving test. They have a good relationship. After we married, we lived in my old house for almost two years until Abby finished high school. She made waffles and watched TV on our couch, just as she always had, and the same stuffed toys were on her bed: Ginger-Man (an orange-brown bear), Bibby, her old monkey. But she never came into our bedroom to tell me something she'd forgotten or to ask if I knew where her headband was. She avoided our room. There was, after all, a different man beside me in our bed, and it was Ian there with his bare shoulders above the sheets, not her father. Or we'd be watching a movie downstairs, and Ian would fart. Abby would leave that room then, making an excuse about homework or calling a friend. We both felt this—the uneasiness of it, the awkwardness, the *wrongness*. There are intimacies that belong only within a family. A real family. Her discomfort and mine, it told me there were ways he would always be a stranger to us.

Love—well, of course I loved him, but there were things I didn't see, and things I didn't understand or know yet. In the chaos and rush of rescue, one cannot slow down for long enough to see clearly and understand. Love—long-lasting love—requires more information. It requires time. When you're drowning, though, there is no time. You are blinded by the waves over your head and the panic of trying to breathe. When you've turned love into survival, the outstretched hand is what matters most.

The noise in my car is getting louder, but I can't think about that now. I feel like someone's chasing me, and I keep watching my rearview mirror to determine if it's true. I must get home as fast as possible. I need to hurry. As soon as I am home . . . What? I don't know. I just need to get there and lock the door behind me.

It's late when I arrive. One of those flyers has blown off a telephone pole, and Ian stares up at me from the gravel parking
strip. I pick it up and crumple it. I shove it deep into my pocket.
Most of the houseboats are dark, except for Kevin and Jennie's—
they're probably up with their baby. Maggie and Jack's bedroom
window flickers with television light. I think I hear footsteps behind me on the dock, but when I look over my shoulder, I see no
one.

Our own porch light is on, but it's obvious that Abby has already gone to bed. I open the front door. I try to be quiet about it.
Pollux, my dear dog pal, my forever friend, little sugar boy, he
sleepily trots up to greet me. I drop my purse by the door, that
meaningless cuff link still inside.

Bed, sleep—how I crave it, even if that dream is there waiting
for me. Fine, come. Let me look. I'm running out of options,
aren't I? It's time to face the facts, no matter what they are.

"Dani."

The voice and the figure startle me. I let out a little scream. I
put my hand to my heart.

"Dani, it's only me."

"Jesus, Ma," I say. "What're you doing here?"

"How can I not be here? You went to the police station today,
baby kid. You met that woman. A girl needs her mother."

I can see a couple of my quilts on the couch. A pillow. A mug.
Abby has set her up comfortably. "You're staying over?"

"Yes, I'm staying over. Well? Does she know where he is?
That Desiree woman?"

My mother looks small in the dark. Without her boots on,
she's shorter than I remember. It's age, I realize. She's shrunk.
Who would have thought it was possible? She'd always been so
commanding.

"Nothing," I say. "It was a dead end."

"Your father called. He said he put some missing-person ads in the classifieds. Who reads the classifieds anymore?"

"He's trying to help."

She grasps my arm. "Dani," she whispers intently.

"What, Ma?"

"There's something I have to tell you."

"Tell me, then."

"I went to a psychic."

I groan. "I can't do this now, Ma. I can't." Dear God, she loves that stuff. Any hint of the mystical, and she's in with both feet, wallet in hand. She's had every kind of brief spiritual fling over the years, with Reiki and past lives and even with an ancient spokesman from beyond. What was his name? Something Indian. An old woman channeled his voice, which must have been a ton of laughs. My mother still has a crystal hanging from her rearview mirror, and it glints dangerously on sunny days. In my opinion, it's more likely to cause an accident than provide good energy. A few years ago she told me my aura was yellow, but I'm sure it was just her cataracts.

"You need to listen."

"I'm so tired. I've never been more tired in my life."

Her grip tightens. Her hand is a claw on my wrist. "It was that place over on Eighty-fifth, have you seen it? I've always been curious about it. They have that sign with the big painted eye? FORTUNES TOLD."

"Ma, it's above an espresso place. I don't see how you can commune with the spirits above the noise of grinding coffee beans."

"She doesn't commune with the spirits. She reads tea leaves."

"Perfect. Regular or decaf? I hope it's one of those teas that promise a new mental state. Calm or Refresh or Awake. Have a cup of tea, gain a new outlook, *and* tell your future."

"Don't make fun. You don't know."

I'm losing patience. "Ma, please. Can't we discuss this tomorrow?"

"It can't wait. She told me that I was keeping a secret. That it's not healthy. I need to say it before it gives me a heart attack."

"Your heart is fine. Your doctor told you that three weeks ago. The heart of a fifty-year-old."

"All night, I've felt these flutters."

"Caffeine, Ma. Anxiety. I'm going to bed." I pull away, but there's that grip again.

"Wait."

"Ma, *please*."

"I *have* been keeping a secret."

"What?"

"I have."

I sit down at the edge of my couch, on top of my quilt. I rub my eyes, making dark circles of mascara, but so what. "All right, okay. You know, so you don't have a coronary tonight."

She sits down, too. She takes my hands. Her eyes are piercing. They glow keen and urgent in that dark room. "What?" I say. "I'm adopted. My father is not really my father. That milkman we had back in California—"

"This is serious."

"Fine. Go ahead." I don't want to hear it. I am suddenly nervous. The thought in my head, the one that's screaming loudest, is: *What has she done?*

"I saw them," she says.

It isn't what I'm expecting. Something in my rib cage falls. My heart accelerates. Maybe I'll have the coronary tonight. "Them?"

"I didn't want to tell you. I didn't want you to be hurt, and then once I didn't tell, it became harder to tell. I *couldn't* tell after I *didn't* tell! But now it might be important. She might know something. I saw them the day before he went missing."

"Who, for God's sake?"

"Mary. I saw Ian and Mary. Together. I'd been walking around Target, looking for birthday gift ideas for Stephanie—what do you get a sixteen-year-old? I was in there for hours."

"You saw Ian and Mary in *Target*?"

"No, I was starving after I was in Target that long, and I went over to that bakery, you know, over by the car place. The one with the good butter cookies? They make sandwiches now. First, it was only a bakery, but now they do lunch. Aunt something? I can't think of what it's called."

"I don't know. It doesn't matter."

"Aunt . . . Aunt what?"

"Never mind! Just tell me."

"It's going to drive me crazy. Starts with a *B*."

"Auntie Bee's, Mom. That's the name. Auntie Bee's."

"Right! That's it. I knew it was *Aunt*. I ordered my sandwich, and I'm waiting for them to wrap it up, and I see them. Ian and Mary. Well, obviously I know him, but I recognize her from that time we saw her at your old grocery store, remember? She got in line right behind you. It was supposed to be intimidating."

"I remember."

Mary.

Here it is. After all this time, after it seemed like the past was receding and the girls were at least coming to our house, his new life still can't compare to his old one. *How* could it? I believe that, I've believed it for a long time. His criticisms of me are all the evidence I need. I'm glad there's an answer here, but I'm sick, too, sick with hurt and regret. *He's with Mary.* They wouldn't keep such a thing from their children, though, would they? They wouldn't let their daughters worry. But this—it's another possibility now; there are more questions to be asked, and with that comes relief. I think, *Thank God.*

"Her hand was over his, Dani. They were sitting at a table together, and I saw it. I can't tell you how furious I was. I said a loud *ahem!* and he looked up."

"He never told me this. He never mentioned it. Are you sure he saw you?"

"Oh, I'm sure, all right. He took his hand back. Snatched it back, the prick. I got my sandwich, and I told the cashier, I said, 'Once a cheat, always a cheat.' Loud enough for them to hear. I was so damn mad, Dani."

"He didn't tell me."

"Well, no wonder. Of course he didn't mention it! I slammed out of there so hard, the bells bashed against the glass door. I've never been so angry. I had my keys in my hand. . . ." She purses her lips together tight. She shakes her head, reliving her fury.

"What are you saying?"

"Well, maybe I shouldn't have done it, but I did. He deserved it." She mimes slicing the air with something pinched between her fingers.

"Don't tell me."

She slices the air again. "Mr. Perfect's perfect car."

"No." I am hoping for a denial, but she only folds her arms and raises her eyebrows in challenge. "You keyed his car? Oh, Mom, tell me you didn't key his car."

"He's lucky I didn't do worse, the bastard."

I moan. "Oh, Mom . . . Oh, God. You shouldn't have done that." *There's a scratch on his car. It wasn't there when we saw him last.*

"No? Wait until Abby is treated like that by some asshole. Mark was bad enough—"

"Mom."

"Mark, now, *he* should have had his balls cut off."

"I can't believe you keyed his car."

"I couldn't stand looking at that thing. Sitting in the lot all shiny and just so, without even a fucking crumb in it. Everything so flawless on the outside, exactly like him. But inside? Ugly. One ugly motherfucker. I'm sorry, Dani, but the way he talks to you? And then there he is with *her*?"

I'm silent. Her bravado is quickly disappearing with my disapproval, I can tell. She looks down at her hands. Pollux puts his paws up on my knees, and I gently push him back down.

"Oh, Mom," I say finally.

"Maybe I shouldn't have done it."

This is my mother in two minutes of one hellish evening, her whole self and her entire history laid bare. She had essentially raised herself under the roof of an aunt who didn't give a shit about her, dropped there by a mother who didn't give a shit, either. Abandonment and the self-sufficiency she'd had the guts to muster had left my mother with a don't-mess-with-me toughness that would occasionally burn fierce and frightening. It was a monumental display but a trick of the eye. There was no fire, not really—only a child waving a plastic flashlight in her own dark night.

"Probably not," I say.

"I'd do anything for you, you know that." She takes my hand. I feel her small, complicated self doing its best to be there for me, and my throat tightens with tears. We make messes, but mostly we're just trying to do the best we can with what we've got.

"I do know that, Ma."

"You're my girl."

Now here is Abby, leaning in the doorway. Her hair is smushed up and coming out of its ponytail. She's never liked to miss out. Even when she was a little bean sprout, she'd try and try to keep her eyes open long past bedtime, just in case. "Hey, is this where the party is?"

"Come here," I say.

She pads over in her socks, reminding me of those plastic-footed pajamas she used to love when she was a toddler. Tonight, all of us are both young and old. Maybe everyone is both of these things all the time. It's our biggest challenge, perhaps, being both. "If this is where we do female bonding, aren't we supposed to put on an Aretha Franklin song? That's what they do in the movies," Abby says.

"Urethra Franklin," my mother says, and Abby snorts.

"Just come here," I say to Abby.

She shoves onto the couch with us. "Double hugs."

I put my arms around them both, give two squeezes as the request requires. "You people," I say, and oh, damn, my voice begins to wobble. In spite of everything, the reason I'm overcome right now is that I am so thankful for them. What is a life without your people? I pull the two of them close. One smells of Jean Naté and the other of apple shampoo. What would you do without your best ones?

"Grateful." This is all that squeaks out. I hate to cry, but tears roll down my nose. I am a mess, and I'm making wet splotches on my mother's robe, my daughter's sweatshirt.

"Oh, Mom," Abby says.

We stay in our huddle until my mother takes a Kleenex out of her robe pocket and blows her nose. "I hate to cry," she says. I know that, of course. Abby hates to cry, too.

"Some party this is," Abby says. Her own eyes are wet.

"*R-E-S-P-E-C-T,*" my mother gives a lame try.

"Sing it, Grammy," Abby says.

Cherished ones, I think.

*   *   *

That night, I am afraid in my very own bedroom. You're supposed to feel safe in your own room, your own house, knowing that the danger is *out there*, outside, somewhere-elsewhere in the dark. Of course, I'd been afraid in my own room before. Under my own roof. As a small child, I used to think that robbers were in the house, hiding in the closet or down the hall, blocking my way to the bathroom. When I was a married woman, the bad guys were inside, too. Here's a funny but not funny thing that happened once. One night, Mark stayed up late to watch TV. When he came to our room to go to bed, I awoke from the depths of a dream and managed to scrabble together only these facts: dark, man figure, my room. I bolted to a sitting position, terrified. *Who are you and what are you doing here?* I'd said in alarmed half-sleep. When we recounted it in the morning, he wasn't amused. Not at all. Sometimes your dreams speak more truth than you'd like to admit.

I was right to be afraid, wasn't I, about what might happen to me? With Mark, and now. I lay awake, thinking about that scratch on the car. That key, dug into metal. I try to envision it: a white line, a thin scar. As the night goes on, it becomes wider in my imagination. A gash. A deep, screaming wound.

I need to see it. What I need to see, actually, is how it will look to Detective Jackson.

I get out of bed. My mother is asleep on the couch (the fluff of her hair is visible from where I stand), and so I step carefully, avoiding the creaks on the floor, same as I used to do when I was a teenager coming in past curfew. I knew just where those creaks were then, and I do now, too.

Pollux meets my eyes but stays in his crescent-roll shape on his bed, bless him. I turn the doorknob slowly, slowly, slowly. The final, opening click sounds as loud to me as a gunshot.

The night smells like deep lake water and damp earth. I love the smell of night; even right now I still love it. I walk as softly as I can down the dock. There are so many people not to wake. I can hear the low moan, the shivery cry, of a cat about to fight.

Ian's car is solitary and still under the streetlight. I check up and down the road, but the street is quiet. Everything is shut up tight for sleep, cars and houses and Pete's Market. If anyone sees me, they might misinterpret the way I bend down and peer at the driver's side door, the way I run my fingertips along the thin white thread.

Of course Ian would have noticed it that day when he got back to the car, and of course he did not mention it, for his own reasons. He would have opened my door for me that evening, and I would have gotten in, and I would have gone to that party with my usual cluelessness. We will have to provide an explanation for this, though. The explanation will lead to other questions. Because, yes, there is damage here. I could never do this, could I? Drag a jagged key against a smooth, perfect surface? This is the sort of anger I've always been afraid of.

But I understand that anger, the desire for it, the desire to succumb to it. I, too, have wanted to gouge and scrape. I had felt the urge that night with my own fingertips on his skin, as he stood on that grass and glared. *Not everything about me is your business.* Oh, I could have dug my nails farther in and made my own thin scar on his flawless skin.

It is the sort of anger I have always been afraid of, yes. But it is in me, too. Ian is and isn't Paul Hartley Keller. And I am and am not Isabel Eleanor Ross.

14

Here is the great irony (or just deserts): You find your soul mate,
you go through hell to be together, and then your soul mate becomes riddled with distrust. If I was dishonorable enough to do
what I did *with* Ian, I was dishonorable enough to do what I did
to him; that's what he thought. His paranoia was the secret lover
of his guilt. They were bound together by betrayal and circumstance. But the suspicion wasn't there only because of our history,
was it? I was becoming more and more clear about that. It was
there because Paul Hartley Keller had gutted Ian's self-certainty.
He'd done it sure and clean as you gut a pumpkin with the edge
of a spoon, and now Ian was sure he could never truly be the sort
of person who could have what he most wanted. Every day he set
out to find proof of that.

We were in bed one morning, legs entwined, sheets tangled.
Abby was with Mark, and so it had been two days of making
love and eating in bed and making love again. We hadn't yet
reached that point with each other where sex became tired,
where your bloated stomach after a too rich dinner took prece-
dence over passion. I was still competing, maybe, and maybe so
was he. His first wife, my first husband—you let thoughts in like

that or you didn't, and if you did, everyone was game: your first
high school boyfriend, that girl he loved in college, his mouth on
other mouths, your hands on other asses. If it got spoken between
you (and, in our situation, how could it not?), jealousy might
grow to need its own room in your house. It would make demands for its favorite meal, but the sex would be good. The sex
would be *great*. You didn't dare let up, because comfort might
mean defeat. Well, we were making up for a lot of time of not
feeling alive, too.

My head rested on Ian's chest. It was one of those times I felt
close to him (confident about my victory?), relaxed, and at peace.
We could lie in bed too long, though. We could go from rested
and snug to restless and irritated. You had to know when to get
up and make coffee and step outside. If you passed that point, it
felt too hot, and your lower back complained, and you needed a
shower, and someone would say something that could be taken
the wrong way. Too long and you could be headed for one of
those lengthy discussions that never get anywhere.

Do you know what a sphragis is? He murmured this into my
hair.

Something Catholic, right? He knew about all that stuff. He
knew all the intricate jargon, the underground pathways of that
particular dungeon. He understood transubstantiation, stations
of the cross, mortal versus venial sins. In spite of the catechism
classes I took when I was eight, all I basically knew was that
Baby Jesus was born in a manger on Christmas. I was even hazy
about the whole Easter thing, to tell you the truth—the rock, the
cave, the there-not-there. Definitely hazy about the palm
branches and about the ashes on the forehead. I looked like that
after I cleaned out the fireplace.

Catholic, yeah. But that's not what I mean.

No. I don't know, then.

It's a plug that some butterflies create.

I hate that word, plug. It's one of the ugliest words.

Other animals make one, too, but butterflies can take it further.

From where my head lay, I could hear his heart beating in there. The sound of a heart always disturbed me. If you were aware of its beat, you were aware of its ability to stop beating.

What kind of plug?

Male butterflies—they make the sphragis out of their secretions. It's like a glue that shuts the female's genitals. Some male butterflies cover her entire abdomen with it. An iron chastity belt.

I sat up. I didn't like where this was going. *Kind of disturbing, if you ask me.*

It's nature. It's natural. It's what he does to protect what's his.

She has to wear that thing around?

Yeah. It's pretty heavy, too. It makes it hard for her to move.

God.

It's meant to last a lifetime.

We'd stayed too long in bed, that was for sure. I got up. I needed air. I reached for my robe. *That's horrible,* I said.

I was wishing I had one for you.

I thought carefully about how to respond. Over the past few months, after each little comment—about my clothes, or other men, or after the lengthy questioning that came after the times I'd seen Mark—I'd tried various strategies to ward off the jabs and the interrogations. I tried reassurance and humor and flat-out anger. Still, his insecurity sat there, stubborn and immovable. No, actually it didn't sit there. It came my way with its fangs bared. A person's insecurity is a creature of the night, out for blood, and for the same vampire reasons: to avoid their own de-mise.

I decided to say nothing. I headed for the door. I was in the hall when I heard him.

Don't worry, Dani, he said. *The females keep finding ways out of it.*

Good, I called back to him.

They just keep evolving, he said.

Here is *another* great irony: You find your soul mate, you go through hell to be together, and then you soul mate pecks away at you with his criticism. *Your laugh is so loud. You're inconsiderate, unplugging my razor without plugging it in again. Your breasts look small in that. You know, Mary never would have cheated.* If I were more perfect, I'd be worth all the trouble he went through to get me, that's what the criticism said to me. He felt a disparity in what we'd given up to be together. If I were more beautiful and more giving, I could make up for the deficit in his column.

But, like the suspicion, the criticism wasn't there only because of our history, was it? I was also becoming more and more clear about that.

Ian hadn't always hunted for ways to condemn me, not at all. Not *at all*. But I'd said that about Mark, too. The thought—the similarities between the two of them—it made me uneasy. They were different men, I told myself. Very different. The truth, though? Well. You can kill a butterfly using different methods. You can use force, grasping the thorax between your fingers and pinching hard. Or you can hold down the wings with the slight, sharp tip of a pin until the heart stops.

We'd like to tow his car to the station evidence-impound garage for further analysis. . . .

I am having difficulty breathing.

We can get a warrant, of course, if you have any objections.

I cradle the phone in my lap. I am underwater. I need to get my head above the surface so I can breathe.

"You need to get a lawyer, Dani," my mother says. "I don't want to hear any more about it. You don't have a choice." She's pacing the kitchen. She looks like hell. She's aged ten years in the last week, or maybe I just never noticed the ways the years have caught up with all of us.

"I don't need a lawyer. Let them take the car."

"Dani. Danielle! This is getting out of control. We're way over our heads. This is crazy!"

"Let them take the car."

"Getting a lawyer—it's not admitting some kind of *guilt*. We need some help! We need to know how to protect ourselves!" Abby is practically begging. She looks like hell, too. She's wearing one of her tongue-in-cheek sweatshirts. This one has Queen Frosting from CANDYLAND on it. The dissonance is disturbing.

"I'll call Nathan," I say. "He'll know what to do."

"Nathan's not a lawyer," Abby says. She and my mother exchange glances.

"I'll call your father," my mother says.

"*Grampy* is not a lawyer," Abby says.

"He knows how to reach that guy . . ." My mother waves her hand around.

"How many times are we going to have this exact same discussion?" Abby says.

It's true. We are repeating ourselves. I have to do something.

"Let me handle this." I attempt to look decisive and in control. I leave them sitting there, and I stride upstairs to our office. In my panic, frustration, fear, fury—take your pick—I accidentally slam the door, rattling those butterflies hanging on the wall. Too late, I remember that we don't have a computer in there anymore. We've got Abby's laptop and my own phone, but likely I'd only get those frustrating online white pages anyway. We've got that old phone book I'd used to look up Kitty's number, but that's back in the cupboard under the kitchen phone. I retrace my steps to retrieve it, and nothing about this looks decisive or in control. Erratic and desperate, maybe. Panicked and chaotic, for sure.

"Frank Lazario," my mother says. "I'll never forget him. Call him."

I cart the phone book back to the office, and I open its fat, sloppy pages. The number might be unlisted. That's certainly possible.

No. There it is.

I dial. I keep my voice low. And then I shower. I want to look good. Funny how that still matters. I do my hair, and I choose my clothes carefully. I keep a nervous eye on the clock until finally it's time to leave.

I emerge from my room, purse over my shoulder.

"Thank God, he can see you today?" my mother asks. "Busy man like that, too. I'm so relieved. Did you mention your father's name? That probably got you right in."

"He doesn't have the great power you think he does."

"You haven't even met him yet."

I mean my father, but I don't bother to correct her. Even after all these years, she's still—ha—*wedded* to the idea that he has some magical abilities that she no longer has access to. I weigh my options. To tell, or not to tell? Someone should know where I'm going. I don't know why, it just seems someone should know my whereabouts.

"I'm not seeing Frank Lazario, Mom."

"Don't tell me you called that lawyer from your divorce. Don't you remember? They had her yacht in the Sunday home section of *The Seattle Times*. No wonder that bill was big enough to bury you. You paid for those oak captain's chairs."

"Ma, I'm going to see Mary." And then, in answer to her stunned face, I walk out the door and shut it hard.

The sun is out, and it's one of those hot spring days that appear out of nowhere. Spring is fickle; spring cannot make up its temperamental mind. It is no day for long pants. I see that now, too late. The heat has gathered in the car, and the seat is warm on the back of my legs. My tendency toward self-sabotage is increasingly revealing itself—I back out of my parking spot and notice a small pool of brown liquid that the car has left behind. That, and now the engine (I guess it's the engine; what do I know about this stuff?) clunks when I shift into drive. The humming and buzzing have also gotten worse. With my window rolled down for a little cool air, I hear it loudly. I'm going to have to drive over the bridge in this precarious condition. *Please, Blue,* I pray. *Please don't stop on 520.* I've always felt terrible for those poor people, the ones whose cars give up right on that two-lane stretch over Lake Washington, causing backups for miles. What betrayal, and what a mess; I'd feel awful if it were me. But now it's not the inconvenience I'd cause other people that I'm worrying about. No, I'd take that problem anytime over the trouble I'm in.

I wonder if Detective Jackson has found that letter yet. Is that why he wants Ian's car?

I can't afford any holdups. I need to get to Mary's as quickly as possible. The walls are closing in on me; I feel it happening. The computers, the car . . . Mary might have information about where Ian is, and, dear God, I need information. She wouldn't keep things from her frantic daughters, would she? Yet who can say what confidences people keep for their own reasons. *Someone* knows what happened. Someone knows where Ian is. Someone has to know. In my heart, I feel Adam is right. *People don't just disappear.*

I steer with one hand and, with the other, I punch button number one on my phone. I imagine a police car pulling me over for cellphone use. I feel a bit hysterical at the idea of it—it would be one of those arrests you see on television, where they pull over a guy who's speeding and find a dead body in his trunk. Bad driving in the wake of my husband's disappearance would speak to my guilt, even if the only rules I'd broken before were minor traffic laws and major marital ones. I stole a library book once. I was too embarrassed to check it out. It was about battered women in the suburbs. Previously, I'd always believed that librarians would be the kind of people I'd love to have as friends. They were smart, open, and well-read. Understanding, definitely. But the folks behind counters can know more about you than you're comfortable with. Librarians, receptionists in doctors' offices, the ladies who work at Rite Aid. The people behind counters know your secrets.

You've reached Ian Keller. Please leave a message . . .

We've become adversaries, that voice and I. It's infuriating, the way he doesn't answer. We're matching wits. One of us will do the other in first, and it's going to happen soon. There are pigments in a caterpillar's blood that allows it to understand days and hours and minutes. It knows when the light is dimming and the days are growing shorter. It knows when it's time to hurry and find a safe place in which to protect itself.

Where are you? Goddamn it, Ian! Speak to me!

Not everything about me is your business.

He isn't dead. I am trying to remain adamant about that. I keep coming back to the same question. I would know it if he were dead, wouldn't I? I would feel it; people say they do. I'm supposed to *be sure*, damn it. Mary will be sure.

He can't be dead! He isn't. But fear may be clouding my sense of certainty. That's what it does, right? Fear stands in front of the truth like an armed guard.

Except that my armed guard—he's becoming unreliable. He's put down his weapon over the last few days, gone off to have a smoke. Truth (was it truth?) is trying to sneak past. Truth is insistent, persistent. There've been these disturbing gaps in my memory, but images are forcing their way in, images that twist and tangle with logic. Those damn pills, that wine. My feet were muddy, but I had been on that wet grass. In the dream, though, my bare feet are on the ground. My hands are shoving against his chest.

I reach for my purse on the seat beside me. I glance at the purse, the road, the purse, the road. The last thing I need is to get into some accident. I feel around inside the zippered pocket. That cuff link. He'd wanted so badly to go back and find it. Why? It was a gift. It had to be. You don't care that much about something you bought at Macy's.

Wait. Where is it? The pocket is empty. I search around in there, beginning to panic. My hand makes contact with my wallet, my hairbrush, a folded compact whose mirror came unglued long ago. A package of mint gum, a folded grocery list. The purse, the road—oh, shit! I slam on my brakes. My fender is a mere inch from the stopped car in front of me. The driver's eyes glare from the rearview mirror. I send profuse mental apologies. The cars have slowed down. We are sitting in traffic now, and I'm going to be late.

A pen, its separated cap, a lipstick—where, where, where? My fingers find some loose change covered in a layer of something sticky. Ah, okay. The smooth jade and gold of that cuff link. Relief. The cuff link is a key in every definition of the word: a clue, but also an object that unlocks a door and sets you free.

Someone gave him that cuff link, and that someone was important enough for him to disappear for. It's the last theory I've got. If not that, then something else happened. Something horrible. I can't think about that.

I switch my gaze; now the game is clock-traffic. I hate being late. I get crazy anxious when I'm late, even in my regular life. It's that profound sense of responsibility again. Or, wait. Maybe it's not that at all. Maybe I'm just too much of a coward to face another person's anger. This suddenly occurs to me. It's a revelation, right there on the 520 bridge. All this time, I've both faulted and congratulated my ultra-responsible self. But she hasn't been as accountable and organized and respectful as I liked to think, has she? She's only been afraid.

Hurry, I plead with the cars. I am dying of heat, beginning to sweat badly. She will see the sweat marks. I roll up my window and try the air conditioner, which hasn't worked well since old Blue was a baby. We inch along, and then, without explanation for the holdup, the traffic loosens and we're moving again. Finally, I'm over the bridge and heading toward the mountain foothills. Even though I'd been out this direction to meet Bethy and Kristen not two days before, this is different. This time I have to drive in to my old neighborhood, past the street where my former house is. Past the swimming pool, and the park where Abby played baseball. Past the elementary school where Abby went. There is a memory on every corner. We rode our bikes there; we had a Mother's Day picnic *there*. We have a picture of Abby in her plaid skirt in front of that JFK ELEMENTARY sign; she's holding her Princess Jasmine backpack on the first day of kindergarten.

I feel a distinct pull when I arrive at my former street. I want to turn and settle into that driveway. I want to unpack some groceries, head up to my old bedroom, and get my cozy clothes on.

There'd been the comfort of routine and familiarity in that place, *home*. But the sick heaviness in my stomach is conveying mixed feelings; it reminds me of the bad memories, too—the raised fists, the anger, the devastation of divorce, and that fax machine by the burbling aquarium, all long gone. Someone else lives there now. Who knows what's in the corner where the aquarium was. Still, the rosebushes out front are ones I planted. I put the bulbs into that ground. Those are my flowers that come up year after year, even though I'm not there anymore.

I don't turn. There's no time for sentimental forays. Besides, it would be too painful to see the house, or to happen upon an old neighbor who still lives there, whose life hasn't changed like mine has. I go on, toward Mary's house. Ian and Mary's house. It looks different. The trees have grown. After living in the city, it seems like the lawns here have gotten wider, the road, too. But these houses are showing their age. The paint colors and the tall, arched brick entryways are almost from another era, when every garage had room for three cars and every bathroom had two sinks. The enormous faux-cement pots from Costco are faded. The tan trim of the windows looks dated.

It's the same driveway, though. So many things change and don't change. Mark had driven up this curve of cement with me as his wife in the passenger seat, a much younger Abby in the back. It had been filled with cars for that party. A badminton net had been stuck in the grass. But today there is only a sprinkler attached to a garden hose set in the center of the lawn. On this warm day, the hose might burn a snake shape into the lawn. Ian would have hated that. I know that about him now, but I never would have guessed it about him the day we first pulled up that drive.

I turn my engine off. My phone is in my lap, and so I return it to my purse. I notice ink on my fingers. There was that pen without a cap, and I'd marked myself with several frenzied lines of blue.

The door has a big gold knocker in the shape of a family crest. It looks intimidating, as door knockers generally do. Using it would be a particular kind of bold move, a statement, versus the polite, less-intrusive song of the doorbell. I ring the bell. I hear a dog go crazy, barking, running toward the door full speed. I hear toenails sliding on wood. I didn't know Mary got a dog. Yes, there he is. I can see his fluffy white face appearing and disappearing in the glass of the side window as he jumps up and down. He's letting me know he has things handled in this place.

"Shush, shush, shush," I hear Mary say, and the door opens.

Mary. She looks different than I remembered. Her face is plain; she'd grown prettier in my imagination over the years. She's gained weight. The boobs that had been a focus of so much attention don't seem sexual anymore, only heavy and ancillary. She wears a violet velour jogging suit and a pair of jeweled sandals. I'm not the only one who is mismatched with the weather.

We'd never spoken after their divorce. Not once. And yet she and I have a relationship that's as full and complex as the one I have with Ian. She's been in my head and in his over the years, and she's hovered over our relationship, steadfast and vengeful, a devoted ghost. But here she is, a regular woman in the flesh, too, with flashing eyes and with her dog under one arm now.

"So annoying." I think she means me, until she squeezes the dog closer to her. She steps aside to let me in. "It's cooler in here," she said. "We've added air-conditioning."

"You got a dog, too." It's an inane comment on my part, yet the dog surprises me. We haven't spoken in years, but I know so much about her. I know that she looked at a million swatches before she had her couch reupholstered and that her mother had gall bladder surgery last year. I know that she was a virgin when she married Ian and that she's afraid of deep water.

"Ken says he curses the day I brought her home. Sophie," she croons. "Be a good, quiet girl." She sets the dog on the floor. Sophie jumps up and sniffs my pant legs intently, getting to know Pollux in his absence. They've never met, but I'm sure she knows plenty about him now. "He says he doesn't even like dogs, but he treats her like his little baby."

Ken. The mention of him so soon—I wonder what it means. Honestly, in all my imaginings, I haven't given Ken that much thought. He's Mary's longtime boyfriend, but they've never married. He'd be easily shoved aside, I've always assumed, if Ian chose to come home. Ian is the lost prize; Ken is someone to go to the movies with.

Mary brushes white dog hair from her velvety top. "Look at this," she says. "What a mess." I follow her past the formal living room, which looks somber and unused—beige carpet, beige brocade couch, beige brocade chairs; a new crystal chandelier that Ian would despise for its drippy excess. Ian and I sat on the floor in that room long ago, listening to his music as the party went on outside. Oh, I don't belong here. It's the house of my rival, and now, inside, all her private details are available to me. They feel embarrassing. Stepping over the threshold seems as wrong as looking in her underwear drawer.

Mary makes her way through the kitchen and into the adjoining family room. She's rearranged the furniture and has painted the room a new color, an unsettling deep olive. That's another thing you do after divorce: You paint. You rearrange the bookshelves or get new ones. You hope Bermuda Pink in the bedroom or Courtyard Green in the bath will cover over the history there. Fresh paint can smell like a fresh start, and he'd have *never* agreed to Bermuda Pink, so it's all you, powerful you, the master of your home and your destiny. I did it myself. Haystack Yellow in our bedroom.

Mary gestures to the large leather couch that bends into an

L-shape. It's huge enough for any Super Bowl party. The television in front of me is the size of a billboard. Why is everything so large in the suburbs? On the coffee table, there's the television guide that came in the Sunday paper, and a box of cheese crackers. The box of cheese crackers is so big, it could feed a tribal village. There's a hairy dog bed in the corner of the room, several dog toys strewn about, and on the side table, an enormous picture of Bethy in her senior year. Her face glows and she looks upward as if pondering her bright future. Someone made pancakes this morning. The smell of them lingers, and I can see the handle of the pan sticking up from the sink.

I try to imagine Ian here. Even though I have memories of him in this room, I can't for the life of me see him here now.

I sit, but Mary remains standing. She folds her arms in front of her. The niceties of weather and dogs are gone. I'm trapped in the plush leather folds of that couch. I might need help getting out. For years she's likely wished to have me cornered. I'm sure she'd love to give me a piece of her mind, and I wouldn't blame her if she did. I'm not afraid, though. More, the purple velour and the Super Bowl couch make me feel a sadness I can't name, and the jeweled sandals hit me with a guilt I always knew I had but never comprehended the depths of. I wait. I wish for and dread what she might say. It's coming—information about Ian that even Bethy and Kristen don't have.

But Mary only stands there with the angry folded arms and glaring eyes of a vice principal dealing with a disrespectful ninth-grader.

"Mary . . ." Where to go from here?

"I don't know what you want from me."

"I thought you might know something," I venture. It's weak. Pathetic. I am hating that weakness more and more.

"Well, I don't. This sounds like a personal problem between you and him."

I weigh this. Would she keep his secrets? Certainly she'd want me to suffer as she had. Why *would* she tell me if she knew where he was? "He's been gone over a week, Mary. I'm worried sick. I'm trying everything, everyone. . . . I think we might need to go public."

She shrugs. "Do what you want. Maybe he just needs time to think."

Standing over me like that, she seems huge. In my head, she's always towered over both of us. "Has he . . ." I can't say it. *Has he talked to you? Come to you for friendship, or more?*

Her laugh is scornful. "You think I know something you don't? Is that what this is about? Because I don't know him anymore. I don't know what's in his head! I haven't known for years. Ever since he started up with *you*. And, in case you haven't figured this out yet, he's your problem now."

"I deserve that."

"You deserve at least that."

I want to apologize. I've wanted to apologize for years. But it's not the time. The purple velour and the folded arms and the blazing eyes tell me it'll likely never be the time.

"I was under the impression that you soul mates would never even have marital problems like us regular people."

"Mary . . ." It was a mistake to come. She doesn't know anything. She doesn't know one damn thing about where he is, either.

She marches across the room. She places her palms flat on the kitchen counter, faces me down. "You're not exactly the person I want to have in my home."

My home—the pronoun sets a fence around the word. My home, my marriage, my husband, my child—the verbal equivalents of those medieval villages set on high rock pinnacles. They kept invaders out that way. "I'm sure I'm not."

"Hardly the person."

"I wouldn't have come unless I had to."

She shrugs again, rolls her eyes dramatically. *So?* I should never have come, never, never, never. The wrongness landslides. I can't picture him here, not at all. I try to imagine him standing beside her, putting his arms around her, the two of them entwined in bed together, and I can't see it. They *were* mismatched, terribly. It is so clear. Another great irony: You find your soul mate, you go through hell to be together, and then, every day afterward, you doubt it'll last.

She doesn't even know me, he'd said so long ago. *She doesn't know who I am. It's not my house. It's not even my life.*

The dried-flower arrangement in a large basket on the kitchen table, the tall faux-gold candlesticks meant to look like they'd come from an Italian villa—it *isn't* his life. Not then, and certainly not anymore.

"What is it you want from me? What *else?*"

I have to know this, anyway. "My mother. She said she saw the two of you in that restaurant. The day before he went missing."

Mary is back in the family room again. She is smiling, nodding her head, pleased. It's the kind of bitter pleasure you get when you realize you've been right all along. "He didn't tell you about it himself." She sits down in the matching leather lounge chair across from me. She stares at me with her blue eyes. Pretty blue eyes, I notice. Lovely, really. Ian said that he had fallen in love with her because he'd been especially lonely at that time in his life. She was social and vibrant, Catholic like his mother, a virgin. But he might have fallen in love with those eyes, too.

"No. He didn't tell me."

"Well, isn't that rich."

I trace the threads on the leg of my jeans with my fingernail. Up, down, in a small square of the tight, intricate weave. The regret and the guilt and the anger all merge into shame.

"Wait," she says.

I look up. The dog has curled up on her bed, and now she watches the proceedings as if they're a salacious but slightly tedious episode of some real-life courtroom trial on television. Mary had loved those shows, I remember. It was one of Ian's complaints, the way she spent her days. He judged. He still judges.

"I get it now. I get why you're here. You don't just think I have information. You think I'm the *reason* he left." She is laughing. "Ian! Come downstairs!" she calls. "Let's break the news to her!" Her voice rises with sarcasm. She tosses her head in disgust. On her bed, Sophie scratches vigorously with one small hind leg. "This is too much, you know that? We met because I *asked* to meet. I didn't want him to hear it from the girls. It seemed only right that it should come from me. You two didn't give me that courtesy."

She holds up her left hand to show me the ring.

"Ken and I are getting married."

I'm shocked. This is a complete surprise. Somehow I thought we'd sit in our triangle for the rest of our lives—Mary wanting Ian, me wanting Ian, Ian in some state of perpetual indecision no matter what roof he was under. I thought the story would go on forever.

"I wanted to tell him personally. Don't you think that's the respectful thing to do? We were married for seventeen years. We have children."

"Yes."

"*Ken* is a good man."

"I'm glad." I mean that. I *am* glad. But had *this* contributed to

Ian's disappearance? Maybe he'd been destroyed by the news. First Nathan's offer, and then Mary's terrible announcement? I'd always had the feeling that Ian thought of Mary as his backup plan. She was there in his old house, patiently waiting for the moment when he'd had enough. She'd open the door and welcome him home with his favorite meal on the table.

She answers the question I haven't asked. "He wasn't bothered in the least. I don't know what I was expecting—maybe a slight show of emotion? It was like sitting with a stranger, and I've known him since I was eighteen. He seemed relieved. For so many years, in the beginning, anyway, he'd acted so jealous, he couldn't stand it if anyone even looked in my direction, and now he couldn't care less. I'm getting *married* and, big deal, so what."

Jealous? Mary at those parties, playing with Mark's tie, flirting with Neal and the other men—Ian hadn't appeared to be bothered at all. He hadn't even flinched. It never occurred to me that he'd been jealous with her, too. It had never even crossed my mind.

"He said he was happy for me. And you know what? I think he was."

I hear the rumble of a garage door going up. "That's Ken now," she says. "He comes home every day at lunch to see me."

Ken barrels through the garage door, carrying bags. "Sweetie pie!" he calls. "I'm home!" He's a big man, with hair combed over his head and a stomach that presses out like a basketball against his buttoned shirt. I know things about him, too, even though we've never met, things dropped into the conversation by Bethy or Kristen. He has season tickets to the Husky games. His own son has a drug problem. He loves hot wings and blue cheese dressing. He once thought he was having a coronary and went to the emergency room, only to find out that it was an anxiety attack.

I saw a picture of him once. He was on a boat with Bethy, on a trip they'd taken to Lake Chelan. His bathing suit has a blue Hawaiian print.

He takes the six-pack of beer from the bag and sets it down on the kitchen table before he notices me. Ian bought that kitchen table. And those bar stools. And that Sub Zero refrigerator.

"Ah! Hello there! Three for lunch?" Ken says jovially. Mary was right. Sophie is jumping on Ken like he's a soldier returning home unharmed from the war, and he picks her up and nuzzles her. The joy-filled reunion is a mutual affair.

"This is Ian's *wife*," Mary says.

Ken freezes dramatically, for effect. He's acting out the stage direction that says, *Ken freezes in his tracks.* He sets Sophie back down; she continues to jump around, wondering where the love has gone. "Well, damn. I need one of these, then." You can tell by the hard, round ball of his stomach that any excuse will do. How lucky that I've provided such a solid one. He twists the cap of one of the beers, takes a swig. "Damn."

"I had to tell her that we don't have Ian hidden in the bedroom."

"For the record, that guy's not going near our bedroom. If he's not dead in a ditch somewhere, then he's a sick bastard to let his daughters worry like this."

In my head, the teams are changing fast. Ian is still mine to defend. "We don't know what's happened. Anything could've—"

Mary interrupts me. "'Anything'? I don't believe 'anything.' He wouldn't have had some accident. That would involve making a mistake, and Ian doesn't make mistakes, in his view." She takes one of the beers and hands it to Ken. He twists off the cap for her and hands it back. "All I know is, they're going to have a lot of questions for the person who saw him last."

I know what she's implying. They've all obviously had their

little powwows. I'm done here, in this place that's no longer Ian's. I get up. I reach for my purse.

"I hope he comes back, really I do. For my daughters' sake. But I have to tell you something." She points her finger at me in case I'm confused about who's being addressed. "You've looked at me with pity? Don't. You did me a favor. Here's one reason, right here." I think she means Ken. I'm expecting her to wrap her arms around his big tight belly, but instead she flicks the handle of that pan in the sink. "I can keep this pan in this sink for however long I like and it's not saying anything about the kind of person I am. See this?" She plucks her shirt again. "He hated me in purple."

"Purple brings out your eyes," Ken, ever the ass kisser, says.

Mary ignores him. "Freedom," she says.

I'm silent. I think it for the millionth time, I do: I admire her courage.

"I'll show you out."

I can hear Ken in the kitchen, crooning lovey-dog talk to Sophie. I've forgotten something. I reach into my purse. "I'm sorry. But . . ." I hold the cuff link in my palm. It's a question.

"He still has those?" she asks.

"From you?"

"From *me*? I hope I have better taste than that. They were from his *father*. Given on Ian's eighteenth birthday. Paul had a pair just like them. *Congratulations, you're a man like me.* What, is he wearing them now? He never wore them when the guy was alive."

His father—*this* was why they were so important?

"The great Paul Hartley Keller," Mary says.

Mary opens the door for me. We look at each other for a moment. She glances down at my hands. One holds the cuff link, and the other has the frantic lines of ink from my uncapped pen.

There's so much to say. I want to pour out my regrets and apologies for the pain I've caused her. I open my mouth to speak, but she gets there before me.

"All this time, I thought you were so powerful," she says.

She closes the door on me and my unfinished business. Through the porch window, I see her figure disappear into the kitchen to join Ken and Sophie. Some things are too big for naïve, tidy apologies.

And then, as I hunt for my keys and get in my car, I think of something I haven't thought about in years. That time when we went for drinks after that concert, Mark and me and Ian and Mary and those other two couples. Mary had been laughing and telling that story about how she'd damaged their car. *You're careless*, Ian had said to her, and I'd felt embarrassed for her, and guilty. It was cruel of him.

I had thought it was who he was inside an unhappy marriage. But it was who he was, period.

I remember something Dr. Shana Berg once told me, that a person generally brings their same self wherever they go. They bring that self to their coworkers and neighbors and to the man who works at the bank and to the guy in front of them who is still sitting at the light when it turns green. They bring that self to every girlfriend and every pet and every wife.

I unlock my car door and toss my purse to the passenger seat. It still has that damn cuff link inside. All at once, I am overwhelmed with sorrow—for Mary, for me, for our children. But maybe most of all for Ian himself. Maybe there was nowhere, no home, this one or ours, where he could be at peace.

I am overwhelmed with sorrow, but I am also something else. Something terrifying.

I am out of options.

15

Old Blue is droning and clunking. The poor baby is critically ill. I feel the dire urgency to get home. Beyond *urgency*—it's a clawing, scratching imperative. It's thunderous buffalo hooves charging over barren land, a rabbit fleeing from a cougar.

It's the heat. Or else I'm having a heart attack. What are the signs? I've read them over and over again in women's magazines. Shortness of breath? Something about pain down the arm, sharp pain, and, yes, I've got that, too. Pain down the arm, pain down both arms, pain radiating from my heart like a sunburst. My palms are sweating. The coffee I drank that morning tumbles and lurches in my stomach.

There's barely any traffic on the bridge, and so I drive as fast as my car allows. Blue Beast seems to be shivering, but I press down on the accelerator, passing a careful driver going the speed limit. The driver is a woman with swooped-up hair and glasses, and she shoots me a look of disapproval. She probably hates people who talk in the library, too, but so do I. People who drive like this—the teen boys who whip wildly around cars, making narrow cutoffs, the ones you see only a vehicle ahead of you at the stop sign at the overpass turnoff—got my mental lectures, too.

See? I'd say to them. *Lotta good that did you, and you could have killed someone.* I'd have given them the look she gave me. She and I—we're about the same age. Whatever she's doing—heading home, going to work, seeing a friend in the city—it's not what I am doing, driving while having a heart attack, fighting some urge to turn fast into the wall of the tunnel I'm passing through. Right now I would choose her life over mine. Door number two, whatever's behind it. I'd take her hated job or her lawsuit or the little bump she'd found in her breast that's worrying her.

I should drive to the nearest emergency room, I think. I'd ditch my car in front and run in and they would put me in a blue cotton gown that tied in the back and smelled like bleach, and they'd cover me with a heated blanket that smelled like bleach, too, that certain hospital bleach, the smell I remembered from Abby being born. The automatic doors I'd walk through would shut and no one could get in to find me. Stern nurses and doctors wearing scrubs and those shower caps for shoes would make sure to keep everyone out of my room. I want a needle in my arm. The cool sheets, the bliss of rest.

Dani, Danielle! You're fine. You're fine! You're okay. My inner . . . who? Mother, God, nurse? She tries to sound soothing. *This falling-apart stuff is no good. It won't help anything. Get it together*, she says.

I don't know what I've done, I confess to her. *I think I've done something horrible.*

That cogent thought, the first admitted one, brings everything rushing up—remorse and Mary and grief and Ian and fear— and I make it through that tunnel and pull off to the side of the road. It occurs to me that people often get hit when they get out of their cars on the freeway to change a tire or investigate an accident. I picture the impact, my body flying, but there are few cars, and this is not what threatens me most.

I heave. I throw up only the morning coffee and fear. The body doesn't know what to do with terror. This is all it can do, and it is certainly not enough.

The Blue Beast makes it home. It sighs with relief when I finally put it into park in its gravel spot. Oh, it is so weary. But I don't sigh with relief. The terror, which is some sort of hunched beast in a dark coat inside my own body, gets down on its haunches. Alarm shoves it aside, sleek and fast, like one of those thin, skeletal dogs I don't like, with the tightly stretched skin and the heads that look like skulls found in a desert. The alarm is there because I see a tow truck on our street. Ian's car is hovering mid-air, set on a red sci-fi Transformer arm—a comical look under other circumstances, one that brings to mind mechanical creatures invading innocent cities. Ian would die seeing it manhandled like that. It seems unnatural, the way its vulnerable underside is exposed. The sight of it is devastating. The fact of the matter is this: Any image of Ian on a beach somewhere is shattered right now as that car is being readied to be taken away.

My mother is standing on the street, watching it, and the guy who checks groceries at Pete's is watching her, because she's yelling. One hand is on her hip, and the other is waving around. She's wearing an innocent little pair of capris and a white T-shirt, and she looks pretty stylish considering that she's losing her mind.

I'm in no shape to do damage control, but she leaves me no choice. Her face is red. "I don't know what you people are doing! Nothing happened to him in that fucking car! Try actually looking for the man, how about that, you goddamn useless idiots!"

She has a mouth and she knows how to use it, I think inanely, but

I am praying she'll shut it. She can only do more and more harm. I run toward her.

"Stop that!" I say. The man operating the tow truck ignores her. I don't understand the procedure here. Is he a cop, too, or is he a tow-truck guy who has a police-department gig on the side? How does it work exactly?

"Dani." My mother is out of breath. Her eyes look wild. Maybe she's the one having the heart attack. Maybe the psychic was right after all.

"Stop that," I snap at her. "Stop yelling! This will do no good."

"Other people were here before, taking pictures of the car. Looking through it. Putting stuff in plastic bags. Then this guy came . . ."

Other people—she doesn't say *police*.

"What do they think?" she says, but we both know. We know what we're afraid of.

The tow truck driver gets out now. He leaves the door open. He heads toward us. He's bald, and he has glasses, large ones that were in style in the 1980s. He has the start of a gray beard, or else he just hasn't shaved. His shirt is blue, the kind prisoners wear. The word *denim* escapes me. He carries a clipboard over to where we stand.

"Don't sign anything," my mother says.

These are the things she knows. *Don't sign anything you haven't read. Get a receipt. Don't give out your credit-card number over the phone. Better yet, don't use a credit card unless it's for emergencies. Credit is a fast road to ruin.*

I sign where he indicates. He looks at me. I know what he's thinking. He's gauging my capacity for wrongdoing. He's staring at my face, wondering what I've done and how I've done it.

But I might be mistaken about that. "You have . . .": he says.

He raises his hand to his own cheek, brushing something off. I put my hand to my cheek, where he's indicated. Vomit.

"You people," my mother sneers.

"Stop," I say. "He's only doing his job."

He smiles. He actually smiles. He tucks his clipboard under his arm. "All righty."

"Thank you," I say. Dear, dear God, why did I say that? Why, why, why? It's a habit, a terrible habit. Here it is again, what I've done for years, madly flinging politeness and compliments at people, the way you throw steaks to a lion. When I've been in danger, I've done it, and when I haven't been in danger, I've done it, too, because how can we ever be sure which is which? Yes, a person generally brings their same self to any circumstance, to tow-truck drivers and furnace repairmen, to snarling, vicious dogs who do not see the innocence of your pizza box. To husbands.

The car disappears down the street on that truck. It's like I'm watching Ian leave. My heart is squeezing and squeezing. I miss him so much I want to fall on my knees. My heart is cracking open. I want to cry out to him to come back. To please, please come back.

He's not coming back. Maybe I do know this after all. *Goodbye,* I say to him in my head. I say it tenderly. I try to tell him with that one word how sorry I am.

My mother is already inside the houseboat, and she's on the phone.

"I'll hold," I hear her say.

She looks at me and then away, staring out at the lake instead. Pollux tries to be positive, giving a small leap, but then he smells the betrayal on my pant legs. Some other dog. He sniffs madly, as if searching my phone for my lover's number. I caught Ian looking at my phone once. No, here's the truth: more than once.

I give Pollux a treat to make it up to him. These are the normal things that I still must do, and this continues to astonish me. How can it be so? Give the dog a treat, change my clothes, pee. They are the odd things that don't belong here right now. I hear Abby on the phone, too. I try to listen in but can't hear much of anything. I put my old sundress on now, and clothing relief washes over me. Ah, it's one of the best feelings, clothing relief, when stockings, or too tight jeans, or a shirt that's new but somehow not you after all, are finally stripped off.

I don't know what to do.

I don't have any idea, and I'm not sure I'm in my own body. The panic has turned to numb horror, and I'm moving underwater and trying to breathe underwater. I can hear Abby in the living room. "Thank you very much," she says. "We would appreciate that. Yes. I'll send you one right now."

My mother also finishes her call. "Thank you. We'll see you then." We are all so polite and grateful and full of fear.

Abby joins us in the kitchen. My mother is speaking only to her. "He's in trial now and all day tomorrow, but his secretary promised he'll get in touch first thing in the morning."

"Okay." Abby nods, as if agreeing to a plan. "They're putting it on the news tonight. KING and KIRO. I've got to send them a picture in the next half hour to make the deadline."

She looks through her phone, punching and scrolling with adept thumbs. "This is good." She shows the phone to my mother, who nods. Then she shows it to me—a photo of Ian that she took—and I also nod. We've all agreed, it seems, on this course of action. Or, rather, they've agreed, and I am going along like a timid and newly hired junior partner. The photo was taken a few months ago, when Ian and I and Abby and Jon, a boy she'd been seeing, went out for the day on the *New View*. It doesn't look that much like Ian; or, rather, it's a version of Ian you don't see too often. His hair is messed from the wind, and he's wearing a gray sweatshirt. You can tell he's on a boat. You can see the bow behind him and the blue of the water, and he looks like an outdoorsman, which he isn't, not really. He's smiling. He looks relaxed. He looks happy.

I almost step in it, the small puddle in the kitchen. No one has thought to take Pollux out. This is what happens when you don't pay attention. I get the paper towels.

"Oh, great, Poll. Super," Abby says.

"Don't," I tell her. It isn't fair—we are the ones who've been careless.

Pollux sees the roll of paper towels and lowers his head. His eyes are sad.

"It's okay," I say to him. "You didn't mean to." I throw away the soggy paper and squirt the floor with Windex. I wash my hands. I go to him and speak into his sweet black neck. "It's not your fault," I whisper.

But he has had enough of his own shame and of my forgiveness. I think he's sick of that whole game. He escapes from my hug and settles down by the glass door, groaning like an old man. He puts his chin on his paws. He stares out at the *New View* and the now choppy waves, and he sighs through his nose.

Of course, it only gets worse and worse: You find your soul mate, you go through hell to be together, but then he doesn't trust you. And then he pecks away at you with his criticism. And then every day afterward you doubt it'll last. And then you wonder how you could have gotten this so wrong. You try to hold on to what made you so crazy for him in the first place. You try very hard to remember what you love.

There are the ways in which you share your life, for one thing. *Share your life*—a phrase like that, it's such a cliché that the words lose meaning. They're valentine and love-song words. But if you do hear them, honestly hear them, they're rather beautiful. To share your life, to have someone beside you who witnesses it— it's the best kind of beautiful; as good as it gets.

A glass of wine would get poured as we waited for dinner to be finished.

Today, when I was having lunch? I was sitting outside at Salvatore's. A woman walking this big German shepherd is coming one way, and this mom with a little girl is coming the other. She's got pink rubber boots on, so she's clunking along.

Seattle kid, with a tiara and a tutu with *the boots?* I asked.

Yeah, but this one is cute. She's about down here. Ian held his hand just above his knee. *And the dog is right down there at her level, and she turns to her mom with her arms up in the air and she says, "Hug!" Not "Up," but "Hug!" Really frantic, like, "Emergency! Hug!"*

That is so cute. I love that so much.

I knew you would.

Imagine if something that big was looking you *in the eyes?*

With those teeth?

Hug!

I would tell him I noticed the maples changing on Ravenna Avenue, and he would tell me he thought his colleague, Mike Reynolds, had a drinking problem. I'd explain in great detail why the pair of jeans I bought were such a super deal, and he'd tell me about the comedian he heard on the radio on the way to work.

My mother bought a new Bible, he shouted in my direction one Saturday afternoon as we paddled kayaks on the lake.

Who buys a new Bible?

Maybe it was new and improved.

His hand would be on my bare hip as rain fell on the roof. His socks would be tumbled with mine when they came out warm from the dryer.

Do you want to try the calamari? His reading glasses would be down his nose as he studied the menu in the dim light of the restaurant.

I've tried calamari.

That's right. The tentacles.

Exactly. The little round pieces that don't have tentacles, fine. But you take your chances. They might put the creepy ones in there.

Hmm, remember? We talked about that in one of our first phone conversations. Food that looks like the animal you're eating.

You told me you couldn't eat fish if you'd seen their eyes.

Honestly, I sometimes have to actively ignore chicken wings.

Let's get the wild mushrooms.

You are both silent after you pass the car accident on the highway. You walk through a department store with opulent Christmas decorations and the bell-ringers out front. He points out the full moon. You ask him to pick up razors for you at the store. You bake him a birthday cake, and he runs back to fetch your purse at the restaurant where you forgot it. You share your life.

Sometimes I would see him anew. Do you know this, do you know what I mean? You catch a glimpse of your beloved, and it's just him you see, not your history or the worries in your own head or the mood of the house in the last weeks, just *him*. His sweet, soft hair. That scar at the bridge of his nose that he got playing sixth-grade flag football. Him being him, in his very own moment, pouring his own self a glass of grapefruit juice while wearing his T-shirt and jeans. He's got bare feet. Suddenly, unawares, you're overcome with tenderness. Your love is like glass, lovely and transparent, fragile, but stronger than you think. You can see the world through it.

When his words pluck you from the air mid-flight, then, and when he pins you and puts the cotton ball of cyanide over your nose: Coming from someone who *shares your life*, it is the worst kind of betrayal.

Ian went to Kristen's graduation anyway, even though he'd been asked not to come. He hid in the back of the gym so he wouldn't be seen. He left before the end, when the families descended and flowers were given and pictures taken.

It was like I was stealing something, when they're my *children. My own babies.*

He spat those words bitterly and turned away from me. As Ian stomped up the stairs and slammed our bedroom door, I flashed on an image of Mark from when I was still in the hospital after Abby was born. Mark had never been happier. He loved babies. (You wouldn't have thought it after what I've described, would you? But no man, no anyone, is ever just an angry person. They are tender and silly and confused, that's the problem. No person is ever one thing, angry or unfaithful or critical or guilty or victimized or weak or strong; do you hear what I'm saying?)

In the hospital, I was wearing a new robe Mark had bought me. It was more expensive than we could afford, and it was so plush, with its striped shades of peach and blue. I'd been looking for him, wobbling down the hall while clutching my newly deflated stomach, because he'd left with Abby in her cocoon blanket. He wanted to let me sleep, but I had woken up and was desperate to see her again. It was as if he'd walked away with my heart or my lungs. I needed her back. Finally, I found him on a green plastic couch in a waiting room. A television was on in the high corner of the ceiling, but he wasn't watching it. No, he was staring down at Abby's tiny face and her rosebud lips, as if he couldn't believe his eyes. He had his pinkie finger in her mouth, and she was sucking on it. I could see how much he loved her.

It felt important to remember that Ian, too, had swaddled his daughters and cradled their small heads and kissed those fat baby cheeks that smelled like apple juice. They once rode on his back and danced on his feet and he took them trick-or-treating, their eyes slightly scared behind their princess masks.

And now they'd made him (and he'd made himself) the jilted lover. He called endlessly. He sent flowers. He begged, and they turned away.

It was too high a price. He said this. *It's too high a price.*

It was also too late to be doing the math.

I wish you wouldn't do that.

Do what?

You were biting your nails. Do you realize you were biting your nails? It's crass.

My heart was in his teeth, as he used to say, and he bit down. No matter how much empathy I attempted to deploy, no matter how hard I tried to see the reasons I loved him, late at night I knew the truth. Way before I went to see Mary, long before he disappeared, I knew it. Dr. Shana Berg had even spoken it, but it wasn't something I wanted to hear back then.

Darkness insists on honesty, doesn't it? Any late hour is brutal with the facts. This is what I came to realize during those sleepless nights after his children had rejected him and after he had turned cruel: Ian and I were not being destroyed by the situation we'd made, but by the ways in which we'd inevitably, with time, revealed ourselves.

Abby phones Bethy and Kristen to let them know the alert is airing. Detective Jackson has provided a phone number for any leads we might get. Now we watch for Ian on the news. When they show his picture, my mother gasps and I have to leave the room. That picture belongs to us. Just after it was taken on our boat, we'd eaten white cheddar on crackers and drunk wine, and that gray sweatshirt is in our closet. I can't bear it. I remember the time when Ian had his picture in the *Puget Sound Business Journal*. He tried to act nonchalant about it, but there are still about ten copies of the article in our spare room. He turned into a bit of an ass for a while afterward. He'd get irritated about taking out the garbage or scraping grease from a chicken pan, and he dressed more beautifully, wearing his cashmere jacket to work, when he never wore his cashmere jacket to work. He was proud of appearing in the press, and I was proud of him, too.

Now, after this piece airs, the phone rings and rings. All night. Not leads—these will be phoned in to the police station, we hope. No, this is everyone who didn't know before now that Ian has disappeared. I never realized we had so many people in our lives. A high school friend of Ian's, Keith Machelli—never heard of him—calls; so does Cathy something, from Très, where he gets his hair cut. There are messages from Fran Sorrel, who was in my old book group, and Jan Clementine, same group. They'd probably stayed close and phoned each other right away. Yeah. They were good friends, if I remembered correctly. I'd forgotten all about them. I'd forgotten these people that I used to see every Thursday night. I'd followed their story line on a weekly basis and then promptly ditched them from my memory after we'd gone our separate ways. There are messages from a former client of mine, Mandy Shepard, and from current ones—Mrs. Yakimora, the accountant, and Jeannie Shore, who teaches Mommy and Me art classes. Ian's old mentor, Bob Good, phones, and so does my next-door neighbor in the suburbs, Margaret Choy. Abby's baseball coach from years ago, Greg Lippincott, leaves a message, too. My father sends his support for this new course of action but grimly urges me to "understand the likelihoods at this point." Nathan has called. And called. And called.

I need to phone him back, but I can't right now. I can't face his kindness.

"I'm making more flyers," Abby says. This has become her corner of operations, and she attacks the job with the no-nonsense vigor of a sergeant in the midst of battle. "The other ones are wet and falling off, and we should use the picture from the news."

There are foam containers of takeout on the counter, and the phone rings and rings and rings. Abby is making the new flyer on her laptop at the kitchen table, and my mother is talking to her good friend Joyce, and I can feel the situation unspooling. The room had been filled with three butterflies and now there are twenty and now two hundred and the gossamer threads that created their beautiful wings are unraveling and unraveling, falling to the floor in ugly, tangled heaps. I need to do something, more than this, more than helplessness or thinking of possibilities that lead nowhere, more than errant cuff links and betrayals that aren't. There *are* no more possibilities. I should put a stop to all of it. I should say it, before anyone says it to me: There is that lie, that letter I never sent to Ian, and mud on the plastic mats of Ian's car and on our sheets.

There is that dream, and that memory, and those damn pills. A black hole of forgetting. Is there a secret self I am not willing to see? If it *was* me, if I have done something . . . *Please, let it not be so.* I need to stop this mad, pointless unraveling, this panicked fluttering. I am making fools of the good people around me.

The problem, the biggest, most insurmountable problem, is that I can't visualize him home that night. Can I see his hand on that key, opening the door? Can I remember anything, him laying down his jacket, his keys on the counter, him telling me good night? His hand on the light switch, *anything*? Wait, go back. Can I see him getting out of the car, walking down the dock? Did I take his arm; did he say a word, any word? There is nothing. Only my dropped shoes, my own bed.

"Where are you going?" My mother holds the phone to her chest so Joyce won't hear.

"Out for a minute. I need to make a call."

My mother's eyes send distress signals. "They might watch your calls."

My stomach is an elevator descending, the cord cut. She thinks of everything.

"Dani . . ." She's pleading. I ignore her. I have a crazy thought: *When I go outside, will there be cameras and lights and microphones?* But it is only the same quiet night it always is. There's a fingernail moon—that's what we always call it; a narrow sliver. Old Joe Grayson has his soaker hoses on; I can hear them trickling pleasantly.

I need privacy, and there is none to be found on that dock. I head toward Pete's. I set my back against the far wall of the store, near the dumpsters, near the empty cardboard crates marked BEE SWEET CITRUS and CHIQUITA.

I will look guilty of something if someone sees me there.

You have reached the office of Dr. Shana Berg. If this is an emergency, please dial 911 . . .

I speak fast. "I'm not sure you remember me. I saw you a few years ago, during my divorce? This is Dani Keller. Dani Hastings? I know you're just getting back from a trip, but I'm hoping I can see you as soon as possible. Tomorrow? It's an emergency." Well, that's something people in their profession surely hear all of the time. A wife found cheating, razor blades on wrists, imminent job loss, and a life not worth living. "Not one I can dial 911 for," I clarify. The open phone line buzzes. "Please."

I hang up. I see a thin tail slide behind a box. You don't want to think it, but there are likely rats all around this place.

While I've been gone, Abby's friend Marcus has shown up, and so has her friend Hannah. Marcus has brought more printer paper and ink in an Office Depot bag. I like them both, I like them a lot, but not right now. The printer whirs and whirs and then jams up. Of course it's protesting these unfair working conditions, hours without a break, overtime. Marcus lifts the lid and he and Abby peer in to investigate, then they slam the lid shut again and the tired whirring resumes. Hannah is creating some website on her laptop, a missing-persons site; who knew. The first time I sent a fax, it was as if I'd witnessed water turning to wine. That was years ago. Still, I'm not young enough to believe that there's a technological solution to every problem. Ian's face stacks up on our desk, another Ian and another. I want to pull the plug of that printer. I want silence. The whirring, the jams, the Ian-faces—I can feel a scream inside, wanting out.

It is close to one in the morning.

"Let's call it a day, gang," my mother says. She's been nervously looking my way all night, as if I'm a bomb that might go off. She can tell that the visitors and the commotion are slicing my frayed nerves, or else they're doing the same to hers. We both understand something they don't. She looks exhausted. Her face is a shade of gray. She's brought me another one of those brown drinks on ice. One for her, too.

I hurry through the goodbyes and the thank-you's and then through the long, supportive hugs from Abby and my mother. I want to be alone. I need to think. I need to figure out the right thing to do.

Another day has passed, and another nightfall, in our dreaded bedroom. Ian's reading glasses are folded and sitting exactly where they've been for days now. In our bathroom, his razor stands up on its end in the cup, still and unused.

I go through it again. The things I know for sure:

The pills before the party. The wine. The need to leave, my aching feet. Something lost. An argument. Feet on wet grass. Fury.

An argument, and then what?

We are home. We. Is it we? Is he there? Is he even there? If only I could remember. I drop my shoes, yes. I get into bed with relief.

Weeks before, a letter. I write this down in a letter I don't send: *I am thinking of leaving you.* Finally this needs to be said, even if the thought of it is killing me. It's killing me because I've failed. I've failed twice. If a person brings the same self again and again to every relationship, if Ian had, so had I. In Ian, I had chosen Mark but not Mark. I had chosen rescue that wasn't rescue. Of course, in the butterfly world, mimicry makes it almost impossible to identify a toxic species. There are nontoxic butterflies with the markings of toxic ones, and there are toxic ones imitating one another. There are control freaks and out-of-control freaks, and at the end of the day they look pretty much the same.

And weeks before that, months—Kerry Park. My wrists pinned. *You've taken everything from me!* Struggling to get free.

Hands shoved against his chest. More strength than I knew I had.

Now that dream. We are back at Kerry Park. We go back because of that stupid cuff link. He is still furious, and so we return. *Fine! Fine, go back, then!* Wrists pinned. Hands shoved against his chest. He is going down, down that ravine.

I cannot remember him at our house that night when we arrived home. I have said that that is the biggest problem, but it isn't. There is something worse, much worse, and the very fact of it makes me sick with horror. The argument that night, it is the small seed-heart of a large growing fear, a guilt fear, which is blooming and climbing like a vine of ivy in a Grimm's fairy tale.

Not everything about me is your business.

Ian! Damn you! No shoes, wet grass, mud.

I grab his arm; I feel the possibility of rage.

What is wrong with you?

I see his furious eyes. I dig my nails into his arm. I do not want to face this fact, I am terrified to, but it is true: I hated him that night. That stupid outfit; the way he came up behind me and whispered that I'd been rude to Dennis Singh and his wife, Stella. *They said so?* I asked. *No, but you interrupted him.* And then Desiree Harris on the lawn and his refusal to say what he'd lost and needed to find . . . No, more than this. Way more. The years I waited for him. The ways I was never enough. His endless monitoring and criticisms and jealousies.

That night, I hated him. Dear God, I had.

I am still awake, and still awake. I get up. Maybe I will sit outside in that warm night and watch the lights of the city. To have those lights right there—it's such a privilege. I forget what a privilege it is. How often do I ever think to really see it and take it in? Maybe the fresh air and the rocking of the dock will calm me.

When I get up, I see that my mother is sitting awake, too. She is also looking out onto the lake, from the couch in the living room. Her feet are on Pollux, who is doing what he does best: giving comfort. I sit down beside her, and we stay like that. You don't sleep when the hunched man in the dark coat is inside your body. You don't sleep when the hours are closing in.

16

The doorbell wakes me. Sometime near sunrise, I'd gone back to my room and had fallen asleep. Now the doorbell is ringing, and Pollux is barking in a frenzy that speaks to his understanding that something is very wrong here. I'm disoriented; I see my phone next to me on Ian's pillow, and it has been ringing, too, I notice. The message light comes on. The doorbell has to wait. It's only nine o'clock in the morning, but my heart has already begun to thump hard. This must be what it's like to live as an animal—as prey, a deer, always alert, always in danger. No. Your heart would do this if you were a butterfly and you'd been caught in a net.

There are two messages. Neither is from Ian. He has been gone only ten days, and his voice is already hard to summon in my head. A person's voice must be the first thing to go, the first thing that flees your memory. I can see him, but I cannot hear him, unless I play his voice mail again. Regardless, he has not called. The attorney Frank Lazario has. He sounds about a hundred years old. And Dr. Shana Berg has called, too. She can see me at eleven o'clock, if I can make it. I can make it. I need answers, and a plan. I can't go on like this anymore.

I put on my robe. There is chaos downstairs now. Abby is shouting, and so is my mother. Who else? A woman. Is it Mary? I am rushing down the stairs. I hear a man's voice, too. My hand is shaking as I hold the rail. What now? *The car*, someone says. *You don't do that for no reason!*

You have no right! My mother shouts.

You can't just barge in here. Abby.

It's not Mary, but Bethy. It's Bethy and Adam, and Kristen is here, too, but she's not speaking. She's only standing there with her arms folded. Bethy's face is red and her mouth is open and twisted, ugly. Adam has one arm raised, and he's wearing a T-shirt with the grille of a truck on the front, and his resemblances to Mark are multiplying. He is a bully, all right, but his jawline has a cold-blooded, sadistic quality. He probably has to sleep under a lamp at night to keep his reptilian heart warm.

Bethy sees me on the stairs. "*You.*" She's shaking with hatred, years of it. "We want the truth. It's not so much to ask." She has Mary's eyes and Ian's bone structure. It's terrible to see him in her then, with that distorted, angry mouth.

"Is this how you want it to go?" Adam says to me. "Because it ain't going to be pretty."

"'It ain't going to be pretty,'" my mother mocks. "Do you think you're the sheriff in the western? Going to draw your gun, big shot? I can't believe you people. You shove your way in here—"

"*We* would have liked to talk to the TV station, but you said Dad wouldn't want that. Then you guys went ahead and did it anyway," Bethy says. "*We're* his kids."

"You call us, and then two seconds later it's on," Kristen says to Abby. "He's *our* dad."

"You're competing over *this* now?" my mother says.

Bethy glares. "Competing? Who's competing? There's never

been a contest. We know that. He's told us a million times! We come first! He's made that perfectly clear. Even if . . ." She waves her arm around, indicating me, this house, our marriage.

"I can't believe we're having this discussion now," I say.

"*Look* at what you've done." Bethy spits the words at me.

"Get the fuck out of here," Abby says.

"Dirty mouth. You're all *evil*," Bethy says. "Look at you. Immoral." Spittle flies from her mouth.

"Look at us? Look at *you*. You come ringing the doorbell like that, you come walking in here—"

"We deserve some answers."

I am in the entryway with them now. "I gave you answers. I gave you all the answers I have."

"Don't say a word. Not another word," my mother commands. She is shaking her finger at me.

"I just want to know where my daddy is. . . ." Kristen starts to cry.

"Believe me, I want nothing more than to—"

"What did you do to him?" Bethy steps toward me.

"You are *crazy*," Abby says.

"We want his things."

"Bethy . . ." This frustrates Adam. It's obviously not part of the plan.

"I want his things! I don't *want* his *things* to be *here* with *her*."

The urge to smack her rises up my arm, and I can feel it surging toward my hand. Hatred —I have more of it now. I have so much that there is a freight train in my chest.

"You people are nuts!" Abby says. "Who ran off here?"

"You want his things?"

"Mom, don't—"

"You want his fucking things?"

It's out of my mouth, and I know it's bad. It's bad and it gets worse, because the room has five hundred butterflies, a thousand, and they are fluttering so hard that silk threads in blues and greens and oranges are unspooling and unspooling and falling to the floor, rising piles of ruined pigment. "Fine." I turn and head up the stairs. Bethy shoves past Abby, and I feel her behind me, and Adam behind her. Kristen is sobbing.

I am raging, and it feels good. It's like every window opening, every trapped creature let out. I am in that office. I grab pictures off the walls, those butterflies. I shove them at Bethy. I shove them at Adam. "You want his things?" I am grabbing books, swiping objects off the shelves. Bottles of relaxing fluid; glass jars. A sweater that is over the chair. I am shoving all this and more at them. A jar falls but doesn't break. It rolls under the desk. "You want him *now*? Now you finally want him?"

"Don't, Mom. Don't!"

"Dani . . ."

I scream at them. My voice is hoarse. I watch myself from a distance and wonder what the hell I am doing. I've lost it. That's what they call this. "Take it! Take all of it. He's *yours*."

Bethy has begun to cry, too. Adam grabs her arm and leads her out of there. "She's fucking bonkers," he says. That's the best he can do? It's a comical word, the sort of word for the person he is: a large child, a cartoon villain.

There is another voice now, calling up at us from downstairs. "Dani? Dani?"

It's Nathan. Nathan, whose phone calls I haven't returned. Somehow we are all downstairs again, and Bethy's arms are full of Ian's things, the sleeve of that sweater is dragging on the floor, and Nathan is there, too. I gave Ian that sweater. He loved that sweater. Nathan looks shocked. He's staring at me as if I'm a madwoman. Adam is shaking his head and muttering under his breath, and Bethy is hovering near Kristen as if they are both delicate, innocent children in a candy house in the woods and I am about to shove them into my oven. Wait, no, a different fairy tale, one involving an evil stepmother and evil stepsisters. *Step* brings out the evil, apparently, on both sides.

"Get them out of here," I say to Nathan. And, by some miracle, he does.

"Mom, is there something you—"

"Don't," my own mother says to Abby.

I see Maggie Long on my way out. She has heard the noise of the morning; I know she has. She's watering her pansies, spying. She and Jack will have lots to talk about tonight over their grilled burgers and green salad made from iceberg lettuce and tomato slices. They will leave the cheese off the burgers because of Jack's high cholesterol. Maggie opens her mouth to speak, but for once she has nothing to say.

I have something to say to her, though. Something to ask. I know I shouldn't do this. But I need to do this. I need to know. This is what's called *digging your own grave*. I am digging and digging, deeper and deeper. I am digging a grave so deep that the walls of earth are falling in.

"Maggie?"

She keeps watering, waiting for more from me. Water is spilling from the top of the basket. It's sloshing over in great waves, but Maggie does not move the hose.

"You remember when Ian and I went to that party? You said you saw us leave."

"Right," Maggie says. It seems like the word takes a great deal of effort.

"Did you see us come back? By any chance, did you see Ian and me return?"

I need only that one thing. One piece of information, something so that I might *know*. *Yes*, she would say, and my nightmare would be over.

"No, Dani."

"Either of us?" My voice is ragged from that screaming.

"You don't know, Dani? You don't know if you both came home?" Dirt is spilling with the water now. It's spilling onto Maggie's tennis shoes. They are the cheap white ones you get in Rite Aid, and now she'll have to put them in the washer and they'll shrink two sizes. She's killing those plants. She doesn't say anything else. She doesn't have to. It's obvious what she's thinking. Her eyes are wide with horror.

Something happened. Last summer. Nine months ago. Feels like forever and it feels like yesterday.

Shana Berg says nothing. She has a notebook on her lap, and a pen, but the notebook is shut. I have explained everything about the party, the wine, the pills. But there is this, too.

His kids, you know. They were still angry with him. We thought we were making progress. They had come over two or three times. He started seeing them —out for coffee, lunch, that kind of thing.

Shana Berg nods.

I've never told anyone this.

This is a safe place, Shana Berg says. It sounds sort of corny. Psychobabble-ish. But it's reassuring, regardless. Her voice is gentle.

It was her birthday. Bethy, the oldest? Her mother was having a party at her house. I don't know if you remember, but they did a lot of that when they were married. It felt empty to him.

I remember.

Well, she—Mary—had this birthday party, and Bethy invites him. He wants to go. He's all excited after being shunned. I think it's bullshit, honestly, but I don't say anything. The whole thing around the kids . . . I wave my arm to indicate the mess it was.

Yeah, Dr. Berg says.

He gets her this really expensive gift. She likes this band—the Whatevers, I can't think of the name right now—but he gets the three of them these tickets to see them in Vancouver. The girls and him. I even get her a present, though I know she won't want it. I've given her other things; it doesn't matter. I keep trying everything I can, but it's reject, reject, reject, which I can understand to a certain degree. Maybe it'll take years before they stop catching each other's eyes and laughing at things I say. I know that. But, Ian . . . Anyway, so he goes to this party at his old house, the house he bought, and it's just like the old days, and there are all his old friends and Bethy's friends, and the neighbors and everyone is laughing and having a terrific time.

Ouch, Shana Berg says.

Exactly. He hovers around the edges of those people in his own house, and he gives the gift and Bethy says, "Oh, this is great. This'll be a lot of fun for us," and she hands the tickets to her mother. He stays for cake, and then he leaves.

Hmm.

He comes home, and he's so down. He says, "They all dismissed me. It was like I didn't exist." He's so down, I've never seen him so down. He's devastated. *And I say, "Let's get out of here. Let's take some food and go to Kerry Park." He doesn't want to at first, but then he agrees. I pack up some nice stuff we have—cheese, bread, a bottle of wine. His face is troubled and dark, but we get there. . . . It's a place we go sometimes, do you know it, Kerry Park?*

I do.

It's right next to Ian's building, but it's a public park. The views are great, you know, because it sits so high up on that hill, with that steep ravine. So we park at his work, and he opens his trunk. I don't know why, because I've got the bags of food and the blankets up front . . . But he opens the trunk, and he takes out that stupid butterfly net of his father's, and I don't say anything, but I think, Really? I mean, you want to tra-la-la and capture butterflies right now? It's summer, and Kerry Park—well, it has all that wild blackberry, and rhododendrons, too, and so, it's true, there are likely a lot of butterflies there then. But I'm just surprised. His mood . . . It seems sort of wacky, and I have this embarrassing image of him running on the lawn. I told you about that collection of his father's?

Shana Berg nods. The trees out her windows are bright green, spring green. They blow sweetly in a sudden breeze, but it's like we're tucked away, even from what's right outside. That fireplace and those books—it feels like a hidden place.

I don't say a word, but he catches my . . . I don't know, unspoken criticism, I guess you'd call it. He does this. He can feel your criticism before you even know it's there. It's weird. He just knows, and he asks, "What?" in that tone, as if he's daring me to say. And I say, "Nothing, Ian." But it's done, and there's no going back. His face gets hard. He was sullen and sad before, but now he's angry, I can see that.

I stop.

Dani? Are you all right? Shana Berg asks.

This is hard. It was . . . God.

She waits.

We arrange the blanket on the grass and sit down. I do all the stuff I do when he gets that way. I say nothing, and then I try to joke. I try to be affectionate. I open the wine, and he drinks his, fast, out of his paper cup. Well, he's right: There are some blue and yellow butterflies right near us, and I point. "There you go," I say, but I can tell this makes him furious. He thinks I'm making fun of him, but I'm not. I only want to soften him out of this horrible day he's had and to let him know I'm not his enemy. I head toward him on the blanket. I'm on my knees. I take a pinch of his shirt to pull him toward me; his favorite T-shirt—it's got a guitar with wings. I try to look him in the eyes, but he won't look back at me. He is staring at those bushes, and he speaks in their direction. He says, with all the sarcasm he can muster, "Soul mates." The words sound cheap and flimsy. The whole idea has become foolish. Our marriage has. It has no weight, you know. Not compared to this rejection by his children. Our great love, all the grandeur we made of it, and it's merely silly and selfish.

I take his chin in my hand. "Sweetie," I plead. I move in to kiss him.

He pulls away. He says, "I ruined my daughters' lives for this.*"*

And he is right, it seems, because right there it's just us. There are no parties and no friends and there's no big house and no adoring daughters and half his money has been given away. There's no commotion of television and neighbors with drinks in their hands. Only the two of us with a loaf of bread on a lawn. Only love, which can't bear the weight of making a life meaningful all by itself.

I exhale, though. I'm pissed. His life is in his own hands, his attitude is his own doing, and if anything is ruining things now, it's that. His lousy attitude. I'm there, you know? Doing my best to love him. To have a good life with him.

He hears that annoyed exhale. And that's when it happens. He takes my wrist. He twists my arm, and I feel a pop of pain near my elbow. I am on my back on the ground, and he is gripping both of my wrists and he has pinned them down, and his face is all fury, his eyes are full of hate, and he says, "I've given up everything for you! My house, my friends, my children. For you."

I cry out, because he is hurting me and because his words are horrible, and when I cry out, he moves one hand from my wrist to cover my mouth. He is covering my mouth and nose, and I can't breathe, and I can see the wild blackberries above me. I think of those butterflies, the way he puts a cotton ball soaked in cyanide into that jar, the way he suffocates them, and I don't want this for myself, I can't allow that to happen, and I get free somehow and put my hands on his chest and shove him with all my might, and he falls backward.

That is terrifying, Dani, Dr. Shana Berg says.

Terrifying, yes, God. But worse, after he falls, it feels like the worst kind of failure. Such a heartbreaking failure. He stands up then, and he rolls up that blanket and walks angrily back to the car, and I get up, too, and I follow. I am holding that sad bag of food and the wine bottle, and his cup has blown in a bit of wind down the ravine, and it's now caught in some blackberry brambles. But I don't retrieve it. The bag of food I'm carrying—it's humiliating and pitiful. I follow, and I'm ashamed of myself somehow. I can't explain it, but I am deeply ashamed. I get in the car. And I realize my shame is no match for his. I know that. He's become furiously cold. He needs to punish me for the way he feels and for what he's just done.

"You weren't the first one," he says. "I cheated on her before, with someone else."

It's supposed to wound me. But it's strange, because it doesn't, not really. A little. Okay, yes, I'm hurt that he didn't tell me before . . . But it makes some sense. It's sort of a relief. He wanted out of that marriage so badly. For both of us—there was love but the need to leave, too.

His anger is disintegrating fast. He is disintegrating. He looks as if he's caving in on himself. He's not angry anymore, but he's shriveling, I swear. When we get home, he lets me out and then he drives off. He doesn't come home that night. He stays somewhere, I don't know, I don't even ask, because I'm glad he left. The next morning, he comes back. He looks destroyed. He stands at our kitchen sink, and he says, "I'm no different than he is." I know who he means, of course

I do. He doesn't mean Mark. That's the funny thing; he's not talking about Mark at all. And now I'm supposed to rush in and soothe him or rescue him or heal his old wounds. I say, "You are not him." But it's a lie. I feel the lie when I say it. I don't mean that I believed Ian was a serial adulterer like Paul Hartley Keller. I don't think that at all. He was never, I don't know, as passionate *about collecting butterflies as his father was. But he* is *his father. That's the horrible truth. He is. He makes the people around him feel small so that he won't feel small.*

And so I say, "You are not him," but I don't mean it. What he's told me, this prior infidelity he never revealed, it matters little to me. There is a bigger betrayal here, and that's the one that devastates me.

I look at Dr. Berg. I am hoping she understands.

He hurt you. He frightened you. He didn't keep you safe. She does understand, thank God.

Yes, the sacred . . . The thing he was never supposed to be . . . I think I could cry. My throat starts to tighten, and I feel the tears there.

There are lots of ways to be unfaithful. All the things you are most afraid of, Dani—they happened right there on that blanket.

I know it. I do. And something changed then. In my heart. Something shifted. I saw what I had done—out of the frying pan into the fire. Or, rather, out of the frying pan into another frying pan. Here it was again. I wanted him to rescue me, and then I wanted to be rescued from him, and I saw this clearly, that rescue leads to ruin. After . . . Something closed off in me. I said, Enough. *I didn't believe in the big dream we'd created together, the big story about soul mates. I believed in a different kind of fate, or maybe just history, the kind that revisits and revisits, the kind that pushes and shoves you toward that one inevitable event where you and your past finally square off. I didn't know how to make it* over, *though. Or if I was brave enough to make it over. God, I couldn't believe I was standing at the edge of some same sinking boat, needing to jump. But it was over. I felt it in my body, if that doesn't sound stupid.*

No.

I wrote him this letter. I told him, My heart was in your teeth, and you bit down. I told him that what he did was unforgivable. That we were finished. That I was leaving him. But I never gave that letter to him. It would kill him if I left. I knew that. I couldn't do it. That letter, though, that I even wrote *it . . . I was done. He'd pushed me too far. And then this party at BetterWorks, like I told you, that fight on the grass . . . And I had taken those pills. All that wine.* I am crying now. I am shattered. The truth spoken is cataclysmic. But I am being heard here, and something about that breaks me even more. *You said that a person can have some kind of blackout . . .*

Yes.

But he's gone. He's gone, and I don't know what's happened, but I know I wanted him gone.

I am sobbing. My nose is dripping, and I'm a mess. She hands me a box of tissues, but I don't think that a box of tissues is up to this job. I need something from her. More than anything, I need her to get what I'm saying, and it seems she realizes this.

I don't know what happened here, she says. *And what I hear you saying is that you don't know what happened here, either. But there are some things I do know, things about you. I know your history. I know that your own anger and rage is terrifying to you. So terrifying that you believe you might annihilate someone just by feeling it. I know this, too: You tend to overcompensate. You tend to be overly responsible.*

She doesn't get it, though. I try again.

I've been having these dreams. We are at Kerry Park that night. He is looking for that cuff link. I shove him with both of my hands. I shove him into the ravine.

She doesn't even look shocked. *It's not surprising you are dream-*

ing about this. Or that you felt blind rage. This doesn't mean that you acted on it.

I wonder if she's heard me right.

I keep dreaming the same dream!

I am blowing my nose, and I don't know what I feel, except that it's not relief. I am only sure that she doesn't get this. Not truly. She doesn't understand the degree of my guilt.

Our time is nearly up, but there is one last thing I need to know. It's crucial.

You said . . . I don't know how to ask this. *A long time ago, you said that people bring their same selves to every situation, to all their relationships.*

Yes.

How is there any hope, then?

She thinks about this. Her eyes are compassionate.

You learn, she says. *You go from there. And then you change.*

It doesn't seem possible, but she is holding out that hope plainly, as if it *is* possible. My heart clutches up.

You evolve, she says.

17

For a time, you are in a cocoon. It's a place of safety. There are comforting threads bound tight around you, soft words and gentleness. But this isn't a place you can stay for long. Inevitable change is pressing upon you. So you must strain and push and press until you are out, out into the most dangerous place of all, the real world, where there are clever birds and swooping owls, where there is illness and bad weather. One day, maybe, you might learn to survive, using your color and speed and your inborn talent for camouflage and subterfuge. Or it all might stop right there. You might fly into someone's glass jar. The lid might get slammed down on what you thought was sky.

Here's something else. I read it in one of those books. The Greeks used the word *psyche* for both *butterfly* and *soul*.

I leave Dr. Shana Berg's office, and I can feel it, a shift in the weather. Oh, what a cliché, but it's true. There's that disturbing electricity in the warm air, and the sky is a muted Northwest gray. It happens often in the spring. A thunderstorm rolls in, and it's something you feel coming in the oldest, animal part of your brain. Already I am restless and uneasy, and the warm weight of negative energy in the air adds its urgency. Dr. Shana Berg—I am convinced she couldn't see how ugly it was, my own mind. All that hatred. That dream is so real when it happens, and I obviously couldn't adequately convey that to her. I don't think she truly heard this: I am shoving him in that dream, and there is horror in that, but it feels *good*, too.

There are new messages. Frank Lazario has called again but says he'll be unavailable until later. And Nathan has also called again. And, yes, I need to talk to him, too.

I get in my car, which is now running on prayers. *Please, please*, I say, to whoever up there is in charge of automotive affairs. Of course old Blue Beast is dying along with everything else. That's how it works. One thing falls apart, and it's some cue for all the others to follow suit. Appliances gang up, lightbulbs riot en masse. The objects in our life, too, just wait for their *fuck-you* moment, after all their years of unappreciated diligence.

I am breaking the law by calling Nathan while I drive, but that hardly matters now, does it? If I've done what my heart fears I've done, I could rob a bank at gunpoint, and it could be no worse. I forgot to tell Dr. Shana Berg this, and it's more evidence: Two weeks ago, I took Ian to work when his car was being detailed. *Your seat is awfully close to the windshield; how do you even see?* he asked. *A person was waiting at that crosswalk and you drove right through*, he said. *Something smells in here*, he complained. I got so flustered that I drove up a curb and ran a red light, giving him more proof of my shortcomings. He finally got out, and as he crossed the street, I imagined it. That cab hitting him. Killing him instantly. Painless but fast. In my head, I'd even repainted the living room. Ocean Mist Blue.

I call Nathan not because he's asked me to but because I need to know the things I don't. That dream—it is possible, isn't it, that we went back to Kerry Park that night? Someone would have seen us, but maybe not. The party was winding down. The parking lot is on the other side of the building. It was dark on that grass, even when we first went back to look for the lost cuff link. We were alone; we had to be. A person can have that kind of a blackout after mixing drugs with alcohol, Dr. Shana Berg said, but it has never happened to me before. Of course not. Jesus. Do you know how terrifying a blank spot is, even a brief one? A dark hole of forgetting and my missing husband and the rising truth about how I've come to feel about him?

He's in that ravine. I know it.

"Nathan?"

"Thank God, Dani. Where the hell have you been?"

The waters of Lake Washington are steely gray under that metallic sky. I wait for the roll of thunder, but none comes. You wish it would go ahead and get it over with, because it's coming, and the air is unbearably suffocating.

I wonder what it will feel like to finally tell it. Thunder and lightning, a downpour, relief. "I went to see my psychologist," I tell him.

The silence between us is heavy. Finally, he says, "I took Bethy out, and we talked—"

But this is not why I've called Nathan. "You said to me about that BetterWorks party, about Ian that night . . . you said he was pissed. You said something like, 'I noticed. I saw.' *What* did you see, Nathan?"

"On the grass. You were arguing. You grabbed his arm. . . ."

"And after that?"

"After that, what?"

"Did you see us on the grass again? Did you see us at Kerry Park?"

"I don't know what you mean, Dani. We were all leaving after that. Did you go back there?"

"I don't remember."

He is silent, and there is only the rattling in my car and the sound of a truck whipping past. Then he sighs. "God, Dani."

"I took these pills. And then I drank wine."

"I don't know what you're saying."

"How do I know . . ."

"Please. Don't say anything more. Look, I know you would never hurt anyone. I *know* that."

"I need to tell them I don't remember. It's only right. Someone should know this."

"No! Dani, no! You can't do that. That would be a crazy stupid thing to do. Have you talked to an attorney?"

"If I've done something wrong—"

"No! You're afraid. You're reaching for some answer. . . . Come on, you haven't slept in days. You've been scared shitless since he disappeared. You can't think when you're this exhausted. Promise me you won't tell the police something like that without talking to a lawyer. Fuck. That would be a huge mistake, Dani. Huge."

"Nathan—"

"*Promise* me."

"Okay. All right."

But listening through fear is like trying to think when someone is shouting at you. It's like trying to save yourself when you look toward the sun and there is only the large open beak of a bird above you, and you are so, so tired. You are too tired, really, to do anything but lay your wings flat and succumb to the outcome that in all likelihood is inevitable.

It does not thunder yet, and does not thunder, and does not thunder. The air is thick with electricity. At home, there is something my mother and Abby are not telling me. It's obvious. Their voices are too cheerful, and they are doing what they can to avoid me. My mother doesn't even grill me about Frank Lazario, whom she assumes I've spoken with. Pollux is trotting around and whining. I take him out, but when he comes back in, he resumes his pacing. He feels the approaching storm, too.

My mother and Abby don't speak at dinner. No one eats the macaroni and cheese one of them has made during the day. There is only the edgy *tink-tink* of forks against plates, food being moved around. There is the sound of ice sliding down a glass as Abby takes a drink of water.

"What?" I ask them, but no one will say.

Finally, before bed, my mother comes into my room. She is wearing her pink quilted robe. This is a robe for reading magazines, for watching *Good Morning America,* and making scrambled eggs. It is not a robe for this news.

She sits me down beside her. She takes my hands.

"They want you to take a polygraph," she says.

I listen to Ian's message again. *This is Ian Keller. I'm not available to take your call . . .* His voice does not sound secretive or adversarial to me anymore. I don't feel frustrated listening to it, only deeply sorrowful. It is the voice of someone who doesn't know the future when you know the future.

When Abby and my mother are asleep, I walk quietly into our office. It is in shambles now. Someone has picked up the killing jar that had rolled under the desk and set it upright on the counter again, but there are bare nails where the framed butterflies had hung, and there is a chunk of glass in the trash can. Something has gotten broken, and I try to determine what that was. Ah, it's the tip of the glass award from the tech magazine, I see now. The pyramid on its black stand has been placed back on the shelf, but it now looks imperfect, as if a bite has been taken off the top.

I open a desk drawer. I take out a lined yellow pad. Ian keeps a stack of them in there. I rethink this. I take out several more. A pen, too.

I do not know how to do this officially. Nathan has warned against it, and so has Dr. Shana Berg, but there are things I don't know and things that I fear, and these facts should be handed over. There are those who have too much guilt and those who don't have enough, perhaps. Still, I will tell what's happened as best as I can and let others judge for themselves. It's the right thing to do. At the end of the day, the truth—your wrongdoings, your good intentions, your human struggles, what you've done and why—is the place you go on from.

It is the whole story.

No, it is a confession.

It is everything I know I am guilty of in this story of Ian and me. All the sins I can and can't remember, all I am heartily sorry for.

I take up my pen. I write:

> *I used to imagine it sometimes, what would happen if one day I didn't come home. Not that I ever considered running off—I could never actually do that, even if I occasionally had that fantasy of driving south and checking in to some hotel. Some place with bathrobes, for sure.*

I write, and write, and the yellow pages fill up, and sometime in the night the thunder rolls in the distance and comes closer and closer until it sounds like it is sitting next to me. It is the dark, hunched man, standing and roaring in my ears, his fist by my face, his hand over my mouth.

It is morning, and my fingers are aching. They are cramped and contorted. There is something else I'm supposed to do. I'm supposed to sign my name, aren't I, to a confession? And so I do.

Dani Ross Hastings Keller
Seattle, Washington

18

Here is what happens next: It stops raining. The hard, driving rain that began after the thunder rolled through has now passed, part and parcel of a Seattle spring. It's a dewy morning, a beautiful one. A day for pardon and peace and absolution. I see that the rain has stopped but that the sun is flashing between dramatic, fast-moving clouds. I take a long shower. I get dressed. My mother is having coffee, and Abby is reading her mail on her laptop at the kitchen table. I am doing something mundane again: I am looking for a bag in which to carry those pages. I see Abby's beloved head, tipped down in concentration. I love that head so much, and that hair, and every little bit of that girl, that young woman. It tears my heart, seeing her, loving her like that. It tears my heart to see my mother in her favorite sweat clothes, her white hair in disarray from sleep. And my sweet old Pollux, oh, yes, him, too. Beloved him. Beloveds, all of them.

Double hugs, I say silently.

I could cry, and so I get myself out of there. I take a bag from the narrow space on the side of the fridge, where we keep them. I go to my room and slide the stack of pages into the bag. There is my wrinkle cream that really does nothing for wrinkles, and my glass-beaded bedside lamp that I love, and my reading glasses. I am in the middle of a book, and my bookmark is still set between the same pages where I'd left off days ago. A life ago. Everything is feeling bittersweet, and so I need to get out of there fast, before I change my mind.

"What are you doing?" my mother asks. I am getting a jacket from the hall closet; who knows what the weather will be.

"Out" is all I can manage to say.

"Dani . . ." She knows; she always does. Abby says the same thing about me. Mother's intuition. Say what you will, but I believe in it. "What are you doing?" My mother's voice is rising in alarm. Abby looks up, questioning.

"Out," I say again. I try to keep my voice steady.

My head is deep in the closet in the hall now. The jacket I want has slipped off its hanger and fallen on the floor behind the rain boots and other shoes. When I get up, my mother is there, staring at me hard. She grabs my arm.

"Dani, if you are thinking of doing anything foolish . . ." She keeps her voice low.

I say nothing. I am trying to hold it together.

"I'm begging you."

And then, can it be? That damn boat. That goddamn boat. The hard rain and the waves have loosened the rope again. I am aware that this is where we began, that morning when he disappeared. It makes me understand that this is some kind of ending. It's silly, maybe, but I want to take care of a problem for them, for my mother and Abby, one I can fix. Before I go, I want to tighten that cleat. It will be one less thing they will have to deal with.

I get that toolbox from the closet. It's the one Mary gave Ian when they were married. I undo the clasps and lift the lid. The tools are lying in their molded plastic places, but the screwdriver is gone. It's odd. I have not used anything in this box since I hung pictures when we moved in, and Ian, as particular as he is, would have always, always returned it to its proper place.

Still, no matter. I can't concern myself with that now. There's no time. I get a knife from the kitchen drawer. I open the doors to the deck and Pollux trots after me.

"Dani, don't worry about it," my mother says.

"That banging is driving me crazy," Abby says. She needs me still. That's what threatens to choke me up. My mother, too. No—truth is, we all need one another.

I kneel on the dock. If someone sees me here, it might look as if I am praying. I fit the tip of the knife into the screw and twist hard. I try to jiggle the cleat, but it feels firm. I wind the rope back over it so the boat is snug once again against the dock.

I get up. It's silly, maybe. But in my heart, I say goodbye.

The stacks of notepads are in the bag, and I am holding them under my arm as I leave. My mother is standing in the doorway. She is pleading with me with her eyes, so I don't look. I don't want anything to dissuade me. I am hoping Detective Jackson will be there in his office when I need him. My mother doesn't know what's in that bag, but she knows it's bad. If she did know, she'd likely be throwing herself down in front of me, blocking my exit. Isabel Eleanor Ross would let this happen only over her dead body.

I hear a noise out there. Oh, really, can it be? Old Joseph Grayson is playing with his electric boat? *Now?* I listen. Yes, there's the unmistakable whine as he zips it over the waves. Why not, though? The sky is all morning purples and pinks when the sun comes out behind speeding clouds. The water is choppy— perfect, maybe, for a post-toke hydroplane race with your ancient hippie self.

At the end of the dock, in the parking lot finally, I unlock my car door. I set the notepads on the seat beside me. The package is almost another passenger; it seems as weighty.

I am trying to hurry. If I don't get out of here soon, I may change my mind. I turn the key. *Please*, I beg. The terrible humming sound starts, and I put my car in reverse.

And that is when there is a horrendous clunk. I put the damn thing in neutral and in reverse again, and again, and again, but the old Blue Beast will not move. Blue is finished. No matter how much I want this, I am not going backward.

I put my head in my hands. I want to cry, but there's no time for that. I need to solve this problem, quick. I will go inside and ask to use my mother's car. It's terrible, yes, to return there after that particular leaving, but I have no choice.

Nothing is easy, I think, *not even this.* I am sure it's the worst kind of bad luck, some cruel trick of timing. What are the odds that the car dies *now?* Yet this is how it goes, one thing happens and then another, a piece follows a piece, things continue to break, as fate conspires, insisting on telling its own story, which (hopefully, finally) you are able to hear.

I get out. I am holding the bag in my arms like a baby, like my own child. And that's when someone begins to shout. A single shout at first, old Joseph Grayson, and he is screaming. He is yelling, *Fuck! Fuck! Fuck!* He's *shrieking.* He's having a heart attack, I think. That's my first thought, anyway. He is screaming like a girl who's seen a snake. No, worse. Way worse.

There's some kind of commotion going on. A door opening and slamming, and now my mother screams. My mother? I know that voice. Dear God, what? They are being attacked; are they being *attacked?*

No. Because now comes the *thud, thud, thud* of shoes running on the hard dock. And Pollux is barking and barking, and Abby is calling my name. She is running down the dock. She has her goofy Toucan Sam shirt on and a pair of cotton plaid shorts and her hair is wild, and she is shouting to me. Old Joseph Grayson is just behind her. Him, with his bushy gray beard and long hair in a ponytail and that tie-dyed Grateful Dead shirt he perpetually wears. My mother—she's trying to run, too. She's back there, running as best as she can.

I am still clutching that bag when Abby reaches me.

"Mom!" She is crying.

And there is old Joseph Grayson, out of breath. He is holding that stupid electric boat. And he is holding one wet and expensive Italian shoe.

19

After the divers arrive to release Ian's body from where he's been tangled in the anchor rope of the *New View,* after the autopsy and the funeral, I stop dreaming of Kerry Park. Instead, I dream the simple, horrible story of that night, told by the singular rope markings on one of his legs and by the screwdriver found on the murky lake floor just below him. He is trying to fix that damn cleat, the drifting boat. It is late, and his mind is so burdened, and he is more than a little drunk. He reaches for the line and loses his footing; he slips, one small misstep, into the lake. One leg is free and one leg is bound, but more critically, he is caught, and he struggles, but the struggle is too much for him. I dream of him underwater, and, most of all, I dream of trying to rescue him.

I toss and turn with a new set of questions. How can it be that no one heard him that night? Hadn't there been a splash, a cry for help? Had the party boat that Maggie Long heard masked the noise? Would I have heard him if I hadn't taken those pills? I do some midnight reading on my returned laptop. I find out that drowning doesn't look the way most people suspect. There is very little splashing or waving and no yelling or calls of any kind. Drowning is quiet and undramatic. Sufferers are unable to yell, using the little air they have left to breathe. People can watch an individual drown—neighbors, friends, loved ones can look right at it with their own eyes—and not even know it's happening.

He had to rescue himself but couldn't. I had to rescue myself but never did.

Months later, my mother is still angry with the police. She has called me from her house. I can hear the television. There is a scraping sound, too, as if she is buttering toast.

"I don't understand why they didn't bring a diver out in the first place." We've had this discussion a million times by now.

"There was no reason to think he drowned. There was a ladder right there, inches from him."

"Still! Accidents happen. A foot gets caught . . . It was late, he'd been drinking . . ."

"Mom. What did they tell us? There've only been two drownings in that lake in twelve years."

"Three now. You could have been arrested!"

"It wasn't clear what happened that night, not at all. Not even to me. Especially not to me."

"Bethy was gunning for you."

We haven't spoken since the funeral, his children and I. Sometimes I wish I had that sweater back.

My mother is crunching, eating in my ear. It sounds like dinosaurs walking the earth. "I shudder to think what would have happened, I do, if that old fool had not lost his boat under your dock."

"I think he's your type, Ma."

"Oh, yeah, baby. *Lately it occurs to me, What a long . . . strange trip it's been,*" she wails. She goes in for a solo guitar riff.

"I'm assuming that's the Grateful Dead." My mother knows her hippie music.

"You would be right."

"Summer of Love."

"Dani?" There is no more scraping or chewing now.

"Hmm?"

"I'm sorry I was such a bitch about him."

Ian, she means. Not old, stoned Joseph Grayson, who is innocent in all this. "You were trying to tell me something important."

"I get carried away."

"Yeah, you do."

"They still should have checked the lake."

I don't blame the police for not suspecting that Ian had drowned, but I don't tell her this. I wouldn't have thought he fell in that lake in a million years. A misstep like that—it'd be so *human*.

Ian never made mistakes. Except for the ones that destroyed him.

I have decided to stay in the houseboat. I am alone for the first time in my life, although this sounds unfair to Pollux. He lives there with me, old pal that he is. I met Mark when I was nineteen years old, as I've said. And then there was Ian.

At first I thought I'd have to move. How could I live there, thinking about him under the water like that all that time? He'd been right there, with that other cuff link still affixed to his shirt-sleeve. And with —*don't think it don't think it don't think it*—that bust of him I had thrown into the lake. I hadn't even known he was there. I hadn't felt it. It seemed like a failure of my love for him. One of many failures.

But then I remembered Ian saying, *I never want to live anywhere else. I could die here and be happy.* Maybe it sounds strange, but that's weirdly comforting. I never got to say goodbye, and this is the last place he was and the rightest place for me to grieve him, grieve us. I could run from here, but there are things I need to look hard at—my own guilt, but, maybe even more, the places where I've been merely human, too.

And I want to remember, I want to keep hold of the good parts, the love, yes, within the complicated whole. Those road trips we took, with the music playing and the windows rolled down. Those heady days before the hard ones, and the hard ones when we struggled toward each other. Those times, God, passionate times, when a look into each other's eyes felt like a long drink of summer.

I found a box in his closet yesterday, tucked way, way up high. I opened the lid and was shocked to see that the box had a leaf in it on a bed of cotton batting. It was a large maple leaf, nearly disintegrating. I didn't understand at first, and then it came to me—a day in the fall when we'd met at the university campus. I gave him that leaf before we said goodbye. He loved me as best as he could, that's what that leaf said. And I loved him as best as I could. But, oh, how we can sink and drown, we with our unforgiving selves.

I see Abby often, of course. My sister came for a three-day weekend. And I see Anna Jane and my mother and my father. I have gone to dinner at Maggie and Jack's and at Mattie and Louise's. I see Dr. Shana Berg. My poor ignored clients have stuck with me as I've slowly returned to work. I hear from Nathan, as well, but I keep him at arm's length. Good-hearted Nathan, who holds my eyes a little too long and brings me food—he looks too much like he wants to save me. I stay pretty close to home right now. It's snug, a cocoon, the setting for the necessary drawing inward that comes before transformation. It's Poll and me. During Ian's disappearance, I was sure that *someone* had to know what happened, and it turns out that someone likely did. I can imagine him that night, his black nose pressed against the glass, his worried eyes. My dear, velvety Pollux, patron saint of sailors, witness to all human faults and lapses. Witness to bad singing aloud and naked dashes to the bathroom, white lies and deadly errors. My very short, fine friend. A good dog.

In this cocoon there is work to be done. Old structures are remade. I think, I write, I read. I try to make peace with myself. I try to remember the simple but difficult truth that we mostly do the best we can with what we have. What a feat that is, too, to do the best we can, given that we've got to drag our histories along with us, like one of those big old Samsonite suitcases from the time before luggage had wheels.

Alone—oh, the angst and the joys of it; who knew? I'm free. I stretch out my legs and eat cookies off paper towels in bed. But, also, I must brave some ancient story that the night is too dark for me to handle. I believed that story for a long time. Believing a new one takes courage. You rip off the sphragis, and the body is bare and vulnerable underneath.

So I will build my own protective layer, made from experience and hard-won awareness. I have promised myself this. I will change, slowly, over months and years. And when I emerge, I will stay away from the hungry beaks of birds and the talons of owls. I will not fear long voyages over water. If I become tired or terrified and the promise of rescue arrives—a boat, a net, an outstretched hand—I will turn my back to it. I will turn my back to it and rise and fly, my tissue-paper wings evolving in midair, becoming strong as the wings of a pterodactyl, soaring now over that hill, and the next, and the next.

Acknowledgments

Heartfelt appreciation to my new publishing family at Random House, most especially Shauna Summers. How grateful I am for your inspired thinking, as well as your talent and generosity. Thank you, too, to Jennifer Hershey, Jane Von Mehren, Gina Wachtel, Marietta Anastassatos, Nancy Delia, Virginia Norey, Leigh Marchant, and Angela Polidoro, for all that you've done for both me and for this book. I am a lucky woman to have my work in your hands.

Gratitude, as well, to all of my old family at S&S, who also made this book possible. Your spirit of goodwill in this endeavor to bridge two worlds makes me love you even more than I already did. Hugs to you, Jen Klonsky. Ben Camardi, and all of The Harold Matson Company, thank you for your unparalleled partnership of fifteen years.

Mom, Dad, Jan, Sue, Mitch, Ty, Hunter, and my dear friend Renata Moran— love you, family. Sam and Nick, my joy and heart, every book belongs to you. And to my sweet beloved, John Yurich—thanks for being both my husband and my one true love.

He's
Gone

A Novel

DEB CALETTI

A Reader's Guide

A Conversation with Deb Caletti

Random House Reader's Circle: You've written many popular teen novels, but *He's Gone* is your first novel for adults. What was the inspiration for your adult debut? Did you have the idea long before you began writing it? And how was the writing process different?

Deb Caletti: You never know how—or when—the idea for a book will appear. This one came right when I needed it, shortly after we'd begun discussing the possibility of me writing an adult novel. The inspiration arrived in much the same way that *He's Gone* begins. I was lying in bed, trying to determine if my husband was home or not. I was doing that thing you do, where you listen for the sound of footsteps, or the toaster lever being pushed down, or coffee being made. And then, rather handily and helpfully, came the thought: What if you woke up one morning and found that your husband had vanished? The idea of writing the book as a confession came quickly afterward, as did the decision to explore the subjects of guilt and marriage, wrongdoing, and the way those old, treacherous voices from childhood can continue to haunt us. I began work on the book as soon as I could, just after finishing *The Story of Us*. Sometimes you have an idea that makes you feel like a kid on Halloween night. Can we just skip dinner, so we can *go*? I wanted to *go*. I couldn't wait to start this one.

The writing process wasn't all that different from my other books. My previous nine young adult novels are full length and fairly complex and character driven, and my readers are already a mixed bag of ages, falling generally in the older teens to adult range. There is always a teen protagonist, but my books also feature adult characters of varying ages—mothers and daughters both struggling with screwed-up love lives, for example, or generations of women with something to say about relationships, family, and identity. I tend to try to push the boundaries of YA, offering more thought-provoking material than readers of that age might be used to, along with a slower, more literary pace. So writing a book for adults wasn't a great leap. The only real difference I found was that the boundaries I always try to push didn't exist anymore. There were no more fences for me to stay in or out of. It was very freeing. I found that, for me, writing within those boundaries is actually in many ways more challenging.

RHRC: *He's Gone* takes place in Seattle, where you also live. Do you feel that your life in the city inspired or influenced the novel? If so, how?

D.C.: Setting has always played a huge part in my books, and I have no doubt that's because I live in such an *evocative* place. I like to approach setting as if it were character, with a character's traits and quirks and moods. Seattle—and the San Juan Islands, and the towns of the mountain foothills that I've previously written about—all have so much character, it's hard to cross a street without seeing something to include in a book. We are bombarded with setting here, which is a lucky thing for a writer, I think. It *offers* itself. *He's Gone* primarily takes place in a particularly eccentric and picturesque part of our city—the houseboat community around Lake Union, where I once lived part-time. It seemed an especially fitting setting for the book. First, there is water everywhere, and these characters are, well, literally *drowning* in guilt. But even more than that, the houseboats and their docks are a little off kilter. Yes, they're charming and shingled and dripping with gorgeous flowers. Ducks paddle by, and so do friendly kayakers. Sailboats swoop out to the lake on a glorious day. But, too, the houses and boats are rocking and clanging. The old piers sway and creak. On a rainy day, it's a little spooky. On any day, it's all slightly deranged.

RHRC: Though the story begins when Ian vanishes, he feels like a fully evolved character by the time we reach the ending. Can you tell us a bit about the challenges of fleshing out a character who is mostly "offscreen"?

D.C.: I like the idea of this, the "off screen" character. I also have one in my book *The Story of Us*. That character, Janssen Tucker, is totally absent until he appears for his one line at the very end of the book. The idea appeals to me because there are a lot of "offscreen" people in our own lives. You can come to know your partner's ex or their deceased parent in a very real way, even if you've never met them. You can come to have very strong feelings about them, an understanding of them, a full picture, just from what you hear. In writing, the challenge to make a character come alive even when he's not on the scene is met in the same ways it happens in real life. You hear stories about the person. Your partner tells you about his ex, but so does his best friend, and so does his mother. Maybe you see a photo or hear a rumor. Maybe you hear a voice on an answering machine.

Ian, in *He's Gone*, needed to be much closer to the reader than Janssen Tucker did in *The Story of Us*. Aside from Dani, Ian is the most important character in the book. It's crucial to *feel* him right there, even though he's missing—to feel the press of his control, to even feel his breath on her face during that picnic. He needs to be so well known that we understand both his complicated emotions and the bind those emotions have put Dani in. Dani's own flashbacks serve this purpose (we actually "see" Ian during those times), but Nathan's accounts of their relationship flesh out Ian's character, as do Isabel's and Abby's. What we see of his relationship with his children and Mary and especially his father hopefully fill Ian in further. What I also felt helped bring Ian close were the times that Dani heard him speak in her head. That's about as close in as you can bring someone.

RHRC: Dani has a compelling narrative voice, and it's easy to take her version of the truth for reality. Ultimately, though, we find out that she's not a reliable narrator. What made you decide to go this route?

D.C.: I went this route because we are all unreliable narrators, not just in the way we tell our stories to others, but how we tell them to ourselves. Maybe *especially* how we tell them to ourselves. All of us create our own versions of an event, of our *lives*, even, not because we're liars, necessarily, but because we can only see and understand the truth from our own viewpoint, and a shifting viewpoint at that. Facing the truth is a messy business. You've got denial, and pride, and the fact that understanding takes time; you've got perspective (or lack of it) and the pesky fact that we can only face the truth we can stand to face at any given moment. I didn't see Dani as being willfully deceitful in the way she tells her story. I saw her as struggling with a hard truth that she hadn't even entirely admitted to herself yet. It's one of the toughest human being jobs, I think, being utterly and completely honest with yourself.

RHRC: One aspect of *He's Gone* that really stuck with us is the imagery involving butterflies. Can you tell us a bit about the inspiration there?

D.C.: My first marriage was an abusive one, and long after I left it, a very good friend, someone who knew me well, reflected on that time. He said, "You were like a butterfly, caught in a net." I never forgot those words. Butterflies became personally symbolic to me. I knew I wanted to one day use this symbolism in my writing—the fragility, the strength, the capture, the escape. Because, yes, there is the helplessness of being trapped, but there is also what happens when the butterfly manages to get free.

RHRC: Did you know how *He's Gone* would end before you began writing it? If not, can you tell us a bit about some of the other endings you considered, and why you ultimately chose this one?

D.C.: I always say that, for me, writing a book is like a wacky Greyhound bus trip—I know where I'm starting and where I'll end up, but I have no idea what will happen along the way. *He's Gone* was different, though. I *didn't* know how the book would end. I struggled with it. I wanted to write the novel as a confession, and so this meant considering the obvious possibility that Dani had indeed harmed Ian. I felt this was the wrong route, though. It would have turned the book into a clichéd abused-woman-kills-husband story, and that felt cheap to me. It would have been a dishonest choice, a disservice, even, to anyone who'd actually been in a similar relationship. In reality, we know who usually ends up being harmed in situations like that, and it isn't the perpetrator. Perhaps more important, though, in terms of my vision for the book, if Dani had been guilty of harming Ian, the story would have become about a violent act and not about what I wanted it to be about—the complexity and impossibility of assigning guilt; the million gray areas of culpability, which can sit right next to our very black-and-white feelings of shame.

After my father read the book, he handed it back to me and said, "I was really glad she didn't do it." And maybe that was the biggest reason that I chose the ending I did. I was really glad she didn't do it, too.

Questions and Topics for Discussion

1. Pollux, Dani's dog, and Isabel, Dani's eccentric mother, bring moments of comic relief to *He's Gone*, even in the midst of all the dark moments and drama. Do you think this adds to the narrative? Why or why not?

2. Whenever someone in *He's Gone* looks for rescue or validation in the form of another person, they end up disappointed—whether it's Dani having an affair with Ian to escape her abusive marriage or Ian attempting to connect with his father. What do you make of this?

3. "Brief moments of goodness are shockingly persistent. You're in the dark, darker, darkest, and yet there's a dog sitting beside you, on his best behavior for a dropped crust, and there's an industrious line of ducks paddling past, and there's a grilled-cheese maestro. Life insists." Discuss how this passage exemplifies the broader themes of the novel.

4. Dani thinks Ian is having an affair with Desiree, but it turns out that Desiree is just jealous of Dani and Ian and covetous of

the life they share together. From the outside looking in, their relationship seems ideal to her. Discuss how all of the characters in *He's Gone* tend to misconstrue situations due to their imperfect perception. What's the author trying to tell us?

5. How did you feel about Ian after reading about the dinner that he and Dani shared with Paul Hartley Keller? Did it make you like him more? Less?

6. There's a ceramic bust of Ian that looks exactly like Paul Hartley Keller—so much so that Dani mistakenly assumes he was the model for it. Why can Dani see the resemblance between the two men only in this one inanimate object? What's the significance of what ultimately happens to the bust?

7. Dani often seems to feel physically threatened by Ian's daughters, particularly the taciturn Bethy. Do you think this threat is real or imagined? What does it say about violence as a legacy?

8. Did your feelings about Mary change when you finally met her in the present-day narrative? How do you think your initial impressions of her were colored by the fact that *He's Gone* is told from Dani's point of view?

9. *He's Gone* is written as Dani's confession, and much of the book focuses on how guilt (both warranted and unwarranted) colors our lives. How do our experiences dictate what we feel guilty for and what we don't? What must we do to be able to forgive ourselves and others? Near the end of the story, Dani holds her confession in her arms "like a baby, like my own child." Why do you think the author chose these words?

10. For most of the novel, Ian seems like a buttoned-up, perfectly controlled person, whose biggest failing is his desire for perfection in everyone around him. Toward the end of the novel we finally find out that he is just as capable of abusive violence as Dani's first husband. Do you think this revelation has more impact because it's withheld for so long? What were your feelings about Ian before you found out the full story of the fateful picnic he took with Dani? What were they like after it?

11. Were you surprised to learn that Ian's affair with Dani wasn't his first? Why or why not?

12. Did you ever believe that Dani was responsible for Ian's disappearance? Discuss.

PHOTO: © JASON TEEPLES

DEB CALETTI is the author of nine highly acclaimed young-adult novels, including *The Nature of Jade, Stay,* and *Honey, Baby, Sweetheart,* a finalist for the National Book Award and the PEN USA Award. She lives with her family in Seattle.

Chat.
Comment.
Connect.

Visit our online book club community at
Facebook.com/RHReadersCircle

Chat
Meet fellow book lovers and discuss what you're reading.

Comment
Post reviews of books, ask—and answer—thought-provoking
questions, or give and receive book club ideas.

Connect
Find an author on tour, visit our author blog, or invite one of
our 150 available authors to chat with your group on the phone.

Explore
Also visit our site for discussion questions, excerpts, author
interviews, videos, free books, news on the latest releases,
and more.

Books are better with buddies.
Facebook.com/RHReadersCircle

THE RANDOM HOUSE PUBLISHING GROUP